'An excellent page turner that positively hurtles along, brimming with menace and plot twists'
Daily Telegraph

'A brisk, event-filled fantasy'
Sci-Fi Online

'An impressive debut ... that brings magic, fantasy and science together'
The Big Issue

'Very well written and consistently gripping'
Carousel

'Exciting and pacy, but with a great deal of thought and thematic depth'
thebookbag.com

'An exciting read with lots of action'
Teen Titles

'Fast-paced inventive writing with original plot involving strange creatures and weird science, it's guaranteed to satisfy the hunger of voracious readers everywhere'
Julia Eccleshare, lovereading.com

'Older readers will be gripped by this gritty, urban, fantasy adventure'
TBK

Also in this series . . .

THE BAD TUESDAYS:

A CRYSTAL HORSEMAN

Benjamin J. Myers

Orion
Children's Books

First published in Great Britain in 2011
by Orion Children's Books
a division of the Orion Publishing Group Ltd
Orion House
5 Upper St Martin's Lane
London WC2H 9EA
An Hachette UK company

1 3 5 7 9 10 8 6 4 2

A catalogue record for this book
is available from the British Library.

ISBN 978 1 84255 643 6

Typeset by Input Data Services Ltd
Bridgwater, Somerset

Printed in Great Britain by
Clays Ltd, St Ives plc

The Orion Publishing Group's policy is to use papers that
are natural, renewable and recyclable products made from
wood grown in sustainable forests. The logging and
manufacturing processes are expected to conform to
the environmental regulations of the country of origin.

www.orionbooks.co.uk

To David

CHAPTER 1

Box Tuesday held the blaze carbine machine-gun at chest height. Its snub nose was levelled at the hammer-headed, six-limbed, scorpion-segmented creature that towered up, only metres in front of him. The creature flexed open its four wings: one pair long and membranous as a dragon fly's and the other pair bearing curved, knuckled spines, long and sharp as scythes.

The spiker was preparing to attack.

Shoulder to shoulder with Box stood Razool, the long, lean snout with the alsatian face, mane of black hair and the scorched skin on his left arm and chest which branded him a mutineer. His blaze carbine was shouldered, trained on the huge creature's armour-tough belly plates.

'They regenerate, so don't stop firing, got it?' Razool drawled from the side of his long, sharp muzzle.

'If I can get in with a mace-blade ...' began Box.

Razool swore quietly. 'Why do you have to take more risks than anyone else?'

Box's dark eyes narrowed. 'I like to get stuck in,' he growled.

'Yeah,' Razool growled back. 'We know.' He cocked the carbine. 'Trouble is, the rest of us have to get stuck in with you.'

Behind Box and Razool stood Skarl and Raxa: Skarl wiry and wolfish, Raxa, thick-set and tall. They were ready to open fire once Box and Razool began to reload. The four of them, in black vests and black combat trousers and boots, were ready to blast as many rounds as it took to smash the hack-winged beast that towered over them.

'Just don't blow my shoulder off, Skarl,' grunted Box. The harsh tongue of the dog-men came to him naturally now, after so many months of living with them, training with them, fighting alongside them.

'Don't get in the way then, when me and Raxa get to work,' retorted Skarl.

'You won't need to get to work,' promised Box. 'Not once me and Razool have finished with this ugly . . .'

The creature's long neck lunged down carrying the wrinkled hammer-head towards them. The lower jaw dropped open like a trapdoor, revealing a massive mouth with fangs like park railings.

Together, Box and Razool blazed at the incoming head.

'Stand your ground,' yelled Razool. 'Spikers regenerate. Keep firing. Keep firing until you've smashed it.'

Box saw the spine-bearing wing-bone windmill over the spiker's head and sail down towards them. 'Zool, watch the hack!' His voice was lost beneath the rattle of the machine-guns. But from behind him another carbine screamed into life, hurling rounds into the bony hack.

'Nice one, Skarl,' shouted Box. That was why you needed

a tight fire team. Just one spiker took a lot of killing. Then his gun clunked empty. Box dropped to his knee, tugged out the spent ammunition block and smacked in a fresh one. Raxa's gun started up.

'Box,' yelled Razool.

Box spotted the hack skimming towards his head. He rolled back, saw it graze his chest and watched it pass clean through Skarl. Raxa stepped forwards, gun blazing, but the instructor had already deactivated the hologram and stepped in.

'Sloppy.' The instructor wore a camouflage jump suit. His lower jaw bristled with teeth like tusks and tufts of fur patched over the grey skin of his face. He pointed at Skarl. 'If that was real, you'd be well gaffed. Probably dead.' Then he pointed at Box. 'And you should have been protecting the left flank of the team, *skin*.'

'Skin': that was what dog-men called humans. And 'snout' was what Box called the dog-men.

'If I'd got a mace-blade, I'd of stopped it,' snapped Box.

They had been taught that where the lower mandible was hinged so that it could open so cavernously, the exoskeleton was pliable and weak. At this spot, a mace-blade could cut through a spiker with ease, decapitating it. But you had to get very close to do this: or the massive jaws had to get very close to you. And if they got that close they would be into you before you could blink. Going for a trap shot was more deadly for the trooper than the spiker.

'Nobody goes for a trap shot,' the instructor said. That was what the instructors always said. '*Nobody*'. He marched away.

The indoor training theatre resounded with the gunfire from the training teams that were still fighting against the holograms. The training rounds they used only had a range of a couple of metres. The holograms registered hits but real bodies would feel their impact like real rounds. Box felt sweat roll down his face.

'Just wait for the real thing,' muttered Razool, clearing a training round from the breach of his carbine.

Box noticed the well-practised way Razool handled the weapon, just like he handled all the weapons and all the drills.

'How long do you think we'll last?' asked Box.

'We'll be up against more than one X'ath at a time,' observed Razool.

X'ath was what spikers were really called, but spikers said it all. Box spat. 'So we don't get to last long then?'

Razool's eyes narrowed. 'We fought our way out of the Fleshings, didn't we?'

Box nodded. He and Razool and Skarl and Raxa, and every snout at this training camp had fought their way out of the Fleshing yards: the arenas on the prison planets where snout criminals and outcasts were used for target practice by the Twisted Symmetry's Dog Troopers. They had fought so well that they had been rewarded by a transfer to the penal battalions. The penal battalions were filled with the roughest, crookedest, most expendable snouts, ready to be deployed into the most desperate battle zones of the Crystal Wars.

'Nobody expected us to make it out of the Fleshings, did they?' stated Razool.

'No,' agreed Box.

'Well, this will be a bit like that.' The tall, lean snout sat down, cross-legged.

'How come you know so much about everything?' asked Box, sitting down beside him. 'And how come they made you a mutineer?'

'When we've got ten minutes, I'll tell you,' replied Razool.

Box licked his lips. 'How long to lunch?'

'Hours,' muttered Razool. 'There's a hunt and destroy exercise next.'

Box groaned.

'Jander, Box,' swore Skarl. 'Do you only think about fodder?'

'Ignore Skarl,' murmured Razool. 'Technically, he's dead.'

'I don't only think about fodder.' Box was definite. 'I think about getting off this planet and finding my sister: finding Chess.' He rolled his thick-muscled shoulders to ease them. All trace of the flabby fourteen-year-old had gone. He was nearly sixteen now and his body was hard and fast. 'And *then*, I think about fodder.'

He didn't know where Chess was. But he knew that the Twisted Symmetry were hunting her; that she was the one they needed if they were going to stop time and live for ever, annihilating everything that wasn't part of them. So the Twisted Symmetry had to be stopped. But more than that, Chess was his sister. He wasn't going to let the enemy hurt her. He couldn't do the things she could, but he could protect her. That was why he had fought his way out of the Fleshing yards and that was why he would fight every inch of the way back to her.

He looked about, at his snout comrades, the friends who had survived the Fleshing yards alongside him. Here he was, a skin who had become a Dog Trooper: fighting the enemy by becoming the enemy. He laughed to himself, dryly.

'Glad you're having fun,' observed Skarl.

'Skins,' muttered Razool, with a shake of his head. 'Weird sense of humour.'

The fighting had stopped. The holograms had been phased out. As the lights of the training theatre dimmed, the fire teams waited in small clumps.

'Everyone up,' barked the senior instructor. 'Everyone out. Leave the carbines at the exit. Collect tunics, helmets and buzz-guns outside.'

Box, Razool, Skarl and Raxa fell into line, tramping out of the huge concrete bunker. This was the second session of the morning. For nearly five weeks they had been steamrollered through basic training: weapon drills, fire team tactics, glue and gore (which was what the instructors called first aid), unarmed combat, general fitness. Box found the fitness training easy and he liked any sort of combat, but most of all he liked unarmed combat. Training with the Dog Troopers had introduced him to some novel techniques, knife-hand neck strikes, open-palm rib smashes, useful against an opponent with a big mouth and lots of teeth where a fist to the jaw would be like punching a shredder.

Box slotted his carbine into the weapon rack and blinked daylight out of his eyes as he emerged from the concrete exit. Rain pattered through the high trees, smacking onto his bare shoulders like cold spit. But after two sweaty hours fighting holograms in the training theatre, he was glad to be out in the woodland. Glancing up, beyond the treetops, he saw a tear in the veil of woodland mist and beyond that, the glinting spray of the asteroid belt that was called the Klanf Causeway. Then the mist rolled over the treetops again, blotting out the Causeway, and now this could have been any woodland.

But Box knew that this was woodland on one of the four moons of a planet called Adron-B; that was what he had heard the instructors call it. He was a long way from home, from the wharf back in the city, on his own planet, where he had lived with Chess and Splinter, his twin brother, and the other street rats. But the wharf had been destroyed when all of this had begun, when the Twisted Symmetry had first come for Chess and she and Box and Splinter had had to run: run first to the Committee, who said they fought the Symmetry, and then run away from everything.

They came to the hut where they had left their tunics earlier. Box pulled his on and buttoned it over his damp vest. 'Splinter wouldn't believe this.' He chuckled quietly.

'Wouldn't believe what?' Razool tugged his tunic over his shoulders.

'Me. Here. Like this.' Box headed for the hut where the helmets were kept.

'Really?' Razool trudged next to him. 'Well, congratulations for being one of us.'

Box's breath fogged as he spoke. 'Splinter's all brains, see. He said he was going to join the Symmetry. He said they would give him an *opportunity*.'

'Yeah?' Razool tried on a helmet and handed it back because it was too small. 'An opportunity for what?'

Box scratched his head. 'I don't think I ever asked him.'

Razool dumped a helmet into Box's hands. 'He sounds about as smart as you, Box.'

'No, he's much smarter,' insisted Box.

'Is that possible?' sniggered Skarl.

It took Box a couple of seconds to decode the sarcasm and then he scowled.

'Box is plenty smart enough,' said Raxa, calmly. 'Smart enough to kick your skinny rump whenever you wind him up, Skarl'. And Raxa was right. Box might only have been a skin, but he was the best fighter of them all. He could use two mace-blades at once, his fists and feet struck like lightning, and he was deadly accurate with a blaze carbine, even on automatic fire.

Box found a helmet that fitted snugly. The damp mist sent a shiver across his skin. He noted that the instructors were warm. On the floor by the stack of helmets, a GPU was humming. General Purpose Units were self-reconfigurable machines. They were packed with microprocessors, sensors, motors and smart particles, and could be programmed to change size, shape and function as required. This one was pumping out heat, but it could easily reconfigure into lifting gear, an automatic medic or a heavy, twin-barrelled machine-gun.

'How are you going to find your sister, Box?' goaded Skarl.

Box's tongue licked across his teeth and he rubbed his chin, pondering. 'I know there's snouts in my world, so they must get there somehow. You reckon we could find transport somewhere, Zool?' His friend seemed to know a lot about things like that.

Razool just shrugged.

'Yeah,' scoffed Skarl. 'And if we found this transport, who's going to fly it? Any ideas, Zool?'

Razool nodded thoughtfully. 'I might give it a go.'

Skarl laughed. 'You're getting as stir-crazy as the skin.'

Razool said nothing.

Box grabbed a buzz-gun. 'I'm not here for fun, Skarl.' He pulled back the battery flap, checked the gun was powered up and slapped the flap shut. 'I'm here for Chess. And as soon as I see the chance, I'm out of this.'

The senior instructor marched out in front of them. 'Right,' he yelled. The chatter ceased so quickly that his voice was still echoing back from the files of thin black trees as the troopers fell silent.

They stood in three rows, thirty in each, breath steaming about them. Every face and body, apart from Box's, was a grotesque jumble of dog and man. Box might have looked different, but he knew that he was a part of the massive army under the command of one figure: General Saxmun Vane. At that thought he licked his lips, which were dry. The General was one of the most dangerous creatures in the universes; Box was certain that if the General knew he was hiding amongst his own troops, his transformation into dog food would be a swift one.

'Pair off,' came the order. 'Move out. Hunt and destroy to the last pair standing. Stay within the taped sector. Anyone outside the taped sector is dead. Instructors will move and fire at will. Anyone shoots an instructor, they get a day in the stable.'

There were no toilets in the training camp, just a huge pit

used by a thousand snouts. Each day the waste was shovelled and hosed to a heap before it was ignited. This pit was called the stable. Nobody wanted a day in the stable. Nobody wanted five minutes in the stable. But the instructors made sure that it was one of the busiest places in the camp.

Boots shuffled over the damp earth. Box and Razool paired up with one another.

'They're not shovels,' screamed another instructor. 'Hold them properly.' There was a general rattling and clattering of metal as the snouts positioned the buzz-guns across their chests.

The buzz-guns looked just like blaze carbines, the standard Dog Trooper firearm, but whereas the carbines pumped out up to five hundred rounds a minute, the buzz-guns were for training. They threw out an electric charge that could sting its target into yelping helplessness. They were good for up to thirty metres and a dial on the battery pack set the charge from one, a slap, up to six, a full punch.

'Set at two,' ordered the senior instructor, 'and goggles down. I don't want you to blind yourselves. Save that for the enemy.'

Box turned his dial to four. He wanted to make sure that anyone he hit couldn't bluff their way through the rest of the exercise.

'What are you doing, skin?' The senior instructor's breath was hot against the back of Box's neck.

'Introducing an element of surprise,' replied Box, and then, automatically because it had been drilled into him, 'Surprise increases combat effectiveness by a factor of six hundred per cent.'

The instructor walked in front of Box and put his bristly chin up close. He sniffed, the nostrils in his black muzzle flaring slightly. Box came to attention with a stamp of his foot, body rigid. 'Sir!' he added.

'Don't joke with me,' said the instructor quietly.

Box knew to say nothing.

The instructor stepped back. 'Right,' he barked at the assembled troops. 'Goggles down. Dials at two.' He glanced over at Box. 'At *two*.'

Razool pulled his goggles into place. 'Four isn't surprise, Box.' He rubbed his wolf jaw thoughtfully. 'Six would be surprise.' He checked the dial on his buzz-gun. 'Ready?'

Box nodded.

The whistle blew for the start of the exercise.

Box and Razool shouldered their weapons and eliminated eight other pairs on the spot.

Surprise: nobody said you couldn't start shooting *before* you ran.

Then they were into the trees, flitting between the trunks before anyone else could get a straight shot. Balls of electric charge crackled across twigs and down the tree trunks or fizzed out in the mist, but Box and Razool zig-zagged into denser woodland. Others followed them, just as Box and Razool knew they would.

Predictability: the twin brother of surprise.

Box slid into a clump of briars. Five metres away, Razool was on his belly, behind a screen of saplings. Three more pairs were closing in, hesitating between giving chase and opening up on one another.

Box was up and running again, but only for long enough

for all six buzz-guns to turn on him. Then he was back down, almost burrowing into the earth, and Razool was up, gun blazing electric blue only metres in front of his bewildered targets.

Three more pairs taken out.

Now, Box and Razool would lie low for a few minutes; let the other pairs whittle one another down before the real job of stalking began.

Box snaked into a dense thicket. Sweat had fogged the inside of his goggles. He pushed them up and wiped his forehead with the sleeve of his tunic. The air was cool so he kept his face into his shoulder; he didn't want to reveal his position by his steaming breath. His eyes rested on the small, horizontal figure-of-eight embroidered on the shoulder of his tunic: the awlis, the symbol for infinity and the mark of the Twisted Symmetry. He was used to it now. He was even used to wearing it.

Shouts and thudding footfalls came through the trees and the thin drifts of mist. Box listened to the crash of vegetation and the high crackle of the buzz-guns. There was an occasional yelp but on two the pain was not so bad. Then he listened to his heart, thumping steadily as his breathing settled. He could actually feel his heart working, and the tight fabric of his tunic rose and fell in a tremor as it beat.

It was strange, how loud your heart could sound, how loud it could be to you, but to no one else. And with that thought, Box knew immediately that something else *was* listening: listening to him and watching.

So many years of creeping through the city, eagle-eyed for slack pockets or unlocked cars, vanishing whenever the crashers turned up, hiding from the hunters, meant that Box knew when trouble was near. There was that sudden sense of nakedness, the tingle beneath his skin, like shivering wings, the weight of eyes watching. But this time, he knew that something was listening too.

Who was watching? Who was listening?

Box raised his face slowly; sudden movements would give him away if he hadn't been seen already. He kept his breathing steady and listened back, but the only thing he could hear was the thump of his heart.

Around him, the near woodland was still. There was the steady tap of rainwater dripping from the thin black boughs, and the cries and howls of snouts from further off. His breath rose like steam, warm on his face. He scanned the surrounding clumps of saplings and boulder-sized nests of undergrowth for any movement but there was nothing. And then, not more than twenty metres away, within a dense thicket, he saw the switches part slightly.

Box's dark eyes narrowed. The switches parted, revealing nothing. But he knew that something in that empty space was watching him, and listening: listening to the beat of his heart.

For a moment, Box was back on the planet Surapoor, where he and Splinter and Chess had met Balthazar Broom. It was hot, it was before Balthazar had started to teach him how to fight and he was warning them about something called a spook. Spooks were invisible and they were used by the Twisted Symmetry to find whoever the Symmetry wanted to find. They found their targets by listening. With only a tiny amount of someone's blood, a spook could listen across time and space for the heart that had pumped it. And however long it took, a spook always found what it was listening for.

Box blinked rainwater out of his eyes. Or was it sweat? A stone's throw from where he lay, the nothingness stirred in the thicket. Inside his chest, his heart thumped.

Without moving his head, Box slid his hand down the buzz-gun until his fingers felt the catch of the charge dial. He rotated it as far as it would go: up to six. Then, minutely, he worked the gun up his chest using his fingers until the muzzle was poking free of his prone body. The spook, if it was a spook, was close enough and still enough to make aiming easy, even with the gun held fast to his body. Box curled a finger round the trigger.

There were all sorts of questions that he could have asked, but Box never liked to waste too much time on questions.

'Listen to *this*, you sneaky piece of skak,' and he squeezed the trigger.

A crackling ball of blue light burst from the gun. It hit the space between the thin branches with a shower of brilliant sparks, and then Box saw it. A slender body, thin as a shadow but silver, with long arms and legs, and an almond-shaped, featureless head trailing waist-length black tendrils like thick cords of hair, which curled and twitched. It had been crouching, using its long, whippy arms to part the vegetation above its head so that it could look out, and the long tendrils had been rippling towards Box as if swept that way by a flow of water. But as the charge struck home, the spook leapt up, thrashing about within the thicket and issuing such a nerve-shearing screech that Box plugged his ears with his fists.

Then the thicket burst open and Box knew that the spook was coming for him. The last of the electric charge danced across its silver skin before the spook vanished from sight, but before Box could begin to scramble to his feet, he was hauled up by the back of his tunic and flung out of the tangled brush.

He struck a tree trunk side-on, the air smashing from his lungs. Even as he rolled to his knees his foot was gripped and his body cracked back as effortlessly as if he were a piece of rope. The spook let go. Box saw the tree coming at him and had time to bury his head in his arms before they hit the solid wood.

At the edge of his vision, Box caught sight of Razool sprinting out of the trees, followed by Skarl and Raxa and two of the instructors.

'What the hell ...' gasped one of the instructors as Box was hauled up by nothing that anyone could see and flung through the air into a wall of saplings.

This time he felt something hit his head and now he caught only shots of what was being shouted, and saw only snaps of what happened about him.

'What is it?'

'Where is it?'

'It'll kill him!'

The voices echoed. Figures danced about him, upside down and in and out of his vision. He wanted to fight back but there was no way of knowing where the spook would come from and it was unbelievably strong. He punched out drunkenly, kicked as he felt something grip his arm, and his foot made contact but he was shaken like a rat just the same.

Then cool air rushed across his face, his head was spinning and he felt the heavy smack of earth.

Legs closed about him: Skarl and Raxa kneeling by his shoulders and standing over him, Razool.

'I can't see it. Where is it?' Skarl, a desperate edge to the voice.

'Watch the ground,' barked Razool. 'It's coming, straight at us.'

Box rolled to his side and angled his face to look where the guns were pointing.

'The leaves. Watch the leaves,' shouted Razool.

'Seen,' yelled Raxa.

'Seen,' yelled Skarl.

Box could hear the spook running towards them and he saw the leaves kick up in a streak.

'Now,' ordered Razool.

The air exploded in a maelstrom blur of electric charge. The silver body became visible, flinging itself into trees, pin-balling from one to the next, long limbs flailing. It shrieked so wildly its cries could have shattered teeth. But the snouts didn't let up. From where he lay on the ground, blood blurring his vision, Box could see Razool, Raxa and Skarl discharging the buzz-guns in a blinding skein, and others were joining them. Only when the spook had vanished, shrieking and leaping into the woods, and the crackling had stopped did Box close his eyes and let the darkness well up.

The darkness didn't last long.

'Not again,' groaned Box as someone grasped his lapels and heaved him to his knees.

'No,' Razool snapped at the instructor, and dazed as he

was, Box was surprised to feel the earth soft beneath his shoulders as the instructor laid him back down.

'Feel your toes?' asked Razool, his rough, hairy fingers pushing back Box's eyelids, steam issuing in sharp snorts from his alsatian snout. He had pulled off his helmet and the mane of black hair hung over his shoulders.

'I'm wiggling them,' said Box.

Cries of 'cease firing' ricocheted through the woods.

'Lucky it wasn't hungry,' observed Razool. 'A hungry spook is a dangerous spook.'

'Yeah,' groaned Box. 'Really lucky. I guess that one was just being playful.' He sat up and felt sick.

'Where is it?' asked the instructor. He looked into the trees.

'It's gone,' said Razool. 'Someone put a spook on him and now it's found what it was looking for.' Razool licked a fang thoughtfully and stared at Box. 'Now, why would someone put a spook on *you*?'

'It doesn't matter what's been put on him,' snapped the senior instructor, and then to the instructor who had spoken with Razool, 'and *you're* in charge here, not the mutineer. We're not playing doctors. You want the skin on his feet? He gets to his feet. Simple.' Box was yanked to his feet. His head spun as if it had just been hit with a mallet. 'You're in the stable, skin. For a week.'

Behind the senior instructor, the gathered snouts parted and two figures in full battle dress and bearing the zig-zag shoulder flashes of the communications corps stomped forwards. Their blaze carbines were slung down their backs, and the long cosh grips of their mace-blades swung from their utility belts as they marched. They stopped in front of Box and the senior instructor.

'Tidy him up, sergeant,' said the first, with a cursory nod at Box. 'The only place he's going is the embarkation zone.'

'Together with the rest of them,' continued the second. 'We have your orders. This company is to join the Zoth-fura battlegroup. Tonight.'

'Tonight?' coughed Box. He was still bleeding from the gash in his forehead, although the strength had returned to his legs.

'Tonight,' repeated the trooper. 'What do you think you're all here for, skin? This push has been building for months, but before the main force go in we need something to distract the enemy. That's why they're sending you lot in first.' Her breath hung about her short-haired head. 'The cannon fodder.' The flat, grey-skinned muzzle twitched a wry, dog-smile. 'You'll be dreaming of the stable when this carve-up starts.'

CHAPTER 2

Chess couldn't believe how stupid she had been. But it seemed that now she had plenty of time to play back her own stupidity. She was imprisoned in space: space that enclosed her like a wall. Like a cell. A cell so small that she could sit or stand or stretch her limbs but do no more. There was nothing to do apart from think how stupid she had been.

'I trusted you,' she muttered. 'I thought you were there to help me.' She kicked out at the wall, vague as mist but impenetrable as diamond.

But Splinter hadn't come to help her. He had come to lead her into the hands of the Twisted Symmetry. She looked at her wrists. The blue bruising had faded into yellow and brown and then vanished altogether, but she could still feel the way she had been beaten to the ground before she could react. And then, there had been coils of blue smoke that had bound her mind and body like chains. And then this cell.

But it was no ordinary cell. It seemed to block time, space, every dimension. Chess let her mind open, unravel the space about her, slip through the space within space. But this time, like every other time she had probed the cell, her mind encountered a barrier that not even she could penetrate.

She yelled at the wall of nothingness. She didn't know what the Symmetry were planning to do to her, but being trapped like this was like being buried alive. Right now, it felt as if anything would be better than this.

Anger and frustration boiled into a scream. But the wall withstood her hammering fist. Chess breathed deeply and felt the heat of rage in her eyes. She ran her hands through her long, curling, chestnut hair. She wouldn't give in. All she needed was a gap: a break in the wall.

And that was when her mind sensed space: space like a jet of fresh air; space swirling into the cell. Somewhere above her head, there was a break in the cell wall: maybe no more than an inch. But Chess didn't need more than an inch.

Instantly she reached for the opening, not with her hands but with her thoughts. To any ordinary person, it would have been useless for escape, but to Chess, it was something that could be opened and expanded as easily as a tent. This was how she had been made; this was the power she had learnt to use.

Her mind and body were rushing: rushing up and out, unfolding from the cell. Almost from a distance she heard a siren scream. An alarm. Now there was light and darkness. She was passing through the steel and concrete of a building, expanding out from the cell all the time. She was emerging from the cell and back into the real world, as swift as thought.

And with the freedom, there came anger, a white, boiling fury at how she had been imprisoned, at how she had been betrayed.

She had only to turn her eyes on steel, her mind towards concrete to decimate them with her fury. Anger and pain fuelled her power and she was full of both.

Figures moving about her, below her: tiny beneath her exploding mind. Gowns of black and silver. Warps: the Twisted Symmetry's scientists and technicians. Chess drove a blinding wave of rage at them and saw bodies fragment into nothingness. And now, above her, there were stars and below her there was rock strewn with buildings and pipelines and corridors.

Chess flung her mind at what she saw, ripping apart rock, stone and metal in explosions of white and orange.

'You wanted me?' she screamed. 'You wanted *this*?'

And then, the sense of slowing, as if a brake had slammed over her soul. There was smoke, blue smoke, coiling about her legs, engulfing her body, wrapping her arms, smothering her face. And she was falling, shrinking: *diminishing*.

Chess struggled to move her arms and legs but the blue smoke fixed them like stone. Even her mind was locked within the confines of her body. She knew that the Twisted Symmetry had contained her again, had acted moments before she had escaped their clutches altogether, before she had removed the entirety of her being from the cell. And she knew that the cell was waiting for her. But she didn't scream with rage. She didn't cry out.

Chess knew that this time she had been too slow, had spent valuable moments unleashing fury when she should have extracted her mind and body from the cell altogether. She had been clumsy. She had allowed anger to swamp judgement. She would not make the same mistake again. Next time she would make sure to slip her bonds entirely. Then she would unleash anger. And there *would be* a next time.

Chess smiled at whoever was watching what was happening. 'You don't know what you are dealing with,' she whispered.

The spaces between the stars shrank, dragging with them thoughts that stretched from nebula to nebula, and from this vastness, four human-shaped figures took form: Malbane, ancient and in a monk's black cowl; Snargis, a beggar, swathed in pus-sodden bandages; Azgor in a red gown, her hair dark indigo but her eyes bright with snake-sharp pupils; and Veer, dark eyed, blonde haired and immaculate in a black suit and waistcoat, and a gold and blue tie fastened with a ruby-headed pin beneath a wing collar.

Four Inquisitors: masters of the Twisted Symmetry.

They stood on a high, metal viewing platform inside a colossal hangar that was a speck on the surface of the forty-kilometre-wide rock which orbited the dead planet, Rath: a rock so loaded with jagged metalwork that it looked like a city skyline bristling with vast pylons and girders which reached into space for tens of kilometres.

Inside the hangar, spotlights dotted the vaulted roof like stars. Save for them, there was no illumination. The spotlights were trained on one point, a space level with the viewing platform and mid-way between the floor, far below, and the ceiling, high above. At this point there floated a fourteen-year-old girl in jeans and a leather jacket, her hair thick and long in chestnut coils, her head slack on her neck. Her eyes were closed. She appeared to be sleeping as she hung in the air and about her swirled streaks of blue smoke, curling, darting, spiralling.

All eyes were fixed on the girl. Even as the clunk of heavy boots approached the Inquisitors down one of the connecting aerial walkways, they didn't switch their gaze. Veer panted slightly and Snargis licked his wet lips and Azgor's mottled fingers clenched the steel safety bar hard enough to bend it. Malbane folded his hands as if in prayer and a smile of the deepest serenity soothed the old lines of his face.

Only when the thud of boots had stopped a body length from where the Inquisitors were standing did Malbane speak.

'Beautiful, isn't she?' Even then, his ancient eyes remained on Chess.

'She's not my type,' growled General Saxmun Vane. 'And anyway, she owes me an arm.' He flexed the skeletal structure of steel rods that was riveted to his right shoulder and curled, then uncurled the gleaming metal fingers.

Three other dog-men, in black leather greatcoats and wearing dark glasses and throat mikes, halted by the General's shoulder. Their heads, part dog, part human, part skin, part hair, turned to face the Inquisitors and their snouts were impassive: fangs hidden behind dark lips.

'I wanted you to see her.' Malbane turned to face the General now. 'To see what we have been working for. To see how close we have come.' He spoke in the common language of Chat.

Now the General turned his jackal-snouted face towards Chess. He was tall and lean, his body cased in a jigsaw body armour of plate and chain, and he wore a long, fur cloak. His savage eyes narrowed as he studied the hanging girl.

'She looks so harmless like that,' murmured the General, roughly. His sleek head cocked to one side as he evaluated what he saw.

'Harmless,' considered Malbane, 'is one thing she is not. We had an incident, only days ago.' The Inquisitor shrugged. 'It seems that there was a breach in the continuity of the Möbius cell. The girl caused a good deal of damage: deaths and so forth.' He waved a hand towards the blue smoke which cocooned her. 'Whilst the xenrian gaolers have infiltrated her sub-atomic fields, she is unable to shift through space, barely able to move, in fact; the dimensions remain closed to her.' Malbane shrugged. 'But for that, she has the potential to destroy us as easily as she destroyed Behrens.'

'There was nothing easy about *that*,' growled the General. He had been at the factory on Surapoor when Chess had destroyed the fifth Inquisitor, Behrens. He had been caught in the explosion of energy; he had his new arm to prove it. He took hold of the guard rail which clanged as his metal fingers closed on it.

'You see her just as her brother, Splinter, gave her to us.'

Malbane cast a glance at Chess. 'The same clothes even. Brought here a little over a month ago, she has been waiting whilst the warps have made their preparations; whilst the cylinders have been shipped in.'

'Take care what she does with all that energy,' warned the General. 'With all that pain and suffering you have harvested.' He inspected his gleaming right arm. 'All those millions of cylinders you have stockpiled, and with just one, she destroyed Behrens.'

Malbane stepped closer to the General. 'In a little over five months, the time spiral will reach the fifth node.'

'The fifth node,' repeated Veer in a hissing whisper.

'The point at which it is most vulnerable,' continued Malbane. 'And the point at which we shall unleash the Eternal.'

'Stopping time and space so the Symmetry can live forever,' yawned General Saxmun Vane. 'I know, I know. All very fine ... *for the Symmetry*.'

'General,' purred Malbane, reaching out to touch Vane's shoulder, where the silver awlis was stitched to black fabric. 'You are part of the Symmetry; you and all your troopers.' He pursed his lips and looked sorrowfully at the three granitic dog-men who stood close by the General. The hanging girl was reflected in their black lenses. 'It is a pity,' Malbane observed with apparent sincerity, 'that you felt it necessary to bring protection.'

'Protection?' mused the General, his rough, low growl of a voice quizzical. 'Well, Malbane, one can never be too careful. One never knows where danger lurks. But the Cerberus agents are only here to keep me company. I am confident I have better guarantees of protection. After all, your precious reserves of crystal and your precious cylinders of energy depend upon *my* keeping them safe.'

The General turned his jackal snout towards the other Inquisitors and a sharp-toothed smile played at the edges of his long mouth. 'So, it is in all our interests that our meeting proceeds smoothly.' He shrugged his broad, lean shoulders apologetically and looked out at where Chess hung. 'It would be a shame if all your precious raw materials were destroyed after you have worked so hard.'

Veer hissed before darkness erupted from the place where his aquiline head had been.

'No, Veer,' ordered Malbane, barely raising his voice. The darkness shrank back to Veer's head but the Inquisitor turned hate-filled eyes on the General.

The three dog-men in the greatcoats stared at the Inquisitors stonily and said nothing. Malbane approached one of them and looked him up and down. 'You military types can't resist your special forces,' he said to Vane, wryly.

'They are necessary,' replied the General. 'The special operations undertaken by Cerberus are important.'

'To whom, General? Important to whom?' Malbane did not press for a reply. He moved closer to the agent and inspected the small silver knife-within-a-shield badge worn on his shoulder. 'The symbol they wear is not one I recognize,' observed the Inquisitor, delicately, and he turned his aged, priestly face towards the General, as if awaiting an explanation.

'The X'ath want crystal because it enables their bodies to

regenerate.' General Vane rubbed his lower jaw. 'And you want crystal because it will allow you to live forever. And it is the Dog Troopers' great privilege to fight and die in the endless conflict which ensues.' General Vane spoke low, without taking his eyes off Chess. 'For millennia, we have fought and died for the Symmetry.'

'The Dog Troopers were created by the Symmetry, *for* the Symmetry,' Malbane reminded the General, gently.

The General snorted. 'Who has been fighting the Crystal Wars for you, these past few epochs? The Dog Troopers. Who protects the cross-universal shipping lanes for you? The Dog Troopers.' He could not prevent his abrasive voice from rising. 'Who protects the Crystal Mines? The Dog Troopers. Who guards your precious deposits of energy, and of crystal? The Dog Troopers.'

The General's lips curled back, revealing the long fangs that were neatly sheathed against one another and he arced his long head round so that his yellow eyes were riveted on the Inquisitor. 'But what I have been asking myself lately, Malbane, is who protects the Dog Troopers? When the big crunch comes, when you "unleash the Eternal" and time and space stop, for *your* eternal benefit, what happens to *my* people?'

'General,' soothed Malbane, as if stung by an accusation.

'Malbane,' accused the General. 'The Plague Breed are sustained by Snargis.' Snargis wrenched up the side of his mouth in a smile which revealed a cluster of thrashing worm tails. 'Azgor's will sustains the Havoc Legions. All of you sustain your chosen servants.' The General's voice reverberated within the vaulting darkness of the chamber and he folded his metal arm with his muscled one, the chains of his armour clinking. 'But it seems to me that when the time comes, no one will sustain *us*.'

'We have made provision for you,' insisted Malbane. 'You have to trust us.' The Inquisitor inclined his grey-haired head, conciliatory. 'After all, General, we trust you. We have always trusted you. Even with the missing shipments of crystal, we have trusted you. By the way, what happened to the commander of those vessels?'

'He was dealt with,' growled General Saxmun Vane. 'Appropriately.'

'Saxmun, Saxmun,' murmured Malbane, and he smiled reassuringly. 'We all have to trust each other.'

'She is here,' whispered Veer, sibilantly.

'Ah, good,' murmured Malbane. 'We begin at last.'

A figure in a long gown, black but criss-crossed with silver strands, approached soundlessly along one of the aerial walkways. Her face was so white it seemed to float out of the darkness and it was crowned by short, bristling hair. Her eyes were hidden behind the pince-nez spectacles that sat on her chisel nose and although her face was thin, her mouth and lower jaw jutted forwards, angular and heavy.

'Greetings, Petryx,' said Malbane, with a courteous nod.

'Malbane,' responded Petryx Ark-turi, the Symmetry's primary warp. 'Azgor, Veer, Snargis.' She nodded at each before turning her round, black lenses on the General. 'General, I am honoured,' she said, without a hint of irony, and without a hint of warmth. When she spoke, she did so nasally, stabbing each word precisely. When she was silent, her mouth remained a tight black line.

General Saxmun Vane grunted.

'You must forgive the General,' explained Malbane. 'Ever since . . . ever since his unfortunate accident he has struggled to be civil, where warps are concerned.'

'But we have done all we can to punish the Traitor,' insisted Petryx Ark-turi. 'It is no fault of ours if he succeeded in extracting his mind before we captured his body.'

'Where is Sprazkin's body now?' asked the General, swallowing back fury as he thought of Lemuel Sprazkin, who had once been the Symmetry's primary warp and whose failed surgical operation to turn the General into a human had left the General's body with a tendency to mutate, without warning, into a chaos of fleshy lumps, extra limbs and flailing tentacles: a tendency that could be controlled only by a serum manufactured for him by the warps.

'The Traitor's body is here, at this station,' said Malbane. 'Brought here so that our primary warp may give it her most intimate attention. But alas,' he shrugged, 'not even a squeal.'

'It has been like torturing . . .' Petryx-Ark-turi selected the right word before spearing it through her nose, 'putty.'

'Two hundred years I have waited,' snarled the General, 'for you to torture putty? I thought the infliction of pain was your speciality?'

'Pain,' observed Malbane, 'is merely the necessary means to a beautiful end.'

Petryx Ark-turi looked out at Chess. The warp's nostrils flared minutely.

Malbane patted her on the arm. 'You have done well to restrain your appetites, Petryx.'

'It has been difficult.' The warp's voice quavered. 'It is always difficult with children, and with this one...' She shook her head. 'Just a small feed would have been...' She exhaled tremulously.

'Just a small feed might have been too much, Petryx,' Malbane admonished her, gently. 'Once you start to feed, it is difficult to stop.'

'I know, I know,' agreed the warp and she inhaled deeply. 'She is perfect.' She turned her spectacles towards Malbane. 'I am glad you are here, glad all of you are here to watch the first fusion.'

'We have been waiting a very long time. We wouldn't want to miss it,' Malbane assured her.

'Not at all,' echoed Snargis.

'Not for anything,' whispered Veer.

From the darkness above their heads, an electric hum began. With no more than that, a giant metal arm ribbed with tubes and strung with cables, unfolded from the heights of the chamber, gleaming as it extended into the focused glare of the spotlights. On the end of the arm was a metallic plate the size of a door, and this plate was encased in copper-coloured windings.

A second arm extended downwards from the ceiling, bearing an identical metal plate. It stopped with its plate opposite the first, and with Chess's body in the space between them.

'Save for the unfortunate incident, the girl has been kept in a Möbius cell until now,' explained Petryx Ark-turi, her sharp, nasal voice stabbing the reverential hush. 'It is the only way to contain a being with her extraordinary dimensional powers.'

'Then how did the unfortunate incident happen?' enquired the General. 'How did she escape?'

'We do not know,' snapped the warp. 'But it will not happen again. She has been sedated: sedated quite heavily, although the effects of that drug will diminish swiftly from this point on.'

Already, Chess was stirring, her loose head lolling from side to side as she emerged from the drugged sleep. Her arms hung by her body, pinned there by the smoking xenrian gaolers.

The air about the metal plates began to glimmer.

'Every minute, eighteen cylinders of energy are loaded into the system. The energy is transferred here.' The warp pointed at the huge arms. The General snorted and looked up at the darkness. 'You won't see the cylinders in here, General,' explained Petryx Ark-turi. 'They are shipped into a different sector of the station altogether, and the energy transferred via the FCAs.'

'FCAs,' muttered the General. 'Very helpful.'

'Flat Coil Accelerators,' whispered Malbane, patiently. 'They drive the energy over three kilometres, exciting it to this pitch.' He indicated the plates, which had become translucent and almost indistinguishable from the hot blur of air about them.

Chess's brown eyes were wide open now. The General could smell the fear. 'For such a powerful creature, she is terrified,' he observed.

The corner of the warp's tight lips twisted out a smile. 'For such a powerful creature, she is utterly helpless.'

Chess was able to move her head from left to right, but her body and limbs were held fast. She didn't look over to the party who had been watching her and the General realized that she couldn't see them: the bright spotlights blinded her from seeing beyond their glare.

He noticed that above the hum, there was a new noise: a whine which was slowly building, as if the darkness had found a voice. The girl had noticed it too; the General could tell that.

As the whine intensified into a high-pitched scream, the air around the plates appeared to become increasingly hot. A liquid shimmer spread outwards from the plates, as if reaching from one to the other, and as the screaming grew louder and louder, a stream of air began to buckle and fork from them both, breaking and curling about Chess's body.

General Vane glanced sidelong at the primary warp whose restrained panting had momentarily distracted him. His lip curled; the way these warps struggled with their artificially engineered appetites disgusted him. There was no honesty to it. If he felt angry, he was angry; if he was in the mood for violence, he would do violence.

Without taking his eyes off the girl, the General whispered to the warp, 'Breathe in my ear like that anymore and I'll use your stupid glasses to cut your stupid throat.'

'Saxmun,' cautioned Malbane from the other side of the warp.

The screaming that cut in blotted out all other noise.

As the ripping shriek seared him to his core, General Vane saw the waves and forks of energy from the two plates stream into Chess's body, as if they were connecting with one another at last, as if the girl was drawing the energy into herself. Her back spasmed, even in the grip of the xenrian gaolers, and her head was flung back but although her mouth was wide open, no sound came out that the General could hear.

With a roar, the last of the energy rushed into her body and then there was silence.

'The agonies of half a million souls released into one small body,' stated Petryx Ark-turi, neutrally.

Chess's head hung forwards, her thick hair hiding her face beneath its tangle. The General thought he could hear the gentle strains of the girl catching her breath.

'The energy transfer will be repeated every minute,' said the warp. Already the whining was re-commencing, the air about the plates shimmering. 'Our stockpiles amount to some four million cylinders, equating to many billions of souls.'

'Trillions,' stated Azgor, parting her dry lips and revealing a dark tongue which slipped across them.

'Energy harvested from so much agony,' mused Veer, eyes closed in serene ecstasy.

'The humans and their children are only a small part,' slobbered Snargis. 'But,' with an eruption of mucal foam from the corner of his worm-infested mouth, 'a most *potent* part.'

'And all to be contained by *her*.' Malbane looked across to the girl.

'I still do not see how one small body can hold so much,' said the General, gruffly.

'Her body is small,' admitted Malbane, voice rising against the building scream of the energy which was roiling from the plates, 'but her spirit is vast. There is no time or place that it will not be able to touch. It will take as much pain and suffering as we can charge it with.'

Malbane was shouting to be heard, and the General noticed an uncharacteristically wild cast to his eyes. 'When the time comes for the Eternal, she will be ready to explode: ready to release enough energy across time and space to draw the universes back into their original, perfect nothingness.'

The scream blotted out Malbane's voice. The jerking fingers of energy met at Chess's body and drove themselves into it. The girl strained against the force fields of the gaolers and then hung limp again.

'All that energy just waiting to be released from her,' said Malbane, calmly now. 'We just have to press the right switch.'

The General snorted. 'The Committee will try to rescue her. Five months gives them plenty of time.'

'Of course they will,' smiled Malbane.

'They will not succeed,' stated Petryx, through her chisel nose. She ground her box-like lower jaw and the General couldn't fail to notice the hard motion beneath the pale skin, as if behind that skin something sharp was moving.

Warps: they revolted him. The General felt an

overwhelming desire to fasten his fangs to the warp's throat and rip it out.

'This warp station is encased in a fractal code,' Petryx was explaining, competing with the screeching energy. 'It surrounds the entire station metasphere and is cross-dimensional, which means that it cannot be penetrated without the access data.'

Conversation ceased as the next energy transfer screamed to its conclusion. In the ensuing silence, Petryx Ark-turi continued mechanically. 'The station itself is well guarded.'

'With?' enquired the General.

'With our own guards,' replied the primary warp. 'Guards that we have designed. And there are other security measures that will prevent infiltration. The Committee *cannot* rescue her.'

'You *hope*,' muttered the General, and his sharp yellow eyes looked out at the girl. She lifted her head, as if looking back at him. For an instant it seemed as if their eyes locked. 'Who knows how this will end?' rumbled the General, huskily.

'You will perform your duties, General. And you will perform them *properly*.' There was no obvious threat; there didn't have to be: Malbane was an Inquisitor.

With a slamming of his heavy, iron-shod boots, the General turned to go. The Cerberus agents moved in between his back and the Inquisitors.

'We have given the Endgame order,' stated Malbane.

'I trust that isn't a warning.'

'Of course it isn't, General, but I thought you should

know.' The Inquisitor waited for the General's reply.

General Vane was silent for a minute before he turned and asked, 'Why should I need to know that you have given the order to assassinate the Committee's personnel?'

'There is no room for error now,' replied Malbane. 'No longer any room for organized resistance.' He smiled benignly, face creased and careworn. 'The Committee must be neutralized.'

'Except Mevrad,' scoffed Vane, knowingly.

'We shall not touch Mevrad,' conceded the Inquisitor.

'You could not touch her even if you wanted to,' laughed the General. 'She is too powerful.'

'She cannot interfere in this.' Malbane folded his hands behind his back. 'We have access to a power every bit as great as Mevrad. For *that* reason, she will not interfere. The remainder of the Committee will be neutralized; the Blood Sentinels too; anyone of significance.'

'Obviously,' sighed General Vane, bored by this catalogue of the Symmetry's targets. 'Why are you telling me what I already know?'

'We have located the boy, Box Tuesday.' Malbane watched the General's face closely.

After the briefest of hesitations, General Vane said, 'Why should that be of any interest to me, Malbane?'

'We put a spook on him,' explained Malbane. 'He left blood on one of the blaze carbines recovered after the mayhem in the Fleshing yard on the prison planet, PURG-CT483. By the way, General, did you know the boy was in that Fleshing yard?'

'There are many Fleshing yards,' replied the General, carefully.

'But there has only ever been one human there,' observed the Inquisitor, with equal caution. He held up a hand. 'No matter. But, the interesting thing is this. Do you know where we traced him to?'

'Amaze me.'

'To a training camp off Adron-B, training with *your* troopers. Isn't that extraordinary, General?'

'Nothing is extraordinary, Malbane. But if you are suggesting ...'

'Please, General,' laughed Malbane, apologetically. 'I am suggesting nothing. I just thought you should know that there was a human hidden amongst your troopers. We all know how you detest humans.'

'He is a boy, you say. Only a boy?'

'His brother, Splinter, is only a boy, as you put it, but he proved an equal match for the Crystal Priests, and that without *our* assistance. The Crystal Priests are a spent force now, due in large measure to the activities of Splinter Tuesday.' Malbane rested a hand on Vane's metal arm, and spoke confidentially. 'What concerns us, General, is the harm that Splinter's brother can do. Of the *use* which could be made of him.'

'This brother, the one in the training camp, remind me of his name.'

'Box,' said Malbane, helpfully. 'Box Tuesday.'

The General sniffed. 'He has days to live. The penal battalions are being sacrificed in the push to soften up the enemy. Don't spend time worrying about the boy, Malbane.'

'We won't Saxmun, we won't,' smiled Malbane. 'But just to be on the safe side, we have sent in our own agent, to do the job properly. We have made arrangements. Wherever Box Tuesday goes, death will track him down.'

CHAPTER 3

'Watch the blast vents,' shouted Razool, voice competing with the background roar of engines and the whirr of turbines.

Box walked in step beside him, both in black combats with kit-bags slung across their backs. Behind them came Skarl and Raxa. The floor of the deck felt hard and flat beneath his boots which was good because beyond the surging troops and the colossal ships which towered about them, the high cranes and container stacks, there was only the yawning darkness of space and then the bouldering arm of the Klanf Causeway, much bigger and much closer than it had been when Box had looked at it from the woods of Adron-B. The moon-sized chunks of rock arced away from them and into oblivion.

'Blast vents?' Box shouted back. He resisted the urge to rub the itching ache on his head where the medics had stitched the gash left by the spook's assault.

There were thousands of troopers, disembarking from the hulking troop ships that had carried them to this vast platform, suspended in the star-spotted darkness of space.

Here, they would receive the combat briefing and their equipment. Then they would be taken into the battle zone. Box's dark eyes narrowed. As usual, the trick would be to stay alive.

Everywhere that he looked, there was massive activity. Flat-hulled destroyers the size of football pitches, cruising in, miles above the deck; roaring fighters preparing to take off; and the small, neat pilot ships that Razool told him were used for reconnaissance and navigation, landing with surprising grace.

'How come you know what everything is?' shouted Box. There wasn't one piece of equipment or type of ship that Razool didn't know the name of.

They passed beneath the engines of a shark-nosed fighter. Box was caught in a surge of bodies and was swept wide of the vehicle as a row of baffles beneath the engines swivelled down and let out a jet of flame with a whoosh.

'Blast vents,' shouted Razool. 'Burning off exhaust gas.' He pulled one of his sharp-toothed grins. 'Biggest flame thrower you'll ever see.'

'Very lively.' Box pulled a fast grin back. The air was hot.

'Lively?' barked Skarl, close behind Box's shoulder.

'Skin-speak for dangerous,' Box heard Raxa explain.

'Yeah?' Skarl licked a fang. 'Seems that this deck's about as lively as combat, with none of the glory.'

'Not much glory in being gaffed by a spiker, Skarl,' observed Razool.

'Gaffed' was what the snouts called being speared by a X'ath spine. Box replayed the holograms in his mind:

hammer heads; long wings; armoured body plates; pulverizing jaws.

'Nobody goes for a trap shot,' the instructors had always barked. '*Nobody*.'

The knife-fanged jaws swoop in: armour ripped, muscle torn, bone smashed. All clean through.

'You OK?' shouted Razool.

'Loving it,' Box shouted back. OK, there were better places to be. But this was just the sort of chaos that could provide him with the opportunity he needed. Out of all this transport, there was a chance he could find something to get him back home. Razool had said some of the ships had a deep-vortex capability. Box just had to find one, and a way of working it. It sounded hard, but so had staying alive up to now and he was still here. He just had to get from here to Chess.

Box gritted his teeth, dark eyes like bullets. He hadn't seen Chess for months. That was plenty of time for the Symmetry to have hunted her down. But wherever Chess was, whatever was happening to her, he would get there.

'Any idea yet why someone put a spook on you?' enquired Razool, not so loudly.

Box shook his head. 'Nope.' No idea at all. And he didn't want to know. At least within this organized chaos, he was well hidden from whoever or whatever might be looking for him. Within the mass of troops, ships and equipment, he was nothing.

Box spotted a weapon-studded cruiser sweeping above them like a colossal manta ray. 'Will we be in one of those?'

'No,' replied Razool. 'We'll be in one of those,' and he pointed to a vast block of iron: square and jagged and solid as a fortress. It sat in a docking station, steam rolling from its blast vents and drifting upwards, veiling the steep entrance ramps. It was waiting for them, and around it sat four more of the same kind of ships, towering up from the deck.

'A transporter-class vessel,' said Razool. 'In this case,' he added, with a sage nod, 'a decommissioned prison ship.'

'Yeah, that's more like it,' said Box with resignation. 'Prison.'

'We're still a security risk, Box.' Razool looked serious. 'The bad snouts, remember? That's why we're here.'

'I'm not a snout,' Box reminded him.

'Don't worry.' Razool patted the silver awlis Box wore on the shoulder of his tunic. 'You're getting there.'

They had stopped; all of them had stopped: a sea of troopers assembled before an elevated platform where there stood five figures, one of whom wore heavy shoulder insignia which showed that he was in charge. Box noticed that all about the area into which the thousands of them had been corralled, there were huge video screens. He noticed also that he was amongst snouts whose scarred, man-dog faces and ravenous eyes, and whose slouching bodies and slaughter-house muscles marked them out as the roughest, most expendable snouts of all.

'This is Klanf 187,' boomed a hard voice, and Box saw that the figure with the shoulder regalia was now standing at a rostrum, on the platform, and speaking into the microphones. At the same time, the all-encompassing wall of screens flickered into light, each screen displaying a green sphere against a black background.

'I am Commodore Lartus. I have responsibility for this battlegroup. This is your briefing.'

Box heard Razool sniff contemptuously beside him. 'What's the matter?' whispered Box.

'Lartus is the matter,' muttered Razool. 'Did you know that incompetence increases risk by a factor of seven hundred per cent?' He shook his head. 'This operation will be very risky,' and his dark eyes slid sidelong to Box. 'Very, *very* lively.'

'You know the Commodore?' asked Box. He couldn't see how a mutineer like Razool could know someone like Lartus.

'Muzzle closed, ears open, Box,' grunted Razool.

'Klanf 187 is part of the X'ath homeland,' continued Commodore Lartus. The image on the screens switched to an aerial view of densely wooded marshlands. 'Your mission is to strike Klanf 187 causing maximum disruption. I repeat, your mission is to strike Klanf 187 causing maximum disruption.'

Now the screens showed a view across tree canopies beneath a brick-red sky. Box saw a loop of asteroids curling into the terracotta distance and guessed that Klanf 187 must be part of the Klanf Causeway.

'See those?' Razool's voice was gruff, low and he pointed at the images on the screen.

At first, Box couldn't see what Razool was talking about. Then he spotted the narrow, silver poles that rose at intervals out of the tree canopy.

'Aerial masts,' whispered Razool. 'The X'ath have

technology. They're smart.' He looked at Box, jet-eyed, intently. 'This is going to be messy.'

'Your landing zone will be here, in the green sector,' boomed the voice. The view changed to a plan in quadrants, imposed over another aerial view of Klanf 187. The green quadrant of the plan was flashing. 'Other battlegroups will be deployed in neighbouring sectors.'

'Who are the people with the Commodore?' asked Box, less interested in the technical diagrams than the figures in the long greatcoats and dark glasses, flanking the Commodore.

'Cerberus agents,' replied Razool. 'Special operations.'

'What's special about this operation?'

'We are. The Commodore is in command of a hundred thousand criminals. Cerberus are here to protect him.'

'Protect him? From what?' Box rubbed his jaw.

Razool chuckled. 'From a hundred thousand criminals, Box. We're the worst of the lot, remember?'

'Five agents can't do much against a hundred thousand of us,' observed Box.

'They can if they're holding close-range nuclear armaments.'

Box frowned. 'No way.'

'Yes way.'

'How come you know so much?' asked Box. 'Seriously, Zool, how come you know so much about all of this?'

'When we've got ten minutes ...'

'You'll tell me. I know, I know,' grunted Box.

'This attack,' continued the Commodore, 'is a deception. After you go in, the main force will launch an assault against the X'ath battle station at the end of the causeway. But since the X'ath will be sending all they have at *you*, the battle station will be vulnerable.'

'Expendable, see?' muttered Razool.

'The atmosphere on Klanf 187 is neutral. Standard equipment will be sufficient. Proceed to the quartermaster units where you will collect weapons and equipment before you embark.' The voice stopped. The images on the screens cut out.

'Not even a "good luck",' grumbled Skarl.

'Not necessary.' Razool shook his mane. 'Commodore Lartus won't waste words on what won't make him a commodore commander.'

The troops were moving again, but Razool stood still. 'In the skin world, before you came to us, you were a swipe, right?'

'A swipe?' Box scratched the black stubble on his head.

Razool lowered his voice. 'A thief.'

'Watch your mash,' warned Box. 'I wasn't *just* a swipe. I was also a burglar, a brawler and a robber. Just ask the crashers. They'll give you a long list of my abilities.'

'Crashers?'

'Police.' Box said the word in his own tongue, but Razool nodded.

'Listen.' His sleek, long-haired head moved close to Box's. 'In those hangars there's a lot of kit. In amongst it will be life-rafts.'

'Life-rafts?' Box scratched his head. 'For water?'

Razool cocked his head to one side. 'Do all skins scratch like you?' But he wasn't interested in the answer. 'Yes, Box.

Life-rafts for water. But we don't need them for water.'

'What do we need them for then?' and Box looked about, as if the answer to that might lie scattered somewhere about the deck.

'Survival,' said Razool. 'They'll be stacked up, after the rations.'

'How'd you know?'

'Because they always are. We're organized, Box. We're Dog Troopers.'

Box raised his eyebrows.

'Well,' sighed Razool, 'the rest of us are. The rafts are compressed, about this big.' He motioned with his swarthy, smooth-haired hands as if they were holding a grapefruit. 'Maybe a bit smaller. We're going to need two. Think you can get them? Get them and hide them in your kit bag?'

'But why?' insisted Box as they entered the quartermaster's.

'Shut up. Come here,' ordered a sergeant, who was directing the troopers into long queues. 'Body armour, utility kit, mace-blades, carbines, ammunition, rations. In that order. Then out.'

Ahead of Box, the troopers were shuffling down a low hangar the length of a railway tunnel, receiving equipment from logistics personnel at kit bays. There were instructions given in grunts, the rattle of metal on metal, the slap of body armour and helmets handed out or dropped to the floor and the hot, sour smell of bodies.

Box strapped on the black, slabbed jacket and thigh shields, and fastened the utility belt with its pouches for food, water, ammunition, emergency dressings, torch, nerve wrench. He asked for two mace-blades because he liked to fight with two but was given one only, the same as everybody else. He fastened the mace-blade to his belt, slung the carbine across his back, beside his kit bag and packed the ammunition blocks into the right pouches. He asked also whether they were going to be issued grenades and an old quartermaster with no nose and one arm told him what he would like to do with a box of grenades and a room full of skins. Then Box came to the rations.

'I want more,' said Box, after he had been given one ration pack.

The corporal handing out the cartons ignored him at first.

'I like food,' persisted Box, as if that made him different from any of the others who were queuing for rations. 'I want more.'

'You can't have more,' explained the corporal with surprising patience.

'But,' repeated Box, loudly and slowly, as if either he or the corporal were very stupid, 'I . . . like . . . food.' And then, to the astonishment of every snout who was watching, Box dropped his carbine from his shoulder, swung his kit bag under his arm and launched himself into a column of cardboard ration cartons.

The astonishment lasted barely a second. Then the corporal kicked the flat of his boot square into Box's chest, and Skarl, who knew how fast and clever Box was when it came to fighting, was amazed to see how Box made no effort to dodge the incoming foot, but allowed it to strike him so powerfully that he was rammed into the next kit bay.

Ration packs cascaded over Box, who was on his belly

with his kit bag under him. There were more staff in the bay now and the thud of kicks to Box's torso were loud enough to silence everybody. Then he was dragged to his feet, kit bag still clutched in his hands.

'If you weren't as good as dead already, you'd die for that,' yelled a sergeant, jaws snapping savagely at Box's face.

'Sorry, sergeant,' muttered Box, with a look of deep shame upon him. 'I was hungry.'

'You was *what?*' exploded the sergeant.

Box lowered his eyes. 'I was hungry,' he muttered, apologetically. 'And I was hoping ... for cake.'

'Cake!' roared the sergeant, outraged.

'Cake,' croaked Box, humbly.

'Get back in line,' shouted the sergeant, and Box heard him mutter to the corporal, 'What is cake?'

The corporal shook his head. 'Something unnatural; a skin thing.' He eyed Box for further signs of deviance.

'That wasn't what I had in mind,' sighed Razool, as he and Box moved towards the exit.

'That was what I call a deception,' whispered Box proudly, and trying not to smile. He opened the mouth of the kit bag so that Razool could see inside. 'Life-rafts.'

Razool raised his brows when he saw the two compression packs sitting on top of the spare vests and combats. 'Good work, Box.' He was impressed.

'Shovelled them in as soon as I was down,' said Box, loudly enough for Skarl and Raxa to hear. 'Splinter would have liked that. It's the kind of stunt he'd of pulled.'

'Splinter?' asked Skarl.

'My brother,' muttered Box. The word felt thick in his

mouth and he pushed away the memories that came with it. Then his stomach rumbled. 'I wouldn't mind some cake though. Or chocolate.'

They stepped out of the hangar. Box threw the kit bag over his shoulder and squinted up at the huge transporter vessels that would be carrying him and the other troopers of the penal battalions into the X'ath homelands. He meant to ask Razool what the life-rafts were for, but then he saw the horsemen. Except that they weren't men, and the creatures weren't like any horses that Box had seen before.

There were fifteen of these horsemen. They strode across the deck, battle-hewn faces set like rock, oblivious to the column of troopers who watched them pass in silence. Their rough armour was thick as granite and bolted together in chunks that were pitted with the star-shaped scorch marks left by incoming rounds. Some had the same limbs and heads as ordinary troopers, but mostly their bodies were a mixture of flesh and metal: glinting optics where there should have been an eye; plates of steel where there should have been a section of jaw or skull; the grey matt of metal where there should have been an arm or leg, with tendons and ligaments of smooth silver.

They carried their helmets under their arms. Box thought that they looked like motorbike helmets, but chunkier, and beside each of the striding soldiers walked a massive creature that was a melding of horse and metal. Their broad, black chests and legs were like iron, their joints robotronic, their hooves clanged heavily over the deck and their eyes were black as death and unblinking.

'Dreadbolt cavalry,' said Razool, quietly.

'They look ... different.' Box noticed that the soldiers paid no attention to the stationary mass of troops who waited for them to pass.

'That's what I like about you, Box,' whispered Razool. 'Your gift for stating the obvious.' He patted Box on the shoulder. 'They're the best. The toughest. Massive strength, massive damage resistance. Bodies hardened by CFR.'

'CFR?'

'Carbon frame reinforcement: normal body tissue reinforced with solarion.'

'What's solarion?' asked Box.

'The densest material in the world. It comes from collapsed stars. It makes the dreadbolts very strong and very hard: like rock.'

'They're not indestructible, though,' observed Box, watching a dreadbolt use a metal hand to check the multi-barrelled lump of a gun he had pulled from his thigh holster, before sliding it back in place.

Razool shrugged. 'They're tougher than anything else we have. And what gets damaged can always be replaced.'

'And the horses?' Box frowned. The black eyes unnerved him. 'If they are horses.'

'Bolts, that's what they're called. They start off as real horses: big horses.' Razool stroked his chin. 'They undergo CFR too. And something called neural sculpting: weird stuff. Like riveting real nerve endings to metal.'

Box grimaced. 'Yeah, weird. What are they for?'

'Smashing enemy ground forces. Destruction. When our ground troops need support and the battle's too close for artillery or air fire, or when we need to soften the enemy up before an assault, they send in the dreadbolts.' Razool pointed to one of the giant, flesh-metal horses. 'A bolt at full charge covers the ground at up to three hundred metres per second.'

'That sounds fast,' said Box, who guessed that was why Razool had quoted the figure at him.

'Almost as fast as sound. And they destroy whatever is in their way.' Razool laughed dryly. 'They smash it to pieces. I mean, *really* smash it to pieces. A full storm at the charge will smash anything out of existence.'

'How many in a storm?' asked Box, with keen interest.

'A thousand dreadbolts to a cohort, ten cohorts to a storm,' recited Razool.

Box did the calculation. 'So that's ten thousand.'

'Well done, Box. Like I said, you're a genius.'

Box ignored the jibe. His attention had focused on the multi-barrelled handguns, the body-length curving swords and the log-headed battle hammers fastened to chains along the bolts' metal flanks, and the mortar-sized guns strapped across the dreadbolts' backs.

'Different weapons,' he observed.

'You need different weapons when you hit the enemy at three hundred metres a second,' said Razool. 'They're pretty handy with their fists too.'

'And they're the best?' asked Box, absorbing every detail of the elite, heavy cavalry, licking his dry lips.

'The best. At destroying things,' said Razool, precisely.

Box nodded. 'Nice.' Then he asked, 'Why don't you just have loads and loads of dreadbolts?'

'Money,' said Razool. 'We build them: *us*. Not the

Symmetry.' That was when Box noticed that beneath the dirt and the oil and the burnt scale, the shoulder slabs bore whorls of colour: snarling dog heads, rearing horses, gold, black and red. Not an awlis in sight. 'They're General Vane's favourites,' continued Razool, 'but the technology, the cybernetics, the solarion . . .' His tongue slid across his long, white teeth. 'It costs a lot of money.'

The dreadbolts had passed. The troopers began to lumber forwards again, heading for the transport ships in a snaking, wide column.

'Boltheads.' Razool shook his mane, and half laughed. 'That's what everyone calls the dreadbolts. It kind of fits.'

To Box's left and to his right, troops were streaming up the long, steep entrance ramps of the transporter ships. The constant bleeping of the loading alarms cut out all other noise. Steam issued from the cooling units at the bases of the vessels, pouring upwards in rolling sheets. Now that he was this close, Box could see the rust-streaked condition of the ships' outer shells, running with rivulets of condensation.

'Why've they put us in the worst ships on the whole deck?' he protested.

'Why'd you think?' laughed Razool, drolly. 'Expendable ships for expendable troops.'

Box passed through double airlocks. Pressed close to Razool, Skarl and Raxa, and hundreds of other snouts, he shuffled along a narrow corridor with peeling paint before emerging in a hall that rose in landing upon landing of barred cells, just like the inside of a prison. Box craned his head to look up.

'Move,' ordered a rectangular lump of metal, the size of a

chest, which hovered several feet off the ground. Box spotted a dozen similar devices floating in the central well of the hall. 'Move,' repeated the GPU. 'Move.' The monotone command was repeated until Box moved, along with the other snouts who were trooping up the stairs and along the walkways.

'Is that all it can say?' Box asked Razool.

'That's all it's been programmed to say,' said Razool. 'It's performing a logistics support function. It doesn't think for itself. It just does what it's told.'

Cell after cell was filled: four troopers to each cell. The ship rang with slamming iron as the doors closed. It wasn't until they had climbed the sheer, open staircases to the fourth landing that Box and his friends came to an empty cell. Leaning over a handrail and looking up, Box reckoned that there were at least another three floors of cells.

'Move,' droned a GPU.

'OK, OK,' grumbled Box, wondering whether it might be interesting to give the GPU a shove, just to see what happened next. What happened next was that he walked into Razool. Box hadn't seen that the snout had stopped sharp, within the entrance of the cell.

'There's someone in here already,' complained Razool, to a passing corporal who was dealing with order on this section of the ship. GPUs hovered up and down the landing.

Box stopped beside Razool and looked in. Against the rust-stained far wall there sat a snout on a kit bag. Body armour and utility kit were strung over the bag as if dropped there in a hurry and the snout was leaning forwards, arms resting on an upright blaze carbine. The black combat trousers, boots and vest were like the combats, boots and vest that Box wore, but the snout's smooth arms, although tightly muscled, were much slimmer than his. He saw bright eyes watching him through the loose black hair that hung over the snout's face.

Box thought that for a snout face, it was a good-looking one: high cheek-boned, short muzzled, fine haired with large, smooth patches of black, human skin. Not just good-looking, almost pretty.

'What's she doing here?' asked Razool, cocking his maned head on one side.

'Our fire team's complete,' added Skarl. 'There's four already, see?'

'She's meant to be here,' said the corporal. 'On orders.' He faced Razool, snout to snout. 'Yours is a fire team of five.'

'You can't have a fire team of five,' insisted Skarl, with a menacing glance at the trooper who remained sitting on her kit bag, arms folded round her rifle and head up now, watching the exchange. 'It won't work with five,' he complained.

The corporal shrugged. 'Your problem.' He looped his thumbs inside his belt and strolled away.

The cells were small, but Razool, Skarl and Raxa still managed to throw their bags on the floor a sufficient distance from their new team member to indicate that she wasn't part of the team. The gate slammed shut behind Box and a GPU hovered on the other side. A thin metal arm emerged from its body and connected with the lock in the barred door. There was a clunk as the door was locked. The metal arm was absorbed back into the GPU which announced, 'Flight time: eighteen hours. Departure in seven minutes,' then slipped away. Box watched it go.

'Programmable matter,' observed Razool, undoing the clips on his body armour and utility belt. 'It's made out of smart particles. Probably got a whole load of other functions: cleaner, drink dispenser, medic, crowd control, as well as gaoler.'

'Very impressive,' murmured Box, whose interest was more deeply engaged by the rotating barrel mechanism that controlled the gate lock, and the rudimentary housing containing it. For a street rat of his abilities, this lock was nursery school stuff.

Razool dropped his body armour and utility belt onto his kit bag before slumping onto it himself.

'What are you doing here?' he growled at the new team member.

The lone, female snout pulled back her hair and tied a piece of cloth in it so that it was held in a ponytail. Because she was unusually smooth skinned, beads of sweat glistened on her shoulders and forearms. For the first time, Box realized how hot it was inside the transporter.

'What are you doing here?' echoed Skarl.

She pulled on her tunic and began to button it up. 'Same as you,' she said, voice as hard as any other snout's. She yanked up the zip. 'Waiting to fight. Wondering how long I'll last.'

'What's your name?' asked Box, un-slinging his carbine and dropping his kit bag by Razool.

'Shera,' answered the snout without looking at him. She whipped up her utility belt and unhooked the mace-blade, spinning the long handle over the back of her hand before releasing the blade so that it whooshed out, directly towards Box's chest. Then she looked at him, her bright eyes catching his as she sighted down the gleaming steel.

'Last one of these they issued me with was blunt,' she murmured. Then she smiled, showing sharp, white, teeth and the blade hissed back into the long cosh of a handle. 'This one will cut nicely,' she predicted.

Box became aware that Razool was sniffing, tasting the air carefully. His friend's eyes had narrowed and Box knew his face well enough to guess that Razool had detected something.

'Why are you here?' asked Razool, as carefully as he had sniffed the air.

'Orders,' said Shera without returning his stare. She busied herself with inspecting the contents of her utility pouches.

A tremor ran through the whole ship. The lights dimmed to a dark red. The alarms had stopped sounding outside the transporter, but inside, a shrill, intermittent bleeping commenced. Take-off was imminent.

Box knew the launch drill. He slipped off the bag and lay, back-down on the floor, arms close to his torso, legs together. About him, the other members of the fire team did the same. This was the best way to ride the massive thrust of take-off.

Razool lay to one side of him and to the other was Shera. He noticed her watching him.

'Comfortable?' he enquired.

'Perfect.' She closed her eyes.

The metal floor began to tremble and through it, Box could hear the roar of the engines from far below. There were no windows in the cells, but he knew that the ship was lifting by the shudders and groans of its body.

A hundred metres below where the fire team lay, the main thrusters were screaming. The ship shook.

'Eighteen hours? If this rust bucket lasts eighteen minutes it will be a miracle,' muttered Box, to no one in particular.

'Nice work, fly head,' said an imaginary Splinter, standing over him.

The mind could play tricks at 5g; Box had been warned about that. He kept his eyes shut. But the imaginary Splinter couldn't be silenced that easily. He knelt so that his mouth was at Box's ear.

'Of all the armies in all the universes, you pick the one where death is guaranteed. Typical.'

Box clenched his teeth as he felt his body compress against the floor. The upward thrust squeezed the back of his chest hard enough to drive the air out of his lungs. He began to babble because of the way the air forced itself out of his nostrils and between his lips: involuntary sounds. Gibberish.

'Your conversational skills remain unchanged, I see.'

Box could imagine Splinter's voice, patient, taunting.

'Tell me, Box, how is *this* meant to help Chess? What exactly are you going to do? Sniff your way back to her? Bark at the enemy?' Splinter spoke with cold condescension. 'You make a good dog, fly head.'

The image was shaken from his mind with a final convulsion of metal and then there was perfect stillness as the transporter began to cruise.

'Heap of skak,' cursed Skarl, rolling onto his kit bag.

'What did you expect?' chuckled Raxa. 'In-flight entertainment and a bottle of strince?'

'Strince?' Box rested his head on the lumpy bulk of his kit bag.

'Drink,' explained Skarl. 'Like wine.'

'Nothing like wine,' murmured Razool. 'More like rat spit. Now, how about some zip while we've still got heads to snore.'

The drone of the engines and the drone of voices from other cells made a dull backdrop against which sleep was possible. Box considered whether the time had come for an exploration of his ration pack; along with the distant rumble of the motors there was the more immediate rumble of his stomach. But he was tired: very tired.

Dog tired, he suggested to the ghost of Splinter, and with a smile at the corners of his mouth, he slipped into sleep.

When he awoke it was to the grip of Razool's hand on his shoulder. The cell was still washed in the dull red light and everyone else was asleep. Razool shoved him again.

'What?' groaned Box, the idea of rat spit alive in his mouth.

'Feel that?' hissed the snout, eyes keen. The ship shook and groaned and shook again. Then there came a boom which echoed throughout the whole vessel.

Box sat up, totally awake. He could feel the pressure of the floor against his palms and thighs, as if he was sinking into it: like when a lift stops, he thought. But a thousand times stronger.

'We're slowing down,' he said, quietly.

Another boom and the scream of metal. The ship groaned to its core.

'Not just slowing down, Box,' said Razool. 'The ship is about to crash.' He smiled bitterly, teeth bright in his long snout. 'This ship and all the others. Like I said, Box, the X'ath are very clever.'

Box opened his mouth without saying anything for the time it took him to contemplate the consequence of an ancient prison hulk carrying twenty thousand snouts crashing into Klanf 187 at high sub-stellar speed. Then he said, 'What do we do?'

'Life-rafts,' replied Razool.

CHAPTER 4

Box scratched his head. With a bending howl, a steel girder spun across the cavernous hall-well of the transporter, hitting the opposite landing with a resounding clang. 'Zool, we're about to hit a planet, not a pond. What use are life-rafts?'

'The X'ath have transmitted false ground-surface coordinates to the ship computers.' Razool was buckling on his armour. Skarl, Raxa and Shera were doing the same. 'It's an old X'ath ruse, useless against better ships but craft like these prison wrecks have skak navigation. Get the life-raft packs.' His mane was edged crimson in the deep red of the cell. 'The X'ath transmission distorts the distance from ground to ship.'

'So the pilot thinks there is further to go than there really is?' asked Box.

'Yup.' Razool yanked tight the draw cord on his kit bag. 'Our pilots will have acquired information visually and seen that there isn't enough run-in to land. So, right now, they're slamming on the brakes.'

The ship howled and shook. Troopers were banging on the bars and shouting to be let out of their cells.

'But, however hard they brake, we're flies and this is the windscreen.' He pointed at the floor. 'At impact, this will be messy.'

Box was digging inside his kit bag. 'Zool, I know we don't have ten minutes,' he said, struggling to be heard above the screaming metal and thousands of snouts who now were yelling from their cells, 'but how the hell do you know all of this?' He emerged from the mouth of his kit bag with a compressed life-raft in each hand.

'How long before we hit the windscreen?' enquired Shera.

'My name,' said Razool, turning to face Box, 'is Commodore Valxata Razool.'

'A commodore?' Skarl's long jaw dropped open, aghast.

'What *is* a commodore?' muttered Box.

'Top brass,' grunted Raxa, frozen in the act of strapping on his body armour. 'Only a bit below the General.'

Box swallowed. 'No way,' he whispered.

'I've fought my way through the Calyx campaigns. I've fought against the X'ath, Krillions and the Galen before commanding my own fleet: eight hundred whales, deep vortex cargo ships carrying pure crystal.' Razool spoke mechanically and swiftly as if reciting instructions.

So this was why Razool knew about everything: about weapons, about spooks, about the X'ath. And this meant he could fly; navigate the vortex even. Not that navigating anything made a difference if the crash pulverized the lot of them.

'My ship was the *Leviathan III*, a deep vortex cargo ship.'

'The *Leviathan III*?' Box repeated under his breath. It seemed absurd, but he was sure he had heard that name before. The ship groaned and shook.

'In the course of my duties, I was ordered by General Saxmun Vane to take shipments of crystal to an alternative deposit.'

'The missing shipments of crystal,' mouthed Shera, as if Razool had just solved a long-standing problem.

'I believed I was following an official command.' Razool snorted and eased the mechanism of his carbine with a clunk before placing it by his feet. 'But it seems that these shipments were not authorized by those who commanded the General.'

'The Inquisitors?' ventured Box. Outside the cell, the metal gantry squealed. The lights flickered. Then the whole ship shook.

'How long do we have?' repeated Shera, quietly.

Razool took a life-raft pack from Box.

'I was court-martialled,' stated Razool. 'They said I had diverted multiple shipments of crystal for my own purposes. Mutiny and piracy were the formal charges, for which the penalty is death.' He shrugged and loosened the toggles on the pack. 'By the General's intervention I was spared death. Instead, I was branded a mutineer and sent to the Fleshing yards: the General's way of giving me a sporting chance.'

'But it wasn't your fault,' insisted Box, momentarily oblivious to the ship's groans. 'You were acting under orders.'

'It seems the General has his own plans for all that crystal.'

Razool smiled, sardonically. 'I was expendable.' He shrugged, pulled the rip-cord and threw the pack against the wall. With a hiss and a flap, the inflatable raft sprang into being, covering the whole wall in a yellow cushion which was jammed between ceiling and floor.

Razool took the other raft from Box and began to undo the restraining straps. 'The General had his reasons, I'm sure. I bear him no grudge, and it wouldn't matter if I did. Loyalty is to the General above all else, Box. Never forget that.' He clenched his jaw. 'But I would like to see my family again. My wife and my whelps.' He gave Box a steady stare. 'You're not the only one who wants to get home,' and he ripped free the cord. The raft inflated instantly, buffeting into Skarl who was knocked off his feet before it finished jamming itself in front of the first raft.

Box realized that the rafts were wedged against the wall in the direction that the ship was hurtling. 'Air bags,' he grinned. 'Nice one, Zool.'

'Emergency crash drill,' nodded Razool. 'In answer to your question,' he said to Shera, 'judging by the time at which visuals must have been acquired and deceleration commenced, and given the relative air density of the Klanf asteroid system, we have about twenty-five seconds left.'

'Skak, sir . . . Zool,' choked Skarl. 'Why wait until *now* to give us your life story?'

The red light was flickering and the squeals of buckling, shearing metal were constant.

Razool shrugged coolly. 'Maybe there won't be another chance. I don't want to go out without saying who I was.

Who I *am*.' He shook his head as if clearing it. 'Right,' he barked. 'Put your weapons on the floor, at the bottom of the rafts.'

Weapons clattered down.

'Arms over heads, knees into chests, backs into the raft.' Razool demonstrated, curling into a ball and forcing himself into the dense yellow rubber of the raft. The others copied him, moving jerkily in the strobing illumination. They braced themselves for impact.

'That's twenty-eight seconds . . .' began Shera.

Box thought he was drowning. His body was driven into rubber so hard it felt like the skin had been flung from his face. His chest wouldn't open and his limbs were paralyzed. Rubber forced itself into his mouth. There was a long, low moan that Box knew was disintegrating metal heard through the suffocating coffin of the life-rafts.

Then total darkness and the sharp groans of the occupants of his cell. The ship had stopped.

Box rolled onto his back, watching the colours spin before his open eyes: dazed but still alive.

There was a sudden clang and Skarl yelped. 'Didn't see the bars,' he moaned before his body shuffled beside Box.

A beam of white light cut the blackout as Razool snapped on his torch. 'Everyone OK?' he asked, quietly.

Everyone grunted.

'Good,' he said. 'But there will be no other survivors.'

There was a very long pause. Box knew that the others would be thinking the way that he was. The exhilaration of having survived the crash-down, followed by the hollowness at the thought of the cells filled with what was left of nearly twenty thousand bodies, followed by the shocking certainty that this fate must have struck the four other transport ships, followed by the spidering realization that they were marooned on X'ath homeland.

Suddenly, the darkness inside the wrecked ship seemed a whole lot darker.

'How many spikers in this territory?' asked Box, as if seriously weighing up the odds.

'More than five,' stated Razool.

'Well,' Box said to Shera, even though he knew she couldn't see him, 'it's just as well you're here, otherwise we'd be even more outnumbered,' and he flicked on his own torch.

'Thanks, Box,' said Shera. 'At least not everybody wishes I'd been strapped to the front of the ship.'

Box's torchlight caught her neat, sleek face and she smiled at him.

'Get your kit,' ordered Razool. 'Weapons ready. We have to get up to the command bay, check the communications equipment is working.'

'Who's going to come for *us*?' asked Shera, coolly. 'Five pieces of cannon fodder out of a whole army?'

Razool was checking his weapon. 'I'm not planning on calling the deck. But somewhere out there, I'll find someone to pick us up. I'm pretty well known in the Fourth Navy. Some people even like me.'

'Like you?' muttered Shera. 'You've got to be joking.'

'You can call in a ship?' asked Box.

'That's the plan,' said Razool.

Box's mind rushed through the possibilities. They might

have crashed but this could be exactly what he needed. 'Maybe you could get me home?'

'One step at a time, Box.' Razool picked up his helmet. 'Can you get us out of this cell?'

Box turned his torch on the bars. The beam wobbled beyond them and into the blackness of the central well where GPUs were floating like sea chests under the ocean.

'*They* survived,' observed Skarl.

Raxa cocked his carbine. 'We have to get out of here, Box. Quick.' The big snout was right. Locked inside the cell, they were at the mercy of whatever came creeping through the darkness. Box approached the iron bars and his torch struck them with a bang that echoed throughout the lifeless ship.

'Not too much noise,' suggested Skarl, nervously.

Shera knelt by Box's side, her blaze carbine close to his head.

'Watch your barrel,' warned Razool in measured tones.

'Just giving him cover,' whispered Shera.

'Where's a helpful GPU when you need one?' complained Skarl.

The whole team was clustered by the iron bars now, helmets on, carbines ready. Raxa pushed Box's helmet onto his head.

'Thanks,' said Box, peering into the locking mechanism with the assistance of his torch.

'No more torches,' said Razool, looking out at the central well and then up.

'It's easy,' murmured Box. 'Just need a wire or something.' There was a tearing sound. 'Here,' whispered Razool, passing the thin, kinked strip of metal to Box. 'Best use for an awlis that I can think of,' he added.

Box probed the innards of the hole with the unwound piece of insignia. 'The power of the Symmetry,' he intoned in a bass voice.

'Don't joke,' warned Raxa ominously.

From the inside of the lock there came a satisfying click. Razool's torchlight revealed the grin on Box's face.

'You know, Box,' said Razool, 'for a skin you're not entirely useless.'

Then, from somewhere in the sea of blackness above there came a solitary bang of metal on metal. It echoed throughout the dead darkness of the ship.

'Here we go,' muttered Raxa.

The bars swung open and Box took the grip of his carbine with his free hand, swinging the weapon level with his hip as he stood.

'OK,' whispered Razool. 'We have to take the stairs up, if the stairs are still there.' Nobody asked what they would do if the stairs weren't. 'At the top there will be service corridors. The command route will be marked with a green line. The communications we need will be down the end of the green line, in the command bay.'

They listened but apart from their breathing, there was only silence.

'I'll take the lead. Box, back me up. Skarl and Raxa at the rear. Only my torch now. We go slowly.'

'What do I do?' asked Shera.

'Do you really want an answer?' Razool clipped his torch onto his blaze carbine.

'Guess I'll stick close to you,' Shera said to Box. 'Or you'll be all on your own.'

Box nodded at her before mounting his torch on his carbine and then turning it off.

Razool's torch beam moved away from the cell.

'I'll go first,' whispered Shera.

'I don't think it will make a lot of difference,' observed Box.

The torch beam turned towards them. 'Shut up,' warned Razool.

From high above, metal clattered, echoing and then silence.

They moved quietly, padding along the walkways, negotiating the buckled metal, ignoring the eerie stillness of the cells they passed, listening for noises. After minutes in which it felt as if they were walking nowhere, Razool said, 'Stairs,' and turned his torch off. 'We climb by touch, up to the top.'

Where the noises came from, thought Box.

'Me first,' continued Razool, voice low. 'Skarl and Raxa wait here until we're at the top. Any problems, torches on and open fire. OK?'

'OK,' confirmed Raxa, huskily.

'Just remember,' added Razool, 'spikers regenerate. So keep firing until they're smashed and down.'

'Sure,' murmured Raxa. 'Now go.'

Razool mounted the stairs, then Box and then Shera. The stairway was steep and the air seemed to become cooler as they climbed. They moved so slowly, so carefully that their footfalls barely dusted the silence and Box strained to hear the slightest noise. All he could hear was Shera's breathing, close by him. They paused on a small platform.

When something clipped the metal several landings above, they froze. It was only a slight noise, but it was a noise where nothing should have been making noise; this was a lifeless ship. Apart from them, nothing should have been moving through the darkness.

Box heard Razool swallow.

Another slight clipping of metal and then a low humming above their heads. Wing beats perhaps. Then silence again.

Box knew that spikers had compound eyes on the sides of their hammer heads, like flies but much bigger, enabling them to gather the least illumination: to see where snouts or skins could see nothing. And the olfactory vents in their thin, wide heads were sensitive to the least odours. He looked about as if he might catch sight of something, and his body armour creaked as he moved his shoulders.

Humming air again, out in the deep well of the prison ship. A sharp clink from the dark: claws on metal.

More than one. Gathering. Waiting.

Box heard Razool swear under his breath. 'Torches mounted?'

'Uh-huh,' breathed Box.

'Backs together,' murmured the Commodore.

Box reached out and felt one snout body, then the other. They retreated into one another, Box shouldering his carbine, elevating it slightly.

'Remember,' whispered Razool, 'don't stop firing.'

A rapid clicking sound, like something opening, and then a strong smell hit Box: raw, putrid.

'Now,' said Razool.

Box's torch beam speared the darkness to illuminate a set of mandibles as wide as a door, opening above his head. The glistening, sword-length fangs struck down.

With a yell, Box pulled the trigger and felt the carbine roar to life in his hands. The torchlight leapt about as he fired, catching flashes of wing, leg, serpentine neck and head as the trap jerked back and came for him again, striking silently out of the dark. He was aware of Razool and Shera firing beside him, the brazen coughing of their carbines, the muzzle flashes, the singing of spent cartridge shells over the metal platform. But Box didn't stop yelling and firing, firing at whatever he could see, rounds streaming into jaws, wings, limbs, the darkness.

Now he felt the wetness on his fingers, and metres from his own face a spiker head was shaking and snapping, in and out of the darkness, black gore spurting from the long cranial bar between its huge, spherical eyes. Jaws wide, the creature struck again. Box remembered everything he'd been taught, stood his ground and kept his finger on the trigger.

At point-blank range, the rounds smashed into the spiker's mandibles, splintering its lower jaw. Even then, Box didn't stop. He tracked a line down to where the creature's long, snaking torso should have been, catching glimpses of it in the torchlight, and he kept firing, slick gouting through bullet holes in the chest scales.

Then Box squeezed and nothing happened: rounds spent.

Five hundred rounds per minute; it had been a quick minute. Box smacked out the spent block and fumbled in a utility pouch for another, fingers slippery with slick. Already the spiker would be regenerating. He felt the air hum as a set of spines smashed into the platform beside his feet.

Firing started up from beneath. Raxa was illuminated in the back-flash of the muzzle, a landing below. Back to back with Raxa was Skarl, firing grimly into the creatures that were flapping and snapping about Box, Razool and Shera.

Box whacked in the next block of ammunition in time to see Shera on one knee reloading as the trap came down at her head. Box swung left and emptied his carbine at the nearest piece of the spiker that he could see. He heard Raxa yell out, but the gunfire didn't stop. There was a high screech, a flurry of wings and limbs, a long neck flung back, an eruption of slick and then a silence, thick with the reek of gun smoke.

'Two,' said Razool.

'Two! Only two.' Box swung his torch about but there was no sign of the bodies, which must have crashed down to the bottom of the well, seven landings below.

Slick was splashed over the helmets, faces and shoulders of Razool and Shera, and Box guessed that he looked no better.

'They take a lot of killing,' he said, wiping his slick-smeared hands on the thighs of his trousers. 'It's more like oil than blood,' he muttered.

'That's why it's called slick,' whispered Shera.

'Raxa's been gaffed,' shouted Skarl.

There was a numbing silence before Raxa shouted up, 'Yeah, but not that bad.'

In Skarl's torchlight, Box could see a patch of blood soaking down the back of Raxa's calf.

'Could have been worse,' added Raxa.

'Medic,' yelled Razool, voice bouncing off the tangled metal of the transporter.

'In here?' Box wondered what Razool was expecting. Then he saw a GPU hover in towards Raxa.

'And light,' shouted the Commodore.

The top of the GPU began to glow, throwing out a dome of light which revealed Skarl and Raxa clearly, although it didn't reach the platform where Box was standing.

Raxa sat down and extended his leg with barely a wince although Box could tell from the amount of blood lost that it must have been a nasty wound. Thin probes emerged from the body of the GPU, bright as steel. Box thought he could discern scissor blades and a glowing lancet. The GPU cut away fabric and began to sterilize and stitch the wound. Raxa didn't flinch, even though the lancet dug deep.

'It's not as bad as it looks,' he laughed up. 'You get a lot of painkiller and I'm a snout. Not soft like you, skin boy.'

Box grinned down, then checked how many rounds he had left before taking a slug of water. After that he rested on his haunches and took some deep breaths.

'Shaky?' asked Shera.

Box stood up and wiped his mouth with the back of his hand. 'That was close.'

'Close?' Razool shook Box's shoulder. 'There's no such

thing as *close*. There's dead and there's alive. Right now, they're dead and we're alive. That's all that matters.' He held Box's eyes in his intense, narrow ones. 'Don't go soft on me, skin. Not now.'

Box pushed his shaven head nose to nose with Razool's snout. 'I don't go soft,' he hissed.

Razool nodded and smiled, teeth bared in the dim light. 'Good.' He slapped Box's shoulder. 'You're a fully blooded trooper now, my friend. One of the best.'

Box eyed Razool carefully. The snout was a commodore. He knew a lot about fighting. 'You reckon?'

'I *know*,' said Razool, earnestly. 'Right,' he said, raising his voice, 'there will be plenty more spikers left so let's get on with this. Not much further to go. Everybody knows we're here now so we can keep the lights on.'

Raxa and Skarl were climbing the stairs, Raxa with a little difficulty but without complaint. The GPU tracked upwards and settled by Razool's side.

'Thanks,' said Shera, who had drawn alongside Box.

'For what?'

'For keeping me alive.' Her bright eyes glinted at him. 'If you hadn't covered me back there, I'd have been spiker meat. And so could you, looking out for me like that.'

Box shrugged. 'Just helping a member of the team.'

'Glad *you* include me in that special group.'

Box smiled. He couldn't see why Razool had a problem with her. 'How does it do that?' he asked, referring to the GPU at Razool's shoulder.

'*Smart* particles, remember?' answered Shera.

'How does *he* do that?' he asked, nodding at Razool.

'The voice of command,' muttered Razool, climbing the next set of stairs.

'Hardly,' scoffed Shera. 'It will respond to any command it's not programmed to refuse. But *he's* the one who keeps giving them.'

'Hey.' Razool turned round, fangs bared down one side of his muzzle. '*I'm* the mutineer, remember? We don't even know what you're doing here: yet.'

'I told you,' insisted Shera. 'I'm part of the team. Orders.'

Razool snorted with contempt and continued up the stairs, the GPU smoothly keeping pace with him.

They saw daylight before they reached the command bay; if it *was* daylight. Box thought that it looked a bit like the dim red illumination of the cells, or the way the world looked when you peered at it through a red cellophane sweet wrapper. It lapped at the far neck of the corridor down which they were advancing, the darkness of the stairways and death-filled cells of the prison ship behind them.

When they reached the end of the corridor, Razool crouched by the open airlock which led to the bay. Box knelt by his side, and Skarl, Raxa and Shera flattened themselves against the opposite wall. Box couldn't see what was on the other side of the opening but he knew that the room was full of light and he could feel the drift of air.

'Cover me,' whispered Razool to Skarl.

'Yes, sir,' Skarl whispered back.

'And don't call me sir,' snapped Razool. 'We're all the same here.'

'Sure ... Zool.' Skarl grinned wolfishly, then nudged the

snub nose of his blaze carbine around the edge of the iron door panel.

Razool rolled round the panel and into the bay beyond, gun first. Behind him came Box, covering the opposite side of the bay.

'All clear.' Box lowered his weapon and assessed the situation. 'Very messy, Zool. Just like you said.'

The command bay was the size of four or five cells. It sat on the top of the ship. The transparent roof and the front wall had been smashed apart so that now they were open entirely to the ochre glow of Klanf 187. The three crew seats had been wrenched from their housing altogether in the crash. One had vanished, probably through the yawning gap in the wall at the front of the bay. The other two were meshed in the chaos of cables and navigational hardware which formed a crash-mangled wall directly in front of the seat housings. There was blood spattered across the shattered monitor screens as if it had been flung from a tin of paint. Box didn't try to look for bodies within the mess.

Above the wrecked roof of the command bay, the terracotta sky was streaked with low cloud.

Razool was kneeling amidst the remains of the hardware, helmet off and carbine on the floor beside him. At his shoulder hovered the GPU, a narrow beam of light emitting from a silver cylinder and directed into the innards of the technology. Glass crunched as Skarl, Raxa and Shera walked across it.

'Communications unit intact,' muttered Razool, but he grimaced and shook his head. 'But no transmission.' His fingers prodded the keys on a board that had remained undamaged.

Box pulled off his helmet and knelt beside Razool, even though he had no idea of how a communications system worked. The GPU changed position to accommodate Box.

'It's basic.' Razool tugged a wire to check it was secure. 'Which is probably why it survived the crash.'

Here I am, thought Box, kneeling beside something that's a bit dog and a bit man, on a planet with a red sky, which is populated by giant, homicidal stabbing things, and talking inter-planetary communications systems in a language that sounds like I've eaten a wasp. The other street rats would never believe it. *I* don't believe it. He laughed to himself.

'What's funny?' growled Razool.

'You won't get the joke,' Box growled back.

But maybe, just maybe, Razool could call a ship in. And maybe this would be the start of going home. Of finding Chess.

Razool stood up and looked over to Raxa who was standing guard with Skarl. 'Have we got company?'

'Not yet,' replied Raxa, limping round the equipment, gun in hand.

Razool sighed and shook back his mane. 'There's nothing wrong with the kit. The problem will be out there.' He jerked his head at the open roof. 'The transmitter panels will have taken a battering. We need to check they're properly aligned.'

Nobody volunteered immediately.

'I'll go,' said Razool. 'I know what I'm looking for.'

'*I'll* go,' said Box. He shrugged. 'We can't afford to lose you, Zool. You're the only one who understands how all this works.' And Box didn't want to lose any time. The thought of getting out of this made his heart thump.

'But the Commodore knows what he's looking for, Box,' interrupted Shera. She pulled off her helmet. 'He knows how to fix it.'

Razool turned on her. 'Who asked you?'

'It can't be that hard to fix,' insisted Box, raising his hands to quell the arguing.

'It isn't,' said Razool. 'You sure you're OK with this? We don't know what's out there.'

'Hey, I eat danger for breakfast,' announced Box.

'He certainly eats a lot of everything else,' muttered Skarl.

'Why not send the GPU out?' suggested Shera.

'I might need to talk, get information back, know the state of the equipment,' snapped Razool. 'This needs a mind, not a machine.' He pointed at the GPU. 'If that was an HFU, it would be different.'

'HFU?' asked Box.

'High Function Unit,' replied Shera, still hard-staring Razool. 'Even *smarter* particles. Intelligent.'

'But it isn't an HFU, is it?' said Razool, patiently.

'Well, no,' admitted Shera.

'Let's get on with it,' grunted Raxa.

'OK?' Razool looked to Box. Box nodded. The snout pointed to the gap in the front wall of the command bay. 'About thirty metres on from there you'll find two flat screens.' He held his arms apart. 'About this big. There's nothing else near them. They should sit square within the chevrons: yellow and black flashes marked on the casing. You just have to get them straight: line them up. Got that?'

'Doesn't sound so difficult,' said Box.

'Not yet,' said Shera under her breath, 'but wait 'til you're out there.'

Box secured the carbine across his back and crossed to the gaping front wall.

'Helmet,' Raxa reminded him.

'No need,' said Box. 'I'll be back quick.' He climbed over the metal ledge and squatted to take a look.

Rising behind him was the canopy of the command bay, battered and glass smashed out. So far as he could see elsewhere, the roof of the ship was strewn with chunks of wood and tree branches and stained with earth. External cooling pipes and panels were bent, dented, ripped or missing. To his right and slightly below him was the gill-slitted mouth of a blast vent, the heat rippling up in a wave as the metal clicked, cooling.

It took Box a while to orientate himself. The vessel had come to rest at a slight angle and was more than half buried in the soft ground. Box recalled that a lot of Klanf 187 was marsh. He knelt up for a better view. The top of the ship was still higher than the tops of the trees and for as far as he could see, there were belts of dense forest, interspersed with open stretches of wetland that were broken by broad bars of dark earth. All of it was stained red by the low, bruised sky. Maybe a mile away, Box could see the half-buried wreck of one of the other transport ships, white lines of steam or smoke rising high about it. A mile or two beyond that ship, there was another, its smoking carcass shattered across a clearing in the forests.

We really are the only survivors; Box's breath hissed out between his teeth.

Then, he realized that the surface of the nearest ship was moving: crawling with spikers.

'Skak,' he gulped, lying flat and rolling onto his back. If spikers were crawling up the other wrecked ships, he could guess what must be working its way up this one.

'What?' Razool's voice was urgent.

Box looked beyond his boots and back over the battered canopy of the command bay on his own ship. Sure enough, there was movement, a break in the lines of bent metal, a dark edge rising and falling, about twenty metres away. Movement again and Box knew that he had seen the dark, knuckly ridge of a wing or a hack.

'Spikers, on the other side of the bay,' he hissed. But he couldn't lie here forever. And if they were going to get out of this, they needed communication. 'I'm going to check the screens. I don't think they'll see me.' He looked the other way, over his shoulder: the way he would have to go.

The roof sloped down and away from him. He rolled to his side, eased the carbine free and then rolled onto his belly. He began to slither down the slope of the roof and away from the bay.

It was easy to spot the transmitter panels. They were raised clear of the exterior of the ship and it was obvious that one of them had been knocked askew. All Box had to do was re-align it.

He placed his carbine flat on the roof, lodging it against the chunky hinges of a service hatch to prevent it from sliding down and away. Then he got to his knees and cast a glance back. The others were at the low, wide opening in the front of the bay wall, covering him with their weapons. There was no sign of movement beyond the canopy. Box took hold of the panel and pulled it in line with the markings on the roof.

Someone screamed his name at the same time as the firing broke out. Hands still on the panel, Box looked back and saw Skarl and Raxa blasting rounds into the back of the bay. The spikers on the other side of the bay must have broken through. Then Razool's voice came again and he heard it as if snapping out of a dream.

'Box, *behind* you.'

Box spun round to see two spikers clattering up the bowed roof shell towards him. He went for his gun but as he did so, it slipped up the roof and away from him. Even with the spikers incoming, he hesitated as he tried to make sense of how a blaze carbine could slip *upwards* without anything touching it. But once it was clear of the thick hinges that had been supporting it, it began to slip downwards with the slope of the roof as if it had been released. Box scrambled but wasn't fast enough to check his weapon which scraped past his fingers and across the roof before vanishing over the edge.

'No,' groaned Box, not at the lost gun but at a mass of scaly, spine-clustered bodies he could see now crawling up the side of the transporter, towards the canopy area. A throng of hammer heads angled his way, compound eyes catching his movements, olfactory vents twitching at his scent. Hacks unfolded.

Box pointed to this mass of spikers that Razool couldn't see. 'There's more of them,' he yelled. 'Loads more.' Then he turned back to see what was coming for him.

The two X'ath were metres away, hacks unfolded to reveal spines that were nearly his height. Traps dropped open, displaying the huge, mucus-strung teeth. The spikers towered over him and with a switch of its wings, one of them leapt forwards, landing on its hind legs and rearing up, displaying its armour-scaled belly and thorax and two sets of clawed forelegs. It snapped forwards, enough to make Box retreat towards the command bay, towards the mass of spikers coming over the curve of the roof.

As Box backed away, he thought he glimpsed a grey, metal sphere in the air, about twenty metres out beyond the ship. But he didn't dare focus on it. His eyes were riveted on the pair of spikers that were coming for him, and as quickly as he thought he had seen the metal sphere, it had vanished.

Box knew he had to get back into the command bay but now five or six of the spikers that had come up the side of the ship were blocking the way. The two in front of him were closing in. He risked a glance over his shoulder and saw Shera at the rim of the cockpit, blaze carbine levelled in his direction. Razool was nowhere to be seen but carbines were blasting furiously inside the bay.

'Give me fire,' yelled Box, turning to face the first of the two spikers.

'I can't,' he heard Shera yell back. 'Weapon's jammed.'

Without covering fire from Shera, Box knew that the

X'ath to his rear would be on him in seconds. He looked to his left and considered whether it would be better to make for the edge of the roof and try to escape that way. But what he saw dead-ended that possibility: a torrent of spikers, racing in a flapping, leaping mass out of the closest wood line and across the open grassland towards the ship.

This was it.

Death comes quickly and horribly in the Final Starfields of the Crystal Wars, the master of the Fleshing yard had promised him.

'Sorry, Chess,' whispered Box, reaching for the mace-blade that hung from his belt. Whatever the odds, he would fight. And if he could take one of the spikers with him, just one, that would be something. But he knew that any moment now, the spines would be into his back.

Then there was a roar, an explosive, roasting roar and as the two spikers ahead of him reared away, Box looked over his shoulder to see a cone of flame fireball from the blast vent, engulfing the X'ath at his back. Wings, hacks and limbs withered and danced, and turned treacle-black in the inferno.

Nice work, Zool, thought Box and without hesitation, he leapt forwards, the steel blade hissing free.

Nobody goes for a trap shot, the instructors always said.

Then again, they had also taught him that surprise increases combat effectiveness by a factor of six hundred per cent.

He heard the blast vent roar again but focused on the near spiker which had only just realized that Box was charging it.

The first hack came down and Box swerved away, the second scythed at his ankles and he pulled up his legs, jumping the long spines. Then the spiker opened its trap and in came the pulverizing jaws.

I'm only dodging a punch, Box told himself. A very, very big punch. And behind the jaws was the weak spot: the hinge that worked them.

The spiker's hammer head came in low like a shovel and as it did so, Box threw himself up and backwards, like a high-jumper, leading with his head and shoulders over the top of the spiker's head, twisting his body. The mandibles closed on the space where Box had been standing while above them, Box corkscrewed through the air and struck down in a flashing arc. The mace-blade sank into flesh and Box sliced hard, whipping the steel round as he spun. His feet hit the roof at the same time as the huge, severed head.

'Now, Shera,' he shouted as the second spiker came for him. He made ready for the incoming attack but these were no holograms; holograms didn't bleed. A spray of slick from the dead spiker's gaping neck, black and slippery as oil, coated Box's legs and boots and he lost his footing. He stumbled back as the first set of spines grazed his chest armour.

'Shera!' he yelled.

Then gunfire. It took a heartbeat before Box connected the incoming rounds with the punching sensation in his upper left arm. The confusion made him hesitate, fatally. The next set of spines caught him in his midriff, between the chest plates and hip shield of his armour. He felt the freezing sensation of the spine as it stabbed clean through his left flank, in at the front and out at the back. He was thrown to the floor and the blade slipped out of his fingers.

Razool's cry cut to the red sky. 'No!'

The huge jaws opened and struck down.

CHAPTER 5

General Saxmun Vane stood in the Operations Room of the hulk-class destroyer, *Show No Mercy*, and watched the view on the occuloid display screen. The view swept left and right and focused in and out as rapidly as an eye, which was what an occuloid drone was: a metal orb the size of a football that transmitted surveillance images, enabling command staff to observe the state of the battle, however distant from it they were.

'And you say all five ships were lost, Captain?' murmured the General, folding his arms and studying the rapid succession of images with fierce concentration.

'Down, *presumed* lost,' clarified the Captain who stood beside him. It was vital to be absolutely accurate with the General.

The General scowled at the red glow of Klanf 187. 'There. That sector. Move in.'

The drone operator, sitting at a desk beside them, touched a small screen and nudged a tiny lever which was adjacent to it. The images zoomed in, filling the huge display screen which was taller than the General.

'And you say that there had been no prior data leak to the X'ath?' The General picked at a piece of meat that was stuck between his teeth. It had been irritating him all afternoon.

'None reported,' came the careful reply.

The General growled, very low. 'So how did they know?' he muttered. 'Unless they were told.'

The Captain knew better than to make suggestions. He said nothing but he had to stifle a yelp of surprise when the General's gloved fist shot forwards to point at the screen. 'There!' he snapped. 'Now. Enlarge forty-eight thirteen to fifty-two fifteen.'

The images wobbled and enlarged and now there was an aerial view of a crippled transport ship, half-buried in earth. Towards the front of its sloping roof, figures were moving.

'Closer,' ordered the General, and his jackal head stretched forwards. He half smiled, then frowned, then snapped orders at the operator: closer, pull back, track left, centre.

'You said there were no survivors, Captain?' growled the General, louder than before.

'I said we *believed* there would be no survivors,' insisted the Captain, as firmly as he dared.

The General's snout whipped round, bearing down on the Captain. 'You *believed*?' he barked. 'I don't care what you *believe*. I'm only interested in what you *know*.'

'Yes, General,' the Captain barked back.

'And let me tell you what we *know*,' snarled the General. 'We know that there are survivors. We know that one of them is very important to us and we know that whatever happens on the roof of that ship, there are about two thousand X'ath about to storm it.' The General had his hand on the Captain's neck.

Then something on the screen distracted Saxmun Vane, made him turn towards it. He released the Captain, who gasped with relief.

'No,' whispered the General, approaching the screen as if he might step into it. 'No. Nobody goes for a trap shot.'

All of them watched what happened next.

The General smiled. 'Good boy.' But when he saw Box go down and the remaining striker move in, the smile vanished.

'We need dreadbolts,' he commanded. 'Immediately.'

'The Fourteenth Storm are in the vanguard, awaiting the assault on the X'ath battle station,' the operator said. 'They are the closest.'

'One cohort,' ordered the General. 'We can spare one cohort for this.'

Already, the operator was relaying commands into his neckpiece.

'They must extract the boy and those with him.' The General's metal fist was clenched. 'Deep vortex travel; we have no time to lose.'

'There is a class one transporter available, General,' confirmed the operator. 'They are embarking now.'

'Good, good,' murmured the General. He patted the operator on the shoulder. 'The ability to follow my orders precisely is a skill I value. We might make a captain of you, craft-master,' and he glanced coldly at the Captain who swallowed but remained silent.

'They are ready, General,' said the operator.

'Send them in, craft-master,' sighed the General. 'My beautiful dreadbolts; send them in.'

The rounds hammered across the ship's roof from the command bay towards Box's legs. Slick erupted in tiny fountains as the bullets raced through the dark pool which had gathered around the decapitated spiker's slumped body. Then, with inches to go, the rounds tracked up, just missing Box and smacking into the second spiker's mandibles as they closed on him.

The creature staggered back and shook its hammer head and Box rolled away as the slick rained down. He gasped as his weight bore onto his wounded left arm and side, but he reached for his mace-blade with his good hand. At the same time, he saw Skarl and Raxa clamber out of the command bay's broken frontage and onto the roof.

The spiker stamped forwards but before Box could slide away any further, it drove one of its hacks down, gaffing Box through his right calf and pinning him to the roof.

Box yelled with pain but his cry was drowned by the burst of gunfire from Skarl and Raxa. The wall of bullets battered the creature and now Razool and Shera were on the roof too, firing alongside Skarl and Raxa and advancing as the spiker staggered back.

The pain pulsed through Box in a sickening wave but he didn't slacken his grip on the mace-blade. He thought he saw one of the big, honeycombed eyes focus on him and Box knew the creature was thinking the same thing he had thought a minute before: if I'm going, I'm taking one of you with me. So Box lay flat, awaiting the sly side-strike of the trap.

It came low, the spiker ducking its long neck and scraping its mouth along the roof to protect its mandibular hinge from Box's blade. Box slashed at the lower jaw and drove his steel into the soft interior of the beast's mouth. The spiker shook its head, wrenching the mace-blade out of Box's hand. Then Box saw Razool's legs standing over him, caught a flash of steel and watched his friend slash up. The spiker's four rearmost limbs flailed, claws skittering on the roof before its huge bulk toppled sideways. The grotesque head bounced along the roof before rolling over the edge and out of sight.

'Don't make me do that again,' panted Razool, his mane coated with slick. He wiped his blade on his trouser leg before retracting it.

Box attempted a grin although his mouth was cloyingly dry and his calf felt like it was in flames. 'You're just trying to keep up with me,' he gasped.

Skarl and Raxa were by him now. Skarl was looking out, beyond the ship. 'This is bad, Zool.'

Box knew that Skarl was talking about the army of X'ath that filled the open grassland and had started to climb the ship. The air rang with the sound of spines hammering up the old metal walls.

'Medic,' shouted Razool. 'And *you*, get here where I can watch you.' He stabbed a finger towards Shera.

Box propped himself up on an elbow and dared to look at the mess that had been made of him. Beneath the blistered sky of Klanf 187, the world was redder than ever.

'Medic,' shouted Razool, again, and he shook his head in anger and despair. 'What a mess.'

'Thanks,' groaned Box.

Razool turned on Shera. 'Were you *trying* to kill him?'

'Don't be stupid,' snapped Shera. 'My weapon jammed and I lost control when it started firing. I'm sorry, OK? It all happened so fast.'

'And you nearly hit him when he was down,' shouted Razool.

'I don't know why,' Shera shouted back.

Razool shook his head. 'And now we've wrecked the GPU. We need a medic and it's wrecked.'

'You didn't need to kick it out of the way. You should have watched where you were going,' retorted Shera.

'I had to stop *you* from killing *him*,' shouted Razool, fist clenched.

'It doesn't matter,' groaned Box, who had managed to sit up, propped against Raxa who had knelt behind him. 'I mean, look at what's coming.' The grassland was seething with gigantic, six-limbed, wing-cracking, hack-bearing bodies.

'OK,' said Razool, more coolly. 'They're coming up that side, mostly. The blast vent is good for a couple more burns. I can use it to clear this approach while you carry him down into the ship, Raxa. At least I can call for help now.'

Razool walked up to Shera, close enough to bite. Then, quick as a spiker strike, he snatched the carbine that she had been holding loosely by her side. 'Skarl, you watch her.'

'Sure,' said Skarl, and his grip tightened on his own blaze carbine.

'Inside the ship we can hole up until somebody comes.

However many spikers there are, they can't all attack at once in there. But out here ...'

Box noticed that Razool's voice sounded tired for the first time.

'Leave me.' It was obvious. Box had lost so much blood and he knew that without help, he was as good as slabbed.

'No way,' snarled Razool.

Shera dropped to her knee and inspected Box's calf wound, which was the one that was bleeding most profusely. 'We need a tourniquet,' she said.

'Leave me,' insisted Box. Without him burdening them, they might even stand a chance.

'No.' Razool was enraged.

'Yes,' shouted Box. 'Look, Zool. *Look*.'

And already, the first rank of clambering spikers was in view, cresting the far end of the ship, beyond the mangled roof of the command bay.

'OK,' said Razool, cool, checking his weapon then slapping shut the breach. 'We fight here. All of us. Together.'

Skarl's narrow muzzle broke a smile and he knocked out his spent ammunition block. 'Last one,' he said, smacking in a fresh block.

'Take hers, Box,' and Razool handed Box Shera's carbine.

Immediately, Box passed the weapon up to Shera. 'If she shoots me now, what difference does it make?' he laughed weakly.

'I didn't mean to shoot you, Box,' insisted Shera.

'I know, I know.' Box managed a feeble smile. 'Anyway, it'll do more damage in your hands.'

'It's done enough damage already,' spat Razool.

Shera ignored Razool. Her eyes locked with Box's. 'Thanks, Box. Thanks for earlier. And thanks for trusting me now.' She reloaded.

Box dug the remaining ammunition blocks from his pouches and handed them out. 'Can you keep me up?' he asked Raxa. 'I'd like to watch the rest of this.'

'Sure,' replied Raxa, voice gruff.

'I'd of liked to make it to sixteen.' Box laughed emptily. There had been so many times back in the city when he'd thought it had been curtains. But he could never have imagined the end being like this. He hoped that wherever she was, Chess was doing better than him.

'We're not done yet.' Razool cocked his gun.

The fire team turned to face the first wave of spikers, blaze carbines ready. In the distance, thunder rolled.

'Wait until they're up close,' said Razool. 'Close enough to make every round count.'

Box could feel his strength seeping away but he worked to focus on what was happening; he didn't want to let go, to miss anything. When time had contracted to heartbeats, every last sensation mattered: the creak of the carbine stocks against shoulder armour, the road-kill stench of slick, the livid stains of his own blood, bright as paint.

'Hey,' murmured Raxa, 'you going to sleep?'

Box blinked and forced his eyes open. 'No,' he muttered. But he did feel tired: very, very tired.

'Thunder. Again,' grunted Skarl as a rolling boom drifted over the forest. Box was sure he could hear the snout's finger tighten on his trigger.

'Wait,' said Razool, steady. 'Wait.'

The spikers were scrambling over the top of the bay now.

Box looked out at the hoard of X'ath below, and the trees stained red by the burnt sky. But then he saw something which puzzled him.

'There's no wind,' he mumbled, hoarsely.

'Like I always say, Box,' cracked Razool, not taking his eyes or his gun barrel off the approaching spikers, 'your talent for stating the obvious is endless.'

'But look at the trees,' insisted Box. 'Look at them.'

The distant trees were moving. Their canopies were bending in a wave that was travelling from the far forest towards them. The front of this wave was approaching faster and faster, and all the time, the drumming thunder grew louder. And now, mixed with the booming rumble, Box could hear cracking and splintering and he saw that the trees were not just moving but were crashing down in an advancing line, as if a tidal wave was thundering through the forest, demolishing everything in its path.

Down in the open grassland, everything had stopped. The spikers froze and then turned as one towards the tree line. But all they could have sensed was the drumming from the forest that was coming closer and closer. They couldn't see what Box had seen from the roof of the transporter ship.

'Some . . . kind of . . . hurricane,' croaked Box.

Razool lowered his weapon as he watched what was happening. 'This is no wind,' he said.

On the roof of the command bay, the spikers had also stopped to watch what was happening, their hammer heads tilting first at one angle and then another as they assessed the situation.

Box's limping heart quickened as the thunder became deafening. It was so loud he realized he was squinting, as if that might reduce its power. Then, in one heartbeat, a wave of metal exploded from the forest. In the time it took for Box's faltering heart to beat again, the wave smashed through the army of spikers, levelling the clearing to a bed of carnage. Only as the tide of metal began to wheel about, skirting the far tree line and coming back on itself, slowing down, did Box identify the huge black horses, metal flanks glinting in the crimson light, and the armour-clad riders, helmeted and sheathing their long, curving swords and heavy battle hammers.

'Dreadbolts,' laughed Skarl, a little crazily.

Box watched the hundreds of bolts pull up on the far side of the open land, dividing into units as commands echoed across the killing ground. The giant horses stamped their feet and shook their heads and snorted, and sometimes they growled, a sound as raw as engines revving.

'No reins,' observed Box.

'No need,' said Razool. Box didn't ask why; he was too tired to talk.

Bolts and riders were spattered with slick from the spikers they had ridden through, the bright decorations of their armour lost beneath the black smears.

Troops were dismounting, setting up communications, and, at intervals along the perimeter of the splintered forestry, lone riders had halted, driving banners into the soft earth of Klanf 187. The banners hung loose in the still air, but as one dreadbolt galloped across the slaughter, his banner unfurled with a crack and Box saw a black, snarling dog head against a field of gold.

'A cohort of the Fourteenth.' Razool rubbed his eyes. 'Someone is watching over us.' Then he said to Box, 'Or watching over you.'

'Ease off that trigger, Skarl,' warned Raxa. 'Maybe the spikers will back off.'

'I don't think so.' Razool kept his weapon ready. 'I know spikers. And this bunch know they're surrounded. They know they're dead, whatever happens.' Razool bared the fangs down one side of his muzzle, taking aim. 'Given those odds, what would you do?'

'Fight,' said Box.

With a clatter of scrambling limbs, the spikers raced towards the fire team, three of them clearing the command bay in a couple of wing flaps.

There were five spikers in all, with more following, their huge, jagged silhouettes leaping and flapping. Box knew that hundreds had boarded the crippled ship so there was no way Razool and the others could hold them off. Once the rate of regeneration had outstripped the rate of fire, the X'ath would be in for the kill. So that gave the fire team a minute at best.

Box could barely sit now. A pool of blood had leaked from his leg and he was slumped against Raxa's thighs. He could hear the mechanism of Raxa's carbine ringing and feel the heat of its barrel.

Riders had drawn up in the lee of the ship, below. Box couldn't see what they were doing but he heard a volley of clangs and saw one wire-bearing harpoon take a spiker clean through its armour-scaled thorax. The creature kicked and writhed on the roof before ripping the spear free. Box guessed that the other grapples had embedded themselves in the body of the ship. The dreadbolts were climbing up.

'Skak,' spat Skarl as he ran out of ammunition. He dropped the carbine and drew his mace-blade.

Now Raxa's breach was open, rounds spent. He tossed the smoking weapon to the roof and Box heard the hiss of steel.

Two spikers were down, with no sign of movement, but the rest were closing in.

'Here we go,' yelled Razool as he hurled his useless weapon at the nearest set of opening mandibles.

'I said they should of given us grenades,' was the last thing Box said before the X'ath came.

But then they hesitated, stopped, and from his position on the floor, Box saw why. A dreadbolt had mounted the roof; just the one. He stood ten metres behind where Box and Razool and the others were clustered and across his arms he carried one of the mortar-sized guns Box had seen back on the deck. The dreadbolt raised the weapon to his chest, levelled it at the spikers and pumped the barrel like a shotgun, as he approached. For the first time, Box heard the spikers communicate: a series of low clicks coming from their closed jaws and their heads moved with tiny shakes.

Two more dreadbolts crested the roof, helmets and armour-blocked shoulders appearing over the edge. Once standing, they un-slung their weapons and advanced, halting behind the first. They raised their weapons. Opposite them must have been gathered no less than thirty spikers.

The first dreadbolt pulled a clip at the neck of his helmet, where it joined flush with the collar of his chest armour.

There was a brief hiss and a finger of steam rolled out from between helmet and collar before he reached up, twisted the helmet and pulled it from his head.

Box was surprised at how human the snout looked: mostly man-skinned with a grizzled, shaven head, a face welted with old scars, thick as veins, and a lower jaw like a bulldog. Only his yellow-green eyes and his bulldog jaw marked him out as a snout rather than a battle-stamped skin.

He approached slowly and spoke with rapid clicks, like the spikers had. He shook and tilted his head in an exaggerated imitation of how Box had seen the spikers move their hammer heads when communicating with one another. One of the spikers stepped forwards, shook its wide head rapidly and issued a stream of escalating clicks. The dreadbolt pointed to the distance and his comrades raised their weapons as if to take aim. The spiker bobbed its head, and then, in one sweep, all the spikers turned and hurried away, as swiftly as if they had been brushed off the roof of the ship.

Box sank back against Raxa.

'I'm Captain Strulf,' said the dreadbolt with the bulldog jaw, kneeling beside Box. He pulled off his gauntlets and put a dry hand on Box's head. 'You put up a good fight, son.'

Son. That was something he'd never been called before. Box swallowed and tried to speak but found it difficult to do more than mumble. He knew he was making no sense at all.

'He's sinking,' he heard Captain Strulf say. 'Terminal rate. I need a stem stick . . . Thanks.'

Box was aware of the dreadbolts moving about him. Now he was lying flat on his back. His body armour was loosened, fingers probed the wound to his flank, and then Box heard the right leg of his combat trousers tear open.

'Gaffed to pieces,' someone said.

Then there was an ice-cold jab below his knee.

'HFU trauma-doc required,' Captain Strulf was saying into the collar of his armour. There must have been a mike there.

Funny how you fasten on the weirdest details at a time like this, thought Box. His eyes focused on the snarling dog heads emblazoned in black and gold on the Captain's shoulder plates. Despite oily smears of slick, Box thought they were brilliant as pictures in a book.

'How come they backed off?' Skarl was saying.

One of the dreadbolts said, 'This is homeland territory. Most of the warrior-bulls are out in the battle zones. The spikers here are bad but they're not the worst. The three of us could have cleared this roof. We let them go if they pulled out quick. We didn't want you guys getting smashed in the crossfire.'

'Suits me,' said Skarl.

Voices drifted in and out like bits of dream. Razool was speaking now. 'Since when has a cohort of dreadbolts been sent in to evacuate the cannon fodder?'

'Orders,' was the immediate reply.

Captain Strulf's fingers were into Box's neck, searching for his pulse. 'We need a deep vortex pilot craft, *fast*. And chain *her* now.'

'Why?' protested Shera.

'Orders,' snapped Strulf. 'From the top.'

There was a rattle and click that Box hadn't heard in a long time but which he recognized at once.

'Thanks very much,' came Shera's voice as the manacles closed on her wrists.

Box reached up and pulled at the dreadbolt's arm. 'She hasn't done anything wrong,' he croaked.

'Don't make them your last words, son,' drawled Captain Strulf.

CHAPTER 6

The little girl with the copper-coloured hair and the barbed-wire tattoo down her cheek used both hands to pull herself up the rope. The rough stone of the shaft was wet with patches of slime that were slippery to her bare feet so she had to rely upon the strength of her stick-thin arms. She caught the rope between her knees and ankles to take the strain. She didn't look down; it had been cold down there and even when she had been down at the bottom of the rope, all that the head torch had revealed was more misty darkness.

Fifty metres of rope and there had been no bottom to the shaft.

Chess had done things like this. That thought made the girl more determined to keep climbing up without slipping, although, being a street rat, creeping and crawling through the dark places beneath the city came naturally to her anyway. Still, it hadn't felt good down there. There was something different about the darkness. Trick's flat tummy rumbled and she thought: hunger, that's what it is.

Down there, deep in the shaft beneath the vaults of the bank, the darkness was hungry.

Once she had clambered clear of the hole, she loosened the rope that she had fastened to the crampon in the wall above it. Then she coiled the rope and left it on the floor by the lip of the drop, just as she had been instructed to do. Now she was to take the unlit passage that ran beneath the bank to the rust-flaked service ladder which led up to the corridors behind the cinema complex next door.

At the top of the ladder it was still dark. Trick pulled off the head torch, brushed her hands over her baggy T-shirt and hitched up her torn tracksuit bottoms. She kept hold of the head torch as she opened the door and emerged, blinking, in a corridor which ran behind the cinema screens.

The third door along, that was the one she had to leave by. Even as she approached it, she could hear the sound of voices talking: big, loud, echoing cinema voices, and then a man laughing and then a woman. There was music. Trick hoped she hadn't missed the end of the film. She had to be clear of the room by the time the lights came up.

But as she edged the door open and slipped through the crack, the film was still running. It was much louder in the auditorium, and the figures on the screen loomed huge at the edge of her vision before the scene switched to a car chase with a man driving the car.

'Would you like to have a go?' the man asked the dog that sat on the rear passenger seat.

'No thanks, I've been drinking,' said the dog.

Everybody laughed and Trick sprinted towards the exit.

In the glare of the screen and the darkness that blotted out the rest of the cinema, none of the popcorn-gorging jacks noticed the tiny shadow of the street rat which flitted by.

Trick ran past the refreshment stalls and through the hall where jacks queued at the counters. Trick's nose and throat were full of the smell of sugar.

'Thieving rat,' somebody shouted at her as she ran for the exit. Someone else actually stuck out a foot to leg her over but she jumped it without a thought and then was out in the late summer evening. By the kerb, a small, cranky car was waiting, engine turning noisily. Trick pulled open the rear door and jumped inside.

'Hello, dear,' said the scruffy old lady who leant round the side of the front passenger seat, the smudged lenses of her spectacles magnifying the rheumy, bloodshot eyes. 'Popcorn?'

'Thanks, Ethel,' burst Trick, salivating at the box of popcorn she had been promised and which Ethel was holding. It was handed over and Trick set upon it like a lawn mower.

'They've got even bigger boxes in there.' Particles of popcorn sprayed from Trick's busy lips as she munched enthusiastically.

'With even bigger prices,' observed Ethel, brushing the damp, chalk-coloured flakes from her plucked, sage green cardigan. 'And look at you, practically spitting a fortune about the place.'

'Sorry, Ethel,' spluttered Trick.

'Don't mind me, dear,' said Ethel, turning back to face the

front. 'It's not my wages that are decorating the vehicle.'

'Seat belt Efel,' said the lanky, flat-capped driver.

'I'm touched by your strict adherence to the rules of road safety, Eric,' said Ethel through pursed and very wrinkled lips, 'but since you have managed to obtain for us a vehicle that travels only a little faster than I do, I shall throw my customary caution to the winds.'

'Suit yourself,' grumped Eric, who made much of checking that his own seat belt was secure before observing his mirrors laboriously and only then, kangaroo-hopping away from the cinema.

A mottled, nail-cracked hand reached up to pull down the sun shield and Trick's eyes were caught by Ethel's which were reflected in the narrow vanity mirror.

'So what did you find?' asked the old lady, as if Trick had been left to roam at a jumble sale.

Trick swallowed. Suddenly the popcorn felt very thick and dry in her mouth. She wished she had more information to give. Morosely, she said, 'Nothing.'

To Trick's surprise, Ethel clapped her hands and the reflection beamed at her. 'Splendid.'

Trick began to chew again and when she had cleared her mouth, she asked, 'Why are you pleased there was nothing after you sent me to look for something?'

'I never sent you to look for anything, my love,' Ethel corrected Trick with a wag of a pink and slightly arthritic finger. 'I merely sent you to *look*.'

Suits me, thought Trick, dabbing the final crumbs from the box.

The gears crunched and Eric swore horribly.

'Eric!' Ethel was aghast. 'We have a minor in the car.'

'I'm ten,' volunteered Trick, who liked swear words.

'It's that gun.' Eric nodded the peak of his cap at the machine gun that had been lodged under the dashboard. 'It keeps dropping down behind the gear stick, so's it jams when I push it.'

'Well, I am surprised at you,' observed Ethel with an indignant flounce. 'Wedging loaded weapons under the dashboard when you're such a stickler for road safety.'

'That's 'ere for *personal* safety,' muttered Eric, changing gear with a jolt.

Ethel's reflection regarded Trick thoughtfully.

'What?' asked Trick.

'Would you like to come to the meeting, my love?' asked Ethel.

'Really?' Trick tried not to show how excited she was.

'Really,' smiled Ethel. She caught Eric's sidelong glance. 'I'm always ready to encourage new talent,' she said. 'Ah! Nearly there.'

Trick pressed her face up to the glass and saw that they had pulled up outside a large fast food restaurant. Although she couldn't read, she recognized the name displayed in big red letters above the huge front windows.

'"On The Hoof",' said Trick aloud, and her mouth began to water again. 'Are we getting more food, Ethel?' she asked, hopefully.

'Not if I can help it,' replied the old lady, pushing open the passenger door with a groan.

Trick followed her out of the car. It was warm in the early-evening sun. They waved goodbye to Eric. Then Ethel marched into the restaurant and Trick trotted in behind her. She thought that Ethel moved surprisingly quickly for such an old lady.

On The Hoof was packed with customers and smells. There was the constant hiss of coffee machines, the clattering of trays on tables, the pinging of cash tills. Close to Ethel's heels, Trick wound her way through snaking queues and ducked under trays stacked with burgers, fries, drinks, pies, dips and ice cream. Her bare feet slithered over dropped fries and bright pink lumps of milk shake and her quick fingers snatched an unguarded apple turnover from a crowded table of diners. She ate the evidence before anyone could have noticed it had vanished.

'It's hard to find anyone in here,' she shouted to Ethel.

'That's the idea, my love,' Ethel shouted back. 'If you want to get lost, find a crowd. Ah, lovely. Here they are.'

'Trick!' Pacer raised a hand. He was wearing his black hooded jacket and was sitting at a circular table at the edge of the downstairs level. Next to him sat Gemma, wispy, blonde hair as unkempt as ever, with a snaggle-toothed grin for Trick. Gemma was only a couple of years older than Trick, and she lived in the remains of the wharf, by the river, with the other street rats. Pacer must have been nearly sixteen, and he was in charge of them all, now that Box and Splinter weren't there. He was tough and smart and normally he didn't have much to say to Trick, but the bright grin that had split his dark face made Trick feel less like a scabby street rat swamped in a crush of jacks. And Pacer and Gemma were Chess's friends, so it felt good to be with them.

Then she saw the tall girl with the long, black hair and the crystal blue eyes. She had got up to fetch a pile of napkins from the island by the wall. Her name was Anna and she was a jack but she wasn't like other jacks. She was friends with Chess and Pacer and she killed people with her sword: killed the enemy anyway. She scared Trick because she looked so perfect, and because she was so clever. And because *she* never seemed to be scared of anything.

Anna's short skirt made her legs look longer than ever. Trick felt smaller and more grubby than usual. Anna looked at Trick and didn't smile. She didn't even blink. That was something else which made Trick nervous of Anna: the way those blue eyes stared like a cat's.

Anna sat back at the table and Trick saw that there was a man sitting with them. He was wearing a pair of shorts and a loose shirt. He gave Trick a friendly smile as Ethel propelled her forwards.

'This is Captain Riley,' said Ethel in Trick's ear. 'He's a member of the Charitable Operations Executive, dear. The COE work for the Committee. They are very, *very* secret.'

Trick looked up at Ethel. 'I've never heard of them,' she said.

'Exactly.' Ethel patted her shoulder. 'In real life he's a policeman, a crasher.'

Trick slammed the brakes on. 'Are we in trouble?' She wiped crumbs of apple turnover from her lips.

'Of course not, dear,' whispered Ethel. 'Captain Riley's on our side, I am pleased to say.' She walked over and sat by the man.

Pacer shuffled up the bench seat and nodded at the

space. Trick squeezed in between him and Gemma. Mouth watering, Trick studied the detritus of wrappers, half-eaten burgers and unopened tubs of sauce that littered the table.

Ethel surveyed the mess too. 'It looks like there's been a battle,' she observed. Her spectacles turned on Pacer. 'I take it you *have* seen food before?'

'We've been waiting quite a long time,' said Anna. Trick thought she had such a clear, clever, jack voice.

'Well you should stick to measuring time in minutes, not burgers.' Ethel smiled benignly. 'It's healthier.'

Trick spotted a piece of bun and shoved it in her mouth. It looked like this was going to be a good meeting; there was plenty to scavenge.

'Trick's been checking out the hole,' Ethel said to Captain Riley. 'It didn't have a bottom.'

'Then we'll watch it,' responded the Captain. 'Watch for the enemy.'

Trick swallowed the lump but it stuck in her throat.

'Don't worry, dear,' smiled Ethel. 'That's a problem for another day. This meeting is for something quite different.' She smoothed the front of her cardigan. 'I had wanted us to meet sooner than this, but the Committee has been waiting for Captain Riley to return.'

Trick glanced at the crasher. His green eyes caught her own. They were friendly eyes, but they were also hard.

Riley looked to Ethel. 'Any news on Lemuel?'

'Lemuel is being a very naughty boy,' replied Ethel, tetchily. 'The Symmetry may have his body, but his disembodied mind is creating havoc in cyberspace.'

'He sent Anna her Link-me,' volunteered Pacer. 'She'd lost it.'

Trick knew that the Link-me was a contraband communications computer. She'd seen Anna use it back at the wharf. Anna was smart.

'I didn't lose it. I left it somewhere.' Anna shrugged. 'But I haven't contacted Lemuel. Yet.'

'Be careful, dear,' said Ethel.

'What about Chess?' asked Anna. 'That's why we're here. What's happened to her?'

Ethel removed her spectacles, polished them on the frayed hem of her thick tweed skirt. Once they were back in place she said, 'I am very sorry to say that Chess is now in the hands of the enemy.'

Pacer swore and punched the table.

'Poor Chess,' whispered Gemma.

Trick stared at a pot of tomato sauce.

'It's my fault,' said Anna. 'I should never have left her.'

'In a way, my love, it's everybody's fault,' Ethel consoled her.

'It ain't *my* fault,' grumbled Pacer, stuffing his fists into the pockets of his black, hooded jacket.

'*If* we are to apportion blame,' said Ethel, casting her eyes towards the ceiling where balloons and streamers hung like ocean wreckage, 'I think that a good deal of responsibility must lie with Splinter, who currently labours under the misapprehension that he is an Inquisitor.'

'No way!' Pacer's hands were out of his pockets.

'Splinter's a bigger fool than I expected,' muttered Captain Riley.

'Splinter is precisely the size of fool that *I* expected,' said Ethel, tersely. 'Although it is vital to remember this,' and she held up a nail-bitten finger. 'The room for improvement is the biggest room in the house.'

Pacer rubbed his shaven head. 'Which house?' he whispered to Anna.

'It's a metaphor, you dimwit,' replied Anna.

'Anyway,' Ethel rapped the table with her bony fingers. 'We have to face the situation, and the situation is this: Chess is currently in the possession of the Twisted Symmetry. She has been handed to the warps who, even as I speak, will be bombarding her with energy the Symmetry have extracted from their billions of victims: from their wars, from their assassinations, from their corruptions, from their dedicated infliction of pain.'

Trick stirred in the seat, aware of the voices of all the people around them, the press of bodies, the faces that were looking their way.

'Right now,' continued Ethel, voice lowered, 'Chess is being subjected to a process that will take her to a breaking point of multiversal proportions. The end of this process will have been timed to coincide with the fifth node, the point at which the time spiral is most vulnerable to change. And at that point the Symmetry will take Chess to the place where the fifth node and the universes coincide and there, they will unleash the Eternal.' Ethel's head craned forwards like a turtle and loudly enough to make Trick jump she said, 'Bang! Time and space will reverse to an unchanging moment that will last forever.'

'That will last forever for the *Symmetry*,' clarified Anna. 'For the rest of us, it's curtains.'

'Nicely put, my love,' said Ethel.

Pacer folded his arms. 'Do we know where Chess is?'

'Captain Riley?' Ethel inclined her head towards the man who sat next to her.

Captain Riley leant forwards and gathered up the remains of the burgers and half-eaten, slightly wet buns. He compressed the material in his strong hands, smoothing the bits of gristly paste that oozed between his fingers, until he had shaped a compact globe the size of a tennis ball.

Anna appraised the sphere of gunk that sat on the Captain's hand and then raised a neat, dark eyebrow at Ethel. 'They've hidden Chess in a cheeseburger?'

Captain Riley laughed. 'No.' He picked up pieces of plastic cutlery and inserted them into the ball until it looked like a sea-urchin with long spines. 'Imagine that this is a model of Warp Station Eight.'

'We'll do our best,' muttered Anna.

'This is mostly rock,' he indicated the ball, 'and these arms are metal. And around the surface there are complexes of laboratories, fission chambers, connecting over-surface corridors.'

'What's that bit of gherkin meant to be?' smirked Pacer.

'Are you taking this seriously?' enquired Ethel.

'I'm not the one making warp stations out of fast food,' bridled Pacer.

Captain Riley said, 'Warp Station Eight follows an orbit about a planet called Rath. We've had a long-range observation team on Rath for decades, monitoring the warp station, and we know Chess is in there.'

'How?' asked Anna.

'We've intercepted communications, even seen a flight in by General Saxmun Vane, and, several weeks ago, we saw a series of explosions that caused massive damage to the station.'

'What's that got to do with Chess?' asked Pacer.

Riley fixed him with a cool, green stare. 'When you see space crack open, see light and darkness vanish, see xenrian gaolers the width of nebula tornado halfway across visible space to contain the chaos, you have an idea that it isn't just matches that the Symmetry are playing with.' Riley tossed the model station on his palm. 'For a few moments it looked like someone was so angry that they were smashing the station out of existence.'

'Yup,' said Anna with a nod. 'That's our girl.'

'So we just have to go and get her?' asked Pacer.

Riley shook his head. 'There's a problem.'

'Only one?' Anna blinked slowly.

'One big one.' Riley grimaced. 'Preliminary investigations have revealed to us that this whole station is encased in an impenetrable field: transparent but impenetrable. A fractal code.'

'And what's a fractal code?' asked Anna, as if Captain Riley were creating problems for fun.

'Difficult to crack,' sighed Riley.

'Impossible,' stated Ethel. 'Without the access data.'

Anna folded her arms. 'So, let me get this right. We know that the Twisted Symmetry have Chess prisoner and we know it's in this warp station. But we can't even *try* to rescue her because the warp station is protected by a force-field: by this fractal code.'

'Without the access data, we cannot break open the code,' confirmed Captain Riley.

'OK,' said Anna patiently. 'So how do we get the data?' She looked from Ethel to Riley and then back to Ethel.

Ethel clasped her hands like a choir girl about to break into song. She said, in an unusually small and croaky voice, 'I have calculated a number of possibilities and there is a *minuscule* possibility that somebody will give it to us.' Her spectacles had slipped to the tip of her nose. She pushed them back into position. 'It is, however, only a minuscule chance.'

Anna's face darkened. 'And if this random act of charity does not come to pass, what then?'

'To tell you the truth, my love,' sighed Ethel, 'unless our people exercise their brains beyond their normal capacity, and unless at the same time they are very, very lucky, I really don't know.'

'We're ready to go,' said Captain Riley, who sounded ready to depart immediately. 'We have plans prepared by agents, plans of the layout of the relevant parts of the station, although they were prepared before the fractal code was activated, before Chess was captured. But until we have the access data ...' He squeezed tight his fist, pulping the soggy model, and dropped the remains to the table.

'So what about Chess?' demanded Pacer, stabbing a finger

towards Ethel. 'What are the Committee going to do?'

Trick fiddled with the seal of the unopened tomato sauce dip. The silence was tight as a vice.

Anna spoke slowly, as if Ethel and Riley were finding it hard to keep up with her. 'The Symmetry are trying to break Chess. We can't just wait for a way of cracking the code to turn up. We have to help her. We have to do *something*.'

There was a desperate silence until Riley said, 'Anna, we're doing everything we can.'

'We're doing nothing.' Anna stood up, ready to leave.

Ethel stood, and took hold of Anna's wrist. Trick could see the skin go white where it was gripped by the old lady's hand.

'Please, dear, do sit back down. I haven't finished yet.'

Anna tugged her wrist from the old lady's grasp. But she sat down.

Trick didn't like the atmosphere. She didn't like the way Ethel went so hard and serious. And she didn't like the way that other people seemed to be watching them.

'You're not just here to watch the Captain make warp stations out of fast food.' The pink eyes loomed out from behind the smudged spectacle lenses. 'You're here for another reason. You're here so that we can warn you.'

'Warn us?' Pacer cracked his knuckles. 'About what?'

'About the Twisted Symmetry. They have given the Endgame order. For all the multiversal machinations of the Symmetry, my loves, this bit is personal.'

Trick wanted to go now. But the others were waiting to hear what Ethel was going to tell them.

'The Twisted Symmetry have been keeping a close watch

on many of you,' said the old lady, pushing a greasy, grey strand of fringe up from her wrinkled forehead. She pointed at Riley, 'On you,' at Anna, 'on you,' and at Pacer, 'and on you.'

Pacer grunted. 'I was thinking maybe they'd miss me out.'

'They've been keeping a close watch on you and a good many others: on scientists and priests, crucial to the work of the Committee; on politicians and world leaders; on anybody whose individual decisions or actions could possibly create a problem for the Symmetry. And now that the fifth node is approaching, the order has been given for each one of you to be killed.'

Trick's finger burst through the cellophane lid of the sauce pot. A jet of red liquid splurted over her fingers and onto Pacer's jacket. But Pacer said nothing.

The heavy silence was broken by Anna. 'Well, they've not been all that friendly up to now.'

Trick looked at Anna closely. Anna really looked as cool as she sounded. But Trick was beginning to wish she hadn't come with Ethel. Maybe it had brought her close enough for the Symmetry to start watching her too.

'So far as the Twisted Symmetry are concerned,' said Ethel, 'things are now too delicately poised to risk any of us messing them up.' Ethel allowed herself a little smile. 'I have to say, you have all proved yourselves capable of causing them a lot of trouble already. But the Captain and I have talked about this, and we think it is safer for you to stay with us, at Committee HQ.'

Pacer's response was immediate. 'No. No way. There's all

the rats at the wharf. I'm not leaving them. I have to look after them.'

'It's too dangerous, Pacer,' insisted Ethel. 'And for Anna. Particularly for Anna. The Symmetry know what is planned for her.'

'That's more than I do,' commented Anna.

'I aren't going away from the wharf. There's little ones to look out for.' Pacer's fists were clenched.

'They're in more danger with you there,' said Riley.

'Says the crasher,' snapped Pacer. Riley sighed and shook his head.

'The Symmetry aren't going to come in tanks are they?' observed Anna, reasonably. 'You always say that they don't like the public to know what they do.'

'Not tanks, dear, definitely not.' The old lady smiled. 'The enemy are a lot cleverer than that. But they *will* come for you.'

Trick looked through the packed ranks of customers, towards the plate front windows. Outside, night was falling.

'We've done all right up to now,' insisted Pacer. 'We can look after ourselves.'

Without thinking, Trick licked tomato sauce off her fingers. She looked across to Anna. Everyone was looking at Anna.

Anna stood. 'You just let us know when you've got the code,' she said to Ethel.

'Don't do something stupid, Anna, just because you're angry,' warned the old lady.

Gemma and Pacer stood up beside Anna. Trick did too. She felt Anna's hand on her shoulder.

'You know, Ethel,' said Anna, 'this isn't about the fifth node, or who wins your war. This is about our friend. It's about Chess. That's the only reason we're here. When you can help us to help her, we'll be back.'

CHAPTER 7

Early morning. Splinter had learnt that the best time was early morning. He had discovered that when he awoke, his thoughts were logical, his head clear, his spirit at its lightest. And then, as he ate and drank his way through the hours that followed, the thick, swirling typhoon of his imagination took hold and he became the King of Rats: ruthless, brilliant, powerful. The fifth Inquisitor. Except that there was no fifth Inquisitor. So long as he ate none of the drugged food and drank none of the drugged wine that was brought to him by the castle servants, there was no fifth Inquisitor.

There had been a coronation; the other four Inquisitors had given him that. And in return? Splinter stared at his thin, naked body in the mirror on the wardrobe door and made himself look into his own, ice-blue eyes: eyes that were smashed with lines of pink from lack of sleep. In return he had given them Chess.

So, here he was, in a spiralling, cylindrical castle that had no top and had no bottom; a castle as endless and tortuous as his own imagination. He had spent hours climbing up and hours climbing down and never did he come to a roof, never did he find a cellar. There was only an endless sky: blue by day and darkest indigo by night. There were servants. And there was Saul.

Saul: his one remaining friend. His ally. And, so long as he hid the food and drink that the servants brought him, food and drink that were so heavily drugged with Dream that he could have believed he was the multiverse itself had he consumed it, he had clarity of thought. And, right now, after all that he had learnt, clarity of thought was more important than anything; more important than ruthless brilliance, more important than power. More important even than being the King of Rats.

Splinter took an unflinching look at his body, at the rewards of his relentless ambition.

Look at your left hand. *Look at it.*

Splinter was nearly sixteen years old, but the skin of his left hand and forearm was as grey and cracked as a dead lizard's. The Hermetic Codex that he had used to save his life had exacted a price of its own: his vitality in exchange for his survival. His left hand was weak now, weak as an old man's. He raised it to his right cheek, which was also webbed with wrinkles and cracked as dry parchment all the way down his neck to his scrawny clavicle. This was the price paid the second time he had used the Codex, draining him of a measure of life to preserve the remainder.

The Codex worked by revealing three occasions on which death lay in wait for Splinter. It had consisted of three small triangular plates. Drawing his own blood with either of the first two plates had shown him how to avoid death, but the third plate could not be used like that; to cut himself with it would have invited certain death. That was the way the Codex worked. And Splinter had seen what that death would be: an ancient, faceless man: the Narrow Man. And the Narrow Man's crystal knife plunged deep into Splinter's chest. But Splinter still possessed that third plate.

Splinter touched his old wounds, tracing the history written into the King of Rats' own body. The weal above his right eyebrow from when Box had blown up the factory gates on Surapoor. The tramline scar from his forehead to his right cheek, cut into him by the metalbacks: mechanical birds constructed from metal and from the nervous tissue of real birds. A long, neatly healed cut down his right shoulder, given to him by the same creatures. Down his left shoulder, the scar left by General Vane's mace-blade. And when he walked, it was with a limp and had been ever since his right ankle had been shattered by cannon shot on Surapoor.

Splinter walked slowly and unevenly from the mirror to his wardrobe and dressed in the black clothes he liked to wear: black trousers and a black, mandarin-collared jacket. Inside the jacket he tucked the crystal knife that the Inquisitor, Malbane, had given him on his coronation; in its side pocket he kept the third triangular plate from the Hermetic Codex, his lock picks and his switchblade. His other possessions he kept at the back of his deep wardrobe. On his feet he wore nothing; his dalliance with footwear was over. Barefooted he had started this journey and barefooted he would finish it. Footwear was for jacks; Splinter was a street rat.

'The King of Rats, majesty? Surely the King of Rats.'

'No,' said Splinter, to the voices that spoke to him less

and less these days. 'Not the King of Rats. Just a street rat.'

.He walked over to close the wardrobe door with the mirror inside it and he studied the tramline gash on his forehead again. It was such a neat scar, thanks to the skilful needlework of Dr Oriana Lache. She might have been a Crystal Priest, one of the Symmetry's principal human servants, but she really had liked him, had actually cared for him.

But Splinter's ruthless brilliance had taken her to her death anyway.

He thought about slamming shut the door on the gaunt, white-haired apparition who stared back at him, but that would have been to make too much noise. His new clarity of thought told him that the coming weeks would be a time for silence. He would need silence and cunning if he was to undo the damage; if he was to prevent from happening the terrible thing he had discovered.

'I didn't want them to hurt you, Chess,' he said as he closed the wardrobe door softly. He walked out of the bedroom and into the sitting room where breakfast had been set out for him: juices, pastries, sausages, bacon, coffee and, this morning, a silver plate of handmade chocolates. Through the open window, the fresh blue sky was endless.

The Twisted Symmetry were stronger then the Committee: Splinter had been right about that. They had bigger armies, better technology, more power. He began to deposit the breakfast provisions into a large, ceramic washing bowl, barely looking at them as he did so. Orange juice, coffee, sausages, chocolates and croissants combined into an oily slop.

But the Symmetry's strength wasn't much good if he ended

up like this. He picked coffee grounds off his fingertips and flicked them back in the slop. Anna had been strong, but it was a different kind of strong from Symmetry strong. Splinter pondered this, rubbing his white hair which was spiky over his head and long down the back of his thin neck. Her strength was her own, that was the difference; she didn't feed off other people. She looked good too. He should have stayed with her when she asked him to. At least his face wouldn't have ended up like some ancient wrinkly's.

Whenever Splinter thought of old things, he thought of Ethel. Or Mevrad, or whoever she was. In fact, these days, Splinter thought of Ethel frequently; her voice gnawed at the inside of his mind. But he was not as quick to ignore it as he had once been. Whatever she had been like in the past, it was Ethel who had made him realize what the Symmetry had been doing to him. Her comment about the Inquisitors feeding him Dream, coupled with his own researches, and the realization that always he thought more clearly in the early mornings before he had eaten or drunk anything, meant that he had guessed what poison the Inquisitors' hospitality really was.

So he owed that debt to Ethel, at least. She might not have gone about revealing how strong or smart she really was, but from where he stood now, Splinter decided that that was the strongest and smartest trick of all. The Inquisitors had actually been frightened of her: he had seen them squirm when she had gate-crashed his coronation. And yet, even after that, he had given them Chess.

'What else could you do?' asked one of the voices, reasonably.

Splinter carried the breakfast slops into his bedroom, opened the wardrobe and reached inside. His stick fingers closed on a little wooden casket.

'I could have refused to help them,' he said, drawing the casket close.

'And you would have been killed,' the voice assured him.

I could have *tried* to refuse to help them, Splinter thought back. I could at least have tried.

The voice had no answer to that, which made Splinter feel more despondent than ever, but also more determined to go through with his plan: his plan to stop what he had witnessed; to prevent it from happening.

He opened the lid of the wooden box and tipped the contents of the washing bowl inside, solid and liquid glugging out like vomit. Although the bowl was larger than the box, not a drop of fluid, not one lump of sausage overflowed. Splinter shut the lid, pushed the box out of sight and closed the wardrobe door. Then he went to wash the bowl.

The white ceramic filled with water and his face was distorted in the shallow ripples. And peering over his shoulder, reflected in the water, was the face of an old lady: an old lady with scruffy grey hair and a pair of grimy spectacles.

'You again,' groused Splinter at the imagining.

'You shouldn't have stolen it, dear,' said Ethel, inside his mind.

Splinter knew that she was talking about the little wooden box. 'You shouldn't have left your portable vortex lying around. And anyway, if I hadn't taken it, I wouldn't have been able to use it to find out what happens to Chess.'

'If you hadn't taken it, dear, we wouldn't all be having to

look for her.' The reflection shook its head. 'It's a question of consequences. Think about all that breakfast. Right now, thanks to you, there is a universe where it's raining sausages and bacon.'

Splinter slapped the water but the voice remained. It was a particularly persistent voice.

'You don't seem very happy, dear.'

He stared into the shimmering liquid in the bowl. 'Chess was happy to see me, when I found her. Really happy.' Splinter laughed feebly. 'Don't ask me why. It's not like I'd ever tried to be nice to her. But after everything that had happened, here, the Inquisitors . . . everything.' He breathed out slowly and felt his chest go tight, his stomach ache. 'It was like her happiness was mine.'

'Happy when she took your hand?' asked Ethel.

Splinter nodded, head bowed.

'And then you gave her to them.' The old voice was gentle, which made him feel worse. 'Gave her to the Twisted Symmetry.'

'Why do you have to go on about things?'

'These aren't my thoughts, dear,' said Ethel.

Splinter turned his back on the bowl. But he couldn't turn his back on the voice. 'How did you find out what happens to her?' it demanded.

'Chess?' asked Splinter.

'Yes, my love. You haven't been looking into anyone else's future, have you?'

Splinter paused, water dripping from his fingertips. 'I looked for mine.'

'And what did you find?'

'I looked in the Omnicon,' began Splinter.

'Ah, yes, the Book of All Things. Something else you stole.'

Splinter sighed. It was only a voice: a voice inside his head. Why couldn't it say agreeable things?

'You've hidden it inside the portable vortex, haven't you?' continued the voice. 'But the Omnicon can't show the future. The pages contain knowledge, but they won't reveal the future.'

Splinter grunted in agreement. 'It won't work when I look for anyone *else's* future, but it will work for mine.'

'Really, dear?' Ethel was intrigued. 'And what does it show?'

'A blank page,' said Splinter, gloomily.

'Hmm. Not very promising, if you want my opinion.'

'I know it's not very promising,' snapped Splinter. 'And I don't want your opinion.' The blank page haunted him. And it was impossible to reconcile with the Narrow Man and the crystal knife, save that neither of them smacked of a happy end. 'Now, if you don't mind, I'm going in search of some breakfast that hasn't been drugged with Dream.' And then, begrudgingly, he added, 'Thank you, by the way, for warning me about the drug. I found out what it does, from the Omnicon.'

I can't believe I'm thanking a voice inside my own head, thought Splinter. But sometimes, the voices were helpful; they made things clearer.

'How *did* you find out about Chess?' asked Ethel. With some gratification, Splinter could tell that she was impressed: at least, her imaginary voice was. He could imagine her standing in front of him, looking like she'd just been woken after a rough night at a tramps' booze-up and smelling not much better.

'Well, the Omnicon might not show the future, but I can use it to find the reachings I need.' Once inside the portable vortex, Splinter could open the vast grid of the mortice-gate which allowed access to the reachings: the invisible, narrow paths that led through the eternal emptiness of the vortex. 'If you know the right reachings, you can find any time, any place.'

'Very clever.' Ethel must have guessed what he had done.

'Exactly,' smiled Splinter, his thin face looking a little younger for a moment. 'I used the Omnicon to tell me which reachings to take, to lead me into the future and to discover what happens to Chess.'

'Didn't you do that for yourself first, dear?' The voice knew him very well indeed.

'Yes.' Splinter felt the vertiginous gloom that had descended upon him when he had followed those reachings and discovered that they led only to nothingness. 'Didn't work for me.' He turned back to Chess. These days, thinking about Chess was something that made him feel better; made him feel that he was doing something that mattered. 'It was an act of brilliance, the way I tracked her through the reachings.'

'Oh, there is no doubt about your brilliance, Splinter,' agreed the voice. 'But it's what you *do* with it that makes me wake in a cold sweat.'

'And I had to be careful,' added Splinter. 'There is so

much emptiness in the vortex, and once you're lost, you're lost forever.'

'But what did you see?'

'I saw what happens to Chess.' The excitement at being brilliant deserted him when he said that, when he thought about what he had seen: his discovery.

'And?'

'And now I have the power: the power to change *everything*.' That thought made Splinter feel a lot better. Power was always uplifting. 'And I'm hungry.' He headed for the door that would lead him to the staircase that spiralled down to the kitchens. 'I'm going to ask Saul to help me,' he said, hesitating with his hand against the wood of the door.

'Can you trust him?'

'You should know, since he works for you.' Splinter laughed. He had first met Saul on Surapoor, and ever since then, Saul had turned up at the most dramatic moments. And he had been at the castle when Splinter had first arrived. That was when Saul had revealed that he worked for the Committee. 'He's like a loyal dog where Chess is concerned. All he ever does is go on about how we should help her.' Splinter sniffed. 'To be honest, I've never liked him all that much, but he might actually be useful now.'

'I think,' volunteered Ethel, 'that you should be careful.'

'If all I did was listen to you,' Splinter retorted, 'I'd spend so much time being careful that I'd never get out of bed in the morning.'

'If only,' sighed Ethel, wistfully. The she said, 'I wonder that you don't leave this castle. You've got the portable vortex, after all. My portable vortex. You can go anywhere.'

'But I'd have to leave the portable vortex here,' explained Splinter. 'Whoever it is. And I don't want to leave it. I *need* it.'

'That's the problem with possessions,' observed Ethel. 'It's hard to work out what's doing the possessing.'

'I'm going for breakfast,' said Splinter.

'Happy stealing,' smiled Ethel.

Splinter shook his head. 'That's enough,' he muttered out loud. And the old lady had gone. Satisfied that the only voice he had to listen to now was his own, he stepped onto the stone stairs.

There was food in the kitchens: un-drugged food. And water. This was how Splinter had sustained himself these past few weeks. It was not difficult for a thief of Splinter's multifarious abilities to slip through the kitchens like a phantom and lift bread, ham, apples, cheese, a jar of marmalade. He never took too much at once. Greed was the principal undoing of most thieves: that and being caught when they found you. But if you weren't greedy, and if you were stealing from the castle larder, you could go on helping yourself for as long as you liked. And if you had a portable vortex in which to hide the evidence: the apple cores, the bits of bone, plastic wrappings, tin cans, so much the better.

His footsteps tapped down the stone steps which would take him to the cold rooms behind the largest pantry. But first, there was a detour to make.

Yesterday, at the bottom of the staircase, Splinter had detected a draught. He hadn't been trying to find one, but for a street rat whose existence had sometimes depended upon noticing changes in the flow of air or its temperature or its smell in the sewers beneath the city, Splinter automatically sensed the air about him. And this patch of air was stirring.

But air didn't just stir of its own accord. It moved when there was wind, or someone or something was moving. Or when there was a hidden passageway. Splinter was particularly interested in hidden passageways. In his considerable experience they led to items of value or means of escape and to Splinter, items of value and means of escape were matters of the deepest interest.

Yesterday there had been footfalls on the stairs above him, descending. Instinctively, Splinter had darted into the first cold room and slithered beneath a stone stillage loaded with hams. Nobody had followed him into the cold room, and he hadn't heard anybody walk back up the steps, which served only to heighten his interest in what might be the cause of the draught.

He was at the bottom of the staircase now. He closed his eyes, centring on sound, smell, touch. Deep silence; nobody was following. The air was cold. There was the smoky, sweet smell of ham and the sharp odour of cheese. And there was a stirring in the air: air moving to his left. The same as yesterday.

Splinter opened his eyes, squatted, brushed a residue of stone dust onto his palm and standing again, threw it into the air. He watched its descent minutely. There was a puff and a swirl amidst the falling dust and Splinter tracked its source back to the wall. His bony white cheek was against the stones at once, clever fingers tracing the mortar, feeling for spaces.

'Ah,' he sighed, and he pushed: one stone. There was a click and then Splinter pushed this whole section of wall. It swung away from him, into a place of warmth and shadow. Satisfied that nobody was near, Splinter slipped through the portal.

It was humid, which he had not expected. Already he felt his forehead prickle with sweat. There were electric lights in the walls, which were built of the same smooth, bulbous stones as the rest of the castle. This room was wide and long and it meandered ahead of him like a river-bed. The ceiling bellied down as if bearing the weight of the unending mass of castle above. There were no carpets and no decorations. Splinter pushed the stone door shut and head ducking slightly, lest he scrape it on the low ceiling, he padded down the hot room.

At the far end there was a wooden door and beyond the door, a room piled high with glass jars, glass cylinders and stacked with what appeared to be empty aquaria, right up to its high ceiling. Some of the cylinders were as tall as Splinter and at the far end there was one that was twice his height and five times his width. Then Splinter noticed that behind one high wall of piled glassware, there was a pair of huge, wooden doors.

'Splinter,' hissed a voice from behind him.

Splinter spun round and then relaxed. 'Saul?' he rubbed his wet forehead with the sleeve of his jacket. 'What are you doing here?'

'Looking for you. What are *you* doing here?'

Splinter didn't answer. He took a long look at the tall, rangy boy with the square jaw, long black hair, big, dark eyes and soft lips. And the nose that had been broken by General Vane's fist. Splinter focused on the big, dark eyes. They told him nothing.

'I'm wondering why someone has built rooms like this, and why they are so hot and why they are secret,' said Splinter, observing Saul's reaction.

Saul shrugged. 'Didn't even know they were here.' He looked about as if seeing the room with the assemblage of glassware for the first time. 'What *are* you doing here, Splinter?'

'Exploring my castle,' replied Splinter. He walked out of the room and headed back towards the secret door. He would continue his explorations on another occasion, without having to share them with Saul. 'How did you know about the door?' He tossed the question behind him as Saul followed.

'I heard you close it. I was looking for you. I'd come to the kitchens to see if you were there. Scavenging.' Saul laughed. Splinter had told him about how he took food from the kitchens, and why.

Splinter thought about what he wanted to say to Saul as he walked. Now was as good a time as any to talk about what he had seen in the vortex. Sweat prickled his brow. 'Why's it so hot down here?' he snapped.

Saul said nothing. When they came to the secret door which Saul had left open, Splinter shoved it shut.

'What?' began Saul.

Splinter spun round. 'Can I trust you?' he demanded.

'What?'

'Can I trust you?' He had hold of the front of Saul's white shirt.

'Why are you asking?' Saul shook his head, confused, disorientated. 'I mean, yes. Yes, Splinter.' He shook his head again and pushed Splinter back. 'You can trust me. You know you can.'

Splinter slumped against a wall, swallowed, gathered his thoughts. He knew he could trust Saul.

'Chess dies,' he said.

'What?' Saul's mouth was impassive but his eyes were wild.

'Chess dies.' Splinter shouted the words because they made him so angry, so unhappy. 'I've seen it, Saul. She dies.'

'How d'you know?'

'From the portable vortex. OK, I've got a portable vortex and I've used it to find out about the future, well, Chess's future.' Splinter knew he was gabbling, words tumbling from his mouth quicker than he could control them. 'I've got an Omnicon too.'

Saul's face was frozen. Shocked. Splinter began to laugh. 'A Book of All Things. There are only two and I've got one. It doesn't tell the future, you see. But it does know about the reachings, in the vortex. So I've used it to take a look.' He laughed some more and realized that his fingers had dug themselves into his white hair.

'I thought she'd be ruling universes or something. I thought she'd be OK; she's meant to be so special.' He choked on his own laughter. 'I don't know what I thought. But what I saw isn't what I want. It's not what I want.'

'I know, Splinter. None of us want that.' Saul spoke gently, put a hand on Splinter's sharp shoulder.

Splinter realized that Saul was kneeling by his side and

that he, Splinter, had slid down the wall until he was on his haunches. His eyes were hot and wet.

'It's sweat. It's just sweat,' he insisted.

'It's OK, Splinter,' Saul assured him.

They stayed like that for a long time. Saul was quiet and Splinter breathed slowly and deeply until his shoulders had stopped shaking. By the time they had stopped, he felt better, lighter. He felt ready.

Saul was sitting on the floor, looking at the shapes his fingers traced in the dust, the stone spotted with drops of sweat.

When Splinter spoke it was slow but resolute. 'We can help her. We can help Chess.'

Saul looked up, eyes intense. 'How?'

After only the briefest hesitation, Splinter divulged what he had planned. 'We can use the Omnicon to find out where Chess is, where the Twisted Symmetry are keeping her. Then we use the vortex to go there. Help her.' Splinter half laughed at Saul's grave expression. 'All we have to do is step out of the vortex, grab Chess and step back. It's so simple. The Symmetry won't have a clue.' Then Splinter paused before saying something he had never said before. 'I can't do it on my own.'

Saul's stern face broke into a smile. 'You won't have to.'

Saul's boots hammered across the wooden floor as he marched into the room, high in the castle. He halted in front of the Inquisitor and turned on him with eyes hot and dark as anthracite.

'I have always known that this was a foolish idea, Malbane. Always.'

'Is that why you have summoned me here with such urgency?' enquired Malbane, hands clasped neatly and priestly face solicitous, patient.

'Of course that's not why I've asked you here.' Saul paced to the window and then paced back. 'He's found out.'

'Found out?'

'About Chess. About what happens. At the end.'

Malbane shrugged. 'He might have guessed as much.'

'He used that silly little box which he hides in the back of his wardrobe. He's hunted through time until he found her: saw the very end of it.'

'I am gratified to hear that Chess is there at the end, just as she should be,' remarked Malbane, not taking his eyes off Saul.

'I am sick of acting as his nursemaid. The King of Rats? Did you know that's what he calls himself? I've listened to him, talking in his sleep. I've listened to him for hours.' Saul clenched his large fists until the knuckles cracked.

'It has all been necessary, Saul. And everyone is grateful to you. *Everyone.*' Malbane cleared his throat and smoothed the front of his cowl. 'Our calculations, forwards and back through time, proved that the King of Rats would succeed with Chess where all other efforts would fail; succeed in being the weakest point. But without your participation, without you earning his trust, keeping him alive, all our calculations, all our planning, might have come to nothing.'

Saul laughed, hollowly. 'Earning his trust has been galling.

That pantomime in the factory on Surapoor with the General? His teeth on *my* neck!'

'The General was none too keen a player,' observed Malbane, under his breath. 'He took a lot of persuading.'

'And the General would have eaten him when he had the opportunity on the prison planet, had it not been for *my* intervention.'

'For which everyone is indebted to you, Saul,' Malbane insisted. 'The General is not always as cooperative as we would wish. You know that.'

Saul pointed to his own face. 'My nose knows that. And then that farce with Lache.'

'If you had not stepped out of time and telephoned Lache, called her home, Splinter might have been shot dead by that fool, Boulevant, and Chess would still be out there.' Malbane's eyes flicked towards the window, as if Chess might have been hovering on the other side of the glass. 'And we would be far from our current, happy position. All of us thank you, Saul.'

'Why can you not organize your own people?' demanded Saul. 'First Lache's servant nearly shoots him dead, then Tethys nearly burnt him alive. Had I not been watching over him ...'

'Saul, Saul, please.' Malbane shook his head. 'Such rage?'

'Would you like to play the part of an agent of the Committee for months on end?' Saul raised a warning finger towards the Inquisitor.

Malbane raised his hands, placatory. 'No, Saul, no. *That* must have been most ... unpleasant for you. You have our deepest sympathy, as well as our deepest gratitude.'

'And all for the benefit of that demented fool, Splinter.' Saul stuck his hands in his jeans pockets and sat against the window casement, his white shirt brilliantly bright in the light of a sun that could never be seen.

'Not for *his* benefit, Saul,' Malbane reminded him. 'For *ours*. Remember that, and how close we are now. Don't let his silly obsessions distract you. He has ceased to feed on what we offer him? No matter. His dreams mean nothing now. He is still captive here; unless he spends his life hiding inside his little box.'

Saul laughed coldly. 'He means to rescue Chess.'

Malbane pondered this, jaws moving slowly as if chewing. 'How?'

'By using his portable vortex.' This time it was Saul who studied the Inquisitor, a glimmer of pleasure in his pitch eyes.

Finally, Malbane let out a long sigh and at its conclusion said, 'That is a pity.'

Saul slapped his long thighs and laughed. 'Malbane, I believe you have grown fond of our King of Rats.'

The Inquisitor sighed again. 'I recognize some of his qualities. They are endearingly familiar.'

'There is still something of the human about you, Malbane,' jibed Saul.

'As there is about you, Saul,' countered the Inquisitor. His ancient eyes looked up. 'Ah, Splinter,' he sighed, and said softly, 'I have tried to keep my side of the bargain.' Then the light died in his eyes and in its place was a void of darkness. 'There is only one solution to the problem of Splinter.'

'Obviously.' Saul flicked back a lock of hair.

'You will deal with this?'

'After all I have had to deal with, *this* will be my pleasure.' Saul left the window and headed for the door.

'We must be sure to be rid of him *forever*,' said the Inquisitor.

A smile slipped onto Saul's face. 'I have the perfect solution. I know how to dispose of the King of Rats for eternity.'

CHAPTER 8

When Box finally surfaced, he knew that he had been out for days. There had been periods when he had come near to that white, ghostly fog of vague movement and blurred sound that floated at the boundary between conscious and unconscious, and there had been times when he had sensed movement on and in his body, a crawling, prickling sensation. But for most of the time he had been out, insensible as clay.

Now there were sounds: the tap of metal, footfalls, groans, snores. There were smells: antiseptic and sweat. And there was light: bright, white light. His eyes were open and he was lying on his back, looking up at a glass ceiling. Box blinked but didn't move. His body felt relaxed, free of pain. He was alive. He let his body sink into the mattress and closed his eyes again.

Down came the hacks, gaffing him through the chest.

With a cry, Box sat bolt upright and opened his eyes. He was gasping for breath but there were no spikers. Of course there were no spikers. The spikers had backed off when the dreadbolts had come. Box rubbed his eyes. He remembered

Shera being taken prisoner. He remembered the soldiers working on his leg. Maybe he remembered being carried off the roof of the marooned transporter ship, but that was as far as his memory went. And now he was here, wherever here was. Box looked about.

It was a hospital ward, big as a platform on a railway station. The roof was glass, supported by girders, and the walls were concrete. There were dozens of beds in rows and in the beds there were snouts. Some looked OK: bandaged, in traction or just sleeping. Others were not so good: sheets wet with blood, bodies riddled with tubes fixed to units at their bedsides. Beside some there were machines, big as the machines that built cars in assembly plants, and the machines worked on the snouts with needles, lasers, blades and soldering irons. Box actually saw a fan of white sparks spray off the arm of one anaesthetized snout.

'How d'you feel?'

Box looked left. A solid, shaven-headed snout in grey fatigues was standing by his bed. His face was badly scarred: old scars but livid. And his lower jaw was bellicose as a bulldog's.

'I'm Captain Strulf,' said the snout. 'Remember me, son?'

Pictures jolted back into Box's memory. 'Yeah,' he croaked, mouth feeling like it was full of glue and flavoured with cat. He rubbed his throat. 'I'm thirsty.'

Captain Strulf fetched a glass of water from a steel sink against the wall opposite. He handed it to Box. 'Nearly lost you.'

Box gulped. Drops of cold water spilt down his T-shirt. He gasped and wiped his mouth with the back of his hand. 'Thanks.' He scratched his head, noticing that the stubble was softer. His hair must have grown a bit. 'Where am I?'

Strulf folded his brawny arms. 'You're in the hospital block. You've been here over a week.'

Box whistled. It had been a long sleep.

'There was a lot of work to do.' Strulf's yellow-green dog eyes were hard, but there was something else about them that Box detected: a pinch of amusement at the corners maybe? As if the Captain knew something Box didn't.

'What work?' asked Box, suspicious.

He followed the Captain's eyes as they tracked down Box's arm; Box looked where the Captain was looking.

'Jander!' he gasped as he saw the screw-threaded socket in his flesh above his right elbow. The hole was over an inch deep and wide enough for him to insert his forefinger. His fingers and eyes ran over the whole of his body. There were similar sockets above his left elbow, behind his shoulders, in his pelvis and in the outer sides of his lower thighs, above his knees. When he had kicked off the thin sheet which had been covering him, he saw his lower right leg.

'Jandering skak!' he shouted.

From below his right knee, there was a metal prosthesis. It was shiny and not at all shaped like a real leg. The central section was solid and cylindrical and at its rear, where his calf should have been, there were three spindly rods. They extended from the heel of his mechanical, jointed metal foot to the pink, warm, genuine hamstrings at the back of his knee. The lower leg had been fitted flush with the knee joint so that the real muscle, bone and tendon merged neatly with the artificial. When he decided to wiggle his toes, the robotic digits moved perfectly and silently.

'Forget what it looks like,' snapped Captain Strulf. 'How do you feel?'

'How do I feel?' mouthed Box. He shook his head. How could he forget what it looked like? But Strulf kept staring at him. Eventually Box admitted, 'Apart from looking like a cheese grater, I feel OK.'

In truth, he felt better than just OK. For a start, he was alive; that was more than he'd expected. The wounds in his arm and flank had been repaired. He understood about the leg. But the holes above his joints were a mystery to him.

'They're called "taps",' explained Strulf.

'Why've you done this?'

'A dreadbolt at full charge travels at three hundred metres per second,' replied the Captain. 'The impact can smash rock. The armour has to withstand some heavy impact. Armour like that has to be part of the dreadbolt; it has to be riveted on.'

It took Box a few seconds to realize what this meant.

'But, I'm not . . .' he began.

'You are now, son,' and Captain Strulf flashed a rough smile, long fanged: some tooth and some metal. 'Get up and I'll show you around.'

Box got up, pulled a pair of black combat trousers over his pants and laced his boots. He didn't rush; he needed to give his mind time to catch up with what had been done to his body. There must have been pressure transmitters in his new leg and foot because the boot felt like a boot should feel, and when he stood, he felt the ground beneath him as he would have done before.

He smoothed down his vest and rolled his shoulders, stretching his neck to iron out the knots in his muscle. Under the clothing, his leg looked normal. He remembered what Razool had told him about how a dreadbolt was made: about CFR. He could feel that his body was harder, more taut than it had been before. His muscles were stronger, his limbs more powerful: far more powerful than any human should be.

However weird it all was, he felt good. He gripped one of the iron struts of his bed. He twisted and the iron bent. 'Nice,' he laughed.

'That's damaging military property,' warned Captain Strulf.

'Sorry, sir,' said Box sincerely, but wondering what else he could test himself upon.

If only he could have told Splinter. Box would have loved to see the look on his brother's face as he smashed a block of concrete with his bare hands, or kicked a hole through a bank vault door. There wouldn't be a prison cell that could hold him now. But Box knew that Splinter would probably say something clever about brains beating brawn; Splinter managed always to come out on top without throwing a single punch.

They headed for the door.

'Where's Razool?' asked Box. 'And Skarl and Raxa?'

'Here. At the garrison.'

'Have they been … done too?'

'Yup,' said Strulf as they left the hospital block. 'You speak our language good, but you say some strange things. "Have they been *done* too?"' He chuckled to himself.

Outside, it was fresh. They walked slowly, Box enjoying the power with which he could feel his body was working. Now he turned on the spot to see where he was. Low buildings were spread about the hospital block. Their outer walls were built of dull, black stone, buttressed at the bottom and curving inwards slightly. The exception was a black-shelled unit, as big as a factory, which overshadowed one end of the garrison. Smoke drifted from its high metal chimneys.

'That's the bolt-works,' said Captain Strulf, seeing what had caught Box's attention. 'That's where we're going.'

Box nodded, savouring the brisk breeze which rolled over the flat, grassy plains that spread out on his left for as far as he could see. He could smell grass and it was good. Looking up and shielding his eyes he saw that there was one sun in a cloudless sky. It wasn't home, but one sun was a start.

It would have been better to have been on a ship, heading for home, but things could have been a lot worse. Box clenched a fist and felt the power surge along his arm. 'Hang in there little sister,' he said to himself. Then he caught Strulf's sharp-eyed glance. 'Where are we?' he asked.

Strulf pointed to flags which cracked and fluttered above the buildings in the fresh wind. Each flag displayed a snarling dog head against a field of gold. 'You're in the Fourteenth now, son. Do you know what that means?'

'Not really,' said Box, enjoying the sensation of air moving over his body. Two hundred metres away, a group of snouts sauntered across a parade ground which was lined with high banners displaying the snarling dog head.

'There are five quakes.' Strulf shielded his dog eyes from the bright sun. 'And there are three storms in each quake, and ten cohorts in each storm. There's a thousand dreadbolts in one cohort, plus support troops: heavy weapons, logistics, transport, technicians. Got the maths?'

'No, sir,' said Box.

'Doesn't matter, son. You're here to fight, not to count. You're a dreadbolt in the Fourteenth Storm. The Fourteenth Storm is part of the Fifth Quake. This is the garrison: our barracks. The Fourteenth are based here.' Captain Strulf slapped Box on the shoulder. 'And you're in *my* cohort. You do what I say, and you stick by me. Understand?'

'Yes, sir.' Box scratched his head. 'A thousand dreadbolts in one cohort?'

'Correct.' Captain Strulf ground his heavy lower jaw. 'There are so many millions of troopers,' he growled, 'and only one hundred and fifty thousand dreadbolts in all. But we're the best.'

Box smiled, squinting at the sun. The maths was beyond him but he liked the idea of being the best.

They took a route in front of the buildings, towards the huge walls of the bolt-works.

'How come I'm a dreadbolt?' asked Box, walking swiftly beside the Captain.

'Someone else's decision,' Strulf fired back, without turning to look at him.

'Oh,' murmured Box, a little crestfallen.

'But if it had been my decision,' continued Strulf, 'it would have been exactly the same.' He stopped to look Box in the eye. 'Son, what you and the others did on Klanf 187 ...' he shook his head. 'We saw the footage just before we went in. I don't give a monkey's skak whether you're a skin or not. You've *earned* a place in my cohort; you *and* your three friends.'

'What about Shera?' asked Box.

'She's earned her place too,' stated Captain Strulf, 'but it isn't here.'

Box could tell that Shera was not a topic for discussion with the battle-ravaged snout, so he said nothing more about her.

They skirted the garrison buildings. Box saw weapons ranges, armouries, barrack blocks and hundreds of dreadbolts who watched as the Captain and Box passed by.

The bolt-works dominated the far end of the garrison. Beyond its high walls there was only open grassland, as far and as wide as the horizon. Now that he was in the shadow of the huge building, Box saw that there were tall, gated arches all along the bottom of the wall, and from within there came the sounds of metal hammering metal, the hiss of gas and the roar of engines. Box remembered that roar and he knew that it was the sound of the bolts.

'Stick by me, got it?' shouted Captain Strulf as they passed beneath an arch and through a gate and entered the bolt-works.

There was too much going on for Box to see it all at once, and he could see only a small part of the interior. There were machines, tall and broad as a man, with hoses bearing drill bits, and gas cylinders. There was a wide, high thoroughfare, as big as a street. There was heat beating over him in waves. And there were stalls like in a stable, and in the stalls there were bolts. From where he stood by the Captain, Box counted more than fifty bolts. But the stalls stretched further than he could see, and he had no idea of what was on the higher levels of the building.

'This part is called the run,' said the dreadbolt captain, indicating the thoroughfare. 'It's where we armour-up and saddle-up.'

The run passed right through the ground level of the bolt-works and up to wide gates that opened onto the grass plains. Right now the gates were closed, but Box could see the brightness of outside through bars in the gates, the light penetrating the hot, musky gloom in stark stripes.

Up close like this, Box realized how big the bolts really were. He watched the closest. Its massive chest was high and full as the prow of a boat and its metal body was smooth as hide and black as pitch. It ate from a trough and when it raised its muzzle, the coal-black eyes looked straight at Box, while blood dripped from its mouth.

'What's it eating?' Box asked.

'The machinery is powered by a nuclear cell,' explained Strulf, 'but inside, a lot of the working parts are biological and so it needs protein. It's eating meat.'

The bolt pulled back its lips revealing grey, metal teeth, and it roared as loud as an engine.

'They're friendly, son, but not when they're feeding,'

warned Strulf. 'Don't look at its food. It'll think you're going to steal it.'

'No chance.' Box was vehement. He'd stolen all kinds of things from all kinds of people, but stealing meat from a giant horse with metal teeth was off the agenda.

'Watch these troopers.' Strulf pointed to four dreadbolts who had just entered the run. They wore black combats. One of them had a steel left arm and a metal lower jaw. Another had a red glow where his right eye should have been. Box knew that this was a scrutator. The optic passed from the front to the back of the dreadbolt's head, giving him almost all-round vision.

'There's a reconnaissance exercise this afternoon.' Strulf pointed at one of the machines with the hoses. 'That's a torque: a static torque. Our troop ships have them. When we're mobile we use GPUs which do the same thing.'

'What are they for?' asked Box.

'Watch.'

More dreadbolts had entered the run and they were standing beside the torques. A siren blared and then teams of snouts rushed into this part of the bolt-house, carrying with them heavy pieces of armour: no more than one piece to each snout. Box could tell that these snouts were young by their sparse bodies, by their soft hair, by the absence of damage.

'Runners,' said Strulf. 'Youngsters, barely out of whelping. If they stick it out, toughen up, stay alive, they can earn their taps: become dreadbolts.'

The runners worked in teams, attaching the plates of heavy armour to the dreadbolts who stood still throughout.

Box saw how the plates were secured, the runners using the drills that were attached by hoses to the torques: powering bolts through holes in the armour plates and into the taps in the dreadbolts' bodies.

The bolt-works were filled with the squeal of the drills. Plate by plate, each dreadbolt was encased in the massive chunks of armour which Box had first seen on the deck.

The armour was clean and now Box could see the detail on the shoulder blocks. The snarling dog heads had actually been engraved into the metal, which was dull and rough as stone. But without smears of slick and oil, the decorations were bright, the shoulder plates glinting gold whorls about the dog heads. There wasn't an awlis in sight.

Runners brought helmets. Box watched as the full helms were twisted into the armour collars, and then ratcheted tight by clips. The front of the helmets had a dark glass band across the eyes and at the back there was a socket. Into this socket was fastened a pipe from the gas cylinders, and there was a loud hiss and a swirl of gas over each dreadbolt's shoulders as each helmet was pressurized.

'When you're galloping at three hundred metres a second, breathing can be tough,' explained Captain Strulf. 'So we pressurize the environment inside the helmet. Helps keep the eyes steady too, son. There's a lot to see.'

'Isn't it too fast to see?' Racing a stolen car at eighty miles per hour meant that Box missed details like one-way street signs and red lights.

'We don't use visuals at high velocity.' Strulf pointed to one of the helmets. 'What looks like a visor is actually a screen. It displays data like speed, distance to target, time to target, weapon locks. And it gives a three-hundred-and-sixty-degree view. There's a lot to look at, son, but it's all inside the helmet.'

With a clattering of metal hooves on stone, the runners began to lead bolts out of the stalls and into the run. They touched the bolts only on their sides, hands reaching up and spread flat against their mighty withers. Even though the casing was metallic, it had the ripple and bulge of skin over muscle, but it was obviously hard, and darker than anything of flesh and blood.

The mounts were saddled. The saddles were leather, and were riveted to the back of each bolt. Down either side of the beasts' girths, metal hooks were embedded in their bodies, standing proud. Chain links hung loose from the saddles, clinking as the creatures approached. There were no bridles and no reins. Box didn't know much about horses but he knew that to control them you needed a bridle and reins.

'How do they steer them?' he asked.

'The bolts do whatever the riders want them to, just by thought.' Strulf scratched his block of a chin. 'Don't ask me the science son; I don't make them. Something about smart particles and neural sculpting.'

Box shrugged. He'd heard of smart particles: GPUs had them. And Shera had said that HFUs had even smarter particles. But he didn't understand how any of it worked, and he didn't care.

'People like you and me, we're better at breaking things than making them.' Captain Strulf folded his arms.

Box nodded and looked at the dreadbolt captain askance. He no longer noticed the crazy, snout eyes or the bulldog jaw. What he saw was someone who knew how things were, someone who was taking time to talk to him. Someone who even called him 'son'. He was under the command of this war-torn snout, a universe away from home and he felt fine. It felt good.

'The bolts are engineered to await our command,' Strulf was saying, 'All I know is that while you're in contact with the bolt it does what you want, goes where you want it to go, as fast as you want to travel. So long as you don't mess with its food.'

Box nodded. 'Just like me,' he said.

Captain Strulf cast Box a quizzical glance and shook his head. 'Skins. Crazy.'

A bolt was brought up to each rider. When it was alongside, it dropped its forelegs and the armour-clad trooper climbed into the saddle. As each bolt stood up again there was a short succession of quick snaps and Box saw that the metal hooks down the creatures' girths had clamped over the riders' lower legs, securing them in place.

Now the run was full of mounted dreadbolts. They towered above Box, basalt silhouettes blocking out the light. There was a stamping of iron hooves on stone, sparks kicking up in orange showers, and sometimes there was a roar, resonating from the mighty chests.

The runners were handing weapons up to the dreadbolts: the long, curving swords and heavy battle hammers that Box had spotted before. The dreadbolts secured the weapons within the chains that hung from the saddles, pulling them tight against the bolts' bodies.

'That's a reaper,' yelled the Captain, pointing at one of the curving longswords. 'Used for slashing down when mounted. And that's a hammer.'

'Used for hammering things,' shouted Box.

'Son, you're a natural,' Strulf shouted back.

The noise was incredible: the hooves, the bolts, the clatter of weapons. Box could see that although there were no reins to hold, the front edges of the saddles were raised, and the dreadbolts steadied themselves by laying gauntleted hands on these pommels. There were twenty dreadbolts and they had manoeuvred themselves into ten pairs.

Box couldn't imagine what noise a full cohort would make.

'Bolt and rider are the weapon, son. Bolt and rider are the weapon.'

A burst of light from the end of the run as the far gate opened. An explosion of sound and movement. By the time that Box's eyes had caught up with the departing troops, they were already galloping across the open grassland.

The air was smoky with the smell of scorched stone and Box's ears were ringing.

'Nice,' he murmured.

The sound of a single set of hoof strikes approaching made him turn away from the vanishing dreadbolts.

'Your turn,' said Captain Strulf.

'You're joking,' replied Box, and he whistled under his

breath as he saw a runner leading a bolt towards him.

'No need for armour or weapons yet,' said the Captain. 'This is just to familiarize yourself.'

Box swallowed. 'I can't ride horses.' He laughed, unsteadily.

'Neither can I,' confided Captain Strulf. 'But this isn't a horse.'

Knowing that he was meant to ride this beast made it seem even bigger. It sneezed and stamped as it was drawn up. But it was the look which the runner gave him that made Box run and spring up and onto the saddle, before the bolt had even knelt down. He was satisfied to see the hint of contempt vanish from the runner's eyes.

'Son, that's one hell of a technique.'

'It's good for getting over walls,' explained Box. Any street rat who didn't want to be gripped by the hunters had to be able to block-hop like a power ball.

The iron hoops grasped his lower leg. His heels found struts which allowed him to bear his weight without the hoops cutting. He rested his hands on the pommel as he had seen the other riders do.

Box took a deep breath and, just for a moment, closed his eyes. He felt the bolt stir beneath him, could actually feel the rumble in its massive chest as it snorted, sensed the working of its muscles, the power of its limbs. All of this at his control.

He was a dreadbolt. Invincible.

'Not too fast, son,' warned Captain Strulf. 'You're not wearing a helmet and it cost a lot of cash to make you.'

'Not *too* fast,' Box assured the Captain. He looked out through the gate, at the open grassland, the huge sky.

'Well? What are you waiting for?'

Box grinned back. 'Nothing.'

CHAPTER 9

As soon as he entered the mess hall, Box realized that the eating was over. But the drinking was in full flow. The air reeked of sweat and alcohol.

The hall was wood panelled and full of tables and benches and dreadbolts. It was one of the largest buildings in the garrison and from its rafters there hung banners, some of them threadbare and some of them mapped with dark stains that hid the battle honours beneath.

'Box!' Skarl was the first to spot him, as Box pushed his way through the hot fug of sitting, standing, drinking snouts. Skarl had been sitting at a small, round table with Razool and Raxa. The table was set with three pewter tankards and judging by Skarl's bleary and poorly aligned eyeballs, the tankards had seen a lot of action this evening.

Skarl slapped Box on the back. Raxa fetched a chair that someone else had left unguarded and dragged it over. Box sat down.

'Hi,' said Box, still giddy from the hours he had spent riding across the plains. 'I think I'm going to like this, as long as I don't starve to death first.' Then he saw Razool's face. 'What's the matter?'

Razool rolled up the sleeve of his black tunic and pointed to the tap above his right elbow. 'What's Mrs Razool going to say about this?' he demanded.

This wasn't the greeting Box had been expecting. He took a sip from the tankard that had been handed to him by Skarl, winced as the bitter liquid kicked the back of his throat, and swallowed.

'I like piloting ships, Box,' continued Razool. 'I never wanted to be a bolthead. But we get shipped here, they fill us with lead and holes and now I'm a battering ram with legs. Any idea why we get singled out for this special treatment?'

Box shrugged, sipped, winced and said, 'I don't know.'

'I like it,' insisted Skarl, cheerfully. He looked about the mess hall with a wolfish grin, then drained his tankard, belched and wiped his muzzle with the back of his hairy hand. 'Best strince I've ever had.'

Box didn't want to fall out with Razool, but he couldn't think of what to say. It wasn't as if he had planned any of this. Eventually, he just said, 'Sorry, Zool.'

'Yeah, well.' Razool sighed. 'We're all still here. That's what counts. How's your leg?'

Box rapped it with his knuckles. 'Not as pretty. Hey, do you think it'll rust?' He took another swig of strince. A dreadbolt strolled by, more cybernetics and metal than original snout. 'At least I don't look like that.'

'Yet,' observed Razool.

'So, what have I missed?' asked Box.

Raxa took a long slurp. 'Lots of training.'

'Lots of riding,' said Razool. 'Riding in formation, riding out of formation, riding and fighting. There's a big horse theme here.'

'They're not horses,' said Box. 'They're bolts.'

'Yeah, well, tell that to my backside.' Razool grimaced. 'At least you don't get saddle-sore flying.'

'Do we get new guns?' asked Box.

Razool rolled his eyes but Skarl hiccuped and said, 'Yeah. HV magnums. They'll blow a hole through anything.'

'HV what?' asked Box.

'High velocity magnum,' explained Raxa. He patted his thigh to indicate where the magnum was carried.

'Oh, yeah. I remember.' Box took another swig of strince. He was getting used to the taste; it wasn't very nice but he was prepared to work at it.

'And the mouse.' Skarl's elbow missed the table but he hit it with his hairy chin. 'I think I need more strince.'

'The what?' asked Box.

'Those guns with the big barrels,' said Raxa.

Box was baffled. 'Why's it called a mouse?'

'Because it makes holes in things.' Raxa drained his tankard in one draught.

Skarl pulled his skew-whiff eyeballs into line. 'It kind of works by a pulling force,' he slurred. 'Instead of shooting into the guts, it just yanks them out.'

Box nodded. 'So it's good against spikers.'

'We're going to find out, aren't we.' Razool fixed Box with a hard stare.

Box shrugged. 'Yeah? And?'

'We don't just get to play at being dreadbolts, Box,' said the snout. 'We're about to go and do it for real.'

Box took a long, slow drink.

Razool leant back in his chair and crossed his arms. 'We're about to embark for a place called the Drakner region. It's a X'ath stronghold. The Symmetry are organizing a massive assault which means the dreadbolts get to go in first.'

'X'ath,' said Box.

'Oh, and just to keep us busy, the X'ath are supported by Krillion mercenaries. Lots of them.' Razool cocked an eyebrow.

'Krillion,' said Box.

Razool leant forwards. 'Is it the strince, or have they filled your brain with so much lead you only do single words now?'

'I don't know what Krillions are,' explained Box.

'Don't worry. You will do. Little guys with sharp faces and enough fingers to hold two automatic weapons in each hand. Oh, and a belief that there's nothing better than dying in battle, so long as you take as many of the enemy with you as possible.'

Box hadn't forgotten that Razool was a commodore. He knew what he was talking about. Box took a slow drink, felt the floor move beneath his feet and stared into the half-empty tankard. It seemed a good time to change the subject. 'What happened to Shera?' he asked, and noticed the swift exchange of glances between the three snouts. 'Well?'

It was Razool who spoke. 'She got taken away. The last

we saw of her was the dreadbolts marching her off the transporter on Klanf.'

But it was obvious to Box that there was more to say, so he waited for Razool to continue. The alsatian-faced snout's eyes narrowed. 'She's a pelt.'

'Like I'm supposed to know what that means?' shrugged Box.

'A shape-shifter,' said Razool.

Box knew precisely what *that* meant. He knew that there were some amongst the snouts who could take human form and dog form at will. When the hunters had first come for him and Splinter and Chess at the wharf, the inspector in command of them had been a shape-shifter.

'How can you tell?' Box asked.

Razool sniffed. 'The smell. It's different.' He wrinkled his muzzle. 'Not as different as yours, but different from normal.' He leant forwards and spoke quietly. 'I knew what she was from the moment we found her waiting for us. But I don't know why she was there.'

'Does it matter?' Box shrugged and drained his tankard. He belched.

'I don't trust pelts,' stated Razool. 'Because they can go skin-side or claw down, they get mixed up in bad stuff. They're useful to all the wrong people.'

'Going skin-side means turning human, like me?' checked Box. 'And claw down means being a dog?'

Razool nodded and scratched his neat chin.

'We reckon that something's going on, Box,' announced Skarl, long tongue slipping out of his mouth for a moment. 'I mean, she tried to shoot you twice.' He hiccuped.

'She said it was an accident,' protested Box.

'Do you believe her?' quizzed Razool.

'Well, yeah,' said Box. 'I do. I think she wanted to help.'

Razool shook his head in disbelief. 'Spooks, pelts, two attempts to kill you? Come on, Box. Any other weird events you've noticed?'

Box scratched his head. 'Actually, my gun fell upwards. That was pretty weird.'

'Your gun fell *upwards?*' Razool looked from Box to Box's tankard and back to Box again.

'Yeah. On the roof of the transporter ship. Just before the spikers attacked me. I didn't *want* to fight them hand to hand.' Box scratched his head, thoughtfully. 'Or hand to spike. Anyway, my carbine slipped *up* the roof and then away from me.'

'Are you sure about that?' Razool didn't sound convinced.

'You're the one saying weird stuff's happened,' Box pointed out. 'I'm only telling you what I saw.'

Razool rubbed his lower jaw. 'That must have been just before Shera shot you in the back.' He exchanged a dark glance with Raxa. A brooding silence thickened.

Box traced a finger round the rim of his tankard, mulling over everything they'd been talking about. One thought in particular was solidifying. 'You're a commodore right?' he asked Razool.

'Well, I was,' said Razool.

Box continued. 'And you commanded a fleet; you could fly.'

'Obviously,' replied Razool. 'OK, listen.' He rapped the

table as he spoke. 'There are four navies. The First Navy is planetary: air and water. With me so far?' Box nodded. 'The Second is interplanetary. The Third covers star systems, deep space. That's the big one. The Fourth Navy navigates hyperspace.'

'And you were in that one?' confirmed Box.

'Yeah. Hyperspace, the vortex, cross-universal shipping lanes.' Razool took a long draught of strince. 'That was what I did.' Nobody spoke as Razool studied the inside of his empty tankard. 'I flew the Fourteenth into the Drakner sector five or six years ago as it happens. In command of the fleet. And now I'm going in again. This time as a bolthead in the Snarling Fourteenth. Life,' he concluded, 'is full of surprises.'

Box nodded. 'I was just wondering. About Chess.' But he stopped talking and shrugged. How could he expect Razool to sort that out for him?

But Razool leant back in his chair and smiled. 'I'm a commodore in the Fourth Navy and you're my friend, Box. We're in this together. We find the right ship and I'll take you to her.'

The colossal hulk of the Class I troop ship, the *Transit IV*, drifted silently through the black void of space. Enclosed within its mighty walls were the Fourteenth and Fifteenth Storms: twenty thousand dreadbolts together with thousands of runners, support troops and crew. And the *Transit IV* was only one ship in the massive Symmetry force that was heading into the Drakner region of the Calyx Nebula. There were thousands of other ships, carrying more dreadbolt cavalry and millions of Dog Troopers. Once, when Box had been up on the viewing platforms, gazing out at the yawning depths, the *Transit IV* had passed close to a supernova which shot the darkness with beads of light, and Box had seen an ocean of silver dots speckle back and he knew that for a moment he had seen the Symmetry fleet spread out across eternity.

But three weeks of travelling through space was drawing to an end. Box and Razool sauntered out of the assembly hall where Captain Strulf had just finished briefing the whole cohort.

'Three days,' Box whistled between his teeth. 'Three days and then we go in.'

Razool nodded. 'We pass through the Drakner Cliff and hit the ice planet X6998 straight away. No messing.'

Although all the other troopers were heading down the corridors, away from the assembly hall, Box and Razool remained a couple of metres from the exit. To the departing troopers, it looked as if the skin and the snout were lagging behind, deep in discussion about the details of the battle plan.

'So what is the Drakner Cliff?' asked Box.

'It's a nebula,' said Razool. 'Think of it as a curtain, about ten light years high but only a couple of hundred metres thick. It'll act like a screen, hiding us. The enemy won't know what's coming at them. Until it's too late.'

'It's about time we got stuck in,' said Box, resolute.

Razool eyed him, coolly. 'There's nothing good about fighting, Box. It's *why* you fight that matters.'

'I know that,' bridled Box. He looked up and down the corridor. They were alone. 'Let's go.'

Razool glanced at the display screen in the wall above the door. The lines of electronic script meant nothing to Box. He had never been much good at reading and snout letters looked impossible. He knew what the display inside the helmets said, and he'd learnt numbers and that was it.

'Are we needed anywhere?' he asked Razool.

'No. Not yet. We're OK.'

Box scowled. 'The only reason they give us duties is to keep us out of trouble.'

'Correct,' said Razool. With a final glance left and right, he crossed to a small metal door in the wall panel opposite. Box followed and together they slipped through.

They were in a narrow stairwell, dimly lit by pale strip lights. The stairs and tubular handrails zig-zagged down so steeply that it was more like descending a ladder than steps.

'And all *we* have to do is ride through the enemy forces that defend the X'ath command station?' asked Box, dropping his voice as he spoke because it echoed so loudly.

'Yeah, Box, that's *all*. But since there will be millions of X'ath and Krillion in defensive rings about the station, they might throw a few punches back.' Razool shook his head as he led the way down. 'The Fourteenth and Fifteenth smash a hole through the enemy defence and then in come the rest of the Symmetry force. The station is destroyed. The X'ath can no longer coordinate their armies. That small bit of the

Drakner falls to us and the Crystal Wars carry on for the next thousand years.'

'Except *we* won't be there after this battle,' said Box. 'Will we?'

Razool grunted. 'That's the plan.'

Box's thigh muscles felt hot with the descent by the time they had dropped to the fifteenth level. He couldn't read the script on the oval door, but the red lightning flashes were easy to understand. They ignored them, the same way that they had ignored them the other couple of times that they had sneaked through this door.

'Lucky I'm with someone who knows so much about troop ships,' grinned Box, as Razool inched the door open.

'Yeah,' drawled Razool. 'And don't you forget it, skin.' He paused and turned his sharp muzzle round to Box. 'And it's not just troop ships.'

'I know, I know. You're an expert on *every* kind of ship.'

The dark lips drew up in a smile revealing the long, sharp fangs. 'Especially deep vortex pilot ships. Come on.'

They slipped through, Box pulling the door shut behind him. Ahead of them, stark on a huge steel platform, stood the two dart-shaped pilot ships, crusted with short antennae and bellied with weapons pods. Their noses pointed towards sloping iron panels the size of a couple of closed drawbridges. Behind the ships, the platform ended abruptly; there was a security rail and then a plunging view down to the dreadbolt run below.

'You sure nobody's going to rumble us here?' asked Box.

'No,' said Razool. 'But I want to check the kit one last time. Make sure the ships are still ready to go.' He gave Box a sharp smile. 'We don't want to turn up and find that the techs have started taking them apart.'

Razool crossed swiftly to the first of the ships. For a Symmetry vessel, it was small, but it was still big enough for them to walk underneath it without stooping. The roof of the hangar was far higher still. Box felt ant-like. But his footsteps resounded off the metal loudly enough for his shoulders to ache with the tension that they might be discovered here.

'It's a shame we can't take it now,' he whispered, following Razool around the ships.

The lean snout shrugged. 'Until we hit the ice planet, the ships are locked down. This whole attack is based on surprise. Nobody wants a loose pilot ship hopping through the vortex and coming out where the enemy spot it.'

'But this can take us ... me, home?' One step closer to Chess: Box felt his heart thump at the thought.

'Yup. In the right hands.' Razool flashed another of his sharp smiles. 'As soon as the fighting's done, we just have to take one.'

Box liked the way Razool spoke like that: when the fighting was over, they *would* be coming back.

'Thanks, Zool,' said Box.

Razool looked at him earnestly. 'I've got family too, Box. A wife. Whelps. I want to see them again. I know what it's like. And I don't forget my friends. If it hadn't been for you, back in the Fleshing yard ...' He shook his head, and half laughed. Razool was about to say something else but then he stopped, knelt down and inspected the floor.

'What?' Box couldn't see the snout's face because it was hidden by his long mane. Razool picked something up for Box to see.

It was a sliver of wood. 'Now, what's this doing here?'

Box shrugged.

Razool glanced about, eyes glinting. 'Seems that someone else has been down here since we last came.'

'It could be from anything,' said Box. But there was no reason for a piece of wood to be here. It shouldn't have mattered, but Box didn't like the feeling that someone else had been snooping down here. He thumbed towards the way they'd come.

'Just want to check the exit doors,' muttered Razool, crossing to the sloping panels.

Box shadowed to the rear of the platform, where the security rail met the wall and he crouched, draped in shadow, to look down. Far below, the run stretched away like an aircraft runway, broad enough to take dreadbolts in ranks of two hundred. The noise once the iron hooves of twenty thousand fully laden bolts went crashing over the metal ramps would be deafening.

There were standing torques, and pipes lining the walls and hanging from the roof for helmet compression, and there were runners and GPUs. The GPUs busied themselves running system checks, and engineering on the ramp. The GPUs all looked the same, until one, out in the centre of the run, started to unfold itself. That was how it looked to Box. Arms and levers extended out of the body of the GPU, and the body itself expanded as if it was unpacking itself from its own space.

Box leant forwards, astonished at the increase in size. By the time the unit had stopped growing, it towered above everything else on the ramp. Numerous arms, bearing drills, soldering irons, pincers and hammer-drives swung upwards and set to work on the helmet compression systems in the roof. Simultaneously, the feet of the unit extended and the extensions broke away, creating two fresh units that opened up in the same way the first one had. Now there were three giant units working on the machinery around the run. About them, the normal GPUs busied themselves like feeder fish.

'Skak,' whispered Box to himself in disbelief.

One of the giant units approached. The top of its body wasn't far below the pilot ship platform. Box drew back from the rail. The unit didn't have eyes, it couldn't have known he was there, but he felt uncomfortable all the same.

'That's an HFU,' said a voice in his ear.

'Jander, Zool, why'd you have to sneak about like that?'

'Because we're *meant* to be sneaking about.' Razool's voice was low. 'A High Function Unit.'

'Oh, yeah, *even smarter* particles, I remember.' Box shook his head. 'Can they do *anything*?'

'They can grow, they can reform, but most of all,' said Razool, 'they can think. They're intelligent.'

Box stood up. 'Let's go.' They'd been down here long enough.

When they returned to the door that led to the stairs,

Razool looked up at the screen above it and cursed.

'What?' asked Box. 'Duties?'

'Yeah.'

'Couldn't you have forgotten to check?' suggested Box.

'If I did, Discipline wouldn't forget to dump us in the skak,' warned Razool. 'That's why they have these screens over every door.'

Box stuck his hands in the pockets of his combat trousers and huffed, ready for whatever they had been tasked with.

Razool wrinkled his muzzle, puzzled. 'I've got to see the Captain. You've got to check out stowage in hold twenty-three: the coffins.'

Box shrugged. 'Could be worse. Yesterday I had to scrub down the training hall, me and about fifty others.' He wrinkled his nose at the memory. 'If we'd been cleaning up after glue and gore, say, stem-pen training, that would of been fine. But there'd been two hours of reaper drills and the sweat was skak.' Box liked stem pens. On Klanf, his life had been saved by the swift application of a stem pen and every dreadbolt was issued with two. The serum of stem cells and adrenalin helped to keep you going while you waited for the medics to arrive.

'We're meant to do duties together,' muttered Razool.

'I'm sure you'll cope without me,' laughed Box.

'It's not me I'm worried about,' rumbled Razool.

'It's all right, Zool. I can check coffins. They don't bite.' Box pulled open the door. 'I'll go straight down from here.'

'Yeah, well don't get caught using the wall shafts,' warned Razool. 'Authorized access only, remember.'

'You're a commodore,' grinned Box. 'So, I'm authorized.'

Razool shook his head and began to climb up. Box hurried down the steep stairs, footsteps almost silent.

Hold twenty-three was on the eighteenth level, near the bottom of the ship. When Box had reached the small door that would lead out of the wall shaft and into the eighteenth level, he listened first, ear against the steel. Satisfied that there was no sound, no vibrations, he opened the door and squeezed into the corridor. The corridor was empty which was to be expected; nobody else had any reason to come down here. Silence hung thick about the flickering lamps which studded the wall at intervals, moon-yellow behind metal cages.

Hold twenty-three carried coffins for the stowage and ejection of dreadbolt corpses. Hands in the pockets of his grey fatigues, Box strolled down the corridor. He'd done this duty before, with Razool; he knew where he was going. He passed the elevator that he should have used to come down here and turned into the corridor which led to a grey panel at the far end, marked with a giant, snout-figured '23' in red.

It was quiet, save for the throbbing hum of engines. Halfway to the panel, the silence suddenly felt so heavy that Box stopped and turned about. If you were a street rat, you knew there was such a thing as too much silence.

'Mr Jumpy,' he muttered to himself, and walked quickly to the end of the corridor. He punched the release pad and the panel slid open. Inside the hold, the light was even dimmer.

Hardly surprising, thought Box. You don't need light in a warehouse full of coffins.

Each hold on the troop ship was cavernous. Box's footfalls reverberated to the deep ceiling and back as he moved amongst the high wooden stacks. At the centre he noticed how resonantly his footsteps echoed and he couldn't resist giving an extra-hard stamp on the floor, although he was careful not to stamp so hard as to dent it.

'Street rat or dreadbolt?' he whispered to himself. 'Dreadbolt or street rat?' It was hard to be sure what he was. He wandered further into the hold, squinting up at the looming stacks of coffins that were piled high as logs in a timber yard. Thick restraining straps bound them fast. He stood at the foot of one of the towering stacks and tested the tension in one of the straps and smiled to himself: dreadbolt *and* street rat. Nice.

He was about to turn back, when he noticed the condition of a coffin at the bottom of the furthest stack. He hesitated before walking over to take a look.

'No way,' he whispered, stopping and squatting down. At the foot of the bottom coffin, there was a gaping hole. Around the hole, the wood had been smashed. The gap would have been big enough to allow him to climb inside.

He didn't know how long the coffin had been like this; he hadn't checked this far into the hold before. Last time, he and Razool had settled for a quick look inside and a leisurely walk back to the bunk room. He'd only walked into the hold as far as he had because he'd been thinking so hard he'd forgotten to cut short his duty.

Then, behind the stack of coffins, there was movement. Box heard something scrape on the floor: something metallic.

He stood up. 'Who's that?' His voice echoed perfectly.

The first wooden box hit him in the legs, knocking them from under him because it was unexpected. He cartwheeled over himself, landing flat on his back. Before he could get to his knees, another coffin fired out, smashing into his face. It should have been enough to stave his head in but his solarion-reinforced frame meant that only the coffin splintered.

Box staggered to his feet as the security strap retaining the stack hit the floor with a slack slap. The whole stack teetered and then the uppermost boxes tumbled down.

He stumbled away from the first but the second nosedived onto his head. He heard wood smash and felt his body take a pummelling as the stack avalanched. Automatically, he crouched, and the coffins smashed over his back and head, driving him to his knees.

By the time the thudding and splintering had stopped, Box was buried under a mountain of wood. He knew that without CFR he'd have been slabbed. But he could move his limbs and nothing was hurting. He burrowed upwards, pushing away broken panels, getting angry. Someone was messing about, and Box didn't like games like this.

But as his head cleared the debris, a stunning torchlight dazzled his eyes and he felt sharp, cold, metal rest against the front of his skull. Box hesitated. CFR made him tough, but it didn't make him indestructible; not even reinforced bone could withstand a point-blank smash with a heavy axe. The broad blade glinted as it swung up. Then it flashed down.

CHAPTER 10

When it came to fighting, Box was quick and smart. He rolled back and kicked up his foot to meet the axe blow: his metal foot. The thud jarred him to his hip and he saw sparks fly. Immediately, the pressure sensors in his leg told him that serious damage had been done to the metal tendons. But he had to get away, now, before the axe fell again. He pushed himself back, arms slipping in the mass of broken wood, blinded by the harsh light. He had to get away, but he was buried in the coffins.

The torchlight blinked out. Darkness flooded Box's vision and then there were footfalls slapping across the floor of the hold. There was the scrape and clatter of panels of wood being dragged away and then he saw Razool and Skarl.

'There's an axe,' panted Box, waving his arm in front of his eyes which were swimming with colours.

'There's nothing, Box,' Skarl assured him, gasping for air. 'There's just this ... this mess. What have you been doing?'

'What happened?' asked Razool, breathless. The two of them must have run here. 'Are you OK?'

'Yeah.' Box laughed. 'Not bad for someone who's just had a couple of tons of wood dropped on his head.'

'Lucky it's even denser than it was before the CFR.' Razool looked Box up and down. 'Not even a scratch. But what the hell's going on?'

'Honest, Zool, someone came for me. With an axe. Just before you showed up. All of this was pushed on top of me and then they came for me.'

'Who, Box?' Razool spoke urgently. 'Who came for you?'

Box shook his head. 'There was a torch, I think. I couldn't see anything.'

Razool's eyes were raking the gloom of the hold.

'They've gone.' Box grunted as he checked the damage to his leg. 'Can't hardly move my foot.'

Skarl was scouting about the coffin stacks, a length of wood grasped in his hand and a hungry glint in his wolfish eyes.

Razool inspected Box's foot. He whistled between his long teeth. 'Some blow. Could have dropped a bolt with that. It's broken clean through the metal. Skarl,' he shouted. 'We need a GPU.'

Skarl nodded and loped out of the hold, the wooden spar still in his hand.

'Thanks, Zool.' Box pushed away the remaining strips of wood. 'Thanks for looking out for me. If you hadn't of shown up ...' He shook his head and laughed wryly. 'Slabbed.'

'I knew something was wrong,' growled Razool. 'I knew it was wrong as soon as we were split up.' He continued to scan the hold as he spoke. 'The Captain hadn't called for me. No one had. What's going on, Box?'

Box had propped himself up on his elbows, legs stretched in front of him. He shrugged. 'I dunno, Zool. But it was weird. I'd found a coffin at the back with a hole in it, and I was taking a look when I heard something. Definitely.' Box pointed at the bottom rows of the stack, which were still standing neatly. 'Behind there. Something scraping. Then a couple of coffins were ... thrown at me. That's what it seemed like. Then they all came down and then there was this axe.'

Razool rubbed his chin. 'An accident,' he stated.

'No way,' insisted Box. 'No way was this an accident.'

'I mean that this was meant to *look* like an accident,' said Razool. 'Whoever did it could have used a gun or a knife, but they chose an axe. Why did they choose an axe?'

'You'd make a good crasher, Zool.' Box frowned at the way his foot wouldn't move as he wanted it to.

'A blow from an axe would be mistaken for a wound caused by the falling wood,' deduced the snout. 'Which means that whoever did this, didn't want anyone to know that you had been killed by *them*. This was meant to look as if you'd been killed by the falling coffins.'

'Very comforting,' muttered Box.

'I don't get it, Box. Spooks, pelts, guns that fall upwards and now this: flying coffins?' Razool shook his head. 'What's going on with you?'

'Someone wants to get rid of me?' suggested Box.

'Got one.' It was Skarl, accompanied by a GPU, the metal

box bobbing by his shoulder. 'Doing maintenance work in the lift. It has an engineer function.'

Razool directed the GPU to Box's damaged leg. 'Repair,' he commanded.

Metallic arms bearing wrenches and a soldering iron extended out of the body of the GPU. Then it set to work, bending, twisting, straightening, soldering.

Razool scowled. 'What's it feel like?'

Box thought about this. 'Like wiggling a tooth, but much bigger.'

'Like wiggling a tooth?' Razool shook his head. 'Some tooth.'

Box laughed as a silver tendon was twisted and then heated with the soldering iron until it melted into his heel. 'Some dentist.'

Footsteps stomped towards them, across the hold.

'Oh, yeah,' said Skarl. 'Strulf's coming.'

Razool swore and under his breath muttered, 'That's me in the skak.'

'You're meant to work in pairs,' fired Captain Strulf, halting ankle-deep in broken wood.

'My fault,' said Razool, immediately. 'I thought you wanted to see me, sir. I thought Box could do this alone and then there'd be no delay.'

The Captain took a couple of seconds to assess the scene. 'What the slicking gaff happened here?' A hot, sour cloud of smoke coiled up from where the soldering iron dug into Box's metal heel. Box explained about the coffins and the axe.

The Captain listened solemnly and when Box had

finished, he said, 'This is my responsibility.' Then he folded his arms and muttered, 'I was warned.'

'About what?' asked Box.

'You stick close to me, understand?'

'Yes, sir,' said Box, but he couldn't stop himself from asking, 'Do you know what's going on?'

Captain Strulf ground his heavy jaw. 'You've got some serious enemies, son.'

Twenty-four hours before the *Transit IV* hit the Drakner Cliff, the viewing platforms had been packed. What Box had seen looked like a view of the end of the world. The height and breadth of space was a rippling iridescence: colossal gas clouds lit with the glow of a billion suns. The might of the nebula had awed the dreadbolts into silence. If light could sing, it sang to him then.

Now, twenty-four hours later, the vision screens were candescent with the surging brilliance of the Drakner Cliff, but the viewing platforms were silent because they were empty. Not a sound disturbed the blazing vision, not a particle of dust stirred. But twelve levels below, the world was a thunderstorm of crashing hooves, roaring bolts, screaming torques, hissing steam, clanking armour, smashing chain, oil-streaked runners pounding the ramps, the boom of the bulwarks as the *Transit IV* ploughed through the energy fields of the Cliff, and the howl of the siren which warned that in three minutes they would hit the frozen surface of X6998.

And within it all, the dreadbolts moved steadily. They

took their positions as the great plates of armour were brought to them by the toiling runners and stood like statues as the torques drove the thick screws into their arms, legs, shoulders, hips. They checked weapons; fastened helmets; mounted the massive, stamping bolts that were led to them. They waited patiently as GPUs, working in flashing teams beneath the roof, operated the helm-compression systems, and as the gas rolled off their shoulders, they nudged their mounts forwards to take their places within the ranks of dreadbolts waiting for the huge front ramps of the ship to drop open.

The Fourteenth Storm would be the first to ride out. Box guided his bolt to its place in the second rank, between Razool and Captain Strulf. As Box drew up, Razool tapped his own helmet and shook his head.

'Sorry,' mouthed Box, although Razool wouldn't have heard him without using the troop communications net, and they had been ordered not to transmit anything yet. But he knew what had upset Razool. At the last instant, Box had managed to end up at the wrong torque station with the result that he and Razool had been riveted into one another's armour. It didn't matter really because the huge plates were not tight-fitting, and although Razool was a bit taller and Box a bit broader, the difference wasn't so great as to create a problem. But Box knew what Razool was like about precision.

Captain Strulf gave Box a thumbs-up and Box returned it. Just before they had gone down to the run, Strulf had said to him, 'You stick by me, son. Understand? You stick by me.' Box didn't plan to go anywhere else. But even the most serious enemies would have been hard pressed to get to him here, amongst the dreadbolts.

The interior lights of the run dimmed to red. The runners had withdrawn. Now, the only noise was the boom of the energy fields against the ship.

Two minutes.

Box checked his reaper, tightened the strap of the mouse, turned up the illumination of the screen inside his helmet, let his mind run through the detail of what would greet them when the front ramp dropped.

It would be light. The ice plain would stretch ahead of them. They were landing twelve kilometres from the X'ath command station. At full charge, they would hit the surrounding defensive positions in about thirty-eight seconds. Eight seconds later, the Fifteenth Storm would smash in from the left flank. Five seconds after that, the air strikes would commence and behind these would come the Dog Troopers. The Fourteenth Storm was to fight out of the command station defence and regroup at a designated collection point.

The lights cut out. Now the run was in pitch darkness save for the dull glow that Box could see in the visors of the nearest helmets. He could feel the *Transit IV* rocking as it hit the surface atmosphere of X6998. The Drakner Cliff would be behind them now and the ice plain only a few miles below.

One minute.

Box closed his eyes and breathed slowly. How did he feel? He was part of a sea of dreadbolts, rank after rank, waiting to charge. He knew that the ensigns with their dog's head banners would be mounted, banner shafts steady in their gauntleted fists, waiting to charge. He knew that at the rear there was the heavy weapons troop, arms cybernetically enhanced, enlarged, powered by robotronics and fitted with rotating gun barrels or heavy plasma punches. He knew that the bolts would be utterly without fear, programmed to charge at the will of their riders. And he knew that on his shoulders, he bore the gold and black heraldry of the Snarling Fourteenth.

How did he feel?

The ship hit the ground and the ramp crashed open. The dreadbolts began to advance.

He had never felt better.

It was bright white light, and the ice was flat to the horizon. The air was biting-cold. To his left and right, bolts clanged down the ramp in long, straight ranks, mounts and riders steaming in the freezing air. The banners cracked open as the cohort cantered forwards, iron hooves kicking up chips of the thick surface ice. His cohort was in the lead, five ranks of two hundred dreadbolts, with nine more cohorts following in formation: a massive wedge that would smash through the heart of the enemy.

The ice thundered. Box looked down and could no longer see his bolt's legs: there was just a dark blur and a cyclone of ice particles. The ice rose in a frantic hail, as if the dreadbolts were pounding through a snow storm. He willed the bolt faster and felt his stomach collapse and the muscles of his face flatten as the beast rocketed forwards.

There came a point when a bolt was travelling so fast that

you no longer had any sense of motion at all. There was only an empty smoothness.

Ten thousand of them thundering like a meteor towards the enemy who, even now, would have no more warning than a cloud of mist on the far horizon.

It didn't matter that Box could see nothing through the white-out. He read the data on the screen display:

SPEED: 270 m/s
DISTANCE TO TARGET: 7.3K
TIME TO TARGET: 27s
INCOMING: 0

The three-hundred-and-sixty-degree view meant that Box could see everything about him: the troops to his rear, the troops to his flanks and what lay ahead. He heard Strulf give the command for maximum velocity and drove his bolt on, lowering his head so that he was shielded behind the beast's huge neck.

SPEED: 300 m/s
DISTANCE TO TARGET: 6.6K
TIME TO TARGET: 22s
INCOMING: 0

Now he could see something in the distance: a dark line at ground level against the white horizon. This would be the above-ground section of the command station. And to his rear and slightly left of him, a raging cloud was streaking forwards: the Fifteenth Storm.

His heart was thumping, his lungs were working like bellows and adrenalin surged like electricity.

SPEED: 300 m/s
DISTANCE TO TARGET: 4.2K
TIME TO TARGET: 14s
INCOMING: 0

Box could see the command station clearly now. It rose stark from the ice, with sheer walls and a curving roof, and for some reason it reminded Box of a gigantic temple: a gigantic temple festooned with antennae and weapon pods. He knew that the vast bulk of the structure was below ground, but the outer region was still enormous, its slate-grey ramparts catching the light with a silicon sheen.

Now he could see what lay ahead, between him and the X'ath command station: gun towers, tracking discs, trenches, bunkers, the tide of troops surging into position. The tiny yellow flashes of enemy fire; the oily haze of hot plasma.

SPEED: 300 m/s
DISTANCE TO TARGET: 1.6K
TIME TO TARGET: 5.3s
INCOMING: 11,837 small arms / 1,807 explosives / 106 plasma

In the last few seconds, detail rushed back and you regained sense: a hurricane of air; an explosion of noise; a chaos of shapes; rounds screaming; heat on his face; fire in his legs; ears bursting; banners streaming.

The Snarling Fourteenth.

TIME TO TARGET: 0.3s

Then a blur of sound: almost slow motion. Ploughing through bodies, buildings, gun towers, vehicles, more bodies. Thud after thud against his mount, against him. Slick streaking his visor. Sound returning. Bolts roaring. Voices screaming. The splutter of small-arms fire. The air bending under the weight of plasma.

Someone was speaking to him. It took half a second before Box realized it was the internal sound system of his helmet.

'Wheel right. *Wheel right.*'

The Fifteenth would be only seconds away.

Box pulled right, his bolt leaping a trench where three Krillion mercenaries crouched, spraying gunfire upwards. Box heard rather than felt the rounds sing off the bolt's metal belly and then he was part of the great wedge of the Fourteenth, swinging right, already heading for the regroup point.

But now they were fighting: the great dreadbolt war machine, clogged by the mass of bodies and machinery it had smashed, hacking and blasting its way back into motion. Krillion, commanded by X'ath, were recovering from the shock, relying upon sheer weight of numbers to take down the dreadbolt cavalry. The dreadbolt heavy weapons units, more droid than snout, fought a blazing rearguard action, their huge, multi-barrelled arms screaming out rounds in a frenzy as the main force withdrew. But the enemy units were fighting back and doing damage.

Twenty metres away, a X'ath warrior bull, massive, armoured segments like boulders, was toting a dual-chambered plasma accelerator, the coils glowing blue within the transparent housing. He stood alone, but with a weapon like that he had already unleashed carnage upon the nearest dreadbolts.

There was a Krillion coming in, by Box's foot. Box kicked out, only vaguely aware of the slight, hooded body spinning into a burning radio tower. He unslung his mouse, aimed, locked range, fired. The bull spiker's chest erupted and the creature crashed down.

'Pull out, Box. *Pull out.*' It was Strulf, voice sharp inside the helmet.

'OK.' Box threw the mouse across his back.

The ground began to hum. To his left, a tornado of ice was approaching.

'Pull out, Box. *Now.*'

Light and noise screamed across Box's path, battering everything before it, leaving only burning wreckage in its wake. The Charging Fifteenth. Of the tens of thousands of X'ath and Krillion who had been advancing after the Fourteenth, nothing was to be seen.

A ripple of booms and the weaponry on the command station came to life. Ice fountained up in a tide a little beyond Box's cohort. He couldn't tell whether any of the dreadbolts had been hit. He thought that probably they had, but already the enemy fire was drowned out by the incoming ground-attack fighters of the First Navy, so fast and huge they made the air groan.

The Fourteenth Storm was regrouping. Box turned his

bolt round and galloped for the banners that he knew would mark Captain Strulf's position. The enemy were rolling into counter-attack mode now, but the Dog Troopers were about to lock with them in a battle that would last for days.

Box's part in this battle was over.

He had made it through, unscathed. But he wanted to keep fighting, to pit himself against the enemy until he had fought to a standstill, as if he had opened a killing flood within himself that needed to keep pouring out. It took every shred of the discipline that had been drilled into him to battle his boiling blood. Ignoring the gunfire which scarred his armour, Box turned his back on the mayhem and sped across the ice.

He skidded to a halt alongside Captain Strulf, ice gouting up in a sharp spray. The Captain had already removed his helmet, as had his signaller and the ensign who still had hold of the tattered battle banner. With their helmets off, Box could see that Skarl and Raxa were there also, and so was Razool. The four of them had made it through.

All about, the dreadbolts were forming into troops, their commanders assessing the losses as they waited for the transport which would take them off the ice.

Box released the collar clips. There was a rush of air, a curl of steam and then he removed his helmet. The freezing air felt great. He hadn't realized how hard he had been sweating.

Captain Strulf looked across and gave him a thumbs-up. Box gave a thumbs-up back. He knew the snouts were watching him and wondered why until one of them said,

'We need a cohort of skins if they all fight like you.' Box was so pumped-up with adrenalin and fight-lust that he couldn't smile straight, but now he knew that he really was one of the team. One of the best.

Life didn't get any better than this.

But Razool was scowling. As usual. 'There's a problem.'

Box noticed then that Captain Strulf had taken the handset from the signaller. Face dark, he barked, 'We're too close.' He was holding an earpiece to his head. 'Way too close. You come in and get us out of here now.'

There was a tin-crackle of a reply.

'*Now,*' snapped Strulf.

Three kilometres away, the ice was hidden by black smoke and balls of orange flame and the air was thick with gunfire. Ground defence batteries hurled thick balls of plasma upwards which coruscated along the underbellies of the Symmetry attack craft.

'The spikers have got enough to worry about,' said Box, hopefully. 'We're out of the picture now.'

'You don't know the X'ath like I do,' growled Razool. 'But Strulf does. They take these things personally.'

Captain Strulf had thrust the handset back to his signaller. He shouted commands, to pull back, to regroup at a point further from the edge of the battle.

'Get your helmets *on*,' he yelled.

Then Box felt heat. He knew there had been sound too: a blasting sound, but it was so loud that it was beyond hearing. It was the searing heat that blotted out all else. Then his ears began to ring and he was wiping his eyes to see what had happened.

Twenty metres away, a deep crater had been blasted into the ice. Around it were scattered pieces of bolt and dreadbolt. And a little ahead of that lay the body of Captain Strulf: face-down, blood-streaked, immobile.

The air shrieked and the next blast came in.

The dreadbolts were driving their mounts away, to gallop out of range of the assault. But Box didn't move. If he got hit, he got hit; if he didn't, he didn't. Blood sang through his head, as hot as the heat of the blast.

Captain Strulf was down. Slabbed. And everyone was pulling away.

Stick by me, son.

'Yes, sir,' mouthed Box, eyes raking the churning battlefield. Incoming rockets shrieked over his head. But Box's burning eyes were unflinching. Then he saw the flash he was searching for, and after a moment's delay, he heard the incoming rocket-shriek again. His dark eyes narrowed. There was a mobile rocket unit, on the periphery of the fighting.

Box's fist tightened on his saddle. The dreadbolts were pulling out, but he *never* backed away from a fight. If they come for you, you go for them; if they smash Strulf, you smash them back.

The bolt began to trot forwards, then broke into a gallop. Box released the reaper from its chains. His helmet had been blown away in the blast, so he tucked his head behind his mount's, eyes shut against the rush of air. The crash of battle grew louder, the hurtling roar of the fighter ships, the rattle of blaze carbines, the hum and whump of plasma weapons.

He opened his eyes. Sound, heat, bodies, machines. He was in the midst of the fighting. This was where he wanted to be. He was a thing that fought, a thing that killed. And suddenly he realized that if this was where it had to end, he was ready for that. This was the place where he had to be.

His bolt stamped down three Krillion mercenaries. He slashed down, back, thrust out, felt the reaper bite, reared up, leapt forwards, flashed the long blade over to the other side of the bolt and galloped right.

Two spikers were manning the mobile rocket unit. They controlled its stalking legs from a cab beneath the rocket racks. It stomped forwards jerkily as they launched the next salvo at the retreating dreadbolts.

Nobody sees what they don't expect to see: not even X'ath warrior bulls. The last thing they expect to see is a lone dreadbolt hurtling full tilt at a mobile rocket unit.

Bolt and rider are the weapon.

Bolt and rider powered into the nearest leg of the unit, Box's head shielded by his mount. The whole unit spun and unbalanced, crashing to the earth in a spray of ice. Box wheeled round, drew alongside and unslung his mouse. Before the thrashing spikers could free themselves from the mangled cab, he had blasted them both beyond regeneration.

But once surprise has been lost, a lone dreadbolt quickly becomes a prize target.

Box shook the slick off his face in time to see two Krillion mercenaries operating a plasma cannon. Their small, caped bodies worked swift as cats. The gears spun, the barrel rotated and dropped, the barrel vanished behind the miasmal blur of energized matter. Box pressed the leg-brace release and threw himself from the bolt as the plasma struck, decimating it.

One reaper, the mouse and one HV magnum against however many million enemy ground troops. Box spat. Not the best odds he'd ever faced.

There were Krillion all about. Rather than isolate himself for an easy shot, he threw himself into the nearest troops. He kicked, parried, felt blades and bullets against his armour, claws rake his face. He must have been too good for them because they were backing away. And then Box saw why.

The spiker bull was unarmed, but it was a phenomenal beast. Its hacks were as long as windmill sails, the spines like gnarled harpoons. When it dropped its trap, the jaws' width must have been Box's own height. His reaper felt like a toothpick.

It came lumbering towards him on four legs, the foremost pair reaching for him. There wasn't time to change weapons, but Box stood his ground, ready to thrust deep into the creature's massive mouth.

There was the roar of a bolt and he looked back over his shoulder in time to see Razool mounted, mane matted with slick, mouse at his shoulder. Razool twisted the breach lock.

'Get down,' he yelled at Box.

Box got down in time for the spiker's huge hammer head to erupt.

'Now get out.' Razool had hold of Box's arm. Box dropped his reaper and swung up and into the saddle, behind the snout. The bolt sprang forwards but it was obvious to Box that the situation was terminally lively. There were X'ath and Krillion on all sides and armed with weapon systems that could blast a lone pair of dreadbolts out of existence with one pull of the trigger.

'What the hell were you doing?' yelled Razool.

'Fighting,' Box yelled back.

Razool heaved the bolt left. 'You skakking idiot.' He was furious.

They cornered at bullet speed, Razool heading through the most open passage he could trace; swerving gun positions, leaping ditches and walls, taking fire all the way. There was open ice plain ahead of them, but they would remain well within range even then.

Box's rage was subsiding. He knew that he had dragged his friend into this blinding lunacy and he guessed that getting out of it was going to take more luck than either of them possessed. He waited for the final blast and heard Razool shout something. Before he could shout back, there was an engine roar above his head, a wave of heat and air pressure over his body and then a huge swirl of steam and ice particles, metres ahead of them. He coughed the frost from his lungs and wiped the freezing water from his eyes.

The bolt had come to a stop and directly ahead of them there was the silver-white gleam of a pilot ship, identical to the ones on the *Transit IV*. The engines were smoking hot. A tongue of flame thrashed the ice from a forward blast vent and then cut out.

'A rescue party?' panted Razool. 'For us?' He wiped his frost-rimed fur and muttered, 'I've seen better landings though.'

The rate of fire to their rear increased, and the air boiled before booming against the outer shell of the craft. The pilot ship had become the focus of intense plasma fire.

Razool drove the bolt to the far side of the ship. Box had to duck his head as they skidded under the stabilizers. The side airlock opened, panels slipping apart in interlocking layers. Razool took them up to the entrance and then he and Box crawled in, hauling their heavily armoured bodies up like dead-weights. Gunfire crackled across the ship's casing, catching Box's heels, and singing along the iron flanks of the bolt, which reared up and galloped away. They barely had time to strap themselves into the small loading bay before the ship began to move.

There were no windows and the bay was in darkness. Box felt his body swing upwards, felt the force of the acceleration on his muscles and guts. He waited for the ship's motion to settle but it didn't.

Razool's voice was gruff as he struggled to contain his anger. 'We'd be smashed by now without this ship. Understand that, you stupid skin?'

Box didn't need his friend to tell him that after everything they'd fought through, every step closer to Chess that he'd come, he'd nearly blown it. He was quiet for several minutes as the ship continued to buck and lurch. Then his stomach began to cartwheel. Box spoke to take his mind off the nausea; and to break the silence.

'I don't want to sound ungrateful, but I've had better journeys.'

'Whose fault is that?' growled Razool. 'I haven't finished with you. But whoever's flying this is more skak-fisted than a strince-filled cadet.' He released the safety harness and stood, swaying as the pilot ship ducked and swung.

There was a door in the bulkhead. He pulled it open. Box freed himself and crawled forwards to see who was on the other side.

'What the hell are *you* doing here?' snarled Razool.

Shera looked back at them, hands grappling with the controls. 'That's no way to say thank you,' she said.

CHAPTER 11

The posters outside The Grand Opera announced *Le Nozze di Figaro*. The deep velvet auditorium was full, and thick with the heat of densely packed humans. Eighty feet beneath Anna was the stage, where a young woman dressed as a pageboy was singing to a young woman dressed as a prettily gowned young woman. Anna had seen them before Kusanagi had tied the blindfold about her face. Now, all was sound and darkness, the weight of the sword in her hands and the pull of the drop below. The violins started to play, rocking gently, and the mellow, soprano voice began to sing happily, ghosting up through the ropes, pulleys, cables and catwalks of the fly loft.

Kusanagi had escorted Anna into the rear of the theatre earlier that evening. He had whispered into the ears of the stagehands who were thick with him, and with their nodachi, their samurai longswords, sheathed across their backs, Anna and Kusanagi had climbed the narrow ladder up the fly tower to the highest lofts above the stage.

As the theatre had filled, they had explored the hidden domain of cables, counterweights, and dark spaces. Anna had committed it to memory for what was to follow. The audience had settled into the plush seats, the orchestra had made itself comfortable with a skittering arpeggio of flutes, a bending boom of timpani and the catcall of one tuning violin to another, and Anna had imprinted on her mind the batons, the support wires, the narrow walkways and the lethal drops. Her survival would depend upon her balance and her memory. Then Kusanagi had bound her eyes with the cloth.

She had done blindfold work before, but never like this.

The music swelled and for a moment, a clarinet partnered the mellifluous voice. Anna shut it out. Concentrate; focus. Kusanagi had brought her here because the music and the singing created perfect distractions from the challenge of listening and moving. And because the consequences of a mistake would be disastrous. The opera house was an ideal training environment.

Anna's bare feet slid along the baton in perfect step with the sword-master who walked a different baton, three metres to her right. He wasn't blindfolded; he performed the moves, steps, the cuts and strikes, and following him by sound alone, Anna shadowed through the fly loft like his double. She listened for the brush of his feet, the rustle of his shirt, the click of ligaments in his arms and fingers, the changes in his pattern of breathing. This is how he had been training her for months, ever since Chess had vanished and Anna had left home.

A brush of fabric, a strain of muscle, a shift in the air and Anna knew he was jumping. With perfect synchronicity, Anna jumped too, flashing between guide-wires that she couldn't see and landing on the next wooden baton in silence, just as the sword-master had done.

He somersaulted backwards, landing with perfect grace; simultaneously, Anna somersaulted backwards but the outside edge of her foot found only the edge of the beam and she felt her weight take her towards the drop. Her knee buckled. Anna arched back, counterbalancing with her head and shoulders, sliding her foot back. It felt as if her heart was already plunging down, ahead of her body. Slowly, she exhaled, cut out the nerves that would make her legs weak if she let them.

The drop and the voice swirled up at her.

She heard Kusanagi's shoulder move, his shirt rub against itself and like a reflection, her own arms rose above her head, positioning the sword for an overhead cut. Her arms were relaxed but her grip was firm. She remembered that there was a rope a metre to her left; severing it would be fatal.

The voice rose, muted by drapes, but still drifting up through the hoisting cables, dreamily.

Ignore it. Focus.

Kusanagi had turned on his heels to face the other way. Neat and swift as a pirouette, Anna turned with him, re-orientating her mental map of cables, pulleys and narrow footholds. The swords cut down together, separated only by three metres of darkness. Anna performed the cut as she'd been trained: pulling with her left hand but not too much force from the right, and guiding the blade across her body so as to cut across herself, not into herself.

The music was beautiful. It was a happy song. Anna could try to control her ears, but controlling the ache in her chest was more difficult; the happiness felt much further away than just the stage below.

And then she realized that Kusanagi had vanished. Inwardly, Anna swore at herself. In half a second's distraction, she had lost sense of the sword-master. Sword held before her, she tightroped along the baton, listening so hard, judging temperature and airflow with her skin so minutely that it was as if her senses were long, smoky fingers, weaving out from her and through the darkness.

The song had nearly finished and in its final bars, Anna thought she heard the click of a tendon not more than a couple of metres to her right. She cut out conscious thought altogether and sensed, her body prepared to react as one with her mind.

The music stopped. The audience began to clap.

Air moved ahead of the incoming blade. Anna slid her right leg back and drew her blade up in a block. The clash of steel was lost in the tumult of applause.

Anna wobbled and she put out a hand to steady herself on a rope that she knew would be there. The blindfold was pulled off.

'It was the flat of my blade,' said Kusanagi, sheathing his sword.

'I know,' said Anna, sheathing her own sword within its black lacquered scabbard. 'I could feel it.'

They jumped to an adjacent gantry and sauntered along it, side by side, insouciant as a pair of cats.

'Always, too much distraction,' said Kusanagi. 'You still let your own thoughts intrude.' His grey hair was scraped back from his face tightly and tied in a ponytail.

'I try to stop them,' explained Anna, 'but I'm not like you. I'm human.' Her blue eyes were deadly serious, her long, black hair swaying as she strolled. Anna didn't actually know what the sword-master was.

One morning he had called for her at the house in Mendoza Row where Anna was staying, and since then, the tall, thin, sharp-faced, silver-eyed sword-master had taught Anna how to lose all boundaries between herself, her sword and the world around them. Kinuq, her first teacher, had taught her how to use the sword and to become part of it. Kusanagi was teaching her how to step out of herself entirely, so that there was no sword and no Anna; there was simply a blade that moved as swift as thought itself.

Kusanagi looked human but he did things that were impossible. She sighed. Knowing what was human and what was possible or impossible had become more difficult ever since she had met Chess.

'You're not happy.'

'Correct.' Anna pulled her hands out of her jeans pockets as they came to the stepladder. Losing Chess had felt like a death. Leaving home had felt like another. Killing her brother's murderer, the Crystal Priest, Fenley Ravillious, was meant to have made her feel better; but Anna had discovered that the pleasure of revenge lay in its anticipation; the act had left her empty. All that mattered now was getting Chess back, but the Committee were no closer to cracking the fractal code than they had been months ago.

At the bottom of the iron steps, Kusanagi was talking to a stocky, bearded man in a leather coat. Anna pulled on her socks and boots and jacket, zipped her sheathed sword inside her hockey stick bag and threw that and her boot bag over her shoulder. It amazed her how many people there were, secreted within the fabric of the city, who were there when the Committee needed them. And how many there were who were prepared to assist the Twisted Symmetry.

In the chill, late-autumn darkness outside The Grand Opera, Kusanagi said, 'Thursday night? At the Eighteenth Shopping Precinct.'

'I've got hockey on Monday and kick boxing on Wednesday,' considered Anna, thinking through her arrangements for the week, 'but Thursday should be OK. Where exactly?'

'The supermarket,' replied Kusanagi, pulling on a long coat which draped all but the plain pommel of his sword. When Anna raised one dark and sceptical eyebrow, he added, 'I have a new exercise. It is an exercise in moving amongst people without being noticed: true invisibility. We fight but must not be seen.'

'Well, it's usually deserted by the Brussels sprouts,' suggested Anna deadpan. 'Let's start there.'

'I like sprouts,' commented the sword-master.

'As I thought,' said Anna, starting to walk away. 'Not human.'

The sword-master walked in the opposite direction, footsteps dying into the city night. Anna shoved her fists into her jacket pockets, and long legs striding swiftly, headed for the smart neighbourhood of Mendoza Row. The traffic on the overpass which banked around the skyscrapers was so thunderous that it filled Anna's head, driving out thoughts.

It felt good; the noise created peace. That was something Kusanagi would never have understood.

But when she was only a couple of streets away from Mendoza Row, and the overpasses and central skyscrapers were behind her, Anna became aware of another noise. Footfalls: sharp and rapid, slapping down the pavement behind her. She looked back and saw a small figure, a child, sprinting in her direction. Barefooted. A street rat. Even though it was dark and the cold neon of the street lights killed detail, Anna recognized the copper hair, the loose tracksuit bottoms and the ragged black jumper. The girl didn't stop sprinting until she had crashed into Anna.

'Trick, what is it?' Anna asked the panting girl.

Chest and shoulders heaving, Trick gasped, 'Hunters . . . at the wharf,' and she kept repeating the words. Then she grabbed the sleeve of Anna's jacket and started to pull.

Anna knew that the hunters had stayed away from the street rats' lair ever since Chess had begun to take on the Twisted Symmetry.

But Chess wasn't around anymore.

Her thoughts speeded up. Something very bad had happened. 'What Trick?' she demanded. 'What's happened at the wharf?' There was the scent of smoke in the little girl's hair.

'You've got to come with me.' Trick was gulping. 'You've got to get away.'

Anna grasped Trick by the upper arms and said, slowly, 'Trick, tell me what happened.'

'The hunters came.' Trick was blinking back tears. 'They burnt it and they was beating and shooting.'

Hunters liked to hurt street rats. It was what jacks paid them to do. It was why they had been so useful to the Symmetry in the past.

'Where's Pacer?' Anna wanted to know that Pacer was all right.

'He got away,' said Trick. 'Most of us got away. *Most* of us did.' Her voice was breaking.

'But why? Why were they there?' insisted Anna.

Trick wiped her glistening nose with the back of her sleeve.

''Cos they was looking for *you*.'

Ethel had warned them that the Symmetry had given the Endgame order. But nothing had happened in the immediate aftermath of Ethel's dire announcement, and, although Anna had been alert for any threat at first, she had grown used to the Twisted Symmetry *not* coming for her. She had thought that maybe they had more important work to attend to. Clearly, she had been wrong.

Out of the surrounding sounds of the city, a new noise came to Anna: a throaty, droning noise. Motorcycle engines. Maybe a couple of streets away. Of course the hunters would be coming in this direction. If they hadn't found her at the wharf, the next place to go would be Mendoza Row.

Trick was tugging at her again. 'Come on, Anna. Come *on*.'

'What about Crazy Boris?' Anna couldn't just leave the retired rock star who owned 18 Mendoza Row to the hunters. But the growl of engines was no more than a street away now.

'Pacer went straight there to warn him,' Trick assured Anna.

'To get a guitar, more like,' muttered Anna, surprising herself by how irked she was that Pacer had gone to warn Crazy Boris rather than coming to warn her.

'Come *on*,' urged Trick.

Anna went with Trick, into a side street and from there, up an alley where soggy cardboard boxes were washed up against iron railings. She heard the motorbikes roar down the main street, five or six of them, and she could picture the riders in their black leathers with the silver death's head insignia and jackboots. They would be carrying pistols and stun sticks and coshes. Maybe machine-guns too. They wouldn't knock on Crazy Boris's nicely painted front door; they would smash it in and enjoy doing so. You had to have an appetite for that sort of thing to become a hunter. Nobody joined the hunters by mistake.

'This way,' said Trick, going deeper into the alley. Without questioning, Anna followed, the pair of them vanishing into shadows that were untouched by the yellow light which leaked between the curtains of the tall houses that backed onto the passage. At the far end there were high, spiked railings between brick pillars. There was a padlocked gate in the centre of the railings, and on the other side the alley continued.

There was a time when Anna would have wondered where they could possibly go from here. But since that time, she had seen what a cornered street rat could do. She watched how Trick took hold of the iron, a couple of railings in, and with her body rigid, walked her feet up the brick pillar while shuffling her hands up the bar. At the top, she actually walked her feet above her head and then vaulted over the sharp points, landing smooth as a cat on the other side.

Anna hadn't just watched street rats, she had learnt from them. She was bigger and therefore heavier than Trick, so navigating the railings as the little girl had done was beyond her. But block-hopping with Chess had taught her what could be achieved with a sprint, a wall, some clever footwork and a reckless disregard for accidents.

Anna walked a short distance away from the railings. She considered the best line of attack and then sprinted at the spot where the bars met the brick. A metre away, she jumped off her right foot and into the wall. She powered up the brick with her left foot and then pin-balled from her right up and off the railings. Her left foot was back on the brick. She kicked off the wall and over the spikes. She landed on the other side in a crouch and with no more noise than the thud of her boots.

Trick stroked her chin. 'Not bad, for a jack. Come on.'

Trick led Anna from the comfortable quarter near Mendoza Row, to a burrow of streets, packed with charity shops, money exchanges and wilting grocery stores. They slipped down a ginnel full of mouldering darkness by the side of a rotten, wood-framed shop called Rough Deals, and entered the shop by an unlocked back door. The door closed without their touching it. When she spun round, Anna saw that standing behind it were Gemma and a tall, olive-skinned man who wore a thick, greying moustache, a long, greying ponytail and an ill-fitting dinner suit that had once belonged to Anna's father. In his hand he held a stout wooden staff, as long as himself.

'Balthazar!'

Whether it was because this philosopher-pugilist from another place and time was a friend to help her against the hunters, or whether it was simply because it felt good to be near an old suit that had come from her father, Anna couldn't have said, but she was glad to see Balthazar Broom.

'It is good you are safe, Anna,' said Balthazar in his sonorous bass. His eyes were bright and bulging in the gloom of the shabby back room. He rubbed his moustache, which, like his ponytail, had been a luxurious black not so long ago. 'Well done, Trick. Well done.' He patted Trick on the head.

Gemma gave Trick a huge hug and they clung to one another long enough for Trick's bone-thin shoulders to stop shaking.

'It seems,' announced Balthazar Broom, portentously, 'that it is now *your* turn.'

'To be hunted?' confirmed Anna.

Balthazar nodded, slowly.

Anna shrugged lightly. 'They'll have to find me first. And then they'll have to catch me.'

'I admire your courage, Anna,' said Balthazar. 'But there are many hunters, and there is only one of you.'

'And the rest of *us*,' insisted Gemma, brightly.

'What happened at the wharf?' Anna was yet to receive a coherent account.

'The hunters came down the river in boats, and there was helicopters,' explained the raggedy, blonde girl, as if she were describing an interesting school trip; except, thought Anna,

Gemma had never been to school and she had never, in the whole of her life, been on a trip to anywhere.

Anna pulled the bags off her shoulders and sat down with them. Balthazar sat down too, resting the staff across his wrestler's thighs. Trick knelt by Anna but Gemma remained standing.

'We were asleep and some of us were awake, because of the stories.' What Gemma said often didn't make sense at first, but there was always a logic behind it. Anna knew that sometimes Pacer told stories to the street rats, particularly the youngest. It was funny, thought Anna, as she pulled open her boot bag, how the way people looked could hide the way they really were. Pacer, with his black hooded combat jacket, shaven head, tough knuckles and street-sharp eyes would have had most jacks calling for the crashers on sight. But it was the same Pacer who organized shelter for the street rats, who watched that everyone got fed and who told stories to the smallest. They thought his scary stories were the best, which they were, because they were true.

'I'm surprised he wasn't keeping them awake with his singing,' muttered Anna. Ever since Crazy Boris had started to teach Pacer how to play the guitar, the top rat had decided he could sing too.

'No, he wasn't singing,' confirmed Gemma. 'But then the hunters started burning the wharf. They wouldn't if Chess was there.'

'Too right they wouldn't,' muttered Anna. 'Chess would have nuked the lot of them. She'd have been miserable for a week afterwards, but she'd have nuked them when it mattered.'

'I wish Chess was back,' said Gemma.

'Me too,' said Trick, earnestly.

'Yeah,' agreed Anna. But it must have been toughest for Gemma. Gemma and Chess had been best friends for years. In fact, as far as Anna could tell, they had been one another's only friends for years. Yet even with what had happened, the little girl with the wispy blonde hair was calm and patient and always certain that things would work out.

'We're going to look for Chess, aren't we Balthazar?' confirmed Gemma.

'Yes, Gemma,' said Balthazar, as if that was the end of the subject.

'In our own way,' added Gemma. 'Won't we Balthazar?'

Anna shot a questioning glance at the man in her father's suit. 'Really, Balthazar?'

'All of us are looking for Chess,' he responded, with pop-eyed inscrutability. He blinked innocently.

Anna pulled a slim case the size of a laptop from the boot bag. She opened it to reveal a screen and keypad. She pressed the ON button. It powered up with a glow that limned the room in dull silver.

'Your Link-me,' whispered Trick.

'Correct,' whispered Anna. 'Good for hacking, tapping, talking and stalking.'

Balthazar chuckled. 'Most poetic.' He dug his pipe from the jacket pocket and began to pack tobacco into the bowl, tamping it down with his big forefinger.

Trick squatted by Anna, the silver light bathing her face, taking the edge off her barbed-wire tattoo. 'What are you going to do?'

'Something secret.' Anna winked at Trick. 'Don't tell Ethel.'

Balthazar gave a buzzing hum of intrigued satisfaction, lit the pipe and inhaled until the bowl glowed and crackled like a miniature furnace. Then he breathed out a plume of aromatic smoke. 'A mystery,' he intoned, and he shut his eyes. 'How excellent.'

'I'm going to consult a friend,' said Anna. 'His name is Lemuel.'

'Sprazkin?' asked Balthazar, opening one eye and then the other. 'Is this wise Anna?'

'I don't know,' said Anna. 'But it's necessary. I haven't spoken to him since Chess was taken. Not speaking seemed wise then. Speaking seems wiser now.'

Balthazar leant forwards, quite suddenly. 'But why? At a time like this, is it safe to trust someone who was once the Symmetry's primary warp?'

'You tell me.' Anna's long fingers were dancing over the keyboard. 'You're the philosopher.' But Anna wasn't waiting for Balthazar to tell her anything, and, save for drawing on his pipe, he remained silent.

'I don't know if he's listening,' muttered Anna. 'I'm using an open message system so if he's out there, everywhere, he might pick this up.'

'Like a broadcast?' asked Gemma.

'Yeah, in a way ... Whoa!'

The screen fizzed and crackled and then a voice came from the speaker, a high-pitched, tinkling voice that sounded amused at itself just for being there.

'Anna Ledward, what a wonderful surprise.' There was a peal of laughter.

'Hello, Lemuel,' said Anna. 'Ethel says you have been misbehaving.'

'Ethel has no sense of fun,' replied Lemuel, a little tersely.

'What have you been doing?'

'Oh, wandering here and there and up and down. There is a lot of cyberspace to explore.'

'Ethel says that you have been causing trouble,' observed Anna.

'Well,' said the voice, pettishly, 'maybe a small financial crisis here, a failure in a long-range weapon system there. But it's only electronic.' Lemuel giggled. 'I've been *virtually* misbehaving. None of it has given me the same pleasure as bumping into you like this.' A tinkle of laughter. 'Well, *virtually* bumping into you.'

Trick gasped with delight at the pink love hearts that appeared on the screen and then popped like soap bubbles.

'Very pretty, Lemuel,' said Anna patiently.

Lemuel dropped his voice, as if sharing a secret. 'The truth is, when you can go anywhere and do anything, you realize that it's the limits in life that make it interesting. Cyberspace is so boring; being real is much more fun.'

'I need some help,' stated Anna.

There was a disappointed sigh. 'And here was I, all excited that you were simply missing me.'

'You know about Chess?' quizzed Anna.

'Yes, Anna, I know about Chess. I know that the Symmetry have her. And I know that she was given to them by that nasty little boy, Splinter, just as I was given to them by him. Did you know they have my body at the same warp station as Chess?'

'No, I didn't.' Anna tried to hide her impatience.

'Yes, they do. General Vane arranged for it to be given to the experts. And who is more expert in matters of pain and its infliction than a primary warp?' There was a modest little laugh. 'Currently, my mortal remains languish in the same zone as Chess.'

Anna said, 'Did you know that the fractal code ...'

'Can't be cracked. Yes, I know. I know all sorts of things in my current condition.' Petulantly he added, 'But I can't do anything. Not really *do* anything.'

'We need to crack the code,' said Anna.

'I can't. I don't know how. It is fiendish in its design.' There was a pause. Then, slyly, Lemuel said, 'But that isn't what's on your mind, is it? That isn't why you've called me up, after failing to speak to me for such a long time.'

Balthazar drew on his pipe, frowning. Trick was close against Anna.

Suspiciously, Anna asked, 'How do you know what's on my mind?'

A superior titter from the speaker of the Link-me. 'Oh, Anna, you underestimate me. I have spread my cyberself out during the course of our little tête-à-tête. I have searched and processed, swiftly and comprehensively, and what have I found?'

'What *have* you found?' demanded Anna.

'You are in a lot of trouble, Miss Ledward.' He tutted. 'The Endgame order no less.'

'I know that,' stated Anna. 'That's why we're hiding in a

rat-filled junk shop called Rough Deals.' She turned to Trick. 'Sorry,' she mouthed, 'about the rat comment.'

Officiously, Lemuel said, 'You would like me to access the hunter net, find out what is happening, maybe cause a little interference giving you time to vanish from your current location. You want me to do that because the hunter system is secure against yours.'

'I'm that transparent, am I?' sighed Anna.

'Like a piece of glass. But I would be delighted to help you, *if* you would do a little something for me in return. *If* you survive the night.'

'Thanks for the vote of confidence,' remarked Anna. 'And what is that little something?' Her face was close to the screen of the Link-me, her straight, black fringe edged silver.

'Bring me back my body. If you get to the warp station, please, bring me back my body. It isn't much of a body, I know, but it's the only one I have.'

'OK,' agreed Anna. 'If I can, I will.'

'Promise?'

'I promise to try my best,' was as far as Anna would go.

'Ooh,' crooned Lemuel. 'I could kiss you.'

Trick giggled as a pair of red lips blew a smacking kiss from the screen of the Link-me.

'There's no need,' said Anna. 'Now, please, tell me what's happening, and what should I do?'

'You are a *very* popular young lady. The hunters are looking for you, everywhere.'

Balthazar was about to speak but Anna kept him silent with an abrupt wave of her hand.

Lemuel was still talking. 'The nearest detachment of officers is no more than two hundred metres from the back door of Rough Deals.'

'What?' Anna reached for her stick bag. Balthazar was already on his feet. She thought she could hear the sound of engines approaching.

'Do not concern yourself, Anna,' insisted the voice. 'We are friends, you and I. I am here to help you, just as you are there to help me.' A little laugh. 'I have already scrambled the hunters' tracking devices. They are already altering their route. You are already safe.'

'Thank you.' But Anna was on edge now. Both Trick and Gemma had pressed their faces to the small, grimy rear window of the shop and Balthazar remained by the door, staff in hand.

There was a distracted humming from the speaker. Its pitch changed and then it chugged to a halt to be replaced by, 'Oh dear. Oh dear, dear, dear.'

'What?' hissed Anna.

'It isn't just hunters that are coming for you, Anna.' More humming. 'Oh dear. Oh *dear*, dear ...'

'Please, Lemuel,' said Anna, trying not to snap at the voice. 'Please, just *help* me.'

The voice was deadly serious. 'It seems that the Symmetry do not underestimate you, Anna. You should be flattered.'

'I'll try to be,' she muttered.

'The Symmetry take no chances: they like to do the job properly. Perhaps they even predicted my intervention. But something nasty is coming for you.'

'What? From where?' demanded Anna, unzipping the

hockey bag, taking out the long sword in its scabbard.

'Through the vortex,' said Lemuel. 'Coming quickly.' He sighed sadly.

'What is it?'

'I don't know. That information has not been given. They're not *absolute* beginners, Anna.' Lemuel sighed again, heartfelt. 'But it will be very, very nasty. You must run. Get out of there.' Lemuel's voice quavered. 'Oh, Anna, I don't think I can help you, and you're not going to be able to help *me* after all.'

CHAPTER 12

Inside a Möbius cell you could move, but you couldn't move beyond the boundary. And a Möbius cell wasn't constructed with space in mind, it was constructed solely to contain a pan-dimensional being. So Chess could stand, sit, stretch her arms out to her sides, but no more. And she couldn't move beyond the narrow confines because the sub-atomic fields of a Möbius cell extended in all dimensions, simultaneously and forever, save for the hollow in which the prisoner sat, stood or crouched.

Chess closed her eyes and leant back against a wall that she couldn't see and which she couldn't breach. She had given up trying to escape months ago. Whatever mistake had led to her near-escape, it had not been repeated. She wrapped her arms around her shins and rested her chin on her knees. Her long, tangled, chestnut hair hung over her face.

Funny, she thought, how I live with the pain of billions, but I still have to scratch my nose when my hair tickles it.

Chess knew where she was and she knew what was

happening and she knew this: that the Symmetry were nothing to be frightened of any longer.

At first the pain, her pain, had been unbearable. The first time her body and mind had been wracked with the torment of half a million souls, she felt as if her own soul was being torn apart and her body smashed, bone by bone. And that was how it felt the second time, and the third. That was how it felt until millions, maybe billions, of souls later, Chess realized that she wasn't being broken: she was being stretched.

With each transfer of energy her mind, her power, swelled like an ocean swallowing rivers. The Symmetry were making her stronger and greater than she could have ever imagined. And so, she began to welcome the energy, to absorb it hungrily, to draw it into herself with an appetite that the Symmetry had never foreseen.

Within the Möbius cell, Chess laughed to herself, ever so softly. Her hunger had caused the warps significant problems. Their machines, with their coils and plates and the extraordinarily complex circuitry with its perfectly balanced mathematics could not cope with the rate at which Chess drew the energy into herself. It over-heated, with the consequence that there had to be system shut-downs more often than the warps had calculated, and so Chess spent more time in the cell than had been anticipated, and she had more time to think.

She thought, she considered, she brooded.

She understood the Twisted Symmetry. Really, she understood them. They were honest: scorchingly honest. Chess had been seared by so much agony, had seen, felt, heard the suffering of so many other beings that she understood perfectly why a multiverse with that much pain should be destroyed. And the beautiful symmetry of it all was this: she was so full of the energy from that pain, that when the time came, she would be able to stop pain, forever. Which, on one view, was all that the Symmetry had desired. True, the destruction of the multiverse meant the destruction of every shred of happiness, every shred of love, but Chess knew she was slipping closer to the Symmetry's way of thinking. She hadn't wanted to, but increasingly, it seemed to make sense.

She picked at a loose toenail and shifted her position. The knight in her jeans pocket was digging into her skin: the chess piece that she had found when she had seen her mother in Knott Street; a few minutes spent with a memory. But time was all about what happened in it, not how long it lasted. And even a few minutes could be worth an eternity.

Chess hummed to herself; an old tune. The words crept through her cracked lips, tired, rasping.

When I was on horseback, wasn't I pretty?
When I was on horseback, wasn't I gay?
Wasn't I pretty when I entered Cork city . . .

The words dried up. Chess had never thought much about how she looked. Sometimes people had told her she was pretty, but she knew that physically, she was in a bad way now. Her skin was sore and bone dry, her hair was rough as a doormat, her nails were broken, her stomach cramped, her head ached, her muscles were raw. Her mind could absorb whatever the Symmetry blasted at it, but her body couldn't.

Chess had always been a realist. At this rate there was no certainty she would make it to the end: to the fifth node. She laughed again, very quietly. How ironic.

She knew exactly what was happening. They couldn't stop her from listening and they couldn't stop her from working things out. She had heard snatches of conversation; she had caught glimpses of her surroundings as the xenrian gaolers transferred her from the Möbius cell to the energy transmission chamber, and back again.

She was in something called a warp station. In about two months' time the time spiral would hit the fifth node, at which point the Symmetry would unleash her, as they put it. And she had learnt that somewhere close to where they contained her, the warps also kept Lemuel.

Poor, sweet Lemuel, Chess thought to herself. Made by others to be used by others. More than anyone else she had ever met, he understood her. He had tried to be good and everyone had treated him badly, so very badly.

However, although she had worked out a lot about her current situation, there was one matter that Chess didn't understand. On three of four occasions, she had seen a figure looking out at her from the place where the warps usually stood in the chamber. The figure was hooded, so she didn't know who or what it was and anyway, the bright spotlights made it impossible for her to see any detail. But it stood there, motionless, watching, and then would leave without saying a word. Chess felt as if she should have known who it was, but the figure's identity eluded her.

She pushed her hair back over her shoulders. What did any of this matter? She was alone. All that she had, the only good thing she possessed, was a memory and its song. That was it. Chess had tried to cling to memories of Gemma and Anna, but her brother, or brothers, whichever it was, had proved to her how empty love was; an emptiness that the Symmetry had filled with pain.

She had loved Box and he had joined the Symmetry: she had seen it. He had turned his back on her from the time he had been apart from her. And Splinter, Splinter in whom she had put all her trust: Splinter had given her to the enemy.

'You silly little girl,' Lemuel had once said to her, and he had been right.

Box and Splinter could have made all the difference in the universes. But without friendship, without love, there was nothing: nothing to balance against all that pain, all that suffering. Nothing was what the Twisted Symmetry wanted, and nothing was what she would give them.

Coils of blue smoke began to pour into the Möbius cell. The xenrian gaolers were coming for her. It was time for Chess to become the final sanctuary of another hurricane of broken souls. And this was what she wanted. Smiling, she opened her arms and let the gaolers take her wrists.

Splinter had the access codes. Once he had located where the Twisted Symmetry were keeping Chess prisoner, and once he had discovered that the warp station was encased in something called a fractal code, a little time spent with the Omnicon had furnished him with all he needed to crack it. He would need to obtain the necessary equipment to transmit the access data and that would require further research, but he was making progress.

This morning's task would be to reconnoitre a government laboratory where ion transmitters were kept secure. An ion transmitter was a necessary piece of equipment for his plan. His plan was a simple one. He would use the ion transmitter to break the fractal code with the access data and with the code down, he could emerge from the vortex, take Chess and return with her, into the vortex. He would have to scout about first, investigate the layout of the warp station, discover precisely where and in what conditions she was being kept. But this could be done. And like the best plans, it was simple.

His brilliance at work. Not even a requirement for *ruthless* brilliance. Splinter was happy to settle for *sheer* brilliance.

And, curiously, he *was* happy. Happy to be occupied with the practical task of a rescue mission; happy to have concrete aims; happy at the thought of extracting Chess from the place where he had put her. Maybe he had developed a hitherto un-encountered strain of *merciful* brilliance? Whatever it was, he noticed that planning and conducting this task was simpler and significantly less painful than the execution of his ambition to become the King of Rats.

Doubtless Ethel would have come out with some tripe about the warm glow of helping others. Splinter was honest enough to know that helping others wasn't what made him get out of bed in the mornings. But he liked the experience of undertaking a mission that wouldn't be universally condemned by the people who knew him closest. And he liked the idea that the very end of everything, that what happened to Chess, could be controlled by his *merciful* brilliance: that he could *stop it* from happening. That Chess would live.

But first, the ion transmitter.

Splinter kept his possessions in his jacket pockets and the crystal knife inside his shirt. Carefully, he touched the sharp corners of the third plate from the Hermetic Codex and a smile born of his cleverness played at the corners of his mouth. It seemed to Splinter that by keeping the plate in his possession, by keeping it close, he would ultimately keep control over it and thus control that particular death. Certainly, he would never have left it where anybody else could find it. When it came to matters of death, you could never be *too* careful.

He opened the wardrobe door and reached inside. His fingers found the little wooden box, his portable vortex, and they grasped it, pulling it close, bringing it to the edge of the wardrobe.

'Ladies and gentlemen,' announced a voice inside his head, 'the King of Rats will now perform his great act of vanishing.'

Splinter ignored the voice. The King of Rats had packed up his ruthless brilliance and gone. Now it was just Splinter. But he knew that *just* Splinter was more than enough.

He opened the box and the light poured out, bathing Splinter's face in a lemon-yellow glow. Vapour tumbled over the wooden lip and puffed across the wardrobe bottom in little clouds. He lifted one long thin leg and put it inside the casket, which accommodated it entirely, despite its size. A shiver ran across Splinter's skin; always it felt cold on entering the vortex. Neat as a flamingo, a pale-skinned, black-suited flamingo, Splinter drew his other leg into the portable vortex before leaning out and pulling the wardrobe door to. It shut firmly, blocking out all daylight.

There was something about the dark security of being hidden that gave Splinter a great satisfaction. He allowed his body to slip within the extraordinary mouth of the little box. He pulled shut the lid at the same time that he realized there was no mortice gate.

And there were no reachings.

There was nothing.

Nothing.

'No,' said Splinter. 'No. No. No.'

And he continued to fall.

Forever.

Saul had waited until the wardrobe door had closed. Always, Splinter pulled the door shut as he climbed inside the portable vortex. Saul had watched this performance so many times before, spying through a hole in the bedroom ceiling.

Now, with the wardrobe door shut, he stood outside it and considered the little wooden box which he was holding: a small box with simple carving on its sides. Splinter's portable vortex.

And the box that Splinter had just entered?

It was a portable vortex, too. But it was a different portable vortex. It had been simple enough to arrange for its construction. Saul had waited until Splinter had embarked upon one of his many rambles within the castle and then he had taken the little box from the back of the wardrobe. The craftsmanship required to construct a replica was unremarkable, and the warps possessed the technology necessary to integrate it with a route into the vortex, thus creating an identical portable vortex: when seen from the outside.

But on the inside it was a very different place. There was no mortice gate and there were no reachings. Saul had instructed the warps to ensure that the replica box should open into a region of the vortex where there was infinite nothingness. Since infinite nothingness was what the vortex mostly was, infinite nothingness was easy to provide.

Once Splinter had entered the perfect replica, he would become perfectly lost. And once something was lost in the vortex, it would be lost, forever.

Saul set down Splinter's portable vortex, opened the wardrobe door and took out its replica: the replica into which Splinter had vanished. He placed the replica on the flat of his hand and studied it for several seconds before striding to the adjoining room in which there was the large ceramic bowl. The bowl into which Splinter had deposited so many breakfasts.

Saul placed the bowl on the table and the replica portable vortex on the floor. Then he raised his boot and stamped on the small box, repeatedly, until it was so many little pieces of broken wood. He scraped these up, all of them, and placed them in the large bowl. Then, from the back pocket of his jeans he produced a box of matches. He struck a match and selecting one spill-shaped strip of tinder from the bowl, he played the yellow flame over its tip until it ignited. When the flames had turned orange and were running up the spill, he dropped it into the bowl.

The wood was dry. It snapped and smoked and the flames danced over it. Saul watched the box burn, nudging the bowl from time to time to ensure the flames devoured every last skelf. Then, just to be certain, he broke Splinter's portable vortex and burnt that too.

Within the hour, the ceramic bowl was full of ash and the room was full of smoke.

Saul went to the window and pushed it open. Outside, the sky was blue: endlessly blue. There was the lightest of breezes. Saul closed his large and beautiful eyes and let the breeze lap his face. Then he went to the table, took the large bowl and tipped its contents out of the window. The breeze took them and carried them away.

'Goodbye, Splinter,' said Saul.

CHAPTER 13

'What are you doing here?' demanded Razool. The pilot ship lurched as it took a plasma hit.

'Saving your armour-plated backside. And his.' It was difficult to tell whether Shera was working the controls, or whether the controls were working her. The ship over-corrected and lurched the other way. 'Mostly his,' she added, with a jerk of her head towards Box.

'*His!*' Razool cast a savage glare at Box. 'He's crazy,' and the snout thumped Box in the chest, hard enough to make Box stagger backwards. 'What's wrong with you?'

'They killed Strulf,' said Box, bemused. The thought of striking Razool back didn't enter his head.

'So?' Razool was really angry. 'They kill lots of people. They might have killed me. They might have killed you. So what? We try to get killed in return? Are you stupid?' He pointed to his own head. 'You use this. Think. Use your brain. If you have one.'

Box knew that Razool was right. He was saying the same things that Balthazar had told him when he was first teaching him how to fight, on Surapoor.

Fight with your head, Box, as well as your heart.

Box felt stupid but that didn't stop him from opening his mouth and admitting, 'I wanted to fight.'

'Really?' Razool's fangs were a bite away from Box's face. '*You* wanted to fight? And I nearly get my head blown off pulling *you* out of the skak.' The snout shook his head. 'We fight when we *have* to. Not because we *want* to.'

'I'm sorry, Zool,' muttered Box.

The ship dropped so fast, both of them buckled at the knee.

'Can you fly this?' shouted Razool.

'Not really,' Shera shouted from the cockpit.

Box rubbed his face with both hands. He felt tired, and heavy with what he had nearly done to himself: what he had nearly done to Razool. 'I just lost it,' he sighed. 'I've been waiting for so long, fighting for so long. I need to get home. I need to find Chess.'

'I'm glad you haven't forgotten that,' said Razool, more gently.

Box's voice was hoarse. 'Underneath everything, it's all I ever think about.'

'Good.' Razool pulled a right-angled metal rod out of one of his utility pouches. He handed it to Box. 'OK, unbolt me before her flying kills us all. Then we're going AWOL.'

'AWOL?' Box didn't know what Razool was talking about.

'We're going to spend a little time away from the front line.'

Once both sets of armour were in a heap inside the small loading bay, Razool climbed into the cockpit. There were two pilots' seats and they were cloistered within a bafflingly complex interior of buttons, wires, dials and levers. There was one narrow window at the front. In a pillar facing the two seats there was a large screen with a pale green glow. Hundreds of shapes moved about one central cross. Some of the shapes were dots and others were the size of a coin. Box guessed that the cross showed the position of the pilot ship and the other shapes were other ships. Their ship appeared to be moving away from all the other ships.

Razool ducked his head under a low-slung cluster of cables, reached up and opened a panel cover on the roof, flicked several switches, punched the panel housing, swore, punched it again and flicked one more switch.

'Nice skills, Commodore,' joked Box.

Razool elbowed a button to the left of his seat. The loading bay airlock began to open.

'Whoa!' yelled Box, grabbing hold of the safety harnesses as the ship dipped right.

Razool thumped the button and the airlock closed, although the ship continued to dip.

'You were saying?' he enquired, gruffly.

Box kept his mouth shut.

Razool took hold of a lever to the right of his seat and pulled it before pressing two switches on the console in front of him. 'Counterforce stability,' he said to no one in particular and at once, the ship was so steady that there was no sense of movement at all.

'Only Symmetry ships out there so we're OK.' He pulled down a keypad on a concertina arm and began to work it as he fired questions at Shera. 'You took this from the *Transit IV*?'

'Yup.' Shera had ceased to handle the controls. It was obvious that Razool knew precisely what he was doing. She crossed her arms and put her boots up on the fascia immediately in front of her. She was wearing a black jacket, black combat trousers and black boots and her black hair was tied back with an oily rag.

Her clothes were clean. Box looked down at what he could see of himself. His jacket was shredded and caked with slick and his own blood, and his trousers were no better, and his skin looked as filthy as if he'd been down a coal mine. Razool looked just as bad.

'You've been on the *Transit IV* the whole time?' interrogated Razool.

Shera stared dead ahead. 'Yup.'

Immediately, Box thought of the coffin with the hole in it. And then he thought of the rest of the coffins. But Shera didn't look strong enough to have done that.

'Why?' Razool spoke out of the side of his mouth as he worked at the keypad.

'I can't tell you,' said Shera.

'You working for us or the enemy?'

Box thought that was a difficult question. Who was the enemy now?

Either way, Shera replied, 'I'm working for me.'

'Doing what?'

'Commodore,' enquired Shera, 'has anyone ever told you that you lack certain, basic conversational skills?'

'Doing *what?*'

Shera ground her neat, velvety jaw as if chewing gum and

drawled, 'I'm the skin's guardian angel. And I owe him a life.'

'Fine,' fired Razool. 'You've just settled the debt. Want to get out now?'

Shera settled into her jacket as if settling into a blanket. 'You know where we're going, Commodore?'

'I'm asking the questions,' grunted Razool, eyes fixed on the controls now, hands dextrous as a conjuror's.

Shera spun round in her seat and looked at Box over the headrest, eyes bright. 'You don't mind if I come along, do you Box?' For the first time she smiled, sharp and white.

Box shrugged. 'I don't mind.'

'Even though she shot you?' enquired Razool.

'That wasn't my fault,' snapped Shera.

'What, and when you tried to shoot him again, that wasn't your fault either?'

'I don't know what was happening with the weapons but it wasn't me,' insisted Shera angrily.

'I don't know what was happening with mine,' volunteered Box, still perplexed. 'But it fell *upwards*.'

Razool flipped shut the overhead panel cover. 'Someone was trying to get you killed.'

Shera huffed.

'One last question.' Razool licked the fangs down one side of his mouth. 'How did you escape? After you'd been taken prisoner, how did you escape?'

'Training,' came the answer. 'Lots of training.'

Razool smiled. 'I know what you are, Shera. But I don't know what you're doing here, or why,' and he turned to her, lips drawn tight on his sharp snout, long canines bared, eyes like jet. 'But I'm watching you. *Understand?*'

'You don't trust me.' She shrugged. 'Too bad.'

'Trust no one,' muttered Box, without thinking. It was just an association of ideas.

Razool nodded. 'Brain engaged again. Good. I'm taking you home, by the way.'

It took Box a couple of seconds to digest this information. 'Home?'

'Yeah. Remember? That place where the people have little teeth and bald bodies, and all the things you go on about, like crashers, and cake and chocolate. And Chess.'

'Chess?' Finding Chess was the thought that had driven him for so long that its reality hit him like a tidal wave. Box shook his head, amazed at the possibility that he might be going home. Getting out of the Fleshing yard, surviving the penal battalions and the crossing into the Drakner: he'd done it, and now here was Razool saying he was going home.

The reality of finding Chess, of seeing her once more was so massive that he could only say, 'Good. That's good.'

'I should hope so,' observed Razool. 'You've caused mayhem to find her.'

Box laughed. It was good to be going home.

'Who's Chess?' asked Shera.

Box was about to say who she was but Razool interrupted. 'None of your skakking business. You're not even meant to be here.'

Perhaps Razool was right. Perhaps it was better to say nothing about Chess to Shera.

'How do we ... I get home?'

Razool pointed to the keypad, and the screen in a panel between his blood-splashed trouser legs. 'See this?'

Box was leaning over the narrow gap between the two seats. 'It looks like a computer.' He was aware of Shera's gaze.

'It's a quantum computer. It can calculate the probability of our ship being in the skin world.'

'Yeah? Really?' Box feigned fascination but the complexities of quantum theory made Razool's explanation fade into gabble. The Commodore, however, was enjoying giving the explanation.

'OK. The computer transmits the data to the hyperbility drive which then translates the ship to the location. Simple. That's how we travel hyperspace.' Razool turned his head. 'Hey, were you listening to any of that?'

'Sorry, Zool,' mumbled Box. 'I think I'm tired.' In truth, he did feel tired. A surging fatigue drained every muscle.

'Back there,' Razool thumbed over his shoulder. 'On the other side of the loading bay there's a crew room. Get some zip if you like. We'll be at our destination in less than an hour.'

Box pushed himself away from the seat.

'Before you get your head down, you better tell me where exactly we're heading,' said Razool. 'I can find your home world, but where do we touch down? I've not tripped skin-wise, but I guess somewhere out of sight would be smart.' His brow furrowed. 'The ship might attract attention, and they've not seen anyone as handsome as me before.'

Suddenly, the practicalities of looking for Chess crashed in. Where to start? At the wharf? But that had been destroyed. At Slack Harry's, the bar where the regulars drank? But Chess wouldn't be there. And they couldn't exactly walk around the city asking people about her; one boy and two snouts, dressed in bloodstained combat gear and looking for a solitary street rat. And what about the pilot ship? They wouldn't be able to appear in the city without attracting unhelpful attention.

And then, instinctively, Box knew what he had to do first.

Find Ethel. She might be a mad old hag, or she might be a witch, but whatever she was, she knew about things. Ethel would know what to do.

Box yawned. 'The Lungs,' he said to Razool. 'They're a kind of forest, on the west of the city. If we land there, at night, there's a good chance no one will see us.' He yawned again. 'Probably you won't be able to find it.'

'Box, I do this for a living. I can fly anything and I can find any destination.' He sniffed. 'Some places might take longer than others but I'll get there. Maybe you'll get a *couple* of hours' zip.'

'OK. Thanks, Zool.' Box patted the snout on his shoulder. 'Thanks.'

'Always happy to help,' said Razool. 'Even a skin as crazy as you.' He flashed a friendly display of long teeth.

Then Box felt Shera's eyes on him. 'Thanks Shera,' he said hesitantly.

'I like you, Box,' said Shera, serious. 'Really, I do.'

Box didn't know what to say to that. He made his way to the crew quarters, knowing that her eyes followed him as he went.

The screen of the Link-me fizzed with a snowstorm of nothing.

Anna pressed the OFF button and clapped shut the cover. 'He's gone. Lemuel's gone. I think he wants us to go too. Go from here.'

It was very quiet in the back room. The air was cold and damp and there was a powerful odour of rot and mouse droppings. Trick was still at the one little, filthy window, face pressed up against the night. Gemma and Balthazar were standing by the back door, saying nothing, going nowhere. The door that led within, to the rest of the mouldy building, was ajar.

Balthazar was the first to break the graveyard hush. 'We cannot stay here, Anna.'

'I wasn't planning to.' Anna pushed the Link-me into her boot bag and took the scabbard from the stick bag. 'Not now we know that something unclassified is coming for us. Well, for me.' She slung the boot bag and the scabbard across her back.

'Something nasty,' Gemma reminded them.

'Yeah, well, I wasn't expecting flowers,' snapped Anna. She knew that they didn't have long. 'Now listen, I need to find Ethel.' To Balthazar and Gemma she said, 'You two, go to Ethel's, but go a different way from me. There's no point all of us running into whatever's out there.'

'Or in here,' observed Gemma.

Trick turned to look at the black bar where the inner door was open slightly.

'Are you sure about this, Anna?' Balthazar's eyes protuberated with concern.

'I am sure, Balthazar.' Anna's hands were on her hips as she gave her orders. The straps of her bag and her scabbard crossed her dark jacket like bandoliers and the slim, rayskin handle of the sword jutted above her right shoulder. 'But,' she continued, 'whichever way you go, you go via Crazy Boris. OK? Check that Boris and Pacer are all right. Then meet me at Ethel's.'

'Anna, I like your plan,' approved Balthazar.

'Good,' replied Anna. 'It's our only one.'

'What about Trick?' asked Gemma. 'She can't stay here.'

Balthazar sniffed the air, sniffed his pipe bowl which he tapped out before dropping it in his pocket, and then sniffed the air again.

'Trick's coming with me,' said Anna. Trick stayed by the window, chewing her lower lip. 'It's OK, Trick,' smiled Anna. 'If there's any trouble, you run, to let the others know. You don't have to stay. But I need someone fast and brave to be a messenger if there's a problem.'

Trick was by Anna's side at once. 'I wasn't frightened,' she insisted. 'I was just thinking.'

'Trick,' said Anna, crystal blue eyes unblinking beneath her straight black fringe, 'you are one of the bravest girls I know.'

Anna knew Chess; they were friends. Trick grinned back at her.

'What's the matter with you?' Anna was irked by the big man's sniffing.

'A smell,' murmured Balthazar, eyes closed. 'A bad smell.'

'Cats,' suggested Anna. 'Or damp.' But she sniffed, and for a moment, caught something in the air that was neither cat nor damp. Something fine, vaporous, almost alcoholic.

Balthazar opened his eyes in a flash. 'Mist.'

Anna looked over to the window. It was fogged with grime, but on the other side the wall at the end of the back yard was clear to see, and so were the tenements beyond.

'No,' said Balthazar. 'Mist from the vortex. A pathway into the deep vortex has been opened.' His eyes were huge. 'Something is coming from the vortex, Anna. It is coming here.'

'The tesseract.' Anna spoke quickly, recalling the device that was no larger than a ball of sticks and which Balthazar could use to navigate his way into and through the vortex. She'd been with him before when he had used it. 'Can't we get away using that?'

'Anna,' rumbled the big man sombrely. 'That would lead us into the very jaws of whatever is coming our way.'

'OK,' said Anna, decisive. 'We have to stick with the only plan we have.' Calmly, she asked, 'Is everybody ready?'

Everybody nodded.

'Good.' Anna strode to the back door and pulled it open. 'Now, run.'

Box heard the door close. The crew room was hot and the edge of the ceiling was illuminated dimly with a red glow which meant that, exhausted as he was, his dozing had been fitful and uncomfortable. It was a small room: bench seats around the walls, a couple of GPUs stowed in recesses and a table at the centre, big enough for six people. There were sleeping pods off the room, a shower, a latrine and a corridor which led to a tiny kitchen. Also in the corridor was a narrow set of rungs running up and down. Box had stuck his head in the pipe-like stairwell and guessed that the rungs allowed access to the engines and the armaments.

He sat up, disorientated at first. He had to blink Strulf's corpse out of his eyes. Then he remembered that he was lying along one of the bench seats and the door to the loading bay was a couple of metres from his feet. A slim, burgundy-edged figure had entered the crew room.

'Shh,' whispered Shera, and Box could see that she had a finger to her lips.

'What are you doing?' Box propped himself up on his elbows.

'Your guard dog's asleep,' murmured Shera, sitting on the edge of the table and sliding along it so that she was right next to Box. 'Even battle-hardened commodores have to sleep from time to time.' Her voice was deeper than usual because she was speaking so quietly.

Shera's body was haloed by the red glow, but her dark eyes still glinted. Box sat further back in his seat, not sure how he felt about the snout being so close to him. Even though her voice was quiet, her breathing seemed loud and he could feel her looking at him: *really* looking at him.

'What are you doing here, Shera?' he asked.

Her smile gleamed in the red-fogged darkness of the hot room. 'Talking.' She shrugged. 'I like you.'

Box didn't want to go down that route. 'No. I mean, why are you here? Why have you been with us?'

Shera sighed. 'I can't tell you, Box. Honestly, I can't tell you. But I was sent to help you. You have to trust me.' She leant forwards and her warm, smooth palm brushed Box's left cheek. Box sat back as if he'd been burnt.

Shera laughed. 'What's it like, being a snout?' she asked him.

'I'm not exactly a snout,' Box replied, trying to laugh lightly.

I sound like an hysterical girl, he thought, wondering whether he should exit from the crew room now.

'I like being a skin,' whispered Shera.

Box swallowed but his mouth was parched. 'So do I.'

'You know, most shape-shifters *like* going skin-side. They *wish* they were skins. That's why they usually hate skins.' She brushed back a stray strand of black hair. 'They're jealous of them.'

'Oh.' Box noticed that Shera was pulling the hem of her T-shirt free from her combat trousers.

'I've been to the skin world.' Shera had slipped off the table and was standing by Box's feet. 'For work. I never liked it all that much.' She shrugged, slim shoulders rose and fell, glowing red. 'But you know what? Going with you will be different, Box. You're not like other skins.'

'I'm not?' croaked Box.

Shera leant forwards. 'You're better.'

'No,' gulped Box. 'No. I'm rubbish. Really rubbish. I'm a street rat. Street rats are at the bottom of everything, and that's me.'

'That's the skin-world, Box. Ridiculous.' She laughed. 'Now, I hope you don't mind, but since that's where we're going, I have to go skin-side. And going skin-side fully dressed is like being buried alive in a sleeping bag.' Her laugh was gentle. 'Please, don't be embarrassed while I change.'

Box heard Shera's clothes hit the floor. He looked for somewhere to look.

The door to the crew room burst wide open and the lights came on. Razool stood in the doorway, eyes puffy with sleep and the HV magnum in his fist, levelled at Shera's head.

Shera turned to Razool and flashed a big smile. Box grimaced to see the long, bare fangs in such a smooth, pretty, skin face.

'Your teeth,' observed Razool, one eyebrow raised.

'Oops. Forgot.' Shera laughed, artlessly.

Razool eyed Shera from top to naked toe and shook his head. 'Sorry Box, but I don't get skins. You all look freshly peeled.'

Box stared at his toes as if nothing in the world could be more alluring.

'Going to tell me what was going on?' enquired Razool, magnum lowered.

'I was changing, Commodore, just changing,' said Shera cheerily, dressing.

Box looked over. 'That's all. That is *definitely* all.'

Razool slammed the gun back in its thigh holster. 'He looks terrified,' he said, and left the room.

Box followed Shera out.

Razool was waiting for them in the bay. 'We're here,' he said. 'The destination marker woke me up. Just in time,' he added, darkly.

'Here? Already?' Box was amazed.

'Hey.' Razool punched him in the chest. 'I said I was good. We're in your forest, near the edge of your city.'

Box nodded. 'OK. Good.' Then he blurted. 'No. *Bad*. The ship'll be seen.'

'It's all right. I can set it in dimensional slip mode when we leave.'

'Make it invisible,' explained Shera.

'Not just invisible,' said Razool. 'It won't be here at all. But it will be in this place when we need it.'

'In the space inside other spaces,' suggested Box.

Razool clicked his tongue against his teeth. 'Moments of sheer brilliance. You amaze me, Box.' Then he held out a handset no larger than a mobile phone. 'We can trace the ship and recall it with this.'

'Don't you want to stay here?' asked Box, suddenly feeling a responsibility, a weight, as if his world was pressing on the outside of the loading bay airlock. 'Or do you want to go? I mean, this is my problem now.' He laughed, almost in bafflement. 'I mean, I'm home.'

Razool snorted. 'You know the answer to that, Box. We help each other. You might be a skin but you're the best friend I've ever had. And you were my only friend when it mattered.' Razool had a way of smiling and looking grave at the same time. 'Loyalty, Box.'

'And I've gone to the trouble of getting changed,' smiled Shera.

'Didn't look like you were having a lot of trouble to me,' muttered Razool.

Box licked his teeth. 'We're going to need clothes. You and me, Zool. Shera's OK.'

Shera smiled at Razool.

'And we need a car, to get to the city,' Box added. 'It's a long way to walk.'

Razool ran his fingers through his mane and cocked his head to one side. 'Where do we get clothes or a car without being seen first?'

Box gave a modest smile. 'Watch the master.'

Night, or very early in the morning. They stood at the edge of the forest, a spit from the main road. On the other side of the road, the forest continued. Behind them were pine trees, dense and wreathed with mist. And somewhere, within the space of those arboreal spaces, the pilot ship was hidden. Looking right, down the long black run of the road, was a sky, orange across the entirety of the treetops: the glow of the city.

'This is where we bring swiped motors,' said Box, the late autumn air cold in his throat. 'Race them down this road. Then dump them back outside the city.'

'Why?' asked Razool, unimpressed.

Box shrugged and shivered, but the cold air anaesthetized the ache from the worst of his cuts. 'Dunno. For a laugh,' he said, grimly.

'Skins,' scoffed Razool. 'They make no sense. Now, remember, no families. No children. No hurt. Understand?' The snout was adamant.

'Yeah,' Box assured him. 'I know what I'm looking for,' and with a sly grin he added, 'It takes a swipe to catch a swipe.'

Dozens of cars had passed before Box spotted what he'd been waiting for: one headlight dim and one not working at all, engine screaming, hurtling down the road like it was trying to take off.

'A Ricochet 59,' he murmured. 'Nice.'

Box waited until the car was no more than a hundred metres away before stepping into the middle of the road.

When Shera went to pull him back, Razool grabbed her smooth, human-skinned wrist and kept her in the trees. 'He can travel through brick at three hundred metres per second. If the car doesn't stop, Box won't be the one calling the mechanics. And watch the guns,' he added, brushing pine needles off the two magnums and the mouse, which lay on the forest floor by their feet.

The music was so loud and the car was going so fast that the driver didn't notice the figure rise out of the mist until there were seconds to go. Automatically, he stamped on the brake, grabbing the steering wheel like it was a snake, writhing through his grasp. The rear end of the car swung left and right and the tyres screamed and the driver's eyes nearly burst from his face.

'Get out of the way,' yelled the front seat passenger, as if that would make any difference.

The car screamed. The driver screamed. The front seat passenger screamed. The back seat passenger screamed. The brakes shrieked. The tyres were chewed by the tarmac, leaving stripes like black crayon, smoking.

Screaming, shrieking, smoking, the car scraped to a halt in time for the chrome front bumper to smash into Box's shins. The bumper squealed, buckled and then clattered off the front of the car. Once it lay still on the floor, there was silence. Smoke and mist rolled upwards, and through it walked Box.

He pulled open the driver's door. 'Everyone out,' he snapped.

Knees weak, shaking, stunned into silence, everyone got out.

Box stood them in a line and looked them up and down.

'He's got holes in his arms,' blabbered one weaselly youth.

'Want holes in yours?' snapped Box. Heads shook. 'Then shut up.'

Nobody said anything else to this youth in torn combats, who was caked in blood and dirt, had muscles like iron and metal holes in the back of his shoulders and his elbows.

Box saw what he wanted. 'You . . . and you. Strip.'

'But it's cold,' said the weasel with jeans cut so fashionably they hung below his underpants to which they were attached by strings.

'Don't worry,' growled Box. 'You can have mine. *Strip.*'

When Razool emerged from the trees, one of the thieves began to scream, but he clenched his mouth shut when the alsatian-faced snout produced an HV magnum.

They exchanged clothes quickly. When they had finished, Box was wearing a pair of jeans and a black T-shirt and Razool was dressed in a pair of black denims, a black hooded top and a black leather jacket.

'Keep the hood *up*,' Box warned him.

Nobody took the stringy jeans.

'What'll we do?' squealed the weasel as Box, Razool and Shera jumped into the car.

'Walk,' suggested Box. 'You need the exercise.' He turned the key and the sports car rumbled. 'Nice.' He revved the engine.

One of the thieves shouted at the open driver's window, 'Don't I know you?'

Box looked at him coldly. 'Maybe.'

'Well, what do we say? If anyone asks, what do we say?'

Box slammed the car into gear. 'Just tell them, Box is back.'

The tyres spun, the engine roared and the car screamed down the road towards the city.

CHAPTER 14

Anna had only been to Ethel's flat once before. It occupied the basement level of a terraced house west of the city centre, but although the terrace was smart, Ethel's flat wasn't. It was a dingy, smelly apartment, rank with the odour of Ethel's two cats, Argus and Sekhmet. After Anna had been there, she'd felt like she needed a good wash. But right now, Ethel's flat was the most desirable location imaginable.

In the depth of the night, that lull before the first inkling of morning, the city was still busy but there were fewer people on the streets. The roads and highways and overpasses still rolled with vehicles, and the windows of the towering office blocks still glittered with light. Occasionally, Anna spotted a bug-eyed, late-night employee drift past a window, wraith-like, shirt sleeves rolled up, as if the office world was a different universe from that which swam in neon-orange fog and freezing night outside.

But with the pavements almost empty, Anna and Trick could flit through the foggy darkness swiftly, taking cover in alleyways or down basement steps whenever they heard the growling motorbikes of the hunters who were patrolling through the mist. There were many more hunters out tonight than usual and Anna knew that was because they were looking for her, and because they were rounding up any street rats they could find. The truce, if it had ever existed, was over; with Chess out of the way, the hunters were tracking down rats with an appetite that was ravenous.

Anna and Trick pressed their backs into the cold bricks of an alleyway that was still thirty minutes from Ethel's flat. Engines rumbling, a pack of hunters slowly ghosted past the mouth of the alley, motorcycle chrome glinting through the drifting vapours. Anna waited until the rumble was beyond hearing, and even then, she didn't unpeel herself from the shadows immediately. She sniffed, seeking the sharp scent of mist behind the air that numbed the back of her throat with cold and the whiff of petrol. But there was nothing.

'OK,' she whispered. 'Let's go.'

They crept from the alley, hugging the walls, aware of the risk of running into foot patrols. At the end of this street there was a small church enclosed by black railings, its high walls and tower looming above the broken trails of fog. The road ran left and right in front of the church. They would need to go left.

They walked, but walked quickly. They had already decided that running made too much noise. Trick was sniffing as she trotted by Anna.

'Runny nose?' asked Anna, long legs going no faster than Trick could manage without breaking into a run.

Trick shook her head and said nothing.

'Cold air?'

'No,' said Trick.

Anna stopped and Trick said, 'I think I can smell that funny smell.'

Anna rested a hand against Trick's arm as she tasted the air, and although the odour was almost imperceptible, she knew the little girl was right. The scent of mist was there, seeping out behind the other smells of the street. Even in the short time that Anna had stopped, it became more intense.

'We keep going,' said Anna, now beginning to jog towards the church.

'Can we run? Can we run?' asked Trick. The least brush of frost hoared her copper fringe. Anna realized how cold the skin was on her own forehead.

'Maybe a little faster,' agreed Anna. The smell had suddenly become much stronger. From the wall to her right she heard a patter of stone, as if a lump of brick had just crumbled. There was a bang, a scrape, another fall of brick debris and then silence: a silence of fog and the sharp smell of mist.

Scuttling, scraping sounds, up the wall to her left and then a shape, swift and slender, onto the roof where it vanished from view.

They had come to the end of the street. 'Maybe,' ventured Anna, 'we run a lot faster.'

But Trick had stopped and was pointing up at the church. Anna followed the line of the little girl's finger and saw two shapes, one on either side of the church tower. Her breath billowed and she wiped her eyes to see more clearly. The figures could easily have been mistaken for gargoyles at first, crouching on the stone, high on the tower. They were narrow bodied and silver-grey, like metal. Their long thin arms and legs were hunched up as they clung to the stone and even through the murk, Anna could see the long iron spikes that bristled around their wrists and ankles: spikes which had been driven into the stone, allowing the creatures to hang, frog-squatting against the wall. Their heads were crowned with long, metal spines too, and were tilted as they watched Anna and Trick below. Their blank, skull-socketed faces were motionless as ice.

'OK, Trick,' breathed Anna. 'They're coming for me. Just me.' She could feel the little street rat's body trembling. 'I'm going to run that way. There.' Anna pointed right, to where a single-storey warehouse sat beneath a gloomy overpass, 'and you're going to run that way.' She pointed in the direction that they would have taken together. 'Get to Ethel's, right? Get help. Get Ethel.'

Trick nodded.

'I'll go first, Trick, OK?' Anna had a firm grip on both the girl's arms. 'They'll come for me. Then you run. You run as fast as you can.'

'OK, Anna.' Trick struggled to speak through chattering teeth.

A third creature had joined the others on the church tower, darting up the wall, left and right, swift and sharp as a lizard.

Anna heard a minute scraping from the rooftops behind and turning round to look, she saw two spine-crested figures, one squatting on the gable-end of each terrace, both looking down at her.

Fog rolled through the streets. There was a gentle fall of stone.

Anna breathed slow and deep. 'Promise me, Trick, you'll run as fast as you can?'

Trick nodded. From the distance came a rumble of motorbike engines.

Anna stroked the barbed-wire tattoo, then began to sprint. With a crunch of brick, the creatures turned and raced after her.

The Ricochet 59 growled down the One Hundred and Third Overpass and sped towards the Cones, the six enormous skyscrapers which soared above every other part of the city skyline.

'A couple of wrong turns,' explained Box. 'I don't drive round the city usually.'

In the back of the car sat Razool, hood pulled over his alsatian face as far as possible, the HV magnums and the mouse beside his legs in the foot well. Shera sat in the passenger seat. Box turned the radio up, tapping the leather steering wheel in time to the hard beat of the music.

'You like this?' asked Razool, taking a swig from the single bottle of strince he'd found in the pilot ship's galley.

'Yeah,' Box shouted at the back seat. 'Your dog ears too sensitive?'

'It's not music,' growled Razool. 'It's just noise.'

'I like it,' shouted Shera, feet on the dash and comfortable in the bucket seat of the sports car. 'I did a job a couple of years back, undercover, in a club in this city. They played a lot like this.' She laughed, teeth bright, white and neat. 'Kind of got into my head after a few weeks.'

'What were you doing in the club?' asked Box, suspicious.

'Work,' replied Shera, breezily.

'Were you a hunter?' Box hadn't forgotten the Inspector, the first snout he had ever met. And one of the worst.

'No,' Shera assured him. 'Enforcing rules isn't my style.'

Box nodded. 'Yeah, I believe that.'

Razool grunted from the darkness in the back of the car. 'Don't believe too much, Box. Our pelt friend says far too little about her *work*.'

With a scream of tyres, Box handbraked the car round onto the opposite carriageway. 'Now we're heading in the right direction,' he said.

'You sure you've driven one of these before?' enquired Razool.

Box turned up the music and Shera grinned, her pretty face flashing beneath the street lamps. But then Box caught something in his rear-view mirror that made him swear.

'What?' asked Shera.

Box scowled. 'Crashers.' The patrol car was racing up behind them, lights strobing.

'Pull over,' said Shera.

Box blinked at her. 'Are you joking?'

'No. Just do it, Box. You'll see why.'

Box heaved a sigh. 'I don't know why I trust you,' he muttered.

'Neither do I,' commented Razool from the back. But Box pulled over, turned off the music and cut the engine. He waited to see what would happen next; he'd been signalled to stop by the crashers many times in the past, but he'd never complied, and when, eventually, he did stop, it was only to get out of the car and give it long legs.

His window was down already so the officer poked in his head and said, 'Lost?'

'No,' said Box.

'OK,' said the officer slowly, condescending. 'Then you must be driving like a moron for fun. Is this your car?'

Box stared ahead stonily and said nothing.

Eyes adjusting to the dim interior of the vehicle, the officer looked Box up and down. 'You been fighting?'

Box was aware of another crasher, coming up on the other side of the vehicle. He was aware also of the way the crasher who was questioning him had dropped his hand to his belt where his sidearm was holstered.

'I want you out,' commanded the officer. 'All of you. Out.'

'Well,' Box said to Shera, in snout, 'that went well.'

'They're both out of the car,' retorted Shera. 'When I say go, you drive.'

'What are you grunting about?' snapped the officer. Then he stared into the back of the car. 'You, take your hood down,' he ordered.

When the shadowy figure did nothing, the officer repeated his demand. 'I want to see your face.'

'He wants to see your face,' said Box, in snout.

'What the hell are you saying?' fired the officer.

Shera caught Box's eye. He inched his right hand towards the ignition.

As the second crasher rapped on Shera's window, the first shouted, 'Show me your face.'

Razool pulled back the hood and roared.

Shera barked, 'Go.'

Box turned the keys and slammed down the accelerator pedal. Tyres screamed on tarmac and the car leapt forwards. At the end of the road, Box cut the corner and the car slid but he turned the wheel into the skid, bounced off the kerb and pulled the nose of the car round.

'See,' said Shera, 'I've given you a head start.'

'Not the way I'd have done it,' muttered Box, hearing the sirens behind him. But he was far enough ahead to lose the patrol car now. With a screech of rubber, he spun the car left and off the main road, knocking down a bollard in the centre of the junction.

'Do all skins drive like this?' asked Razool.

'Would you like to have a go?' asked Box, negotiating a side street of double-parked cars.

'No thanks. I've been drinking,' said Razool, and he took another slug of strince. 'But if you want my advice ...'

Box turned the radio back on, louder than before. Shera laughed. Box laughed. This felt good: good music and a good chase with the crashers. Even after they had lost the crashers, Box kept the music up and his foot on the gas. But in this part of the city, the mist had thickened, filling the streets with clouds that glowed in the neon and made it difficult to see. There was a crossroad up ahead so he eased up, although he was still going faster than any jack would have dared. He wanted to get to Ethel's.

It would have been easy to miss what was happening down

the street that ran off the crossing, but as he flashed by, Box caught a glint of chrome and three dark figures surrounding one small one.

Three hunters; one small street rat. Not fair, thought Box.

He stamped on the brake and turned off the radio.

'What now?' asked Razool, as the radiator ticked and the cold fog swirled.

Box put the car into reverse and backed up until he was level with the street. He peered through the murk. The hunters had dismounted and were pushing a little girl from one to the other. One of them grabbed her hair and yanked it and she shrieked, a terrified wail that cut through the fog like a razor. Another hunter whipped out a slipjack, an extendable cosh, and waited for the hair-pulling to finish. He slapped the cosh against his gloved palm patiently. His silver death's head glinted on his shoulder.

When Box slammed shut the car door, it was like an anvil strike.

When the hunter with the slipjack saw the figure marching out of the mist, his eyes narrowed and he waited, cosh in hand. The figure was unarmed but heavily muscled. No matter; he knew the places to strike to put the hero down. A thin smile curled the edge of his lip.

'You can stop there,' snapped the jack-booted hunter as Box strode forwards.

Box didn't stop. His eyes were riveted on the creep who had the little girl's hair in his gloved fist.

As Box pushed past the first hunter, he slashed at the side

of Box's knee cap with all his strength. He might as well have been striking an iron post. He howled and dropped the cosh, arm jarred to the shoulder as Box snatched the stun stick out of the next hunter's fist and snapped it between his hands.

Then he felt the jab of a gun barrel against his temple and the hammer clicked back to strike. The hunter let go of the little girl with his other hand and sneered. 'Say goodbye.'

Shera kicked up and high, so high that Box could have sworn she did the splits standing. The gun spun out of the hunter's grip. Fast as a snake-bite, her right hand struck sideways, into the hunter's throat. Box heard the hunter's voice-box crunch before he dropped to the ground.

'Thanks,' said Box.

Shera smiled brightly. 'I told you, Box, I'm your guardian angel.'

Hood down, Razool raised his HV at the two remaining hunters. Guns were dropped to the floor. Razool growled an order.

'Go,' translated Box.

Before the bikes had cleared the street, Box was kneeling by the little girl. He noticed the barbed-wire tattoo on her cheek.

'Trick?' he whispered.

The little girl with the copper hair threw herself against Box's solid body and began to cry. She kept saying his name.

How long since he had heard a human say his name: a street rat, one of his own people? He didn't know what had been happening, but it was good to be back. It felt right.

'Hey, Trick, what's going on?' Box squeezed her in his arms to let her know she was safe.

Trick pulled her face from his chest. 'We need Ethel. I've got to get to Ethel but they stopped me. The hunters stopped me.'

'What's happening? Why'd you need Ethel?'

Trick wiped her face on her jumper sleeve. 'There's things going to kill Anna. Down there.' She was pointing down the street, past the church tower which broke the mist a hundred metres off.

'Who's Anna?' asked Box.

'Chess's friend,' sniffed Trick.

An electric heat coursed down the back of Box's neck. 'What's going to kill Chess's friend?' he growled, peering into the fog the way that Trick was pointing.

Anna knew that she would never outrun the creatures; she would have to hide and hold them off until help came. If she could. And if she couldn't? If she couldn't, they would kill her as they had been sent to do.

She sprinted around the side of the low warehouse, scanning it for a way in. Footfalls came after her through the fog and she heard metal spines smash brick as one of the creatures flung itself at a wall and swiftly scrambled up and onto the flat roof.

Long grass had grown between the paving slabs. It was wet and it soaked Anna's jeans as she ran round the back of the building. Behind the warehouse there was rubble-strewn grass littered with the rusty skeletons of prams and bicycles, corroded oil drums and crumbling chunks of foam from the insides of car seats. The premises had one rear window which was protected by an iron mesh. Anna's fingers seized on the rusty mesh and she pulled. It sprang away easily.

She grabbed a lump of concrete from the long grass and bashed out the glass, then hoisted herself over the jagged ledge, making sure not to roll over the bare skin of her hands. She landed flat on the cold floor. Outside, the creatures were rustling through the grass. The roof rapped hollowly under running feet.

Anna was in an empty room. There was a door that she knew would lead into the rest of the building. She wanted to barricade herself against the creatures if she could, so she crossed to the door and pushed. It opened. This next room was bigger, running the length of the rest of the warehouse. The walls were lined with metal shelving and there was a desk and metal chairs. Grilles had been fastened over the windows.

Figures were climbing in through the smashed rear window. Their barbed heads and limbs were black against the orange fog outside.

Anna entered the long room and slammed the door shut. Cracks of neon from the metal-shuttered windows sliced the darkness. She pushed the desk across the bare concrete floor, jamming it up under the door handle. It hit the door at the same time that something whumped into it on the other side.

'OK, OK,' whispered Anna, backing into the centre of the room. 'Breathe slow. Breathe slow.' She closed her eyes, ignoring the hammering of metal on wood, the squeal of splitting timber, the ripping open of the roof. Then her right hand reached behind her shoulder and silver cut the dark as she drew her sword.

The door was nudging the desk back at the same time as the wood was being pulverized; plaster began to collapse from above her head as the roof was torn up. Anna shook debris out of her long, black hair and stepped back. Now she was standing in the centre of the room.

With a crash, a spike-ringed fist smashed through the door. It was snatched back, levering out a whole panel. At the same time, the ceiling to Anna's right caved in, plaster and rafters collapsing with a huge billow of dust. Now a frenzy of kicking and tearing sent the desk screaming back and smashed the door to smithereens. Four lithe, metallic bodies slipped through the opening, long spines catching the wan light.

Anna glanced over her shoulder to see two more figures drop through the hole in the roof. They landed, crouching, and one of them swung its wrist down at the floor. It watched the girl, eye sockets black, soulless, as it dragged the spine through the floor, gouging a deep rut in the rough concrete.

There was no way that help would be here in time.

The six creatures encircled Anna. She stood with both hands holding the sword, lightly but firmly, and she turned on the spot to watch them, counting the number of vicious limbs. She would fight like a demon, but she knew that this time, that wouldn't be good enough.

Anna's lips moved as she whispered to herself, 'I need a little miracle. Just a little miracle.'

CHAPTER 15

The wall erupted.

There was a man, a young man, and he had bulldozed straight through it. Lumps of brick bounced off his broad shoulders and crashed across the floor.

Without breaking his stride, he kicked a steel chair hard across the length of the room. It rocketed into one of the metal bodies. The creature exploded into tiny fragments which glittered in the air before fading and then vanishing altogether.

Sword in hand, Anna watched agog as he blocked a wheeling metal arm with his own forearm before delivering a crunching roundhouse kick that smashed the assailant out of existence.

Now two creatures attacked. The man ducked a spine-encrusted fist and jumped a scything ankle before catching one long, metal leg in his hand. As he did so, he dived to the floor, flinging the leg and the rest of the metal beast behind him and into the body of the other. The air was filled with the sound of glass shattering as the two collided and then were gone.

That meant two were left, and the dust was still only settling from where this figure had exploded into the warehouse.

He had rolled up and back onto his feet as the fifth creature sprang at him. His back was to the desk. Even though there was only a moment to think, Anna saw how the man's coal-dark eyes watched his leaping adversary, calculating. The spike-bearing wrists slammed down, and it was only with a heartbeat to go that he rolled aside. Anna had to stop herself from gasping.

Spikes thudded deep into the wood of the desk. Before they could be whipped out, the man had his hand on the back of the creature's neck. He rammed its head down so hard that the crown spikes whammed full depth into the wood. Then he delivered a spinning kick, turning full circle in the air to send the front of his shin straight through the narrow body.

The shimmering dust was settling as Anna saw the final attacker spring to a wall and off the wall towards the man's head. He hadn't seen it. But Anna had seen enough to realize how to fight the metal assassins; had realized that she had to strike through their bodies. As it flashed through the air, so did Anna's blade, and the two met in a detonation of glassy fragments.

The man turned in time to see the last fragments vanish. His ox-broad chest was heaving, his short, black hair was full of brick dust and his forearm was bleeding.

Anna sheathed her sword and put out her hand. 'I'll say this only once,' she said. 'That was amazing. My name's Anna Ledward and I am very, very pleased to meet you.'

The young man looked at her, frowned and looked about the room before eventually saying, 'My name's Box. Box Tuesday. Where's my sister?'

'Box?' repeated Anna, gobsmacked. She had heard Chess talk about her brother, but she had never said he was anything like this. He looked about eighteen, not fifteen, had been sculpted out of blood-spattered muscle and he had a stare like a machine-gun on rapid fire.

'Chess said you'd joined the enemy.' As soon as she had said that, Anna knew how stupid she sounded and wished she hadn't said it at all.

'Chess gets things wrong,' was all Box said in response. He walked past Anna and she saw the holes above his elbows.

'You've been hit, badly,' she gasped.

'No,' said Box, still taking stock of the room. 'Those are for bolting on my armour.' He looked about again. 'No more spindle rippers. Good.'

'Bolting on your armour?' laughed Anna, smoothing her fringe with her fingers. 'What, they just screw it on to you?'

'Yes,' said Box and he turned his eyes on Anna. 'You talk like a jack.'

Anna put her hands on her hips. 'Oh, here we go. The "you're a jack and I'm just a street rat" routine.'

Box looked her up and down, shook his head to himself and walked over to the hole in the wall, where two more people had appeared. Anna followed behind him.

'Thanks would be polite,' she said.

The machine-gun stare turned on her. 'Thanks? For saving *your* backside?' He rubbed his jaw, licked his teeth in a way that Anna had never seen anyone do before and then he almost smiled. His face was much nicer when he smiled. 'OK, thanks. It might have got messy if you hadn't of stepped in like that. But where's my sister?'

Anna knew that the answer wasn't a good one. 'Captured,' she said, cautiously. 'By the Twisted Symmetry.'

The smile vanished.

Then Anna saw what was waiting for Box by the smashed wall. There was a young woman in black combat gear. Her hair was tied back in a ponytail and her eyes were sharper and smarter than her pretty face first appeared. But it was the tall, rangy creature with a snout like a dog's, a smooth-haired face and a long mane that made Anna take a step back.

Even though he wasn't looking at her, Box must have been aware of her because without turning round he said, 'It's OK. His name's Razool and he's on our side. He's a Dog Trooper. A snout. And this is Shera.' Then Box began to talk with Razool and the young woman. Their language was harsh and guttural and utterly meaningless to Anna.

Trick slipped into the warehouse and against her side.

'Just listening to them gives me a sore throat,' whispered Anna.

'It's Box,' said Trick, and Anna could tell how proud the little girl was. 'He's just given the hunters a good kicking.'

'Yeah,' whispered Anna. 'From the look of it, Box could give anything a good kicking. Sparkling conversation might be more of a challenge, but in the kicking department, he's a natural.'

She watched Box talking with the others before adding, 'He's *nothing* like Splinter.'

Trick could tell that it wasn't a criticism.

They collected the weapons from the car and then walked to Ethel's flat. Nobody stopped them, even though they strode through the fog making no attempt to hide, and Anna knew that this was because everything had changed. Box had returned from wherever he'd been and this was something the Twisted Symmetry had never expected. For the time being, the enemy had been wrong-footed, and for the first time in a long while, Anna felt as if her safety did not depend upon *her* efforts alone. Tonight at least, nothing else would attack them. Anna felt a little lighter, a little happier, and she knew that it was because of the person who was marching through the fog beside her.

Anna watched Box carefully: how he talked quietly with Razool; how he joked with the woman who moved with the lithe strength of a panther and whose name was Shera; how his face was the sort of face that set itself entirely by what he was thinking. He was inhumanly strong and tough as iron, literally it seemed, but he wasn't complicated: not complicated like Splinter and not complicated like Chess. But he was here to look for Chess and plainly, he was going to keep on looking for her, smashing down as many brick walls as it took until he found her.

He hadn't spoken to Anna since asking if she was coming to Ethel's with the rest of them. So Anna chatted with Trick and noticed that Shera was watching *her*.

Anna didn't like the way the woman observed her, sidelong. In particular, there was something about her eyes that didn't seem right: an animal intensity. They glistered when she laughed, which she did a lot, but it was when she was serious, when she was concentrating, that Anna saw the fierce heat within.

They were at Ethel's flat within twenty minutes.

Down below the pavement level, light leaked through the filthy net curtains. Box led the way, followed by Razool, Shera, then Trick and finally, Anna. Box rapped on the door.

'Not making your usual entrance?' quipped Anna.

Everyone looked at her without laughing.

'It's a joke, Fido,' she said to Razool, who didn't understand her.

The door was opened by Pacer.

'Box?' he asked, tentatively. Straightaway, Anna could tell that there was more than just Box's reappearance on Pacer's mind.

'Pacer!' Box laughed. 'Your hair's grown.'

'Yours hasn't,' said Pacer. He frowned. 'Are you OK, Box? You look ... different. You look like you've been in a war.' Pacer considered the way Box looked at him and said, 'OK, maybe you *have* been in a war. You better come in.'

'Don't worry about Razool,' said Box as they filed past Pacer. 'He's with us.'

Pacer nodded. 'Nice work, Box. You've made friends with Wolfman.' Then he saw Anna and smiled, but the smile was drawn. 'You made it.'

'Nearly didn't,' said Anna, relieved that she was back with someone who spoke with her normally. 'Box showed up in time. A lot of action and then a lot of silence.'

Pacer looked sceptical. 'Box and silence occupy two different universes.'

'Perhaps he's changed since you last saw him,' suggested Anna, entering the flat and wrinkling her nose at the taste of cat in the air. 'Just take a look at his arms,' she whispered.

'The muscles?'

'No, the holes somebody's drilled in them.' Anna gave Pacer a knowing look.

'Holes?'

Anna nodded. 'For his *armour*.' Then she asked, 'What's the matter?'

Before Pacer could answer, there was a crash of chairs from the kitchen. Anna ran down the little hallway to see Captain Riley on his feet, his chair on the floor behind him and his nine-millimetre pistol at Razool's head, whilst the tall Dog Trooper had whipped out a handgun the size of a power drill which was in the Captain's face. Razool's lips were drawn back and Anna could see his teeth which were very white, very sharp and very long.

'Boys, boys, boys,' said Ethel, dumping her knitting on the small kitchen table as she stood up and raised her pink and wrinkled hands. 'Captain, you must put your gun down first.'

'I don't see why,' Captain Riley hissed through gritted teeth.

'Because you were the first to draw and therefore it is only polite for you to be the first to *with*draw.' Ethel frowned censoriously. 'Come along, dear.'

Captain Riley eased his finger off the trigger and lowered his weapon. As he did so, Razool's muzzle relaxed and he holstered his handgun.

Ethel smiled. 'There. Now, that's better isn't it?' Then she spoke to Razool in a language that Anna didn't understand and which wasn't the same as the language she had heard Box speaking earlier.

'It's Chat,' said Box, who must have guessed how baffled she was. 'A kind of universal language. Well, snouts speak it, and Ethel does. I do a bit, too.'

Anna nodded and muttered to Trick, 'What a relief; it turns out I exist after all.'

Trick grinned at her.

Box was watching Ethel and Razool but he added, 'He's telling her he's a commodore in the Fourth Navy and she's apologizing for Captain Riley's behaviour.'

'That's rich,' muttered Captain Riley. 'She's usually the first to shout, "Get stuck in".'

Anna said, 'Thanks, Box. Is Shera in the navy too?'

Before Box could answer, the woman in black combats pushed herself away from the wall against which she'd been leaning and said, 'No.'

Courteously, Ethel inclined her head towards Razool, who inclined his head towards her, and then she said to everybody, 'Now, we're all on the same side so let's be friends.' The kettle whistled on the hob. 'Trick, my love, would you make everyone a nice cup of tea?'

Trick turned off the gas flame, poured the boiling water into a large metal teapot and then began to lob teabags from a finger-smeared tin into the pot.

'Now, I know that not everybody knows everybody else,' began Ethel, resuming her seat, 'but on this occasion, introductions will have to come at the end.' She removed the knitting needles and the skein of purple wool from the table and dropped them in the lap of her baked bean-stained gingham apron. Then she clasped her hands together and said, 'We have far more important things to talk about first.'

Captain Riley was sitting back at the table. So was Commodore Razool, although Anna could sense how on edge he was. For that matter, Captain Riley looked none too at ease sitting across from a high-ranking Dog Trooper. Box stood behind Razool, translating occasional phrases into growl-speak for Razool's benefit, and Pacer sat on the stainless steel sink, pensive. Shera leant against the door frame. Trick clattered crockery.

Anna propped herself against the end wall of the little kitchen.

'May I say how lovely it is to see *you*, dear?' and Ethel reached up and pinched Box's dirt-smeared cheek between her nubbly finger and thumb. 'Although,' she added, with a look of disappointment, 'you look like you've been fighting again.'

'It was nothing much, Ethel, honestly,' muttered Box.

'And,' continued Ethel, 'they don't appear to have been feeding you properly. You're all *defined* and I'm not at all sure I approve of what they've done to your joints.'

'It's for my armour,' explained Box.

'Is it, dear?' Ethel raised a thin grey eyebrow. 'How remarkable. And what have you become? A knight of the realm?'

'No. I'm a dreadbolt.'

Ethel pursed her already well-pursed mouth. 'Hmm. I'm

not sure that's an aspect of your character we need to encourage. However,' she beamed, 'I'm sure your strapping muscles and extraordinary perforations will all be helpful in the long run.'

'You haven't changed, Ethel. Have you got food as well as tea?' Box smiled.

Much better with a smile, thought Anna.

'You know me, dear. There's always something in the back of the cupboard. I never throw away a slice of bread. But first, to business.'

Trick poured out tea for everybody except Razool, who made it clear he didn't want any.

'We have a number of problems,' began Ethel. 'There is the Endgame order, which very nearly cost us at least one of you this evening. And there is Balthazar.'

Pacer caught Anna's eye.

'It seems,' explained Ethel, 'that Balthazar has decided the time for unilateral action has come.' When nobody said anything, the old lady elaborated by announcing, 'He has taken Gemma to go to look for Chess.'

Pacer spoke up. 'After we went to see Crazy Boris, who it turns out was all right and was singing with his plants ...'

'Singing *to* his plants,' corrected Anna.

'I was there,' stated Pacer, snappy at the interruption. 'He said he was singing *with* his plants. Well, after we got there, Balthazar said that Gemma wanted to help Chess and that they had to go before it was too late.'

Two cats entered the kitchen, one large with dozens of dark spots on its grey fur, the other, sleek and tortoiseshell. They bounded onto the kitchen table in silent unison and sat there, blinking at everybody. Anna watched the tall, black-maned Dog Trooper closely.

'It's all right,' crooned Shera from the doorway. 'We don't chase cats.'

Anna felt embarrassed for some reason, and wondered why the woman said 'we' when talking about snouts.

'Balthazar used his tesseract and they just went.' Pacer clicked his fingers. 'Like that. I saw them go.'

Even with the tesseract, Anna couldn't see how Balthazar would get through the fractal code when nobody else could. 'How can he hope to help her?' she asked. 'If we can't get through this code, why can Balthazar?'

Ethel sighed wearily and looked down into her teacup. Her scruffy, grey fringe stuck out like dirty goose feathers. 'We have been in this position before with Balthazar Broom. He has an amazing knowledge of the vortex. He was a Guide long before he met any of you. If anyone can navigate a way through the code, he can. However, it will not be a safe passage, nor would it enable us to mount the type of operation required to effectively achieve our aim.' She sighed again. 'As ever with Balthazar, great knowledge does not walk hand in hand with great judgement.'

Ethel slurped some tea. Anna observed how the pale lips puckered over the rim of the cup like suckers to draw up the steaming liquid. Ethel sighed, this time with satisfaction, smacked the asbestos lips together and continued.

'Balthazar is correct about this, however: Chess is entering a critical stage. Her mind, her thoughts will become increasingly distorted, by anger, by despondency. She will *want* to destroy. She will believe that that is *her* choice. She will not understand that that is exactly what the enemy wants.'

'So, Balthazar is right then,' said Pacer.

'No,' insisted Ethel. 'He is wrong because he *cannot* do this. The enemy hold Chess secure. He doesn't know where or how. He simply has the means to bypass the code and a head full of disastrously good intentions.'

'That little girl is in a lot of danger,' muttered Captain Riley.

Anna knew that he was talking about Gemma. 'Do we know exactly where Chess is?' she asked.

'We have drawn plans, thanks to the stalwart work of the COE.' Ethel pointed to a row of cupboards. 'Up there. Plans of the relevant parts of the warp station. Plans indicating the circumstances in which Chess is being kept.'

'How've you got them?' Anna was astonished.

It was Box who answered her question. 'Dermacarts.'

Anna had no idea what he meant. 'Is that human, dog, Chat or a language all of your own?'

'Actually,' said Box, 'I can talk with lizards too. Psychopathically.'

'*Tele*pathically, dear,' corrected Ethel, gently. 'But your appetite for the exotic is one of your unexpected and remarkable attributes.'

'How's your appetite for spikers?' joked Shera.

Box held up a finger and thumb with barely a micron of air between the two. Shera laughed. She said something in dog to Razool and Razool half laughed too.

'I still don't know what a dermacart is,' said Anna, aware that she sounded pettish, even though she didn't mean to.

Ethel smiled at her reassuringly. 'It's a map, my love. Made out of human skin. Our agents burn them into their own skin and when the enemy find them and kill them and send the bodies back, unwittingly, they send us the map too. A sad and distressing tactic, but a highly effective one.'

'It's how we first stole a slice of the Twisted Symmetry's brain,' said Box.

'Oh,' said Anna. 'I know about that.' And now I sound like a four-year-old. And I'm older than him by at least a year.

'We have the plans,' said Ethel. 'We have the means of transport, thank you, Commodore. We have the team, or we will have, once the boys have made proper friends. But, what we don't have is the means of breaking the code. And, until we can break the code, we can't help Chess. It's a frustrating state of affairs, my loves.'

A telephone rang.

Ethel dug under her knitting and into the front pocket of her apron and produced the mobile which she put to her ear. Her brow creased deeply and then, quite suddenly, she smiled with delight. When she spoke, it was in the same language in which she had greeted Razool. Anna stood with arms folded, wondering what it was that had elevated Ethel's mood so dramatically.

'This was where we first saw a spindle ripper. In this kitchen.'

It took Anna a couple of seconds to realize that Box was talking to her.

'Pardon?' she asked.

'In here,' repeated Box, 'was where we first saw a spindle

ripper. See that broken plaster on the wall.' Anna could see the cavity inches from her head. It looked as if a chunk of wall had been scooped out. 'Yeah, that was where it tried to hit me. Nearly got us too.' Anna nodded, not wanting to stop this unexpected torrent of information. 'I batted it away with a frying pan. It floored Splinter with a tin of beans.' Box laughed but looked embarrassed. Anna noticed that Shera was watching her as he spoke. 'Anyway, that was how I knew about spindle rippers. That was how I knew how to fight them. If you'd of known that, you'd probably have been all right.'

Anna shrugged. 'I think I needed the help. There *were* six of them.' She noticed Ethel motioning to Captain Riley for a pen and paper.

'Shut up, Pacer,' snapped Box. His face was red and Anna wasn't sure whether it had turned red before or after he'd told Pacer to shut up.

Pacer was smirking. Shera looked at her combat boots, face expressionless.

'Well, now.' Ethel beamed as she replaced the telephone in her apron pocket. 'For those of you who don't speak Chat, and for those of you who do but weren't listening,' one bleary eye swivelled towards Box and then came back in line, 'that was very, *very* helpful. The help does come at a price, but then help usually does.'

Anna noticed Ethel glance towards Box again as she said that.

'What price?' asked Anna, suspicious.

'A price that I am sure we would all agree is worth paying. Worth paying for *this*,' and Ethel tapped the open page of the pocket notebook that lay on the kitchen table.

'Who was it?' asked Box.

'I'm afraid my mystery caller has to remain just that: a mystery caller.' She held up the notebook so that all of them could see the mathematical symbols she had scribbled down during her telephone conversation. 'But here, my loves, is the access code we need.'

It looked like a very long and over-stuffed equation. Anna thought that Ethel looked very pleased with herself when she said, 'That wasn't who I expected to hear from, but I did expect to hear from somebody.'

'You said there was a *minuscule* possibility,' Anna reminded her.

'It's the possibility that matters, not how minuscule it is.' Ethel chuckled and poured herself another cup of tea. 'Anyway, enough of mathematics.' She took a deep slurp and smacked her lips before smiling through steam-fogged spectacles.

'Now, my loves, it's time to rescue Chess.'

CHAPTER 16

From the moment he had smashed through the wall and seen the girl standing her ground against six spindle rippers, Box had thought two things. First, he had thought that she was probably the most beautiful girl he had ever seen. And second, he had thought that she was one of the bravest.

But his blood had been up and he had wanted to know about Chess, and Anna had been like a bossy jack. It had been difficult to talk to her normally. And he didn't really know what to say to her after that so it had seemed safest to say nothing. And then, when he had decided to say something, to tell her about the spindle ripper in the kitchen, it had sounded like he was boasting and Pacer had started taking the rip. So Box had decided to go for silence again. He tried not to look at her too much.

But she was fast; he had seen how quickly she could use a sword. And she was clever. He could tell that by the way she spoke and by the way that she talked straight with Ethel and Ethel didn't treat her like an idiot: not like the way Ethel spoke to Splinter when he had given her mash.

Box wanted to know about Splinter, but the fact that nobody mentioned him meant that he wasn't sure what he would be told if he asked. So he waited for the right time, and watched how clever Anna was with the Link-me she had taken from her bag.

'Are you sure about this, dear?' Ethel was asking.

The Link-me sat on the kitchen table, between the two cats, and Anna sat in front of it on a chair, fingers working the keys like a concert pianist.

'None of us knows how to use the access data,' said Anna. 'Lemuel is a warp. He was once their primary warp. He'll know what to do. We just need to get him to come with us. We need him in the right mood.'

'Hmm,' hmm'd Ethel. 'He has so many different moods, good luck if you think you can find the right one. And how will you get him to come along?' Ethel was standing, cup and saucer at her chest and looking over Anna's shoulder. 'A creature like Lemuel is not given to altruism.'

'He likes me,' stated Anna.

Ethel cleared her throat more briskly. 'That would be a very good reason for a young person like you to stay away from him.'

'I'm not that young, Ethel.'

'You're sixteen as I recall. That's young enough.'

'Nearly seventeen,' muttered Anna. 'And anyway, there's something he wants.'

'There always is,' observed Ethel, sotto voce.

'His body. He wants us to get his body. It's at the warp station. At the same place as Chess.' Anna struck the return key. 'Hello, Lemuel.'

The bird's eye lens on the top of the Link-me glinted. The screen remained dark.

'Still with us, I am very pleased to see,' came the dulcet voice of Lemuel Sprazkin. 'I had every confidence in you.' He sounded less than convinced.

'It wasn't me,' said Anna. 'It was Box.'

Box felt his neck go hot when Anna said his name.

'Then all of us owe a debt of gratitude to Box Tuesday,' said Lemuel, with genuine sincerity. 'It seems that in the great playing field of the Crystal Wars, you have your very own horseman. He's quite the knight.' A rill of laughter burst from the Link-me.

Anna was businesslike. 'Lemuel, we have the access data for the fractal code. We need you to break the code so we can get Chess. Probably you will need to upload yourself back into the Link-me, which I know is a come-down from your current cyberspatial position. But in return, we will find your body and bring it back.'

There was a very long pause during which Box was convinced that either the Link-me had lost power or Lemuel had decided to vanish. He heard Razool scratching his chin, thoughtfully, and Box told him what was happening.

'*Has* the power gone?' asked Shera.

Anna shook her head, eyes fixed on the screen. 'No. It's powered by a nuclear cell.'

'That was *my* idea,' said the disembodied voice, emerging at last from the Link-me. 'It is interesting, is it not,' mused Lemuel, 'to consider that had the General not sought my surgical assistance in the first place, you would not be in a position to ask for my assistance now?' Lemuel sighed wistfully. 'Cause and effect; there is, in fact, no logic. And just as puzzling as good and bad.'

'Lemuel.' Anna's voice was penetrating. 'Is this a yes or a no?'

'It is,' said Lemuel, with a tremulous cadence, 'a yes.'

Ethel rattled her cup and saucer and cheered, 'Splendid.'

'But, you must bring my body back here, and only upload my mind once I am back here. Do not put me back in my physical frame whilst I remain within the purlieu of my former comrades.'

'We won't Lemuel, we won't,' Anna assured him.

Trick began to clear the empty cups. The cats bounded from the table and padded from the kitchen.

'But we need you in the Link-me, Lemuel,' added Anna. 'We need you in the Link-me for you to come with us.'

'Ah, yes.'

'Ah, *yes*.' Anna was uncompromising. 'We will be relying on you. We need your mind with us, not just floating about in cyberspace. It's Lemuel in the Link-me, or it's no body. That's the deal.'

'And maybe,' suggested Lemuel, 'at some future date, an opportunity to meet you properly?'

Ethel choked on a mouthful of tea.

'No body, no meeting me properly,' dictated Anna.

'I am putty in your hands,' declared Lemuel.

'I need you to be putty in the Link-me.'

'Very well then,' sighed Lemuel, 'I shall simply imagine that this is an elaborate game.'

'A game with one life. Don't forget that,' warned Anna. 'But thank you, Lemuel. Thank you.'

'I shall prepare myself,' said Lemuel, a little sorrowfully. 'And then I shall tell you how to Link-me me.' There was a highly amused titter.

Razool spoke quietly to Box. 'So the talking's finished?'

'Pretty much, yeah. We've got the data to break into the warp station. We've just got to check out the maps, sort what we're taking, and that's it. Thanks, Zool, This was never your problem.'

Razool shrugged. 'There's no plan. We keep going and see where it takes us.'

'Home, for you, eventually,' said Box.

'Yeah,' grunted Razool. 'Eventually.' He noticed that Pacer was standing behind Box. 'He can't come.'

'Who? Pacer?'

Razool nodded. 'I'm not flying corpses for fun. Whoever he is, this is out of his league.'

'He's my friend,' began Box.

'Then tell him he's not coming.' Razool was adamant. Without another word, he folded his arms and stood by the door, opposite Shera.

Box rested a hand on Pacer's arm.

'What?' It was an accusation, not a question.

'Listen, Pacer,' began Box, switching from snout to skin-speak without thinking. 'When they did this to me, I stopped being like you.' He pointed to the tap above his right elbow. 'Not any better. Just different.' It was hard to know what to say, because Box knew that Pacer wouldn't want to hear this, whatever he said. 'It means that if someone hits me with a piece of iron, the iron breaks. But you're still one hundred per cent genuine human. I mean, look.' He pulled up his trouser leg to reveal the metal beneath.

'Is there a lot more of you like that?' he heard Anna ask.

'That's it, but that's enough,' muttered Box, wishing that she hadn't seen his metal leg: not yet.

Pacer was plainly astonished, but he still said, 'I get it; it's only robots on this rescue mission, yeah?'

'No,' explained Box, 'but it's not going to be great for humans. Not for normal ones anyway.'

'Yeah?' snapped Pacer. 'What about her then? What about Anna?'

She was looking at them. Box knew his face was flushed. 'We need her for Lemuel,' he said, but thinking also that her sword and her brains put her in a special category. But he knew also that there was more to this special category than just a sword and bravery. He tried to ignore how Anna was watching them. Watching *him*.

Pacer bit his lip.

Box had tried to be gentle but putting it straight was simpler. 'This is too dangerous, Pacer. It's not about being brave, it's about not killing yourself. You go, you'll die. You're not coming. That's it.' It felt terrible to talk like this. Pacer was an old friend and he had been there for everyone. And now Box was telling him that he wasn't up to this.

Pacer clenched a fist. His teeth were gritted.

'Don't,' Box warned him. 'You'll break your knuckles.'

'You tell Chess I wanted to come,' he said, speaking slowly, finger in Box's face. 'You do that, right?'

Box nodded.

'You tell her, I didn't care how dangerous it was. Because I don't. Got it? I don't care what happens. I want to help her.' His voice was hoarse.

'Of course I'll tell her,' said Box. He definitely would. If he lived that long himself.

Anna held Pacer's arm. 'Hey, Pacer,' she said, softly.

Pacer stepped away. 'Just make sure she knows, right? I don't care about me. Chess is the only thing that matters.' And without another word, Pacer marched out of the kitchen and out of the flat.

'That's really hurt him,' Anna said to Box.

'You think I don't know that?' fired Box. 'This isn't about making Pacer feel good. It's about getting Chess out and trying to stay alive at the same time.' He went to speak to Ethel, wishing that he could talk to Anna without sounding either wound up or stupid.

Box was the last to leave. Ethel was ushering people out of the front door as if at the conclusion of a delightful tea party.

'You're going to have to coordinate this, my love,' she said to him. 'A great deal depends upon Captain Riley and Commodore Razool, but there is, amongst other things, the language barrier.'

'Ethel,' began Box.

'And I know we need a few days to prepare. For example, your current outfit is a little casual for active service.'

'Ethel.'

'And you need to catch up on your sleep. If dreadbolts need to sleep.'

'Ethel.'

Ethel looked at Box as if she had only just realized that he was a being that did more than merely listen to her. 'Oh, Box!' she gasped, clapping her hand to her mouth. 'How selfish of me. There's that slice of bread I promised you.'

'No, no.' Box shook his head. 'It's Splinter. I need to know about Splinter.'

Ethel exhaled slowly before putting her arm about Box's heavy shoulders. She steered him back into the flat. 'I think that for this, dear, you will need another cup of tea.'

For the next four days, the pilot ship was their base: they slept there, they ate there, they planned there. Razool was able to dislocate it from the Lungs, in the same way that he had concealed it. That meant they were well hidden. When the time came to make the move to Warp Station Eight, the hyperspace jump would be almost immediate.

Box had done his best to keep up with Razool's explanation of wormholes and interstitial particles, but, apart from expanding his snout vocabulary, he had failed to grasp the mechanics. All that Box understood for sure was that cross-universal travel had more to do with mathematics than fuel.

Funny, thought Box, how someone who looked so much like a dog could be so smart. It just went to prove what Ethel always said: appearance could be deceptive.

'What did Ethel say about Splinter?' Anna had asked him.

'That he's dead.'

'Dead!'

'Well, lost, in the vortex she thinks,' said Box. 'But that's as good as dead.'

'I'm sorry,' said Anna. 'I'm so sorry.' Her eyes had been bright and Box realized that a film of tears was welling on her lower lids. 'I've lost a brother. His name was Richard. It hurt. It still hurts.'

'Yeah. It does. I'm sorry, for you.' There wasn't anything else that Box could think of to say. He didn't know Anna at all really, he didn't have a clue who Richard was and he still couldn't absorb what had happened to his own brother.

After all these years, he still didn't understand Splinter, or what he had done, and he couldn't fathom the way his mind worked, except that it was smart. But, maybe, not so smart. It was hard, thinking about him; Box didn't know whether it made him feel angry or sad. So, he tried not to think about Splinter at all and to fill his mind with preparations and with thinking about what lay ahead of them.

But before the subject had been closed, Anna asked, 'Was it the Symmetry?'

'Mostly, yeah,' said Box.

'Same with Richard,' said Anna. 'That's why I want to keep on killing them.' She smiled brightly although her eyes were still wet. 'Funny, how we've both lost brothers.'

'Yeah,' said Box. 'Dead funny.' But he managed to smile so Anna would know he didn't mean to be nasty.

There was equipment on the ship. Razool had found the craft's log book which included an inventory of what equipment was available, from fuses to stem pens. What wasn't stowed on the ship had been obtained by Captain Riley from the COE. He had provided Box with black combats, boots and body armour. There were half a dozen blaze carbines and plenty of ammunition on board and Box still had his HV magnum. And he made sure to slip a stem pen in his thigh pocket. Razool was comfortable in his skin clothes but he accepted an armoured vest and a fresh pair of boots from Riley.

Box was relieved to find that Riley and Razool found it easy to get along in one another's company, after the initial confrontation in Ethel's flat. It seemed to Box that battle-hardened veterans had a way of communicating which didn't require subtle conversation. A shared fascination with weaponry and tactics appeared to be sufficient. But one matter which was a cause of complaint for Razool was his armour, or its absence.

Soon after they had first returned to the ship, Razool complained that his dreadbolt armour had gone missing. He had been right, too. When Box came to look at what had been left on the loading bay floor there was no sign that Razool had ever left his armour there. Even imagining that it had somehow fallen out of the ship when they had first come to the Lungs was fanciful. So Razool and Box were left with the mystery and Shera was left with an even greater degree of distrust from Razool, although Box couldn't see how the missing armour had anything to do with her.

Shera still had her own combats and she armed herself with weaponry from the ship: a carbine, two pistols, two knives.

'Not taking any chances,' Anna had observed.

'Just being careful,' had been Shera's response. She was careful enough to request body armour from Riley too.

But Anna travelled light. She accepted a pair of black combat trousers and a black, loop-shouldered vest, but turned down the body armour. 'It's a trade-off between speed and safety,' she explained to a curious Shera. And no guns, pistols, knives or grenades, noticed Box; just her sword.

Box had watched how she handled the sword when it was in its slim, curved scabbard, how gentle she was, how respectful. It was like she had a relationship with it: like it was a person. And when she had exercised in the woods, when Razool had phased them back in to pick up more supplies or for Captain Riley to consult with the Committee, he had watched how she moved with it. He had watched her whilst he was talking with Razool and Shera, whilst cleaning weapons, whilst exercising his own body, and he noticed how her sword work was so different from the way they fought with the mace-blades: how swift and how neat. How smooth. And she could fight just as well with her eyes shut.

After watching her a couple of times, Box decided that Anna was gentler in her fighting than she was in her talking. But just as clever.

'You must like it, being back with skins,' Shera had said one afternoon. Box had stopped to catch his breath after a series of burning shuttle runs with Shera and Razool, and his eyes had been drawn to Anna who was walking back through the trees, sword across her back in its scabbard. Shera was looking at *him*.

Razool didn't trust Shera, but Box did. If she'd wanted to slab him for whatever reason, she'd had her chance when he'd been on his own with her in the crew room. Whatever else had been going on, she hadn't tried to slab him. In fact, Box liked Shera. She was easy to chat with and she laughed a lot.

'You really like her, don't you?' said Shera. 'You really like Anna.'

'I like the way she looks,' said Box, and he shrugged. 'Doesn't mean I like *her*.'

Shera had straightened her ponytail. 'It helps.'

That had been two days ago. Now they were confirming final details before Razool and Shera settled into the cockpit to take them to the immediate vicinity of the warp station.

The dermacarts had been spread out on the crew room table. The parchment-like sheets were scrawled with ochre diagrams and annotations: the last mortal remains of some of the Committee's most determined agents. Captain Riley leant over them. His body armour and submachine-gun were by his feet, but he was ready for the operation to commence, as they all were. Over his black combats was chest webbing with a couple of nine-millimetre pistols. There were grenades, a torch and ammunition pouches clipped to his belt, and on the left shoulder of his jacket was the grey star in a purple circle that was worn by COE agents on active service.

Riley's finger tapped one of the diagrams. 'This is the complex where the energy transmission takes place. You can see the route of the flat coil accelerators, the FCAs, along here.'

'The Committee's agents are very thorough,' observed Shera, and she ran her fingers delicately over the dermacart. 'This is a very clever idea.'

'Yeah, well it's *our* idea.' Riley looked serious.

Box knew that Riley had been unhappy about revealing the dermacarts to Razool and Shera, but Ethel had insisted that there was no alternative.

'I won't say anything,' smiled Shera. She had chosen to stay skin-side even though her visit to the city was over. Her dark skin was a rich brown in the track lighting of the crew room.

'Once the code is down, Razool will get us in here.' Riley's finger slid to what must have been a corridor right next to the FCAs. 'Just make sure you get the layout in your heads. There'll be no time for maps once we're in.'

'I have committed them to memory, Captain.' Lemuel's voice came from the Link-me which sat open at the centre of the table. 'Just as I have memorized the access data you were kind enough to show me. I will be available for consultation at any time. I may have turned my back upon cyber-power, but it's good to be back amongst friends.'

'The Link-me will stay on ship,' said Anna, 'but all of us will be in contact with one another and Lemuel through the ship's communications net.'

'In combat, communication is key, wouldn't you agree, Captain?' maintained Lemuel, very chatty.

'I agree.' Riley grimaced at the Link-me and shook his head.

In snout-speak, Razool asked Box, 'Does the freak in the machine ever shut up?'

'I'm waiting to find out,' muttered Box.

'The freak in the machine speaks snout,' objected Lemuel, his highly strung cadences strangely sinister in the dog-tongue. 'And since you are going to be depending upon him, you will show a little more courtesy, Commodore. After all, somebody like me probably designed your gene pool.'

Razool gave Box a look which meant that had he a hammer in his fist, the mission would be cut short right now.

'OK, now remember,' Riley said, having waited patiently for the exchanges in snout to conclude, 'getting in should be the easy bit. It gets difficult from here.' His finger came down on a hexagon at the end of the FCAs. 'Chess will be in here, and we'll be relying upon Lemuel to confirm exactly where.'

'Another *starring* role,' proclaimed the voice from the machine.

'She's going to be in one of two places,' continued Riley. 'Either in the energy transmission chamber itself, or in a Möbius cell. We can't break into a Möbius cell so we have to time this for when she's in the transmission chamber. And inevitably, the area will be guarded,' warned Riley, 'but we don't know how.'

'There's quite a lot we don't know,' interrupted Anna.

'Welcome to reality, Anna,' responded Riley. 'We have to react according to what we find. We'll be in communication with one another,' he pointed to the earpieces and throat mikes on one of the benches, 'and in communication with Lemuel. Lemuel, if Chess isn't in the energy transmission chamber, if she's out of phase and in the Möbius cell, we need you to let us know. We can only get her out while she's in the transmission chamber.'

'Never fear, Captain, I shall orchestrate this perfectly,' promised Lemuel.

'It has to work, Lemuel.' Riley was grave.

'You *have* to trust me, Captain.' So was Lemuel.

In the silence which followed, Box adjusted his belt and considered whether he could stomach some chocolate before they went in. His stomach didn't feel much like food; his body was gathering itself for what was about to happen. But Box had yet to encounter a situation where he was rendered incapable of eating chocolate. He found a bar that Ethel had given him, wedged in one of his ammunition pouches, and he ate it with satisfaction.

'Let's run through this one last time,' said Riley.

The first to speak was Lemuel. 'Once the ship is in position, off the station metasphere, I transmit the access data via the ship's equipment, to which the Link-me has been connected. That will break the fractal code, allowing us to approach. Next, as the Commodore takes us in, I enter the station mainframe.' Lemuel giggled modestly. 'One can do these things when one is composed principally of data oneself. And when one is a primary warp.'

'*Has been* a primary warp,' corrected Anna, pointedly.

Riley brought Lemuel back to business. 'Once inside the mainframe, Lemuel will do two things.'

'First,' announced Lemuel, crackling slightly over the Link-me's speaker, 'I shall seal off the energy transmission area. This will prevent other parts of the station from interfering. I will be able to access plans and systems, but I do have limitations. For example, as an *ex*-primary warp, I know that within the transmission area, the system will be self-supporting. I will not be able to override the controls. I can guide you, but you will have to operate the system.'

'And second?' asked Anna.

'Second,' and here there was a pause. Box could sense the excitement in Lemuel's voice. 'Second, I shall find Chess, and establish what state she is in.'

'By this point we will have left the ship,' said Riley. 'We move up this corridor with a GPU in support for medical back-up and illumination, if necessary. By the time we are here,' he indicated the outer edge of the hexagon where the route in ran parallel to the FCAs, 'Lemuel will have established Chess's location. When we know Chess is in the transmission chamber, Lemuel gives us the situation, we go in and we pull her out.'

'And then,' added Lemuel, 'you pull me out. I will have located my body, and I shall guide you. Don't let me down.' With palpable menace, the ex-primary warp added, 'Your success in this depends upon my body.'

'We'll get it, Lemuel,' Anna assured him.

'And Balthazar and Gemma?' demanded Box. They had discussed this before and Box remained unhappy with this part of the plan. As far as he was concerned, they *had* to rescue Gemma; Balthazar too, if they could.

'We get them out. *If* we can,' stated Riley.

Box clenched his jaw and stared at the plans.

'Listen, Box, I don't want to leave that little girl with the warps.' There was no doubting Riley's sincerity. 'But Chess is our priority. If we don't get her out, that's the end of everything.'

'Hey, skin,' growled Razool.

'What?' growled Box.

'Do you really think he's going to leave the little girl?'

Box shrugged.

'He's got whelps of his own.'

'You know that?'

'Yeah, I know that. How do you think we pass the time while you're gawping at the girl with the sword?'

'I don't gawp,' protested Box.

'You were kind of looking at her just then, Box,' teased Shera.

'Now focus on the mission,' said Razool. 'You're a soldier. We go in there, we get the job done, we pull out. And we'll bring Chess and the girl with us. He can't say that but it's what he'll do. It's what we'll all do. Got it?'

Box nodded. 'Yeah. Got it.'

Razool shook his head. 'Skins: soft as whelp butt.'

'Finished?' asked Riley.

Razool nodded.

'OK,' said Riley. 'Time to go.'

Box knew that Anna was looking at him, so he looked away, made sure his ammunition pouches didn't rattle when he shook them, checked his HV magnum, did anything to avoid having to look at those cool, unblinking eyes, because whenever he looked at them, he either said something stupid or became mute as a mollusc.

The best thing was to think about Chess. Thinking about

Chess cleared everything else: cleared thoughts about Splinter and Anna; focused him on what was about to happen. This was what it had all been about: the Fleshing yards, the penal battalions, the dreadbolts. He missed his little sister, he wanted her back, he wanted to stop the Symmetry from hurting her. Whatever was happening, they'd be with her soon. They'd get her out. And Gemma too.

He slammed the HV back in its holster.

Shera put her hand on his shoulder, gently. 'You OK?'

Box nodded. 'Yeah.'

Then she smiled and kissed his cheek. 'Just remember, Box, I'm your guardian angel.'

Gemma held Balthazar's hand. It was enormous. In his other hand was the staff. He used it to help identify the reachings on their way through the vortex, tapping the narrow and invisible surfaces as they walked through the misty-white nothingness.

She didn't know for how long they had travelled because there was no night and no day, and she felt neither hungry nor thirsty. But all the way, Balthazar had entertained her with stories. He was a very interesting man.

She knew that Ethel had once told him off very badly. Chess had told her about that, and that was why he was on Surapoor when they found him; or he had found them. It was where he'd been sent as punishment. But before all of that, he had been a Guide. Guides worked for an organization called the BIG Cooperative, or BIG for short, and their job was to navigate paying customers through the vortex.

Guides knew everything about the vortex. That was why Balthazar had been able to help her squeeze through a horrible, turbulent part that he had called the fractal code.

'Only room for a big one and a little one to pass,' he had said, which had made her feel special, even if it had been frightening.

There were all sorts of rules that Guides had to follow, but it turned out that Balthazar wasn't very good at following the rules, which was part of what led to him getting into trouble in the first place. When he'd been punished, he had kept his wooden staff, or thumper, to give it its proper name, but they had removed the metal base which was what Guides could use to smash reachings in an emergency.

All in all it had been a very interesting journey through the vortex, particularly, as Gemma had pointed out to Balthazar, for someone who had never been through the vortex before.

'We're here now,' said Balthazar.

'Already?' Gemma was surprised. The time had gone very quickly.

'Yes. Look.'

Gemma looked ahead, at the drifting vapours that looked like all the other drifting vapours. But this time, there were shapes and textures beyond the vapours: darkness, metal, maybe a ladder.

Balthazar collapsed the little ball of sticks which was called a tesseract and which he looked through to help him find their way along the reachings.

'Next time I use this it will be to take Chess home,' he said.

Gemma gave Balthazar's hand an extra-hard squeeze.

CHAPTER 17

Box was in the loading bay of the pilot ship. The GPU emitted a dim red glow. Beside him were Anna and Captain Riley. Shera and Razool were in the cockpit. After the momentary suspension of sensation during the jump through hyperspace, he could feel the ship drifting now, slowly descending to one of the docking bays that gave access into the energy transmission zone. His blaze carbine was in his hands and Lemuel was in his ear. Lemuel was in everybody's ears.

Lemuel was giving instructions to Razool in snout. 'Dock at the bay located at eighty degrees and three thousand, four hundred metres from our current position. I have entered the mainframe: I'm inside the station communications system. They haven't identified our incursion through the fractal code. It appears that the Symmetry have identified two interlopers. Humans. A man and a girl. By a happy coincidence, they have attributed the ripple caused by our passage through the code, to them.'

Anna was against Box's right shoulder.

'They know about Balthazar and Gemma,' he whispered. He heard Riley swear quietly.

'We have to get to them first,' was all Anna said.

I don't think it's going to be so simple, thought Box to himself. Getting Chess out would be lively enough, and they were honour-bound to extract Lemuel's body, too. Balthazar and Gemma created yet more uncertainty in a situation that was already lethally unpredictable. All of them were desperately reliant upon Lemuel Sprazkin.

Trust no one, Ethel always said.

Box checked his HV magnum was secure. He'd checked it about three times already. They couldn't have been more at the mercy of the Twisted Symmetry's *ex*-primary warp. But they *had* to trust him.

'Lemuel?' It was Shera's voice, friendly, close in the darkness, not speaking snout.

'Yes.'

'Why do you want your body back?'

They were flying into a warp station, embarking upon a rescue mission that would be as lively as it was uncertain, and he was listening to a disembodied conversation like this. It seemed so ridiculous that Box realized he was smiling to himself.

'With some authority,' said Lemuel, 'I can say that being a mind without a body is not a lot of fun. Omniscience and omnipresence are all very well, but without a body with which to taste, touch, enjoy beautiful things, they are merely long words. Being in a body is the only way of coming close to being human, and being human is designed for intensity. There is nowhere else I'd rather be.'

'Would you like to be a human, I mean a *real* human?' asked the pelt. This wasn't just curiosity; Box could hear longing in her voice.

Lemuel thought for several seconds, during which the ship continued to drop, before saying, 'I like trying. But it is complicated if it doesn't come naturally, as you must know.'

'Love is what makes it complicated,' said Shera.

'In my opinion,' observed Lemuel, 'love is what makes it work.'

The hard vowels and growls of snout-speak came over the net. 'We're nearly there, Lemuel. Give me a sit-rep,' requested Razool.

Lemuel's report switched between skin and snout-speak. 'The situation is as follows. I have shut down the alarm system connecting the energy transmission zone with the rest of the station. I have sealed off routes in and out, although none of this will become apparent to the enemy until they try to react to our infiltration. Inside the docking bay there will be drones.'

'Which are?' asked Anna.

'Workers. Engineered by the warps for basic staffing tasks. There are two sections to the docking bay: a reception unit and beneath that, a guard room.'

'What guards?' asked Riley.

'Drones again. Basic humanoid structure and physiology.' Lemuel hesitated. 'Three unarmed in the reception unit. Four armed in the guard room. The guard room will give access to the service corridor that follows the FCAs to the transmission chamber.'

'And Chess?' As far as Box was concerned, this was the important thing. Everything depended upon Chess being in the right place. And knowing where she was would make it feel as if he was a little bit closer to her already.

'She is in the transmission chamber,' said Lemuel. 'Undergoing the energy transfer process.'

'Right.' Box's jaw clenched as tight as his fist. Now was the time to get in and get her out.

'We're there,' said Razool.

'Everybody ready?' enquired Lemuel.

Box heard the metal clamp and the gas seal on the other side of the loading bay door.

There was a series of acknowledgements over the net.

'Good,' announced Lemuel. 'Then let the party commence.'

The door slid apart. There was a short connecting tunnel at the end of which was a transparent, metal-reinforced panel. Box could see movement on the other side of the panel: two, no three bodies in blue boiler suits. Hairless heads, pasty skins, shark-eyes, thin mouths, no noses but two slits in the front of their faces.

'Could have made them prettier,' was Anna's initial observation.

Box felt the press of bodies as Shera and Razool joined the rest of them in the loading bay. Weapons and bodies were jammed against one another, and the GPU.

'We have to take them out without alerting the guards below,' said Riley. He reached down to his boot. 'Knife,' he whispered.

'Or a quick assault through, and down to the guards fast,' suggested Box.

'No, too much noise,' disagreed Riley. 'Too much time for armed response.'

'Not if we're *really* fast,' insisted Box.

He heard Anna huff, felt her supple, strong body push against his and then she had dropped into the short tunnel.

'Anna!' Riley's voice crackled over the net.

Anna's sword remained across her back. She strode up to the entrance panel, slapped the door release, marched into the docking unit and felled the first drone with an elbow strike to the throat and the second with a spinning roundhouse kick to its head. The third had time to snatch a wrench before Anna blocked its swing with her left forearm, punched it straight to the face twice with her right fist and sent it hurtling backwards by a jumping front kick to his chest.

'Come on,' she said, as the third drone slid down the wall to the floor.

'The rippers didn't stand a chance,' muttered Box as he and the others jumped into the docking bay entry. Razool and Riley were at the front.

'We have to be fast,' urged Lemuel.

'We are being,' snapped Box, Shera marching at his side, and carrying a blaze carbine too. Behind them came the GPU, ordered to stay at the rear until called in.

Anna was at the top of a staircase. Her eyes were bright and her black hair gleamed in the white light of the docking unit. She looked over to Riley and Razool and held up four fingers, then immediately indicated two to one side below and two to the other.

Riley nodded, left his submachine-gun down his back and ripped the two pistols from his chest webbing. He vaulted the handrail, landing halfway down the metal stairs, arms outstretched in opposite directions and angled down slightly. Both pistols coughed twice. Riley holstered them and nodded to the others.

Anna strode past Box and patted him on the shoulder. 'Don't worry, Box,' she whispered. 'I'm sure we can find you a small wall to headbutt.'

'Didn't notice you complaining last time,' he muttered, but he was relieved to be making progress.

The VDUs and monitors in the docking unit and guard room didn't matter: they had Lemuel. When they were not communicating, his flow of information was constant.

'Through the exit door you enter the FCA service corridor. It runs for approximately three hundred metres and then you come to the first section of the energy transmission area. The area is divided into a central chamber, which is where you will find Chess, and an outer area which connects with other routes in, and importantly, the containment units which is where *you* will find the rest of *me*. You will have to cross the outer area to enter the central transmission chamber . . .'

'OK, Lemuel. That's enough for now,' said Riley, who was at the door which would lead to the FCA service corridor.

'I am your eyes and ears, Captain,' remarked Lemuel. 'And you are my hands and feet.'

There was a steel wheel in the door. Riley spun it and the

door swung inwards slowly. Razool knelt at the emerging opening, the HV in his darkly haired hand. Behind him, back against the wall was Shera, blaze carbine against her chest. As soon as the way was open, they checked the corridor was clear. Razool gave Riley a thumbs-up.

Box could see that at the far end of the corridor there was a high doorway, as high as the entrance to a dockyard warehouse. This would be the entrance to the transmission chamber. It was dark within, but as they watched, they heard a high-pitched screeching and then the darkness began to flicker with a stark, electric-blue illumination. The screech rose in intensity, the dancing light became arc-weld bright and then there was a rush of silence and darkness.

'What the hell was that?' murmured Riley.

'We've got to get to Chess.' Box stepped into the corridor. Shera rolled round the door to cover the opposite direction.

'OK, Lemuel,' said Box. 'What's in there; what will we find?'

Lemuel's response was immediate. 'Chess will be suspended, aerially, between two metal plates. There will be stairs up to a control platform from where you will be able to shut off the energy that is currently being fused. You will be able to release Chess.'

'Can't you?' insisted Box.

'No, I've explained before, that part of the station is sealed against external control; very wise, if you want my opinion. So, you will have to get in there, if you want to get your sister out.'

'Lighting?' asked Riley.

'There are spots in the ceiling but nothing else. The chamber is currently manned by the primary warp and two others. So three warps in all. A trio.' And a little peal of laughter.

'And guards?' Riley spoke quietly but urgently. 'Armed guards?' He unslung his submachine-gun.

'They have access to this area, but there are none patrolling at the moment.'

'None that he sees,' cautioned Anna.

All of them were in the corridor now. It was empty. They had a clear run to the transmission chamber entrance. Shera was relaying information to Razool in snout.

'Come on,' urged Box. There was no need to wait any longer. They had to get to the chamber, take out the warps and shut down the system. It would be straightforward, so long as they were fast.

But Lemuel had more to say and the way he said it made Box's skin go cold. 'Something tells me that there is excitement amongst the warps in that chamber. Something tells me that they are about to ... feed.' His voice swelled into the last word, hanging upon it longingly.

'Gemma,' said Anna.

'Now,' shouted Box. Carbine at his hip, he began to sprint towards the high, dark entrance of the transmission chamber.

Gemma and Balthazar had emerged from the vortex onto a catwalk. In front of Gemma was a desk of dials and switches and out in the darkness that faced her was a girl, caught by the piercing beams of spotlights and hanging in the air.

'Chess,' gasped Gemma. She looked awful: her hair was matted over her face, her eyes were sunken, her cheeks were haggard.

'Chess,' shouted Gemma, voice reverberating throughout the huge chamber.

Chess raised her head. Her cracked lips moved and faintly, she said, 'Gemma?'

Chess was suspended between two flat sheets of metal which were attached to robotic arms. The arms reached down from the darkness. Gemma couldn't see what was holding Chess in the air, but there was blue smoke coiled around her arms and body.

'What's happening?' Gemma asked Balthazar, her eyes filling with tears.

Balthazar shook his head as he looked at the controls. 'I have brought us to exactly the right place, but this is more complicated than I had expected.' He rubbed his thick, grey-black moustache, perplexed. 'I had hoped to snatch her and take her home.' He sighed. 'But now . . .'

'What did you expect?' The figure loomed out of the darkness only metres from Gemma. Gemma gasped as the thin woman in the black and silver gown stepped closer. Her hair was short, like bristles, she wore tiny black spectacles clipped to her hard nose, and she lifted a hand and pointed the middle finger at Balthazar.

A long needle, thin as hair, extended from the gap between finger and nail and pricked Balthazar's neck as he opened his mouth to speak. The huge man croaked, collapsed to his knees and fell flat forwards.

Gemma looked up. Behind the woman with the black glasses stood two more people dressed identically to her. One of them was bald and his head looked as if it had been stitched together from two halves because a thick, ugly scar passed from the bridge of his nose right over the top of his cranium. The other didn't have a face at all. There was a metal grille from its brow to its lower jaw, and pressing against the thin bars of the grille, almost pushing through, was what looked like glistening, red meat.

'Save the old one for later,' said the female with the black spectacles, and she kicked the motionless body of Balthazar Broom.

'Gemma,' shouted Chess.

The bottom part of the woman's face began to move as if something hard was stirring behind her tight lips and jaw.

Gemma stepped back, unable even to scream.

The female spoke. 'But we shall eat the young one *now*.'

Box and Razool were at the front, powerful legs driving them forwards. Box focused on the entrance to the chamber and what he would find beyond it. There would be no time for thought; there could be no hesitation. Acquire targets: fire. He knew that Razool would be thinking the same. Back to back, they could cover the chamber within a matter of seconds. The warps wouldn't be expecting them.

Surprise increases combat effectiveness by a factor of six hundred per cent.

Then, someone walked into view. A figure in a black gown, criss-crossed with silver lines, just like the gown Lemuel had been wearing the first time Box had seen him. A warp's gown: a warp.

Razool was raising his magnum.

Box prepared to drop to his knee to take aim.

'Warp approaching,' Lemuel was saying.

The warp's hand dropped to its belt, as if taking hold of something. Then the warp vanished.

Razool and Box hesitated. But a moment later, the warp came into view again in exactly the same way as before. However, this time there were four other figures with it: drones, but they were naked and their bodies were as featureless as dough. Their forearms were silver, like metal, like the arms of the dreadbolt heavy weapons units. The drones turned to face down the corridor, raising their metal forearms, which Box now saw were barrelled, like chain guns.

'Get down,' yelled Captain Riley.

There was an instant to think.

As the barrelled forearms of the drones began to turn, Box and Razool caught one another's eye. Both of them knew that to be anywhere in the corridor would be instant death. So everybody had to get out of the corridor.

Razool dropped his left shoulder and rammed himself into the left wall of the corridor.

Anna was standing beside Box. With his left arm, he grabbed Anna round her waist and then drove his right shoulder into the wall next to them. There was an explosion of concrete as he bulldozed through the wall, holding Anna tight and protecting her body from the impact with his own. They landed on the other side, with Box on the floor, Anna on top of him and a covering of concrete lumps and dust over them both.

The rounds from the chain guns crashed down the corridor, raking walls and floor until the dust was like smoke. Box heard them pinging off the casing of the GPU that had been following.

Anna brushed the dust off Box's face. 'I've never jumped through a wall before,' she said, 'but I think I could get used to it.'

Box's arm was still around Anna's waist. Her body was warm and strong, and even though it was dim where they were lying, her eyes were bright and very close to his. For a moment they said nothing. They just looked at one another. Box felt as if he could lie like that, looking at Anna's eyes, without ever having to get up again. But there was a burst of gunfire from across the corridor.

'Don't you think we should join in with everybody else?' whispered Anna.

'Yeah,' said Box, unenthusiastically. He slipped his arm from around Anna's waist. At the same time, he realized how uncomfortable it was, lying on his blaze carbine and shards of concrete.

They were in a channel that contained a huge pipe. The pipe ran parallel to the main corridor and was as thick as Box was tall. Along its surface were narrower pipes and tubes, interrupted by valve wheels at regular intervals.

Light entered the channel via the hole smashed in the wall by Box. Box scrambled across to the hole. Outside, the corridor was dust, gun smoke and screaming rounds. Nestled in the breach on the other side of the corridor were Razool and Riley. Riley's submachine-gun coughed furiously, while Razool was blasting with his magnum, taking cover as the return fire came in. Shera moved in the dust behind them.

'They won't go down,' Riley was saying over the net.

'I've hit two but they're still standing, Box,' shouted Razool in snout.

Box pulled out his HV and leant against the wall.

'They should be down. They should be down,' Riley kept complaining.

Anna's voice came over the net, cool and clear. 'Where are we, Lemuel?' Box could see her inspecting the pipeline in the gloom.

'You and Box are in the FCA duct,' came Lemuel's voice.

'Carrying the energy to the transmission chamber?' confirmed Anna.

'Constantly,' came the reply.

Box waited for a lull in the firing before moving up the duct a little way and elbowing a fresh hole out of the wall. He snatched a glance through the hole. The four drones were in a line at the end of the corridor, barring the way to the area immediately outside the transmission chamber. And behind them stood the warp they had first seen. Rounds pounded in and Box pulled his head back.

'They're taking no damage,' he reported to whoever was listening. 'They're just standing there. They're not even wounded.'

Apart from a fierce exchange of gunfire, there was no response. But they couldn't spend forever pinned down like this.

Box remembered his training: in a contact, take out the commander when you can. He had had a clear view of the warp. He took the HV in his left hand and waited for the current exchange of fire to cease. There was a smack of concrete falling from the roof of the corridor and hitting the floor. He counted to three. Then he leant through the gap he had elbowed, dropped the magnum level with the warp and squeezed the trigger.

The magnum blasted and the round whammed into the warp, smashing him to the floor. The drones were slow to react. As two sets of smoking, gun-barrelled forearms turned towards him, Box let off two more rounds.

WHAM. WHAM.

Both hit home, straight into the bare chests of the drones. But unlike the warp, they remained standing. Not only did they remain standing but their bodies seemed to absorb the HV rounds. In fact, Box could have sworn that they enlarged by a few inches and returned fire with even greater intensity than before.

'I don't get it.' He rolled away from the gap in the wall and leant against the pipeline. 'I hit them and it seemed to make them stronger. How do we fight something like that?'

Lemuel chortled. 'I know what you're up against. They were in development when I was the primary warp. They might even have been one of my very many bright ideas.'

'Yeah, well stop congratulating yourself and start telling

us what we have to do,' came Riley's voice over the net.

'Don't get shirty with me, Captain,' warned Lemuel.

'Come on, Lemuel. Tell us about your bright idea.' Anna was still inspecting the pipe.

'Endotherms.' Lemuel laughed knowingly. 'They feed off energy. You shoot them and they absorb the energy into their bodies. They grow; become stronger. Isn't that clever? And so simple. They make perfect guards. The more you fight, the greater their might.' Lemuel cackled. 'Oh, I like that: the more you fight, the greater their might. I'd be a whiz in advertising.'

'Lemuel,' snapped Anna, 'how do we kill them?'

The warp considered this momentarily. 'I don't think you can.'

'Can we follow this wall cavity up the corridor?' asked Riley. 'Get in that way?'

'No, Captain,' said Lemuel. 'The passages don't cross the outer area around the transmission chamber, and the chamber itself is encased in solid concrete. It's a sealed unit once you get across the outer area: too thick even for a dreadbolt to make holes in.'

Anna looked at Box. 'They feed on energy. How do we stop them having energy? How do we take energy away from them?'

'I don't know.' Box couldn't fathom what Anna was talking about. 'Make them do some exercise?' he joked.

'Yeah, very helpful, Box,' snapped Anna, exasperated.

'Well how should I know?' protested Box. 'I do the walls; you do the science.'

—[301]—

'Got it!' Anna slapped the pipe. 'Lemuel, do the FCAs get hot?'

'Of course,' replied Lemuel. 'Very, very, very hot.'

'And how are they cooled?'

This time, when Lemuel chortled he said, 'You clever girl.'

'I don't get it,' said Box.

'Endotherms feed on energy, right?' said Anna.

'Right,' said Box, none too sure what Anna was driving at. But he liked the way she thought things through. Sometimes her mind was like a blaze carbine on rapid fire.

'So intense cold will have the opposite effect. It'll slow them down, maybe even stop them.'

'Correct,' interjected Lemuel with approval. 'Around the FCA pipeline, there should be a cooling jacket of subsidiary pipes carrying liquid coolant under high pressure.'

'I can see them.' Anna was standing over the pipes, a silhouette with hands on hips.

'The gas flow is controlled by valves,' continued Lemuel.

'Yup. I can see them too.' Anna turned to Box and said, 'OK, I know what to do.'

'Let's hear it,' said Riley. 'We're low on ammo and going nowhere.'

Anna gave orders swiftly. 'Razool needs to go up the passage about thirty metres. When I say, I want him to smash out the wall; create a distraction. When the guards open up, we'll get them with the freezing coolant.'

'Best plan I've heard so far,' agreed Riley.

Box relayed the instructions to Razool as he followed

Anna along the pipe. He didn't get the science but that didn't matter. They were here to rescue Chess, not to provide target practice for a gang of crash-test dummies with chain guns. He pushed the blaze carbine on its strap behind his back and holstered the magnum.

The endotherms were blocking the end of the corridor and Box and Anna knew where that was because they came up against solid concrete.

'OK,' said Anna, voice close in the darkness. 'How are your muscles?'

'Superhuman.' Box grinned. It was nice to be able to give a reply like that when asked the question, particularly when it was Anna asking the question. He pulled a torch from his webbing and clicked it on.

'Thanks.' Anna worked back along the pipeline. 'OK. I'm going to turn this wheel to shut off the coolant. See this?'

There was a junction where all the cooling pipes conjoined to become one pipe before entering the concrete. Box nodded.

'We're level with the guards. You're going to pull this pipe free, smash the broken end through the wall and I release the coolant. It comes out under high pressure and we hope it works.'

'You're telling me.' Box took a quick look at how the single coolant pipe was bolted to the FCA pipeline. He'd need to free enough pipe to pull it across to the wall.

Anna turned the valve wheels firmly shut on either side of Box's chosen fracture point. Box kicked off eight U-bolts with the heel of his boot. The insulated coolant pipe squealed as he wrenched several metres free. He twisted it back and forth until the section of pipe sheared in two. A cloud of icy vapour rose from the broken ends of the pipe.

'It's like having my own human tool kit,' smiled Anna.

'Yeah, a tool kit that has to save your butt on regular occasions.' Box grimaced as he tugged the open-mouthed pipe to the wall.

'OK, Zool,' he said. 'It's demolition time.'

Out in the corridor, there was an explosion of concrete followed by a blazing exchange of gunfire.

'Now!' Box rammed the mouth of the pipe into the wall. It cracked through the concrete. Anna spun the valve open. Box pushed himself back as freezing liquid sprayed out like water from a fire hose. Through the vaporizing fountain, he saw all four guards turn, stagger and cease moving altogether as the freezing liquid reduced them to a state of total inertia.

'It worked,' said Box, looking out at the pink-grey figures, immobile as stone.

'Of course it did,' said Anna, turning off the valve. She patted Box on the cheek. 'It's called science,' she whispered.

They stepped through the breach in the wall made by the pipe, cautiously negotiating the evaporating pools of coolant. Razool, Riley and Shera were already walking up the corridor towards them, the bullet-scored GPU at their rear. But there was no time for congratulations.

From inside the transmission chamber, white-blue light crackled as energy screamed through the air.

'I'm getting Chess.' Box ran for the opening into the chamber. It was dark on the other side of that opening.

Lemuel had told them to expect three warps. But warps weren't endotherms; the body in the black and silver gown, slumped on the floor outside the chamber proved that. Box unslung his carbine.

Anna was at his heels.

They had to move fast. Box wanted to get Chess out now, and if Lemuel was right, anything could be happening to Gemma: warps loved children.

Box dashed through the vaulting entrance. Immediately, he found himself back outside the chamber. Suddenly, Anna was by his side. Both of them ran at the entrance again. But the moment they seemed to pass it, both of them found themselves back outside again.

'What are you doing?' asked Shera, astonished.

'I don't know.' Box looked at the opening as if there might be something he had missed. 'We can't get through.'

Riley was looking left and right, down the passages that ringed the chamber. 'We *have* to get through.'

'We have a little problem.' It was Lemuel, crackling over the net, and sounding tense.

Immediately, Box knew that this was not going to be a *little* problem.

'What?' asked Riley.

'The energy transmission process will continue to run. There is now, however, no cooling system in operation. This is most unfortunate. Over the coming minutes, the whole system will experience a temperature rise of stellar proportions.'

'Meaning?' Riley's teeth were gritted.

'By my calculations, this zone will go into meltdown in

approximately twelve minutes. The whole warp station will be a raging ball of flame approximately thirty seconds after that.' Lemuel sighed pitifully. 'And we were doing so well.'

CHAPTER 18

Shera whipped out a knife and pushed it deep into the nape of the neck of each of the static drones in turn. 'Severing the spinal cords,' she smiled. 'We don't want an action replay when these dummies thaw out.'

'What about the door?' demanded Anna.

'The problem,' said Lemuel, defensively, 'is that the plans don't show everything. And whilst I'm chatting with you, I am also having to withstand the primary warp's efforts to trigger the alarm and re-open this area to the rest of the station.'

'Can you do that?' asked Riley. 'Can you hold the area?'

'Fortunately, this is a contest of primary warp against primary warp and I am every bit as sly as Petryx Ark-turi,' tittered Lemuel. 'Quite a lot slyer, in fact. And this has distracted the warps from their feeding. But since this whole station will vaporize within the next quarter of an hour, the contest is entirely academic.'

Anna was at the entrance to the chamber. 'Whenever we go in, we come straight back out.'

'It must be a teleport-based system,' observed Lemuel.

'I have never encountered this particular application before, but it seems that there is a teleport screen across the entrance. It will transport you back outside once your body has crossed the threshold.'

Box scratched his head. 'But it can't be impossible to cross, otherwise how would the warps get in?'

'He's right,' said Anna.

'Don't be too amazed,' muttered Box.

'Well, what about the warp that we saw?' Shera motioned to the body. 'He must have been about to go in.'

In his mind, Box replayed the final moments before they had taken cover in the walls. What did the warp do? Before they saw him with the endotherm drones, what did he do?

His hand was reaching for something: reaching for his belt. Box had assumed he was going for a weapon, but he never had a weapon, not even after the fighting started. However he *had* vanished and then reappeared.

Inside the transmission chamber, the air shrieked and flashed.

Out here, Box was sure it was already beginning to feel warmer.

'His belt.' Box was at the body. 'He went for his belt.' He worked his fingers along the belt until they came to a black cylinder the size of a tube of sweets. There was a silver button on the top and a clear band around the centre. He held up the cylinder.

'Look,' he shouted and then, because he couldn't resist doing so, he pressed the button.

Everybody was staring at him open-mouthed. Box realized

that *he* was open-mouthed. He was also standing near to the chamber opening again, with nothing in his hand. It was as if he had never touched the cylinder. It was as if he had been transported back in time by about thirty seconds.

'Did I blink?' Razool was holding his HV loosely by his side. 'Did I just miss something?'

Box could see that Anna understood what had happened to him immediately. Even though Box could feel time ticking through his body, running out, Anna paused, long fingers by her face, blue eyes thoughtful as she tried to piece it all together.

'If we go in through the door, we come back out. If we use the warp's device, we go back in time about thirty seconds, which, incidentally,' she observed, 'is how he must have been able to fetch the guards instantly, while we were still standing there. And somehow, the warp would use that device to get through this entrance. Now, how does that all work?'

'Why've we stopped?' grumbled Razool, in snout. 'As I understand it, we've hit a critical point. The warp station's about to explode and we stand still while she starts talking.'

'She's thinking,' replied Box, earnestly.

'Yeah, Razool,' said Shera. 'Box is watching thinking happen. They don't teach that at bolthead school, do they?'

Captain Riley was kneeling by the warp. He didn't touch the little cylinder, which was back in the belt, but he was studying it. 'This must act like a key.'

Anna clicked her fingers. 'Got it.' Her eyes were intense.

'Passing through the entrance triggers the teleport. But there will have been a moment when you *were* in the room on the other side. So if you get the timing exactly right, pressing the teleport key will take you back to that moment: you'll be back in the room.'

'Ooh, she's right,' cooed Lemuel with delight. 'The teleport key takes you back in time without having to cross the teleport screen.'

'But how do you get the timing right?' asked Riley.

'Count to thirty and hope for the best?' suggested Box. Anna and Captain Riley both looked at him as if he had said something incredibly stupid. 'Well, have you got a better idea?'

Anna walked over to the warp's body and removed the cylinder from his belt. 'There must be some way of timing it,' she observed, inspecting it closely.

'Can I just go in and get my sister?' asked Box. 'And Gemma?'

'I'm going with you,' said Anna. 'Chess is my friend. And the key must work if we're in contact.'

'And what about the timing?' scowled Box.

Anna shrugged. 'Let's count to thirty and see what happens.' She smiled. 'It's the best suggestion so far.'

'But what about my body?' complained Lemuel. 'No body and it's the barbeque for the lot of us.'

'We'll get your body, Lemuel,' said Riley. He slapped his chest webbing and pointed down the passage, around the side of the chamber.

Razool gave a thumbs-up and then said to Shera, 'You're coming with me and Riley.'

'No.'

'Yes.' The HV was in his hand, which hung by his leg. 'I haven't forgotten what happened on Klanf. If you think I'm leaving you with Box, you're more stupid than I bargained.'

'She's OK, Zool,' said Box.

'Like hell she is.' Razool shook his mane. 'I've watched over you, Box. And watched over her, made sure there's no opportunity for her. Now, if I'm wrong, I'll say sorry once this is over; *if* we make it out. But I'm not going to let her prove me right.'

He raised the magnum.

'What are they *doing*?' Anna was at the door, waiting for Box but unable to make sense of what was going on between Razool and Shera.

'I'm here to *protect* him,' insisted Shera.

It sounded to Box as if Shera was begging, but Razool was unyielding. 'There's no more time. You come or I shoot. I don't care.'

Box knew Razool wasn't bluffing. So did Shera. But as she left, he heard her say to Razool, 'Saying sorry when you're wrong won't bring him back.'

'Box. *Box*.' It was Anna. 'Forget the growl-fest. We're going in.'

Box joined her by the door, carbine in his hands.

'Ready?' asked Anna.

'Always,' said Box, face set like a rock.

They entered the chamber together. And then they were back outside. Box placed his hand against the small of Anna's back and both of them began to count. Somewhere around twenty-five, Box spotted the clear band on the key glow red. Then the glow vanished. They hit thirty and Anna pressed the button.

They were back outside.

'It must be the red light,' said Anna. 'I reckon it's a timer. Going through the teleport screen must activate it. We have to press the button as soon as the light appears.'

'Well, let's get on with it,' urged Box.

Again they entered the chamber and were teleported back outside. But this time they didn't count. They watched the cylinder until the red light flashed on. Then Anna's thumb pressed down.

For a moment, Box's body felt as if it was simultaneously stationary *and* rushing. Then, they were in a vast room, so high and shot with darkness that he couldn't see the roof.

Box blinked up through the glare of spotlights. All around the high walls, fifteen or so metres above the floor, the chamber was ringed by walkways. He could pick them out by the way the light bounced off the tubular steel of the handrails. Knotting the walls were pillars and tubes, dense as entrails. There was one flight of metal steps which led up. And suspended in the air, level with the walkways, was Chess. Box knew it was Chess at once, even though she was partially obscured by swirling, blue mist.

'How do we release her?' Box hated to see her hanging there like that. He was desperate to get her down and then out.

To the front and back of Chess there was a metal plate. As Box looked up, he saw the air about the plates begin to shimmer. At the same time, there commenced the high-pitched screech that he had heard from outside the chamber.

'I can't see anyone,' said Anna, voice hushed.

'I can't see *anything*,' complained Box, squinting. The spotlights were so bright that they made it impossible to see beyond the stark spars of their beams.

He cradled the carbine in his left arm, shielding his eyes as the light began to dance across the plates and then to reach out with jagged, electric fingers from each towards the other.

'What are they doing to her?' he whispered, voice lost behind the rising scream of the energy. 'What are you doing to her?' he yelled.

He could barely see Chess through the cocoon of blue smoke, but he could see that her body was directly between the two plates. It looked as if she was about to be riddled with fork lightning. He couldn't believe that she could survive it.

'No!' Box's scream was lost in the screaming chamber as the bolts of energy flashed into Chess's body.

Then there was dead silence and a tired voice said, 'Box?'

'What are they doing?' Box's voice was hoarse. He stood below Chess, turning, trying to see clearly through the lights. Anna was by his side. Box could feel her senses alert, penetrating the darkness around them.

'It's too late.' The voice struggled and was very quiet. 'You can't help me, Box. I don't even know if you *want* to help me. Did you join the enemy, Box? Did you join them?'

'No.' Box's voice echoed back at him. 'No. Never. I never

joined them. I've … I've been with them, while I've been looking for you. Don't you believe me?' Box didn't know what else to say.

'Go. Get out,' said Chess. 'For your sake, while you still can. Get out now.'

'No. I've come to take you home, Chess. I'm not leaving here without you. How do we get you down?' Box looked across to the stairs. Hadn't Lemuel said that stairs led to a platform from which the process was controlled? 'Just tell me what to do. We haven't got long.' He tried to stifle the tremor of anxiety that crept into his throat.

'Just leave me. I'm all right.'

Box wondered how Chess could possibly be all right and then he heard her laughter: ragged, broken, desperate laughter. Quiet laughter. It was hard to tell whether this was laughter or sobbing, in fact.

'She's not all right,' Box said to Anna.

'Surprising if she was,' muttered Anna, 'after four or five months of this, you'd get a little frayed around the edges.'

Something moved, up on the balcony at the top of the stairs, facing them.

Automatically, Box pulled the trigger. Rounds sang across the walkway. But nothing else moved and he released the pressure.

Anna's sword was drawn.

'Box?' The voice came from where Box had been firing at. 'Box?'

'Gemma?' He hadn't heard her for months, but he recognized her voice immediately.

'Well done, Box,' said Anna. 'You nearly blew her brains out.'

'I didn't know,' protested Box.

'There's three of them,' shouted Gemma. 'But you can't see them.'

Above him, Chess started to laugh again.

Box could pick out where Gemma was lying, a little mound on the platform floor at the top of the stairs, just below where he'd been firing.

'Is Balthazar there?' Box shouted up.

'He is, but he can't move,' came the reply.

Anna was looking about the chamber, sword held out in both hands. 'There's movement, Box. I can hear it, but I can't pin it down. Something's moving.'

'We've found Balthazar and Gemma,' Box said into the mike in snout. 'And Chess. But there's something in here and we can't see it. We need back-up.'

Razool's voice came through. 'But we can't get in, remember? And it's getting very hot out here.'

Anna had the key. She'd slipped it into the back pocket of her trousers after they'd entered the chamber.

'Just get out,' laughed Chess. '*Get out.*'

The plates began to shimmer again.

'They must be near to you,' shouted Gemma, voice shaking. 'Please don't let them get you, Box. Please don't let them come back to me.'

'Where *are* they?' growled Box, through gritted teeth, gun at hip level. He turned back to back with Anna, below Chess.

The air flickered white and blue.

And then, like it was surfacing up through water, a long, pale face wearing small black lenses swam at him out of the darkness, and Box felt something prick the side of his neck, so thin and so sharp that it broke through his skin.

The paralysis was instantaneous. The blaze carbine slipped from his hands, he dropped to his side, banging his head on the floor, and rolled onto his back. He felt the HV being tugged from its holster, heard it go spinning across the floor, heard his carbine kicked away, saw Anna look down at him, sword in hand.

He could see and hear everything that was happening, but he couldn't move at all. He was utterly helpless.

The energy roared and the chamber flashed. Box tried to shut his eyes against the dazzling illumination directly above, but he could barely flicker an eyelid. Half blinded, colours swam before him, even after the transfer had ended and the room had returned to darkness penetrated by sparse beams of light.

He could see Anna, her tall body, the sheen of her hair, the silver glimmer of her sword. Her eyes were wide open, but she wasn't looking, she was sensing. Yet, there were three warps out there, invisible. They could be anywhere. They could do anything.

'You will not see us.'

The nasal voice was hard and sharp. Box remembered listening to it when he and Chess and Splinter were hiding in the Riverside Prison.

'At our will, the metamaterials within our gowns render us practically invisible,' said Petryx Ark-turi, the Twisted Symmetry's primary warp. 'That you have rendered yourselves so *defenceless* will be a source of lasting pleasure. Two such young, healthy humans. There will be so much to feed upon.'

Box could hear Riley and Razool and Lemuel in his earpiece but he wasn't able to summon sufficient strength even to whisper a reply. Anna had removed her earpiece and her eyes were closed. She was poised at the foot of the stairs.

Box saw a shadow cut through one of the spot beams behind her. He wanted to shout out, to warn her. He felt his heart would burst, but apart from a twitch of his fingers, he could do nothing.

The warp must have been almost upon her.

And then, like a snake-strike, Anna's sword was thrust backwards, the long blade vanishing up to its hilt, the tip reappearing a short space beyond. Another hiss of air and the blade was out, the girl spun, and at neck level, the sword sliced. There was a loud slump of body and a head with a metal vent for a face rolled across the floor, coming to stop only a metre from Box's own face.

Even with the head lying there, even with his own body so helpless, Box was amazed at the way Anna moved and fought. It was as if she could see. It was as if the warps had not made themselves invisible at all.

Anna had stepped away, away from the stairs, away from the spots. All Box could see now was a shadow, darker than the other shadows, and, at its centre, a silver blade. The warps might have made themselves invisible, but from where Box was lying, it was difficult to tell who was stalking who.

He *could* twitch his fingers.

Box used all his strength to flex them again. It was like trying to open a vice with his fingers alone. He felt sweat run from his forehead, down his cheek and by the corner of his mouth. It tickled. But it wasn't just the effort of trying to move his hand which made him break a sweat. It was the heat inside the chamber. It was a lot hotter now. He could feel it in the air he breathed.

Voices came to him over the earpiece: arguing, shouting. Time was running out. Outside the transmission chamber, nobody was sure what to do.

There was a ripple of strength down his forearm. Box only needed one hand. He flexed his fingers and moving his hand by degrees, so as not to draw attention, and because it was so difficult to move it at all, he began to work it towards his thigh pocket.

The energy was building again, but this time the system was groaning as well as squealing. The huge metal plates shuddered on the robotic arms as the power pulsed through them.

Anna leapt high, a whip of light lashing through the shadows at where she had been standing. As the whip came down again, she somersaulted backwards, then struck up, her sword blinking out of the dark, the blade vanishing. The whip of light faded. With two hands, Anna pulled the blade free and struck again, the long, curved sword flashing over her head in both hands and sinking deep into the darkness that was the warp's body.

But one warp remained. Anna shook blood from the blade and turned to look into the centre of the room.

Box's hand worked into his thigh pocket. His fingers closed on the stick-thin case of the stem pen. Sweat coursing down his face, he worked to flick off the cap. Charging through walls had been much easier than this.

Swift footsteps. No attempt at stealth at all, and out of the air marched Petryx Ark-turi, perfectly visible.

The transmission plates shook and energy screeched like train-brakes slamming.

Anna waited for the warp to come to her, sword by her side.

Box was a rat: he knew a trap when he saw one. There was no way the warp would have revealed herself like this without a surprise for Anna.

No, get away from her, he wanted to shout. But his lips twitched no more than a drooling wrinkly's.

Anna drew back her sword, preparing for the neck strike: the strike she had used to such deadly effect twice before. Now that the primary warp had made herself visible, there was no way that Anna could miss.

Box wanted to scream. The warp *wanted* Anna to go for a neck shot.

Anna struck, fast as light.

The blade clanged against the warp's neck, glancing off as if it had struck metal. The blow must have jarred Anna's arm, because she gasped and took a step back. Her sword arm was still outstretched. The warp struck back, not as fast as Anna, but fast enough. With one hand she grasped Anna's right wrist and with the heel of the other, she struck it so hard that Box heard the crunch of bone breaking. The sword fell to the floor. Anna groaned and the warp kicked the legs from under her.

Box's thumb cracked open the top of the pen. His finger gripped the shaft. Without pulling it from his pocket, he pressed its nose against the head of his quadriceps, just above his knee, and pushed the button on the top.

The needle shot home, an injection of fire and ice into his flesh. He felt the serum spread like vitriol, through his leg, into his belly, coursing up to his chest, neck and arms; damage repaired, muscles quickened. His breathing deepened, his fists clenched, his head moved.

Anna was on her knees, clutching her wrist and Petryx Ark-turi stood over her. Box could see the HV magnum some way across the chamber from where he was lying. He couldn't see the blaze carbine at all.

'We haven't met before,' said the primary warp, walking around Anna. 'Your smell is unfamiliar.' She twisted every word she spoke through her sharp nose. 'But you are powerful. Very powerful. I sense that this was not the end expected for you.'

'It's the end for all of us,' Anna snatched at the words, through the pain in her wrist, 'if you don't shut up.'

How quickly could he get the magnum? Then he heard Anna catch her breath and saw the warp yank her to her feet by her long black hair. Petryx Ark-turi was behind Anna now, her arm across the white throat, her hard, box-like jaw against the side of her face, the pince-nez spectacles reflecting the spotlights.

'You have such beautiful eyes,' stated the primary warp. 'When they made me, it was without eyes of any beauty whatsoever.' The warp sucked in air through her nose, thin nostrils working like the gills of a fish. She exhaled with pleasure. 'I will enjoy feeding on you, but I shall keep your beautiful eyes. I shall keep them for myself.'

Box rolled across the floor and was up on his knee with the HV in both hands.

'Let her go.' He stood slowly, gun raised.

Petryx Ark-turi pulled Anna's body harder across her own, and square in front of Box. 'Humans are so pitiful when they love,' she hissed. 'They do such foolish things.'

Box stood his ground, but he knew that it would be almost impossible to hit the warp without risking Anna. Without much thought, he repeated what he had heard Lemuel say. 'Love is what makes it work.'

'I don't think so,' spat the warp. From her face there came a cracking noise and beneath the skin of her jaws there was movement, as if something hard was struggling to get out.

'You can watch if you like.' But the warp's words were mauled by whatever was happening inside the bottom part of her head.

'Get Chess and go,' choked Anna. 'Leave me.' Her eyes were bright beneath the glare from above.

Box needed to be clever. He needed to think like Anna. There had to be a way out of this.

With a sound like meat being stripped from bone, the lower part of the warp's face began to tear open. Within, there was the glistening of flesh and metal.

And then, Box knew what he had to do.

'Do you trust me, Anna?' he asked, gun still outstretched. 'Do you trust me?'

Anna's crystal blue eyes locked with his and she nodded.

Box levelled the HV magnum at her chest and pulled the trigger.

CHAPTER 19

WHAM.

The HV round blasted through Anna's body and through the warp, knocking both of them off their feet and to the ground. Box didn't stop to look at the mess he had made of Anna. She was groaning, but already Petryx Ark-turi was clawing her way towards him. The warp might have been down but she wasn't out. But that didn't matter to Box.

He knelt by Anna, lifted her dying body. Her eyes were open and they looked up at his, glazed, uncomprehending. She was warm in his arms but loose, as if the strength had flowed out with her blood.

'Trust me. Trust me,' Box kept saying. He reached for her back pocket and found the teleport key.

Anna's eyes began to close. Box pressed the button on the key as the warp grabbed hold of his ankle. And then . . .

He was lying on the floor of the transmission chamber again. He could see the HV magnum some way across the chamber floor. Anna was kneeling, clutching her shattered wrist whilst Petryx Ark-turi stood over her.

It had worked. Not exactly as Box had planned; he hadn't

bargained on bringing the warp back with them. But he had won a little time, and that was all he needed. They were all back where they had been before Petryx had taken hold of Anna and before the warp's face had started to change. And this time, Box wouldn't waste valuable seconds scrambling for the gun.

He was a dreadbolt. He needed no gun.

Anna was still dazed by what had just happened and so was the warp. But the wound to Anna's chest had vanished and as Box leapt to his feet, she had the presence of mind to scramble away from the warp, who was only just piecing together what must have occurred. Before Petryx Ark-turi could descend upon Anna, who was still on her knees, Box was standing between them both.

The chamber hummed as if the walls themselves were overloading with power. The air was hot.

Above him, Chess was talking but he couldn't hear what she was saying over the violent crackle of the transmission plates.

'You cannot save either of them,' hissed Petryx Ark-turi, 'and you cannot save yourself.' Her head jerked left and then right as if gripped and shaken by something from within. 'You are just a human, a foolish human.' Her thin mouth contorted as she spoke, so that the sharp, nasal sounds were slurred.

'Don't you realize our work is done?' she continued, pointing a gown-draped arm upwards at Chess's body. 'She has more than enough power to serve the Symmetry's need. All that remains is to position her in the correct place at the right time.'

'Anna,' said Box, calmly, 'go up the stairs, get back in contact with Lemuel and release Chess.'

'She goes nowhere,' spat the primary warp, who stepped to the foot of the stairs that led to the control platform. Her box-like lower jaw jerked and bulged with a sound of cracking. 'I am hungry,' were the last words she uttered before the bottom of her face ripped open.

From her nose to her neck, the skin tore back as if splitting away under tension. Out of the glistening, red flesh burst a writhing clutch of bright silver tubes. They twisted and thrashed like snakes, and amongst them bristled sharp blades, long and thin. The razor points flicked like worm tails.

The little black lenses remained clamped to the top of what remained of the primary warp's nose, but her chest and shoulders shook as more of the blades and silver feeding tubes erupted from her bulging neck. Then she came for Box.

Box stood his ground. Petryx Ark-turi stamped towards him, light glancing off black lenses and hungry metal.

'Get back,' he heard Anna yell.

Gemma shouted his name, desperate.

This was Box against the Twisted Symmetry's greatest intelligence. But in that moment, Box knew that the great intelligence had made a huge mistake. Outwitting him was always a possibility, but a straight fight was his territory, however ugly the opposition.

Box drew back his fist and as Petryx Ark-turi thrust her head to drive it into his chest, Box drove his fist forwards as if he was aiming to smash a hole through the far wall of the transmission chamber.

He felt his knuckles connect with the front of Ark-turi's face, pounding metal, pulping flesh, and then his fist burst clean through the back of the warp's skull. Arms flailed at Box's arm, which was buried full length through the creature's head. He lifted a boot and kicked the body away.

'It's hard to be smart with your brain on the end of my fist,' said Box. Then he knelt down to wipe the mess from his arm on the warp's computational gown.

Anna was at his side, her sword in its sheath and her right hand supported by her left. Above them, the plates screamed and the chamber groaned.

She placed a hand on Box's shoulder. 'Thank you,' was all she said, but Box loved the look in her eyes.

He managed a grin. 'I wasn't sure it would work,' he confessed.

The look vanished. 'What?'

'I mean, I *thought* it would. I was pretty sure it would.'

'You shot me and you weren't sure it would work. I could have been dead, you idiot.'

'I preferred thank you,' muttered Box, making a mental note *not* to explain his thought processes in future.

Anna eyed him severely. 'Well, thanks.' Her eyes had a bit of that look again. 'I don't know how you do the things you do, but I'm glad you do them.'

Box didn't try to explain anything. 'Contact Lemuel. We don't have long. We need to get Chess out of here, whatever's going on inside her head.'

Anna was talking over the net, relaying what had happened. Box could hear everything as he helped Gemma down the stairs. She was shaking and there were deep cuts scored up the length of her right arm. Box didn't need to ask how they got there. He sat her on the floor by the chamber opening whilst Lemuel and Anna determined the operation of the controls. The first thing they did was to clear the teleport lock, which was possible now that they had control of the workings of the chamber.

Razool and Shera ran through the opening.

'There's no need,' said Box when he saw the weapons in their hands.

'Are you OK?' asked Shera, looking about the room for the first time.

'Better than the opposition.' Box indicated the heap that lay on the floor at the bottom of the stairs.

'Rough surgery,' grimaced Shera.

'Come on,' said Razool. 'We have minutes.'

Inside the doorway, the GPU was tending to Gemma.

'Where's Lemuel's body?' asked Box.

'With Riley.' Razool pointed at the doorway. 'He's taken him back to the ship. Then he peered up, frowning. 'Is that your sister up there?'

Box nodded.

Razool shook his head. 'What kind of a place is this?'

'A hot one.' Box wiped sweat from his face. 'You take Gemma. I'll bring the others.'

'Come on,' Razool said to Shera. 'He can manage this bit on his own.'

Up on the platform, Balthazar was regaining control of his body. Box shook him as Anna began to operate the controls to release Chess. He could hear her and Lemuel talking quickly.

'There will be a line of switches with symbols that look like pieces of spaghetti,' Lemuel was saying.

'Seen,' said Anna.

'Click down the two on the right.'

Box heard the switches click and then Anna said, 'Next.' She was leaning over a panel of instruments, her right arm hanging limp by her side as her left worked the controls. Box knew that her right arm must have been hurting like crazy, but her concentration was unbroken.

'How are you doing?' Box asked Balthazar.

Balthazar sat up. He clutched Box's wrist. 'You didn't fail us. From the start, I knew you wouldn't fail us.' His big eyes were transfixing. 'You have come such a long way.'

Box clapped the big man on the shoulder of his dinner suit. 'Yeah, well, we've still got a long way to go. How much longer, Anna?'

It was Lemuel who answered. 'Not long. The transmission apparatus should be retracting now. Then we can lower Chess and dismiss the gaolers.'

A tremor ran through the whole chamber and the energy plates shook. Between them, Chess stared out from swirls of blue smoke, almost dreamily, and for the first time, Box saw the state that she was in. 'We don't have long, Lemuel.'

'As if I don't know,' came the terse reply.

'Can you walk?' Box asked Balthazar.

In response, Balthazar grasped his staff and stood.

'Go,' said Box. 'Out of here and down there.' He pointed in the direction of the corridor outside. 'There's a ship waiting. We haven't got long.'

But Balthazar was staring out at Chess. 'What have they done to her? What does this mean?'

'How should I know?' snapped Box. 'Just get out, Balthazar. Now.'

'Things happen for a reason, Box,' Balthazar said quietly. 'There is a reason for everything.' But he took the stairs, slowly, his staff banging beside him.

With a metallic squeal, the plates began to rise.

'OK,' said Anna. 'I'm going to lower her.' She glanced at Box. 'Chess is going to need you once she's free.'

Box stayed long enough to put his hand on Anna's shoulder. 'Thanks, Anna,' he said. 'Thanks.'

He couldn't think of how to say anything more although there was a lot more that he wanted to say.

He headed for the stairs. The steel handrail was hot to touch. When he came to the bottom, he could feel the floor shaking. Even with the transmission units shut down, the FCAs were still conducting vast quantities of energy and generating massive quantities of heat.

Box heard Lemuel instructing Anna on what to key into the panel, which dial to turn. He looked up to see the blue smoke suddenly pour to the floor like a waterfall that had just been released. When it hit the floor it spread out in great, rolling waves. The streamers that remained trailing up, into the air, brought Chess down. She spiralled slowly as she descended, landing gently on her feet. But her legs gave way immediately and she collapsed, hair heaped over her head and spread across the floor as she lay face down.

Box was by her side at once.

'Chess.' He clutched her shoulders, pulled her up. 'Chess.'

'Box?' she smiled, raw lips cracked, eyes sunken. 'I thought you'd left me. I thought ...' she laughed weakly. 'I thought you'd joined the enemy.'

Box squeezed her tight, feeling the bones through her frail body.

'I haven't *ever* left you,' he choked. '*Ever.*' She was so weak. He wanted to give her strength. He had so much of his own, he felt that there must be a way of giving her his. But all he could do was to hold her so tightly she couldn't slip through his arms, slip away from him again.

Anna hesitated by them both as if waiting and then said gently, 'Don't be long, Box. I'll tell them to get everything ready.' With barely a sound she left the chamber, walking down the corridor on her own, sword across her back, right hand held close to her chest.

Chess's forehead was damp, her hair plastered with sweat. The floor shook. But Box had to hold her for a little longer. Then he would carry her to the ship and they would go. He'd get her away from this demented place. After the prison, the planets, the battles, he had found her. It didn't matter that the warp station was breaking about them; he would keep her close to him for a few seconds more. So he held her and whispered her name. And in the darkness behind them, something that had bided its time for weeks saw its final opportunity.

Razool and Shera were strapped into the cockpit of the pilot ship. Lemuel had said they had less than five minutes left before the energy transmission zone would go into meltdown.

Right now, Lemuel's body lay on the crew room table. Around the table sat Captain Riley, Balthazar and Gemma. Riley was tending to the wounds on the little girl's arm. Lemuel's body was badly damaged from the malevolent attentions of the warps, and it possessed only the most basic senses, but it was still in working order which pleased Lemuel, who was very excited at the prospect of taking it home to have it fixed. But not even he suggested abandoning Box and Chess. Not yet.

The rows of instrument lights flashed as Razool made the final checks. Under his direction, Shera ran through system drills on her side of the cockpit. Razool regarded her sidelong. He knew that by human standards she was pretty but he still wondered at the bareness of her dark skin, without its soft covering of fur.

'When are you going to stop pretending to be a skin?' he asked. They spoke in snout, unconnected to the net.

Shera shrugged and reached up to flick a switch. 'When I choose.'

Razool's narrow, dark eyes were thoughtful. 'If I didn't know you better,' he muttered, 'I'd say you've taken a liking to our skin friend.'

'You don't know me at all, Razool,' Shera muttered back.

Razool sniffed. 'You never take your eyes off him.'

'Neither do you,' she retorted.

'That's because I'm making sure you don't *accidentally* shoot him again.'

Shera bit her lip and then said, 'How long have we got? I can feel the whole station shake.'

─[331]─

Razool wasn't to be distracted. 'I know what you are, Shera.'

'Really?'

'Yeah. Really. Tell me, how did you escape when you were taken prisoner?'

'Basic techniques,' replied Shera, airily. 'Slipping shackles, dislocating joints to squeeze through bars. That sort of thing.'

'And somehow smuggling yourself into a coffin so you could follow us; follow *him*.' Razool watched every reaction, eyes like darts.

'That wasn't me who attacked him in the hold.' Shera folded her arms and stared ahead at a view of low buildings, connecting passages, rock and darkness. 'You're right that I'd smuggled myself in. But I wasn't there when he was attacked.' She clenched her jaw. 'I should have been but I'd gone to ground elsewhere. I thought he'd be safe on the ship.'

'Really?'

'*Really*.'

Razool asked his next question casually. 'How long have you worked for Cerberus?'

'About seven years,' answered Shera, just as casually.

'Want to tell me why you've been hanging around?' Razool laughed, dryly. 'I'll be honest, Shera. There was a time when I'd have smashed you as soon as spit, but now?' He shrugged. 'I don't know. You seem to like him too much to hurt him.'

Shera laughed bitterly and shook her head. 'I stole a pilot ship, *this* pilot ship, from the troop ship to save you from certain death. Don't you trust anyone?'

Razool shrugged, leather jacket creaking.

'OK.' Shera turned her eyes on him. 'Let me tell you what this is about, Commodore. I don't see it makes any difference now, not when we're all about to be blown to the other end of the galaxy.' She brushed a strand of hair from her face. 'Your friend, Box, isn't universally popular. It seems that the senior management, the Inquisitors, thought he might cause a problem for them.'

The docking bay groaned and a tremor ran through the pilot ship. 'I can't imagine what gave them that idea. Anyway, I was tasked by the General ... you know, General Vane?' asked Shera sarcastically.

Razool raised one eyebrow. 'Of course.'

'I was tasked with close protection duties. I was told to guard Box, that nothing was to hurt him. The General didn't tell me everything but he told me he had plans for the skin: plans that wouldn't be approved of by everyone. He told me that Box might turn out to be very useful.'

Razool murmured, 'Box is here, pulling Chess out: out from where the Symmetry want her. The General must have planned this all the way down the line.' Quietly, he added, 'But why does he want Chess out of here?'

'The General told me to say nothing about what I was doing.' Shera smiled wryly. 'It seems that the General doesn't trust the Inquisitors, and they don't trust him, but there's a stand-off; neither wants to make it obvious how much they don't trust the other.'

Razool nodded. 'Which is why the General's used Box to get Chess out; or to try to.'

'Yeah, well the management aren't that stupid. The

General told me that the Inquisitors had despatched an agent of their own to kill Box.'

Razool leant forwards, dark brow furrowed.

Shera shrugged. 'My job was to protect him, whatever the cost to me. That's why I was sent, Razool. For all your suspicions, *that's* why I was sent. You spent a lot of time looking the wrong way.'

'You should have told me,' said Razool, quietly.

'My orders were to say nothing, to protect the General.' Shera sniffed. 'You know what?' There was a catch in her voice. 'I found that I wanted to look out for Box. I really wanted to. I've spent my life taking the skak for everyone else, risking my life for dirt, and here was this guy, a skin, and he was nice to me. He even saved *my* life whilst you'd have been happy to see me gaffed through the heart.'

Razool was silent.

'And when things went wrong, on Klanf, it hurt when I was held responsible.' Shera heaved in a breath. 'I was going to be sent to the Fleshings, for mission failure. Can you imagine that, Commodore? What it feels like to be blamed for something that isn't your fault? To pay the price when you were trying to do the right thing?'

'Yes,' replied Razool gruffly. 'Yes, I know what that's like.'

'But I like Box: I really *like* him.' Shera wiped her eyes. 'So I thought, why not look out for him anyway? There was an assassin, the Inquisitors' agent still out there; still is, for all I know. And, I mean, it wasn't as if I had a great career ahead of me.'

Razool nodded slowly. 'This all explains the spook. But when you shot him, what was happening?' He tuned into the radio. 'How long are they going to be?' There was no reply. 'Communications are down,' he said to Shera. 'It'll be interference from what's happening out there. But they're taking too long. Far too long.'

'Don't think I haven't gone over that shooting a hundred times.' Shera shook her head. 'It was like my gun wasn't my own. It was like something else was in control.'

Razool grimaced. 'That's the bit I don't get, because you were the only person holding it, Shera. And if I hadn't nearly broken my shins falling over the GPU to get to you, you'd have smashed him.'

'Yeah, but what about Box's gun?' asked Shera defensively. 'He says it moved without him even touching it. He says it moved upwards, *away* from him at the moment he needed it.'

Razool didn't speak for a moment. His mouth was open slightly as his mind raced. 'Oh no,' he said.

'What?'

'Get the log book. The ship's log book.'

'The ship's log book?' asked Shera, bemused.

'Down there.' Razool pointed to an alcove on the far side of where Shera sat.

Shera dug out the fat manual. 'Why?'

'When we touched down at this warp station, the ship had three GPUs, right?'

Shera nodded. 'Yeah.'

'Look in the book,' said Razool. 'Check the equipment roster. How many GPUs *should* there be?'

Razool's eyes were fixed dead ahead as Shera riffled through the pages. 'Two. Just two.' She looked at Razool.

'GPUs employ powerful magnetic fields,' said Razool. 'Box's gun was pulled out of his reach at a crucial moment. And your gun jammed when he needed fire support, but began to fire at him when he was vulnerable, and it *kept* firing until I smashed into the GPU by accident.'

'What? You're saying a GPU did it?' Shera shook her head. 'It can't be, Razool. It can't think like that. And anyway, a GPU from Klanf couldn't end up here.'

Razool was speaking quickly. 'It's falling into place.' He glared out of the window as the warp station shook. 'My armour . . .'

'Went missing from the ship.'

'No. It didn't go missing. It *changed shape*. GPUs can change shape, right?' Razool thumped his seat. 'Listen, start at the beginning; think it through. After the shooting, the GPU from Klanf must have made its way back with the dreadbolts, and ended up on the *Transit IV*. I mean, who's going to notice one GPU knocking about the place?'

'So it was the GPU that went for Box in the hold?'

'Yeah, after it had infiltrated the ship's messaging system and split us up; so it got him on his own. But the attack doesn't work; we turned up. *But* GPUs can morph, right? They do it all the time. So it morphs into armour; substitutes itself for his armour. If we hadn't ended up in the wrong armour, it would have smashed him in the Drakner. But once we get onto this ship, it switches back to being a GPU.'

Shera was frowning. 'I don't get it. A GPU can't do that. It can't think. It doesn't have a mind. It can't *plan*.'

'No.' Razool turned to look at Shera. 'A GPU can't, but

an *HFU* can. An HFU has intelligence. Why couldn't an HFU act like a GPU until the right moment? If the Inquisitors wanted Box dead, why not send a machine to do the job? An intelligent machine?' Razool tilted his head back. 'How have I missed it? All this time it's been tracking Box down, right in front of us.'

Shera looked at Razool as if he'd just pulled a gun on her. 'Razool, in the transmission chamber, did you tell the GPU to tend to Gemma?

'No.'

'But it went in there, to tend to her. And nobody told it to. Razool, it's not a GPU, is it?'

Razool's eyes were electric. 'Where's it now?'

Hoarsely, Shera whispered, 'It didn't come back to the ship with us.' She ripped off her seat straps. 'Razool, it's still in there with Box. We've left him alone with it.' She was out of the straps, and out of the seat. 'I don't want Box to be hurt. I . . . he *mustn't* be hurt.'

She leapt from the loading bay and sprinted into the warp station.

Box had Chess in his arms. She weighed nothing. The air in the transmission chamber was almost too hot to breathe now. He was heading for the exit.

'Pacer wanted to be here,' Box said. 'You should know that, Chess. Pacer would have risked his life for you if we'd of let him.' But she was asleep, and sleep seemed to have released some of the pain from her face, softened the drawn, cracked skin and lips.

'We're going home, Chess,' he whispered. 'We're going home.'

Maybe it was a shadow falling across him, but suddenly Box knew that they were not alone. And then, from behind him, there was noise: metal sliding, the hum of robotronics, the thump of something powerful hitting the ground, the rapid clicking and ratcheting of multiple weapons preparing to fire. Still holding Chess's limp body in his arms, Box began to turn round.

The machine was unpacking itself, just like Box had seen the HFU do on the *Transit IV*. It extended outwards, legs and arms cantilevering until it stood as high as the viewing platform. Its lower limbs were set on the floor like foundations, its joints powered by thick pistons. Its body ended flat with no head but supported two arms bearing clusters of gun barrels which made the endotherm drones and even the dreadbolt heavy weapons units look like toys.

Box turned to see the multiple barrels lock on him and begin to rotate, and to see a shape hurtle in from his right. He had time to drop to his knees and roll Chess to the floor, as Shera dived between him and the machine.

Her pistols blasted, rounds sparking off the metal body and, at the same time, the gun barrels screamed. The only thing between Box and those barrels was Shera. Box somersaulted away unharmed. Shera hit the floor as if she'd been slung there, every round that should have smashed Box taken by her own body.

Box had half a second that the machine had not accounted for. He charged forwards, driving his shoulder into one of its cumbersome legs. The impact felt like his body had been lump-hammered and the leg barely moved. A fist the size of a car bonnet swiped him clear.

The floor shook, a metal-buckling squeal rent the walls of the chamber and behind it all, a shrill wail cut the air.

Box felt the wetness of blood down his cheek. Kneeling, he pulled out the HV magnum and blasted three rounds in quick succession into the robotronics housing in the machine's left arm. Sparks gushed, followed by smoke, but the arm still moved jerkily. It was able to lift, align itself with Box and fire.

Box dived away, rounds snapping across his metal leg. Now the machine stamped towards him. It moved much more swiftly than he had expected. Before he had backed off, he felt a blow to his back that spun him flat across the floor. His head struck the ground hard, so hard that he could see light flashing across his eyes.

He blinked, groaned, and the machine was standing over him. To his left lay Chess, to his right, Shera. He could smell the hot metal of the warp station as the temperature rose to melting point.

Light continued to flash and flare in his eyes as he looked up.

There was nothing left to do. Lying there, Box spat out a gobbet of blood. At least he'd fought his way back to Chess. He'd keep fighting now until he knew nothing else. He raised the magnum.

This was how it would end.

CHAPTER 20

The sound was so wild it was like the air was being torn. Metal drummed and thundered. The brightness was unbearable. The last thing Box saw before screwing shut his eyes was the maelstrom of energy fork out of the darkness and explode into the top of the machine.

Metal sheared and squealed. Box rolled over Chess's body. Magma-hot lumps splashed down, scorching the floor, and the temperature soared as the machine began to vaporize.

The sound-tornado cut out. Above him, hot metal spat and fizzed. Box turned about, brushing embers from his top, ignoring the pain and smell of his own charred skin. Over him stood the lower half of the machine, scored by rivulets of molten metal. What remained ended in a jagged, blackened twist, as if something had torn the entity in two. The top section, with its limbs and gun barrels, had vanished entirely.

The energy plates smoked.

'Anna?' Box saw her shape, up on the control platform.

'Thank Lemuel,' Anna shouted back. 'I just followed his instructions.'

But Box was looking across to where Shera lay. He knelt

by her and rested a hand on her face, no longer skin-side. He looked at where she had taken the rounds, taken them for him. There was no chance of resuscitating her now, no chance of bringing her back to the life that must have been gunned out of her before she had even hit the ground.

Anna had hurried down from the platform. 'I didn't know she was different,' was all that Anna said when she saw Shera lying there.

'There's a lot we won't know,' said Box, his throat so tight it hurt. He blinked heat from his eyes. 'I guess she liked being a skin.'

'Box.' It was Razool. 'You can't help her.' His hand dropped to Box's shoulder. 'We have to go.'

Anna's right arm was held to her chest. Her left dropped to Box's other shoulder. 'You couldn't have stopped this, Box. None of us could,' she whispered.

Razool spoke carefully. 'In about one minute, this whole area will blow. And thirty seconds later, so will everything else.'

'Get out *now*,' yelled Riley from the door.

Razool's grip tightened, dragging Box to his feet. 'All of us wish we'd done things differently sometimes,' he said, voice gruff. 'But there's no more time to say goodbye. Chess needs you.'

Chess was stirring. Box lifted her. Razool and Riley were already running back to the ship. Anna was waiting for Box in the corridor. Box and Chess were the last to leave the chamber where Chess had spent the last four months. Box ran to the ship with Chess in his arms, leaving the darkness smouldering over Shera's body and the remains of the machine sent by the Inquisitors to kill him. By the time he reached the ship, his eyes were streaming.

'It's the heat,' he said, as he passed Chess up to Riley who was waiting in the loading bay.

The air was almost unbreathable. Behind him, a series of detonations boomed down the corridor. Riley helped him into the ship. Box rolled into the bay in time to hear Razool say, 'We're not going to make it.'

The airlock closed and immediately, the ship detached itself from the docking unit. Chess lay on the loading bay floor, eyes open, silent. Riley jumped into the second pilot seat. Box and Anna watched what they could through the narrow cockpit window from the doorway in the bulkhead.

'We can't do it.' Razool cursed. He pulled the nose of the ship up and began to speed out of the warp station. They felt the tremor as the transmission zone erupted.

'The code is down,' said Lemuel over the net. 'Break through the gap, then you can make hyperspace.'

'Thirty seconds.' Razool's fangs were gritted. 'But we're not going to make the exit point.' He heaved at the levers in front of him. Box could feel the ship shake.

'We're off the station,' he said, optimistically.

'When the station blows,' said Razool, 'the fire ball will be about the size of a small sun. We won't have a hope.'

The ship's engines were screaming as it streaked away from the warp station. Through the door to the crew room, Box could see Balthazar nestling Gemma in his arms.

Riley and Razool were silent now.

'This is it,' Box whispered to Anna.

Anna turned her face towards Box, eyes softer than he

could ever have imagined them. 'Box,' she began.

The inside of the cockpit flared yellow, there was a hypersonic boom, and Box's world became a world of heat.

'No,' said Chess. She was propped against the loading bay wall, one hand raised, fingers outstretched.

About the airlock, through the roof, up from the floor, long tongues of flame had frozen, as if cut dead as they had licked their way in from outside. The cockpit was still bathed in fiery yellow, yet the glow neither intensified nor faded and the blasting heat had vanished. But although it felt as if everything outside the ship had been freeze-framed, Box was still aware of what was happening and he was able to move and talk, and so was everybody else.

'Chess?' Box knelt by her, bemused.

'This is Chess's thing,' Anna whispered in his ear. 'Stopping time, playing origami with space, destroying universes when the mood grabs her.' Anna patted his back. 'You should get to know your little sister better.'

'Balthazar?' Chess's voice was as cracked as her lips.

The big man came to the crew room door. 'Chess,' he murmured, 'you are miraculous.'

Chess managed a broken smile. 'It would have been easy to end it all *now*,' she said. 'But that is not the way to finish it. I need you to find a way out of here, out of this ship.'

'Surely . . .'

Chess cut Balthazar off at once. 'No, I can't. I *can't*.' She laughed in the way that had made Box feel so uncomfortable when he had first found her in the energy transmission chamber. 'I owe all of you this, at least. But don't ask for more. Don't make me do more than I *have* to.' Her hair hung over her face crazily. 'I don't trust myself,' she whispered.

Balthazar nodded. 'I understand, Chess. I understand.' He reached into his jacket pocket and took out the tesseract. 'This might be difficult.'

'Balthazar, if anyone can trace a route into the vortex from here, you can.' Chess smiled, closed her eyes and rested her head back against the bulkhead.

'Chess.' Anna's voice was acute as a cattle prod. 'Don't you dare go to sleep now. We need you to concentrate.'

Chess laughed, eyes remaining closed.

'Did you know, I only have one brother?' she half laughed. 'Which one is it?'

'What are you on about?' asked Box.

'She's just worn out,' replied Anna, gently. 'Don't listen to her.'

Gemma came over to sit by Chess, pushing her slight body close. 'I'm glad you're not dead,' she said.

Chess laughed a little more and opened one, darkly ringed eye. 'I don't know, Gemma. I don't know. It's such a horrible world.'

'It's not so bad here,' said Gemma, nestling her head against Chess's shoulder.

Incredulous, Anna murmured in Box's ear, 'We're sitting on the edge of a nuclear inferno, Chess is deciding whether or not to call last orders on the universes, and Gemma thinks it's not so bad.'

'I've missed you,' Gemma was saying. 'But you're here now. So that's good. And I didn't even need a leaf.'

'She is mad,' whispered Anna. 'Sweet, but mad.'

'Gemma, Gemma,' sighed Chess, ruffling the little girl's wispy hair.

'I think,' announced Balthazar, who had been studying the space about him through the little ball of sticks, 'that I have found the way back.'

Pigeons roosted on top of the iron mesh that covered the inside of the windows. Their chirring had been so constant that Box no longer noticed it. Beneath the bleeping of the monitors, and the busy footsteps of the doctors and technicians that clipped across the hard floor, and the clatter of trolleys carrying medical equipment, the pigeons were almost beyond notice. But Box was watching them, remembering how there were pigeons roosting here when he had first come to Committee HQ with Chess and Splinter. It seemed such a long time since they had first come to the old city bus depot. And now there was only him and Chess. And it was hard to know whether Chess was really with them anymore.

The room was long, concrete-floored, bare brick-walled and about the size of a small car park. And about as welcoming, thought Box, despite Ethel's efforts. Chess lay in an iron bed halfway down the chamber. Around her bed were drips, ECGs, monitors and a troop of surgeons, physicians and nurses. They had patched her up, inserted IVs to boost her nutrition and mineral levels, and gathered more data than Box would have believed a single body could generate.

'The problem,' Ethel was saying, 'is not when she will be

on her feet. She'll be up and ready as soon as she wants. The problem is what Chess will *do* when she's ready.' Ethel's teacup clinked down onto its saucer. '*That's* the problem.'

They were sitting in a temporary parlour that had been erected on Ethel's command at one end of the long room. There were a couple of decrepit sofas that had been purchased hastily from a junk shop, a table, low chairs and a row of tapestry-covered firescreens which served to delineate what had become Ethel's parlour from what had become the makeshift hospital ward. They also helped to retain some of the warmth that was generated by the two-bar electric heater which Ethel had contributed to the furnishings.

Chess was not the sole convalescent. In a bed on the opposite side of the spartan chamber lay Lemuel Sprazkin. The blankets were tucked up to his long, crescent-moon, bone-white chin, and his limbs were swathed in bandages. The medics had spent three days in the operating theatre in the cellars of the old bus depot, repairing the extensive damage that had been inflicted on his body by the meticulous work of the warps. Now he was surrounded by a battery of medical hardware and was sleeping. His mind continued to reside in Anna's Link-me, where it awaited transfer back to his physical structure when it was ready.

'My mind is in such a ferment,' Lemuel had explained, 'that my mortal form would pop if the two were joined at this juncture.'

So, Anna, whose right wrist had been repaired by the accelerated ossifiers of the Committee's medical technicians, continued to be the custodian of Lemuel Sprazkin's mind.

But with the Link-me powered down, even that mind was put to rest.

Box sat on one sofa beside Gemma, whose right arm was bandaged to the elbow. She rested against him. Her warmth was good and she was sleepy: sleepy and happy. Anna and Balthazar sat in the other sofa. And Ethel was perched on a wooden chair. Riley and Razool were at HQ too, but they were two levels below, where Riley was demonstrating the capabilities of some of the COE's prototype weaponry on the firing range. Apart from one distant but discomforting bang, the demonstration had not intruded upon Ethel's tea party.

Box no longer had the teleport key. Ethel had relieved him of it soon after their return, explaining that it was a 'regulated item'.

'Messing about with time is all well and good in a warp station, miles away from anywhere,' Ethel had said. 'But who knows what would happen if there was an outbreak of the same nonsense here in civilization.' Box could recall at least one occasion when Ethel had been responsible for an outbreak of that sort of nonsense herself, but he hadn't argued with her.

Box didn't feel much like talking. His cuts and burns had ceased to bother him, but his sorest feelings were on the inside. The cold white fog on the other side of the grimy windows looked exactly how he felt. He kept thinking about Shera, and how there wasn't anything of her left, and about Chess, who didn't seem to care about anything, and about Splinter, whose absence hurt more, now that Box's thoughts had had time to catch up with him. And about Anna.

Box couldn't work out how he and Anna had been so together one moment and were so apart now. Not apart just because they were sitting on different, hessian, frayed, bare-spring, rat-chewed sofas, but apart because after the heat of what had been happening less than a week ago, everything seemed cold. After Balthazar had led them like a chain of war-wounded through the vortex and back to Committee HQ, Anna had been spirited away by the medics and had returned two days later with a repaired right arm and a ton of quietness.

The shrill tone of Ethel's mobile telephone cracked the silence as if it was china. Ethel dug it out of her pocket and pressed a button with great deliberation before holding it to her ear. She spoke in Chat. Box was too occupied with his own thoughts to pay a great deal of attention, but that changed when he heard her talking about a price that had to be paid: a bargain to be settled.

Ethel covered the face of the phone with her hand and said to Box in a voice barely above a whisper, 'There's someone to speak to you, dear. Now, listen to me. You are to agree with what he wants you to do. You *have* to agree, for *our* sake.'

'What are you talking about, Ethel?' asked Anna, her face drawn.

'There was a price to be paid, my love, for the access data we used to crack the fractal code.'

'So?' Anna frowned.

Ethel smiled at Box. '*You* are the price, dear.'

'What?' exclaimed Box, as if he had just woken up.

Ethel thrust the phone towards him. 'I had to make a decision quickly. Without the data, we would never have got Chess.'

Before Box could respond, the phone was in his hand. Scowling at Ethel, he put it against his ear. The person on the other end of the line spoke snout. Box didn't realize who it was at first.

'Box Tuesday?' The voice was hard and gruff, even for a snout.

'Yes.'

'I have had to deal with you from a distance. I have had to ensure that I am not held responsible for your activities. But you have liberated the girl exactly as required. You have performed *exceptionally*. And always, I believe that exceptional service should be rewarded.'

Then it dawned on Box to whom he was speaking. Suddenly his mouth felt as if it had been filled with ground flour. 'Yes, sir. Thank you, sir.'

'Captain Strulf was an exemplary officer,' said General Vane. 'It was necessary for you to serve under him, for your protection and development. I am sorry that your bodyguard's performance was less than desired.'

Box wasn't prepared to let anyone speak about Shera like that, not even the General. 'She was perfect. She was perfect and you as good as threw her away ... sir.'

The silence that followed made Box think that maybe he had put himself back on the menu. But eventually the General said, 'I have a problem. I have a cohort of the Fourteenth Storm that is without an officer commanding; sadly, Captain Strulf is no longer with us. I would like you to assume command. I am informed that it will be a popular appointment amongst the troops. Not that popularity is of any concern to me.'

But Box had done what needed to be done and now he was home. He was back in the city. What was happening in the Crystal Wars, in other universes, was surely something he was no longer part of. Anna had looked over at him. Box didn't mind fighting, but he didn't want to go. Not now.

'The General gave us the access code. In return we have to give you back to him,' hissed Ethel. Anna's eyes opened wide. 'And there is more for you to do: for the General; for *us*; for *Chess*.'

'You will wish to accept this great honour at once, I am sure,' growled the General.

Box swallowed. How could Ethel do this to him? But how could he refuse to do what was necessary for the Committee? For Chess? 'Yes, sir,' he said, mechanically.

'I have a particular task for you, Captain. I shall arrange for your collection from the Committee's headquarters within the hour.'

'Within the hour!' gasped Box.

'I am sorry that I cannot arrange for your transport sooner.'

'Yes, sir. Thank you, sir.' Box's stomach sank to his feet.

'Thank you, Captain. And please, send my regards to Mevrad. Working *with* her has proved to be most rewarding.'

The phone went dead.

'What is it?' asked Anna.

Box felt too sick at the prospect of leaving to be able to answer. He just looked at Ethel. '*Why?*'

Ethel fiddled with the loose skin around her fingernails.

'I wish this could all be different, my love. But we don't always want to do what we *have* to do. You have to go with him. I wouldn't say so if it wasn't going to help us, dear.'

'So Box has to go, just like that?' demanded Anna. Her blue eyes were shining, her jaw clenched.

'The Committee needs the General's help.' Ethel took the telephone from Box and tucked it away. 'Missing shipments of crystal? The release of Chess? The General has a plan of his own, my loves, a plan that will help us, and Box has a part to play in it.' She attempted a smile. She was the only one who did.

Silence squeezed Ethel's parlour like a hydraulic press. Even Balthazar had been struck mute, although Box guessed that after the two hours he had spent in a small room with Ethel, he had been subjected to enough noise to last him a week.

Ethel rattled her way through another cup of tea, apparently oblivious to the unhappy silence. Then she said, 'Now, we just have to wait for Chess to decide what she's going to do.' She crossed her legs in a superior and knowing way.

Box could hardly bring himself to look at Anna. The prospect of having to leave made him feel as if he'd been floored by a battering ram. But to hold back the ocean of silence he said, 'I know we got Chess back, which is good, but what have we actually done? I mean, if she might go off on one and wreck everything anyway, how is our getting her out of there going to make any difference?'

'My love.' Ethel fixed Box with a stare so intense that his broad shoulders sank back into the sofa. 'What you have done, what all of you have done, makes *all* the difference in the universes.'

'Let me explain,' began Balthazar, but his suggestion was impaled on a steely glance delivered by Ethel.

'Balthazar,' said the old lady, 'I shudder to think what damage even an explanation could do in your well-intentioned hands.'

'I only mean to help.' Balthazar's bass voice was quiet.

'What you *mean* to do, and what you *do* do are always so contrary, my love.' But Ethel smiled kindly. 'Let me explain.' Ethel uncrossed her legs and re-crossed them the other way.

Box tried not to look at the veins which were so varicose they made Ethel's calves look corrugated. 'In a little more than one month, the time spiral will reach the fifth node. At that point, anything might happen. But if Chess had remained in the grasp of the enemy, only *one* thing would have happened. Her spirit would have been broken entirely, they would have positioned her exactly as they wanted and . . .' Ethel indicated universal destruction by a shrug of the shoulders.

'Great,' observed Anna. 'So this way, she only *might* destroy everything.'

'You know, my love, for such an intelligent girl, your grasp of the power of the possible extends only to the way in which you wield that sword of yours. The point is this: because of what you have done, Chess might *not* destroy everything. In fact,' added Ethel, with a hint of a smile, 'she might choose to do something extraordinary.'

'But it *could* all go wrong?' asked Anna, carefully.

'It could, dear. Of course it could,' replied Ethel, equally carefully.

'Chess will do the right thing.' Gemma's voice was sleepy. She barely opened her eyes. 'She always does.'

'I hope so, my love,' said Ethel, a little tensely. 'Quite a lot depends upon it, you see.'

The conversation died. Box wanted to talk but he couldn't find anything to say. The minutes he had left here were running out and the desperation of waiting was like being buried alive.

A man in a white coat emerged side-on through the firescreens.

'Ah, Mr Stilson,' said Ethel. 'Fresh from your electrodes, no doubt. How are our patients?'

'Stable,' said the man in a voice devoid of any warmth whatsoever. 'Eric has rung down. There are visitors here.' Stilson's gimlet eyes momentarily flicked towards Box.

'Goodness. Sooner than expected,' said Ethel with a lame attempt at cheeriness.

Box saw Anna look at him. It was a look that would have made it much easier to talk with her if she'd looked at him like that earlier.

'They are here for *you*, dear, you know that don't you?' Ethel said to him.

'Yeah,' he said dully, but looking at Anna. He didn't want to let go of Anna's eyes.

'Perhaps, Mr Stilson, you'd be good enough to send a message down for the boys. The Commodore must join us.'

Box glanced at Ethel.

'Our sharp-toothed friend did share some of his plans with

me, dear,' said the old lady. 'Not *everyone* thinks I'm as mad as a bat.'

Mr Stilson huffed in a way that was intended to let Ethel know he wasn't there to act as her messenger; but he left the makeshift parlour and headed for the internal telephone all the same.

'Well,' announced Ethel, looking at her lap and tugging at some loose threads on her skirt, 'the time has come to break up the party.' She patted the tops of her thighs. 'Come on, my loves, Box must go outside now.'

Box looked at Anna and she was looking back at him, and he realized this: words were not always the best way of saying things. They seemed to be saying more to each other now than they had done since they'd first met. And now he realized that there were so many things to say: things that had nothing to do with spindle rippers, or warps, or the best way of neutralizing the enemy. He wanted to ask her about her brother, and how come she was so off-grid, and what she wanted to do now that Chess was back, and what she liked to eat. Box realized that he knew almost nothing about Anna. He didn't even know what made her happy. At last, he'd thought of a thousand things to talk about and suddenly there was no time to talk.

Ethel's hand was on his shoulder. 'Come on, my love. It's time to go.'

Dreadbolt or not, it took every gram of strength to stand. He rested Gemma flat because she'd fallen asleep.

'I'll stay here, with Gemma,' said Balthazar, and as Ethel left the parlour he said in Box's ear, 'The universe knows what it wants, Box. If *it* wants what you want, nothing can stop that. Time, space, the greatest armies cannot come between you and what the universe wants.' He patted Box's back. 'You have become a mighty man, Box. The universe is on your side.'

Box nodded but couldn't think of anything to say and he could see from his old sparring-master's eyes that nothing was expected.

'What was he saying?' Anna asked Box as they followed Ethel through the makeshift ward.

'The usual stuff,' muttered Box, feeling as if he'd been gaffed through the chest. He stopped by Chess's bed to kiss her forehead. 'So long, little sister,' he whispered.

Every step to the old bus depot exit was leaden. The silence between him and Anna thickened like the fog. When they came out in the parking bays at the front of the depot, beneath the clock whose hands were still positioned at three o'clock, Box felt utterly incapable of speech.

The fog was thick about the old brick buildings and it was cold. Drawn up on the roadside opposite were two black saloon cars, one behind the other, engines running, windows blacked out. Standing beside the front of each car was a man. The men wore black suits and coats, and dark glasses. Ear-piece wires coiled down their necks. Their arms were folded.

Box heard Razool's boots scrape to a halt beside him, heard his friend sniff the air, three times, sharply.

'Pelts,' he said. 'Cerberus agents.'

The black-suited man by the first car strode over to them, the heels of his shoes clipping the tarmac.

'Commodore Valxata Razool,' he said, speaking in snout.

'By the General's order, you have one week shore leave. You are then to resume your duties.'

Razool sniffed. 'My duties as *what?*'

'As a commodore, sir. On attachment to the Fifth Quake, Dreadbolt Cavalry.'

Razool nodded and turned to Box. 'I think I see where this is heading, my friend. You and I have not seen the last of each other,' and he smiled a muzzle full of sharp teeth. 'Thank you.' He slapped Box's shoulder. 'I get to see Mrs Razool and the whelps. I get to show her my modifications. And all of it due to you.' Then his dark eyes narrowed. 'You are a good friend, Box. In my world, that is the greatest thing we can say.'

Box nodded. 'Same in mine, Zool.'

'Come on then,' Razool said to the pelt. He followed the agent over to the front car, but halfway there he stopped and without turning round, he shouted in snout, 'If she was a snout, I'd have to smash you for her. Don't blow it, Mr Tuesday.'

His voice echoed about the foggy bus depot. Then Commodore Valxata Razool climbed into the back of the car, and with a swish of tyres, he vanished into the fog.

'It's your turn, dear.' Ethel's head barely reached Box's chin, but her grip on his hand was surprisingly strong. 'Shall I walk you over?'

'No,' said Box. Ethel let go. His mind coursed clumsily through a thousand things to say. 'Do you want to walk over with me?' he asked Anna.

'OK,' said Anna.

They walked to the waiting car in silence. The pelt moved

to the rear door and pulled the handle. Box tried to think of the right thing to say. Anna's blue eyes were wet.

Think of something, think of something, think of something, his voice shouted at him.

Anna put out her right hand. 'Perhaps we might shake hands at last,' she tried to laugh.

Box took her hand.

'Get in the car please, sir,' said the agent.

Think of something, screamed the voice.

'Goodbye, Box,' said Anna.

Box couldn't speak. Words weren't his strength anyway. He stepped forwards, arm around Anna's back, and kissed her. And she kissed him.

'Sir,' said the pelt, after Box had forgotten he was there.

Box still held Anna's hand, even after his arm had slipped away from the strength and warmth of her body. He grinned.

Anna blinked water from her eyes. 'Be careful,' she said, hoarsely.

'And you,' he said. 'Whatever happens, wherever they send me, we'll see each other, right? Nothing will stop me.'

Anna laughed and tried not to cry. 'I know. There's nothing.'

Box held her in his eyes for a moment, then entered the car.

Anna stood in the parking bays until the silence was so deep she could hear the fog falling. Then she walked back to Ethel who was waiting, head bowed, beneath the clock tower.

Don't miss the other books in THE BAD TUESDAYS sequence . . .

Children everywhere are disappearing.

Orphan, Chess Tuesday, and her brothers, Box and Splinter, don't want to be next. But they are being tracked by two powerful enemy organizations, each intent on destroying the other . . .

Who is good and who is evil? Why do both sides need the Tuesdays? And can anyone escape the Hunters? Chess, Box and Splinter are about to embark on a terrifying mission to find out.

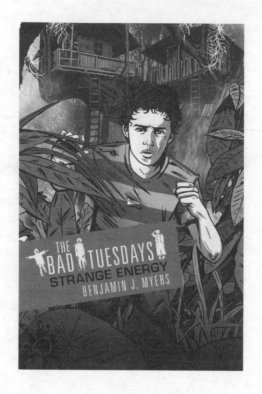

Time is running out.

Chess and her brothers, Box and Splinter, are caught in a bitter struggle between two ruthless organizations.

Now they face a terrifying choice – carry out a dangerous mission for the Committee, or try to outrun the evil Twisted Symmetry alone.

Chess wants to take the mission. But it could prove fatal. And it will lead the Tuesdays into the heart of the very organization that is hunting them . . .